Praise for *New York T...*

SUSAN SQU...

ONE WITH THE SHADOWS

"Full of colorful characters, romantic locales, and vivid details of 1820s life, [*One with the Shadows*] has a delicious pace and plenty of thrills, and her vampire mythos is both mannered—almost Victorian—and intriguingly offbeat. Bound to net a wide audience of paranormal fans, this one may even convert devotees of traditional historicals." —*Publishers Weekly* (A Best Book of the Year)

ONE WITH THE NIGHT

"Superb . . . captivating . . . With her usual skill and creativity, Ms. Squires has crafted a novel that is passionate, heartbreaking, suspenseful, and completely riveting."
—*Romance Reviews Today*

"Few writers combine a sensual romance within a supernatural thriller as well as Susan Squires consistently does. Her latest is a terrific Regency vampire romantic suspense starring two courageous heroes battling one hell of a meanie."
—*Midwest Book Review*

"This is an incredibly unusual take on historical vampire stories. Susan Squires delivers an exciting story."
—*Fallen Angel Reviews*

MORE . . .

THE BURNING

"A terrific tale . . . the story line is action-packed."

—*Midwest Book Review*

"Blazingly hot and erotic."

—*Romantic Times BOOKreviews*

"Marvelously rich, emotionally charged, imaginative, and beautifully written."   —*BookLoons*

"A fantastic erotic vampire thriller."   —*Fresh Fiction*

THE COMPANION

"A darkly compelling vampire romance . . . the plot keeps the reader turning the pages long into the night."

—*Affaire de Coeur*

"Bestseller Squires charts a new direction with this exotic, extremely erotic, and darkly dangerous Regency-set paranormal tale. With her ability to create powerful and tormented characters, Squires has developed a novel that is graphic, gripping, and unforgettable."

—*Romantic Times* (4½ starred review)

"Travel through Egypt's deserts and London's society with two of the most intriguing characters you will ever read about. You will encounter a dark world that is intense, scary, and sexy, and a love that will brighten it . . . powerful and passionate . . . captivating . . . Squires has a wonderful ability to keep her readers glued to the edge of their seats."   —*Romance Junkies*

St. Martin's Paperbacks Titles By
SUSAN SQUIRES

One with the Shadows

One with the Night

The Burning

The Hunger

The Companion

One with the Darkness

SUSAN SQUIRES

St. Martin's Paperbacks

This is a work of fiction. All of the characters, organizations, and events portrayed in this novel are either products of the author's imagination or are used fictitiously.

ONE WITH THE DARKNESS

Copyright © 2008 by Susan Squires.

All rights reserved.
For information address St. Martin's Press, 175 Fifth Avenue, New York, NY 10010.

ISBN: 0-312-94104-8
EAN: 978-0-312-94104-8

Printed in the United States of America

St. Martin's Paperbacks edition / June 2008

St. Martin's Paperbacks are published by St. Martin's Press, 175 Fifth Avenue, New York, NY 10010.

10 9 8 7 6 5 4 3 2 1

To Jen, for making me think twice. And to Harry, for teaching me how to live with a human of the male persuasion, and why it's worth trying to understand one.

1

Florence, Tuscany, 1821.

HER FRIEND, EURIPEDES, used to say, "Time cancels young pain." Euripedes was wrong. After eighteen hundred years, the thorn of regret had festered until it was like to poison her.

Contessa Donnatella Margherita Luchella di Poliziano drifted onto the balcony of the Palazzo Vecchehio. The scent of star jasmine hung in the air as twilight deepened into indigo. Summer in Florence gave precious little darkness, an inconvenience to her kind. Below her in the Piazza del Signoria the usual throng of women crowded around Buonarroti's statue of David. It had been modeled after her son, Gian, in 1504.

Gian was the bright spot in her life. It was so rare for her kind to be blessed with a child. He was like his father, Jergan—as handsome as Jergan had been, as much of a leader. But Gian was vampire, like Donnatella, born in A.D. 41 in Rome, and Jergan had been human.

Her eyes filled. She could have changed that. She hadn't had the courage to make Jergan vampire because the Rules forbade it and the vampire Elders always enforced the Rules. So she had watched the only man she ever loved grow old and die. Such a short time she'd had with him! Half a century? No more.

She shook herself and turned inside. The library smelled

of the lemon oil used to polish the heavy, dark furniture. Her gaze fell on her favorite painting. Botticelli had rendered Jergan as Neptune rising from the waves, based only on Donnatella's description. The likeness was remarkable in view of the fact that the artist had never seen him. Green eyes. Long, dark hair. Body sculpted by a warrior's training. The painting and her son were all she had left of Jergan.

If only she had known the regret that waited for her, she would have found the courage. She could have infected him with her Companion, the parasite in her bloodstream. Then he would have shared her more-than-human strength and senses, the healing, the power to compel men's minds, the ability to translocate. There had been one moment— he'd been wounded; she'd almost done it then, used that as an excuse. The Companion would have healed him. Of course the Companion also demanded its host drink human blood. How could she have asked him to take on such a burden? To be thought a monster . . . Still, if he'd survived the infection, they would have had forever together.

Of course, if he'd died, then she'd have had no time with him at all.

And it was against the Elders' Rules. If one made a vampire every time one fell in love . . .

She straightened her back and daubed at her eyes. The Elders were wrong. She would have been stronger for having Jergan by her side, a man who understood her, loved her. He made her whole.

The clock chimed ten. Already she had missed the first act of the opera. This was fruitless longing. There was no going back. It would do her good to get out of the house. She rang for Maria. The rust silk, perhaps. It made her complexion glow. And her garnets. She opened the secret compartment in the wall and removed the large puzzle box containing her jewels. The bas-relief on the box had been carved by Buonarroti, showing Adam and Eve in the garden. Adam's likeness was amazing. Buonarroti always had a better feel for the nude male figure than the female, for obvious reasons.

She sat at her dressing table and pressed open the box as she had a thousand, thousand times before, twisting just the right way. The box popped open as it always had.

But this time a tiny drawer in the edge popped open, too. Donnatella blinked. What was this?

She pulled open the tiny drawer. A folded piece of paper lay inside. A note? But who could have put it here? Had one of her maids learned to open the box? But even Donnatella didn't know how she had sprung open this special little drawer. . . .

She set the box down and unfolded the paper. Holding it to the light, she recognized Buonarroti's cramped hand. Really, how could such a brilliant artist write so badly?

"Go to the catacombs under Il Duomo. Take the main corridor from the north end directly south. Behind the end wall is something Leonardo says will make you happy, Donnatella." It was signed "Michelangelo" in just the scribble one could still see on the base of the *Pietà*.

Whatever could he mean?

And why leave a note for . . . for more than three hundred years inside a puzzle box? Why, she might never have opened the little secret drawer. He'd never showed her how when he demonstrated the box back in 1501.

Maria knocked discreetly and let herself in. She bustled about, opening the wardrobe. "Which dress would you like tonight, your ladyship?"

"The rust silk," Donnatella murmured, still staring at the note. *"Behind the end wall is something Leonardo says will make you happy. . . ."* Not likely. Only one thing would make her happy, and it was nearly eighteen hundred years too late to get it. She hadn't even admitted what it was to herself until tonight. Buonarroti could not have known. Whatever was behind that wall would long ago have crumbled to dust. Finding a pile of dust was definitely not worth missing that new castrato at the opera.

No, she was *not* going to go chasing off after some daft dream that Buonarroti could never fulfill. No one could fulfill it, and to think otherwise for a single second only indicated just how close to madness she was drifting.

But what else was left for her?

She rose so suddenly the chair toppled over. "Never mind the rust silk, Maria. Get the dress I wore when we reorganized the wine cellar."

The maid's eyes widened. "Your ladyship is never going to wear that dress to the opera!"

"No, I am not. And find my sturdiest half boots." She rang the bell again. It sounded as though she'd need a tool for demolition. A blacksmith's sledgehammer perhaps. Bucarro, her faithful majordomo, would know where to procure one. A footman peeped into the room.

"Get Bucarro," she ordered. This was insane. But she was going to the catacombs.

DONNATELLA STOOD ALONE in her rooms in front of a full-length mirror, the sledgehammer and a lantern concealed under her cloak. She dared not meet any late-returning revelers in the streets carrying a sledgehammer and dressed for dirty work. So she called on the Companion in her blood. Power raced up her veins, trembling like the threat of sheet lightning in the air around her. A red film dropped over her field of vision. To anyone watching, her eyes would now be glowing red. *Companion, more!* she thought. And the being that was the other half of her answered with a surge. A whirling blackness rose up around her. Even light could not escape that vortex. She watched her reflection in the mirror disappear. She pictured the Baptistery of the Duomo in her mind. Not many living knew about the catacombs beneath it anymore. The field of power grew so intense it collapsed in on itself, popping her out of space. The familiar pain seared through her just as the blackness overwhelmed her. She gasped.

The blackness drained away, leaving only the dim interior of the octagonal Baptistery. She did not bother with the lamp. To humans the mosaics of the dome above her would be lost in shadows, but she saw well in darkness. The place felt like the crossroads of the world. The building itself was clearly Roman, almost like the Pantheon, but the sarcophagi on display were Egyptian, the frescoes Germanic in flavor. The floor, with its Islamic inlay, stretched ahead to the baptismal font. Her boots clicked across the marble. Behind the font was a staircase. She ran down into the darkness without hesitation. Below, the walls of the vast chamber were of plain stone, the floor above supported with columns and round arches. Marble tombs of cardinals and saints lined the edges. It smelled of damp stone and, ever so faintly, decay.

But this was not her destination. A large rectangular stone carved in an ornate medieval style lay in the middle of the floor. It was perhaps four feet across and six feet long, six inches thick. Setting down her sledgehammer, she stooped and lifted. *Thank the gods for vampire strength.*

She dragged the stone aside so that it only partially covered the opening. A black maw revealed rough stone stairs leading down. The smell of human dust assailed her. Rats skittered somewhere. Now she took out her flint and striker and lit the lamp. Stepping into the darkness, she turned and lifted the stone above her once again. It dropped into place with a resounding thud, concealing the stairs. Holding the lamp high in one hand, she started down. Light flickered on the stone walls on either side of the staircase. Catacombs at night were the stuff of nightmares for most of the world. But she was not afraid. She was the stuff of nightmares, too.

The stairs finally opened out on a maze of corridors, each lined with niches to hold the bodies of the early Christian dead. Most were filled now only with piles of dust or sometimes a clutter of bones. Occasionally a skeleton hand still clutched a crucifix or some shred of rotted fabric fluttered in the air that circulated from somewhere.

Before she headed into the maze, she got her bearings. She must find the north side and locate a corridor that led south. That would take her back under the nave of the main building of the Duomo. She took a breath and started out. It took her several wrong turnings to make her way to the north edge of the maze, but she was rewarded by finding a long, straight corridor that led away from the main catacombs.

This was it. She knew it. Whatever Michelangelo Buonarroti thought would make her happy was at the end of this corridor. She was foolish. There was no doubt about that. Buonarroti couldn't know what would make her happy, and if he did, he couldn't give it to her. Traipsing around in catacombs on a treasure hunt that would no doubt prove disappointing if it wasn't useless altogether was a sign of just how desperate she had become.

But she *was* desperate. She didn't know how much more she could take of the gnawing regret that had overwhelmed her in the last years. So, foolish as this was, however likely to end in disappointment, she couldn't turn and walk away. She started down the corridor.

It ended abruptly in a solid wall of plaster. She set down her lantern, her stomach fluttering no matter how she tried to tell it there was no cause for excitement. Hefting the sledgehammer, she hauled it back and slammed it into the wall with all her strength. The plaster crumbled, revealing carefully cut stone that fitted exactly together. Dust choked the air. This would take some doing. Again and again she swung at the stones until she could pry at the ruined corners. Her fingertips were bloodied. No matter. They healed even as she glanced at them. But wasn't she going about this the wrong way?

Instead of trying to pry the stone out, she shoved it in. It toppled into the darkness. She pushed a neighboring stone and then another until she confronted a yawning chasm, coughing.

She lifted her lantern and stepped through the cloud of dust into the darkness.

And gasped.

What stood towering above her was a maze of a different kind. Giant gears and levers interlocked in some crazy pattern that was positively beautiful. The metal gleamed golden, still shiny with oil. At points in the mechanism, jewels the size of her fist were set, red and green and blue and clear white. Those couldn't be real, could they?

She stood dumbfounded, staring. What was this thing? A machine of some kind. But what was it for?

It was long minutes before she could tear her eyes away from the beautiful intricacy and look around the room. There was no dust except for the puff that had wafted in from her exertions with the wall. The place must have been tightly sealed to keep out even dust. How long had it been sealed? Probably since the note was written. Besides the machine, the room contained only a simple metal chair and a table to match, golden like the machine, sitting in a corner, unobtrusive. On the table was a leather-covered book.

Disappointment lurked at the edges of her mind. A

machine could not give her back happiness, no matter what it pumped or measured. And yet there was something almost otherworldly about this most human of creations.

She pulled out the chair, sat, and drew the book toward her. The cover had mold on it. Even a sealed room couldn't keep out mold. Carefully she opened it. The first page startled her. "For Contessa Donnatella Margherita Luchella di Poliziano, from her friend Leonardo da Vinci. I dedicate to you my greatest work."

Shivers ran down her spine. Twice in one night she had received notes from friends dead hundreds of years. They must have expected her to open the notes long ago. They'd never believe she was still alive three hundred years after they'd written them. Whatever they wanted her to know or do with this machine, she was very late in accomplishing.

She turned another page.

When you read this, for I know you will, you will have found my machine. Magnificent, isn't it? And only I could have designed it.

Leonardo, the dear, always had quite an ego. Still, the man was amazing. He was probably right about the machine.

I could never find enough power to test it, and yet I know it works. Or at least in one possible reality, it works. But really it is all too complicated, even for one of my intellect. I must find a way to get you here. Something you will keep by you through all the years, something valuable. A piece of art? You love the arts. Buonarroti, that dwarf, will know something. But of course, whatever I do works, because you are here, reading this, and I know you are reading this because . . .

Or it doesn't work, and everything is changed, and I never built the machine, or wrote this explanation, and I am not who I am, and you are not who you are. . . .

Well, never mind that. I have no choice but to fulfill my part in this epic, or this tragedy, whatever it turns out to be.

So here is all the truth I know: what you see before you is a time machine.

Gods, do you jest? She looked up at the machine that filled the space. It gleamed in flickering lamplight, towering above her. The jewels sparkled as the light caught them. The possibilities flickered through her in response. What if she could go back? Undo the decision that took Jergan away from her, have at least the hope of happiness? This might be the one thing that *could* make her happy.

Her eyes darted back to the journal. But Leonardo had said he'd never tested it. . . .

You are asking yourself how it works. If you care to read the journal, you will know. But if you are in haste, know this: time is not a river but a vortex, and with enough power man can jump into another part of the swirl.

Or perhaps man can't, but you can, my dear Contessa, you who are not human. Do you think I did not notice the hum of energy about you? I measured it without your knowledge, and was astounded. The people around you think it is vitality, a force of personality. They feel it only as an incredible attraction to you, but I know better. Your power is real and it is incredibly strong. It keeps you young and heals you. The you of today thinks I did not know those things about you, either. But the you who you will be told me in the past. It is the knowledge of this source of power that inspires me to build a machine worthy of its use.

My only regret is that I will not live to see it used. But you, who started me on this quest, told me you must not find it until after I am dead, or too much would be changed. It will wait for you, who live forever, to use it when the time is right.

So, my dear Contessa, pull the lever. Use your power. Think of the moment you want to be your now as you jump into the maelstrom. That will influence the machine. You will end up in the moment you imagine. At least I think you will.

But be warned: the machine will go with you but it cannot stay long in another time. To return, you must use it again before it disappears and returns to the time whence it came. I do not know how long it can stay with you. I do not know what will happen if you make it back to the time you are in now, or what will happen if you don't. I give you only the means to change your destiny, or perhaps all of our destinies. Use it if you will.

Donnatella sat there, stunned. She couldn't think. A time machine? If so, it was one that confused even the grand intellect of the one who made it. The possibilities thrilled through her. Could going back change what happened? If she changed what happened, couldn't it have some unintended consequences? How could one possibly risk that? She took a sharp breath. What if Gian had never been born? Could she bear that? What if making Jergan vampire made him unable to father Gian? She'd often thought the only reason she conceived was that Jergan was human. She found her throat constricting at the thought.

But no. She'd conceived Gian before Jergan was wounded. If she made Jergan vampire at the moment he was close to dying and not a moment before, she'd still have her son.

She leafed through the pages of the journal. Lord God in heaven. Was this possible? Complicated drawings, long blotted passages containing theoretical explanations of the vortex of time, records of Leonardo's useless attempts to find enough energy to power the machine, all flipped past her. She stopped and read a few passages. She was doing it only to delay the moment of decision.

And why? She knew what she would do here. Once she had been too timid to break the Rules and grab for the prize. Now she was willing to risk everything, everything but Gian.

Her heart thudded in her chest as she rose from the table and stared up at the great machine. Did her Companion have enough power to run it? She had fed recently and translocated only once tonight. But who could know? She might just test the theory—pull back if she got some initial result. But she wouldn't. What if timidity ruined everything as it had so long ago? What if she drained herself in an experiment, making the real effort impossible?

It was all or nothing.

She swallowed, her eyes filling for the second time tonight.

The handle of the machine was a brass lever about two feet long and topped by a glowing jewel. She reached out for it. The great diamond fitted her palm exactly.

She pulled. There was a creak, but nothing else changed.

"Companion," she called on her other half out loud in

the wavering lamplight. A surge of power shot up her veins. A red film fell over her field of vision. Above her, the early-morning light would be filtering into the nave of Il Duomo. The priests would be moving quietly about, tending the votive candles or kneeling in prayer. The machine was still.

"Companion! More!" The whirling black vortex of translocation began to swirl around her feet. She couldn't allow that. She pushed it down but kept the power humming in the air. There was a great grinding sound, and the largest of the metal cogs in front of her began to move. Still she called the power from the parasite in her blood that was part of her and more than her. A white glow formed a halo around her. Every detail of the cavern stood out, sharp-edged. The movement of the gears cascaded down from the great, cogged wheel to the hundred smaller ones. The jewels sparkled. Gears whirled ever faster until the eye could not follow them.

"More!" she shrieked into the hum that cycled up the scale, and lifted her arms in supplication. Her Companion was at its limit. Was that enough?

Nothing more was happening. The machine was faint behind the white glow. Her body stretched itself taut with effort. What now? She couldn't hold this level of power forever.

Ahhhh. The destination.

She thought of the moment she had almost decided to make Jergan vampire. Emotion poured through her as she stared at his wounds, not knowing if he would survive them. She could feel the machine move even faster. It was just a blur beyond the corona of her power. And then it slowed. From somewhere outside herself she saw her body standing, glowing, in front of the great machine as it creaked almost to a halt, it moved so slowly. Had she failed? The power still poured from her body into the room. A feeling of incredible *tristesse* came over her. She would not win through. Her only hope of happiness, or of giving Jergan his own forever, faded.

It was only luck that she had met him at all. Her friend Titus had talked her into buying a slave as bodyguard. Poor Titus. . . .

Everything snapped back to motion and she felt herself being flung like a stone in a slingshot into more and more speed. The jewels lit up. They magnified the power into colored beams that crisscrossed, swinging in arcs across the stone ceiling. Pain surged into every fiber of her body.

Then, blackness.

2

DONNATELLA LAY WITH her cheek against cold
stone, aching in every joint.

She opened her eyes. They wouldn't focus. She blinked
several times, but it did no good. It was dark, though normally that didn't hinder her. What was that smell?

She pushed herself up, fighting nausea. Had Leonardo's
wonderful machine done what it was made to do? *Breathe,*
she told herself. Air rushed into her lungs in desperate
gasps.

The place smelled like a charnel house. The room
wavered into focus. The dull gleam of the great machine
loomed above her. She blinked again. The giant gear
creaked to a stop. The smaller gears slowed. Where was
she? In the dimness behind the machine she saw the niches
of a catacomb. She thought for a moment she had just
transported a few feet into the maze under the Baptistery
without changing times at all. But these bodies were only a
few years dead at most, thus the smell of putrefaction. Cru-
cifixes were clutched in moldering hands. Flesh still clung
to bones.

These catacombs were still being used. Where were
the narrow confines of the subterranean passages underneath Taurus's arena? That was what she had been thinking of. . . .

But she hadn't thought about the moment she had planned. She stumbled to her feet. She had thought, right at that last incredible moment, of the day she met Jergan.

That was, what, a week before the day she failed to make the right decision? It didn't matter. She would just make him vampire immediately and return to the machine and her own time. But maybe these were the Baptistery catacombs of Florence at a time when they were new. Had she changed times but not places? If she was in Florence, she had a journey of a week or more to Rome ahead of her to get Jergan, and back again. . . . The machine would surely be gone by the time she returned.

Then there was no time to be lost. She stumbled away from the giant machine and felt along the walls until her hand touched the cold, mushy surface of putrefying flesh, still moving with the maggots that spawned in it. She jerked her hand back and stared into the darkness. The squeak of rats was plain. She picked her way down the corridor, keeping her hands to herself until she stumbled against something. Stairs. She looked up. There was a line of very faint light in the darkness above her. She headed upward.

A great stone door stood slightly ajar, letting in moonlight filtered through something. She pushed on the stone. It creaked open, resisting, revealing a garden bright with the light of a full moon. The doorway was cut into a rock wall and covered with a thick mat of trailing wisteria vine. Now the vine was rolled aside like a cascade of hair. She was not in Florence.

This was her garden in Rome. Lord, she had forgotten how beautiful it was with the sundial, telling no hour at the moment, and the carefully tended beds of herbs, the olive trees. Not much was blooming. It had been January when she bought Jergan. The wisteria kept its leaves, but no purple flowers floated like shed tears upon the walkway. The

garden was empty, the gardeners who worked in daylight
long retired. She turned to the house. Her house. Her name
had been Livia Quintus Lucellus then. And this house was
the center of her effort to ease Rome back into a republic.
Impossible as that had turned out to be. Of course a woman
could have no public power. She could not hold office, and
office was everything in Rome. She could not vote. She
had power only through a man: husband, father, brother.
But Livia had always thought on a larger scale. She gathered power through many men. Most of the senatorial class
came to her audience room to consult her, unofficially of
course. But her name had the power of her wisdom and her
cunning behind it, and was whispered in the corridors of
the Forum.

She moved silently toward the house, keeping to the
shadows. Wonderful Leonardo. She had a chance to rectify her horrible mistake. Ahead, servants were tending
braziers in the house, which was open to the elements inside its courtyard walls. She looked down. Her everyday
dress made in 1821 and sturdy half boots seemed out of
place here. But perhaps she was invisible to those who
lived in this time. What would happen if she ran into herself as she had been? This might be the night after she met
Jergan. If so, he would already be in the house somewhere. Her stomach did a little somersault of anticipation.

Then she frowned. This wouldn't be so simple. She
couldn't just make Jergan vampire immediately. That act
must be consensual—otherwise it was a violation worse
than rape. She'd have to wait until he knew what she was,
got over his horror, if that was even possible, and perhaps
felt something for her. That would never happen before
the machine returned to 1821.

So she must wait, use his wounds in the arena a week
hence as an excuse as she had planned, and hope he

would forgive her. What if he resented being vampire so much he ended in hating her for what she'd done?

She stood, wavering, in the garden. What a tangle. She took a breath. Well, maybe she could tell him what she was earlier than she had the last time she'd lived through this. Maybe she could tell him that she loved him sooner. Perhaps that would allow his acceptance when she'd finally did the deed. She certainly wasn't going back down those stairs to Leonardo's machine and run home to her own time without even trying to get what she came for.

Ahead she heard voices. She slid through the columns onto the marble floor patterned with deep green and white triangles arranged in circles and ringed in rose-tinted stone. She had always loved that floor. Several senators were being escorted out the front door.

One voice was familiar. Titus Delanus Andronicus, always a trusted advisor. "You should buy bodyguards, Livia. Good, strong backs who can wield a sword and are broken for the arena."

"I can take care of myself, Titus." Was that her? Did she really sound like that?

"But that is just the problem. Gaius has arranged two attacks, and twice you have eluded death, even though you spurn a retinue. I don't know how you survived. Neither does anyone else. And they are starting to wonder. You can't afford curiosity."

"True." He didn't know how true. She hated having to bow to convention. But she least of anyone could afford close scrutiny of her actions, not only because she plotted against Gaius Caesar, but also because if they found out that she was as strong as any ten men and could dispatch her attackers single-handed . . . well, they couldn't kill her, but her life in Rome would be over, and her plot to rid Rome of Gaius a failure. She heard herself sigh. "You Romans find all your slaves about you a comfort. You dislike being alone. But I am from Dacia, and those are not my ways."

Dacia was the Roman province that included what was, in 1821, called Transylvania, though Rome held no sway high in the Carpathian Mountains where she had been born. There only the Council of Elders ruled.

"Well, then buy one well-broken, brawny brute who knows he will be killed most painfully if you die. That will motivate him to protect you. And it will still the wagging tongues."

Donnatella could now see Titus, the white toga of a Roman citizen bordered with the rich purple band of the senatorial class and embroidered with the pattern of his family. Now where was Livia? She meant, where was *she*? Or at least the she of long ago. How disconcerting . . .

"I dislike brutes who know only how to shed blood." The voice that must be hers was almost petulant. The conversation was all coming back to her now.

Titus threw up his hands. "Then train him as a body slave and have your pleasure of him as well. I don't care, Livia. But get some protection whether you need it or not. I know you dislike the sunlight. Let me accompany you to the night market."

Dear Titus had always respected her privacy. He did not ask her too many questions about how she had survived the attacks. And of course, he had been right about needing a slave as camouflage. Donnatella moved closer and edged around a column. Had Titus known more about her than he let on?

"Very well, Titus. I am putty in your hands," the earlier her sighed.

Titus laughed. "Quite the opposite, my beautiful witch,"

he said. "You have all of us old men under a spell, I am certain."

Donnatella peered around the column.

There she was, her former self, hair piled in intricate knots of shining black, a flowing *stola,* a tunic sort of thing, made of fine red wool embroidered with gold hanging from one shoulder, fastened with a jeweled broach and bound at the waist with a girdle of golden mesh. The face was the image her mirror had shown her for two thousand years and yet it startled her. Her skin was fine, of palest olive, her eyes dark, expressive pools fringed by long dark lashes and slanted slightly. Her lips were full and she had prominent cheekbones. The whole effect was slightly exotic, not quite Roman. Her *palla* wrapped around her petite, almost delicate form, giving the *stola* shape. She felt the energy vibrating around her former self. Donnatella vibrated in sympathy.

And then the vibrations in the air cycled up until they were almost painful. The woman who was herself turned, eyes wide in shock. Their eyes locked. Vibrations rocked Donnatella. She felt as though she was disintegrating. She stepped forward into the room, pulled, sucked almost, toward Livia. Shrieking, Donnatella clutched her belly. And then she was hurtling toward the form of Livia, a mist, disintegrated into a million, million tiny pieces.

And then nothing.

LIVIA HAD THE oddest feeling she was being watched. Her Companion itched in her veins, though she had just fed. She couldn't be hungry. "Very well, Titus, I am putty in your hands."

Titus was saying something. She couldn't concentrate on what. She looked around. And there was a woman dressed very strangely, staring at her. With her own face! Livia's vibrations ramped up until they were almost painful. She stared at the woman in shock.

And then the woman with her face wasn't there. She simply disappeared. She didn't translocate, for there was no telltale sign of whirling blackness. The air seemed to waver. A mist formed and the woman with her face simply ceased to be. Livia shook her head to clear it. She felt so strange—full to overflowing and nervous. Something knew her, knew all her secrets, even the ones she had not told herself. Shocked to her core, she shuddered. What had happened here?

"Livia, are you attending to *anything* I say?"

Livia jerked her gaze to Titus, who was frowning at her in concern. "Of . . . of course, old friend. You were saying something about the night market. Did you . . . Did you see anyone standing there? A woman. She would have been right in your view. . . ."

Titus raised his eyebrows. He was spectrally thin, his brows gray streaks over brown eyes wise for having lived only a single lifetime. "You've been working too hard."

"Oh." So he hadn't seen anyone. Had she? It had just happened and yet the memory seemed to be slipping away from her. She pressed a hand to her forehead. "You're right of course. Forgive me." What had she seen? A woman?

"Come," Titus said, taking her arm. "Let's to the night market and buy you a body slave, and then you are going to come home and rest. Unless you'd rather go to Neronius's banquet. He has all that Syrian gold to thrust into society, and he means to do it up lavishly tonight."

"Spare me a night of overindulgence and I'll give you your trip to the night market."

"A fair trade, my lady," Titus laughed, and guided her

out into the night. "And my bodyguards will provide your protection until you get your own."

She clapped her hands. "My litter," she ordered Lucius, who appeared from nowhere at her signal.

THE NIGHT MARKET was a new idea. Roman citizens usually conducted business in the morning and early in the afternoon, then retired to rest. They gave the evening over to socializing, on either a grand or a simple scale, whatever they could afford. But Livia was glad for the new idea. As she was a vampire, even bundled up against the rays of the sun her skin itched painfully, and any glimpse of flesh was burned in seconds. She was old and could heal burns, but she only braved the daylight in emergencies. As she alighted from her litter, she felt a thrill of excitement unwarranted by the familiar bustle around her. She didn't even want to be here, she reminded herself. And yet something important was about to happen. She felt it at the base of her spine.

Why did she feel that she had done all this before?

Something inside her poked to get out. A memory? She pushed it down.

She would buy a slave tonight. It would be a barbarian slave.

Where had that thought come from? Really, her brain was feeling quite disordered. She shook herself mentally. *Keep your mind on your task. Conspirators can't afford to have disordered thoughts.*

There were perhaps still some slaves left from the "triumphal" march Gaius Caesar had staged two days before, upon the army's return from the north. He had gone to conquer Britannia but lost his nerve. The army stalled on the shore of the channel. He had them gather seashells, proclaiming "victory" over Neptune. All Rome was whispering after the triumphal march of the soldiers followed by wagonloads of shells and a hundred slaves, some Gauls who had staged a brief, ill-conceived rebellion and some spies and scouts from Britannia. The army was deeply shamed. The Senate protested the waste of funds. It would make her job with the Senate easier.

She was alighting from her litter when a clatter of boot heels on cobblestones and metal on metal alerted her that the Praetorian Guard was near. She glanced up and saw a troop of Caesar's personal army coming up the street. They looked like evil insects, armored entirely in black, each helmet sporting a black brush of horsehair. Short swords were strapped to their thighs, and they wore greaves that covered their legs to their knees. The crowd skittered aside for them as they marched forward. What were they doing at the night market?

As they drew closer, she saw that the captain of the Guard, in charge of Caesar's personal safety and one of his closest confidants, was in their lead. The whole city feared Cassius Chaerea almost as much as they feared his master.

Livia feared Chaerea for another reason entirely. *Let him not stop,* she thought. *He mustn't even look at me.*

But he raised a hand. His cloak swirled back. The troop stopped, took one marching step in place, and stilled. Chaerea had a face hardened by years of battle and more years of palace intrigue. It had deep lines carved around the mouth and an ax blade of a nose. His eyes had seen every cruelty Imperial Rome could present.

"Livia Quintus Lucellus," Chaerea said, nodding crisply, "I heard that you were attacked last night by three men." He did not even acknowledge Titus.

"It was nothing. I was unhurt."

"You lead a charmed life."

He was right about that. It was a fact she did not want blurted to the world. "They were bumblers," she said, though they hadn't been. They had been dressed as ruffians, but she was betting they were ex-army, the way they wielded swords. She realized others near her were listening intently to her and Chaerea's exchange. Soon the whole city would be buzzing about her too-miraculous escape. "Several generous bystanders helped me," she lied by way of explanation. "And did not remain that I could know their names and thank them properly." Even Chaerea must not know how she had vanquished her attackers.

"Alas, the Guard apparently cannot keep the city entirely free of brigands. My apologies."

"I am here to buy a bodyguard," she said, to reassure him.

"I would buy a troop of them, if I were you." He nodded again. Then he held up his hand and motioned the Guard forward.

Titus breathed a sigh of relief. "That man makes my stomach churn," he muttered.

Surrounded by several burly slaves armed with short swords, he led the way into the busy market. The air was filled with the chatter of bargaining, the cries of the vendors hawking their wares, and the smell of cooked meat, spices, and cedar boughs. Dyed cloth in many colors, produce from the lands beyond the Tiber, carved wooden bowls—you could buy anything at the night market. The slave vendor stalls were at the back, surrounding a simple raised platform on which stood several posts with shackles for the auctions held once a week. The place was a warren of stalls. You could buy scribes, accountants, galley slaves for your barge, men to till the fields of your estates, or females to be hairdressers, laundresses. Of course Romans also bought slaves used for more intimate activities, such as bathing and sex. In Rome anything was possible.

"There's a likely seller." Titus pointed. He had gathered his toga over one arm. "He specializes in combatants for the arena."

Livia cast her eyes over the stock, brawny men with dead eyes. Not barbarians. These were likely from the provinces to the east, Judea or Syria. Roman men and women clustered around, prodding muscle, asking about their training. A shivery feeling wafted through her. What she was looking for wasn't here. She knew that as surely as she knew her own name. "I want more than muscle, Titus."

Titus sighed. "I doubt you'll find one who can slaughter at your command and play the lute into the bargain."

"I don't want a lute player." But intelligent, a core of strength and courage . . . maybe she was looking for character. One couldn't judge those qualities in a slave market. But she knew she would recognize the one when she saw him.

They kept going. The slaves all seemed alike, none what she wanted. She glanced to Titus. He didn't relish shopping. But she vowed she would see every slave in the market until she found the one she wanted. He was here. "Why don't we split up? I'll scout ahead," she offered.

"I'm not leaving you alone. Your enemies are everywhere."

"Give me a couple of your bodyguards as escort. Look out for any slave that seems like he has a brain in his head as well as a ribbed belly."

Titus nodded brusquely, pointed at one of his slaves, and started off to the left. Livia looked around. She felt so strange. It seemed as if she had done this all before. She moved through the crowds. The electric energy of her Companion made people part in front of her like water before the prow of her barge. Let the bodyguards keep up if they could.

"New shipment!" she heard a vendor yell. The cry sent shivers down her back. She knew that cry. "Fresh from Britannia." She pushed through the clot of onlookers.

Somewhere in her mind she registered the barbarians who sat half-naked with slumped shoulders and hunted eyes, chained to posts. Even in the brisk January night, the scent of men unwashed and the lime used to kill their vermin hung in the air, along with the sweet aroma of blood from half-healed wounds and the astringent smell of the *acetum* used to disinfect them.

But all that receded. Her eyes were drawn to a giant of a man in the back. His wrists and ankles were shackled to two posts by chains of only two or three links so that, though standing, he was spread-eagled and unable to move. His hair was dark like any good Roman's, though long and tangled, held away from the sides of his face by some tie at the back. His beard was rough and untrimmed. He wore only a scrap of cloth about his loins, the better to reveal his muscled shoulders, chest, and corded thighs. Those muscles had not been acquired in some gymnasium but were created by hard work. His flesh was paler than a Roman's, though he had spent time in the sun. He had a light dusting of dark, curling hair over his chest and belly. A wound in his left shoulder still seeped. No one could say he wasn't attractive. Yet it was his eyes that riveted her. They were light: translucent green like the shallows of the Mediterranean. They burned with hatred. She felt she had known him always, though her rational mind knew this was the first time she had ever seen him. Her throat seemed to close. She had done all this before. She swayed as something inside her seemed to be trying to get out. A thought? A memory? She squeezed her eyes shut.

She took a breath. That was better. She'd pushed down whatever weakness assailed her. Her eyes returned to the barbarian.

A gaggle of three men clustered around him. They were talking. . . .

"You can't want him for your brothel, Graccus," one laughed. "He's incorrigible. Your patrons want slaves to spread their cheeks willingly."

There was much tittering. "Enough fruit of the poppy and he'll take direction." The one called Graccus was an oily-looking creature. His pomaded locks lay in curls around a face that was lined with a heavy sensuality. "And if he does not, some like the pleasure of forcing a big man. I'll just chain him."

The slave's muscles bulged as he strained against his bonds. He had broken out in a sweat in spite of the fact that he was nearly naked in the cool winter night of Rome.

"Well, he isn't much good for anything except a brothel," another said. "You could never trust the brute, and who wants a slave like that?"

Graccus mustered his courage and approached the barbarian. "His body wants shaving, except for a patch around his organ." He poked the man's biceps with his ivory walking stick. The barbarian gritted his teeth. She could see his jaw clench. Emboldened, the others surrounded him, touching shoulders, tweaking nipples.

"Be careful, Roman dogs," he growled in accented Latin. They leaped back as though they had been struck.

Where did a barbarian learn to speak the language that ruled the world?

Graccus drew himself up to retrieve his dignity and managed a chuckle. He turned to his friends. "Yes, fruit of the poppy and daily beating. I'll enjoy seeing him on his knees. Perhaps I'll use him myself." He looked around. "Seller! You there!"

A small man in a surprisingly rich tunic and toga looked up. He was waiting on two women. "Yes, citizen? Ahhhh, you have good taste. He is magnificent, is he not? I shall be with you in only a moment." He turned back and continued extolling the skills in hair dressing of the female slave the two women were considering.

Graccus looked sour. "Well, let's see more of him. I would know whether my patrons will find his genitalia sufficient." He stepped near enough to the barbarian to tear the cloth from his hips and toss the pieces away. The barbarian lunged against his bonds with another growl. But now Graccus was surer of himself. He only grinned.

"He's well enough," one of the others said. That was an understatement. The barbarian was impressively endowed.

"I'd like to see him eager." Graccus walked behind the slave and slapped his buttocks.

One of the others moved in. They were going to tease the slave into an erection. That would keep them occupied. Livia glanced to the slave trader. He had finished with the women. One of his slave assistants was escorting them to the front. Graccus and his friends were now focused on the barbarian. He roared his protest as they touched his genitals.

Livia knew what she would do. And it felt right and true.

She slid over to the slave trader, Titus's bodyguards in tow, before he could approach the men. "Kind sir, how much for the barbarian?"

The trader looked startled. "That one, my lady? He is no woman's slave."

"I shall be the judge of that. How much?"

A calculating look came over the trader's face. She could see the price rising in the face of her open interest.

"Two thousand dinars."

Steep. But what did she care? "Done." She did not even glance toward the barbarian and his tormentors, though she could not help but register his roars of protest. The trader led her to the front of the stall and wrote out a receipt. She paid him from the purse she had concealed in the folds of her *palla* and took the scroll that said she owned a new slave.

"Let me get your property, my lady," the trader said. They turned to the back of the stall. The three men clustered round the straining barbarian, laughing as he tried to twist away. Blood dripped from his wrists where he had pulled against his shackles. They had him fully erect and one was still jerking on his rod. He spat at them. It was his only means of defiance.

Graccus wiped his face and laughed. "Oh, he'll be a joy to break."

"I agree," she said. The three yanked their gazes up, as did the barbarian. He flushed in shame. "Now unhand my new slave, sirs, so I may begin."

"What? But I am buying him for my brothel!"

She waved the receipt scroll. "Too late." Her bodyguards stepped up behind her. She turned to the trader. "For the price I just paid, you can throw in a pair of shackles."

The trader nodded and clapped his hands. Slaves appeared with the required bindings. They unlocked the barbarian's wrists from the poles and chained them behind his back before they released his feet. His ankles, too, were bloodied. Those green eyes stared at her, burning with intensity, as though he was still not sure what had just happened to him. Excitement churned inside her. This was the start of something—she didn't know quite what. "Come quietly, slave," she ordered, putting all the force of her personality behind her words, just shy of raising her Companion for compulsion. "You two—see that he does." Two of Titus's bodyguards nodded. Each took one of the slave's arms and dragged him forward while Graccus remonstrated with the trader.

"You knew I wanted him," Graccus was saying. The trader only shrugged. He couldn't have gotten two thousand dinars for a slave bound for a brothel.

"Let's find your master," she said to the bodyguards. They pushed into the market throng.

"There you are," Titus called, hurrying over. Livia saw him frown as he registered the barbarian. "Livia Quintus, what is this? You've never purchased this creature!"

"I have, Titus. He was a soldier, therefore skilled in martial arts. He even speaks Latin."

"Livia, return him at once. This is no slave for a woman."

Livia turned to her new purchase, seeing him through Titus's eyes. His rod was still full, if not erect. Bloody and sweating, he looked fierce, with those intense green eyes and all that hair. But he was the one she wanted. She knew that as certainly as she knew her own name. "Once we clean him up you won't recognize him."

"He needs more than a bath to make him suitable."

"You were the one who suggested a slave, and now that I've meekly done as you ask, you rail at me."

Titus rolled his eyes. "Meek? I would welcome meek."

Livia gestured her entourage forward. Titus sighed and fell in step. "I just hope you haven't bitten off more than you can chew."

"If I have, I shall sell him. Now, to my litter."

3

HE'D BEEN BOUGHT by a woman. This did not bode
well. Jergan had hoped he'd be bought for his strong back
and sent to labor in some Roman's fields or to pull an oar
on a galley. Those things he understood. It would be
painful never to see Centii, his home, again, but he would
bear it. Instead a woman had bought him for who knew
what purposes.

Rome loomed around him. Huge stone buildings everywhere, triumphal arches. The place was like no other he had
ever seen. He'd been marched naked through the streets
yesterday, *paved* streets, along with the other captives and
wagons holding an astounding number of seashells. The
soldiers who had captured him were not happy about the
seashells, but he put it down to the insanity of Rome. Rome
was insane. Word of its indulgence in orgies and cruel
games had spread across the world. Those brutes who had
raised his cock in the slave market were no doubt just the
beginning of his ordeal. The thought of their touch still
made him squirm. If not for them, the woman might not
have noticed him.

Or maybe he could not escape notice. He was a clear
head taller than any Roman man. He had not seen light eyes
except on other captives. If the woman had not noticed him,

he might be in a brothel, being raped and beaten. Could anything be worse than that? In Rome, perhaps the answer was "yes."

He was hurried out to a litter. It was all he could do not to limp. But he wouldn't let these Romans see him weak. The woman stepped inside and closed the veils of her litter while the men shackled him to one of the poles. The richly dressed man walked round to the other side. She did not treat him with the submission required of a woman to a husband or father in his homeland. And what man would let his wife or daughter buy a slave like Jergan? He must be a friend. The bearers lifted the poles and started out of the market.

People and litters still crowded the streets. Did Romans never sleep? Jergan was conscious that he was naked. He jutted his chin up. He refused to be ashamed.

Two women whispered together, then hurried up to him and . . . and touched him. He growled to frighten them away. It didn't work. Soon he had a small, clucking crowd following him, touching biceps and shoulder, buttocks—even his privates. The guards only grinned. He stopped ducking away from his tormentors and resolved to ignore them. He would think of Centii: the rich fields, his family eating under the trees of the orchard in the summertime. He couldn't hold the image. He felt his cock rising. Curse the life of a soldier. If he had been relieving his needs regularly with a woman, they would not be able to tease him so. He strode ahead, gaze stony, willing himself flaccid. It wasn't working.

"Halt," her voice barked out from inside the litter.

The bearers lurched to a stop. That only gave the chattering leeches clinging to him a better target for their foul caresses. His owner poked her head out from among the veils. This close he noticed that she had a vitality, a force of life that almost hummed about her. A scent of something exotic, spicy and sweet hung around her.

"Get back, whores," she said, low but so intensely her words seemed to echo in the air around her. "He belongs to me." To his amazement the women stepped back, shock in their eyes.

"You three, keep them away from him," she ordered the guards. Her head disappeared inside the hangings. "Proceed."

The men around him, chastised, drew their swords. The women backed off, murmuring epithets. Several spat upon Jergan.

Before they could start forward again, a litter squeezing through the narrow street from the opposite direction halted their progress. This litter was wide, its gauzy hangings bordered in purple and embroidered with gold thread. It took eight burly Nubians to bear it by the ornately carved double poles that sat on their shoulders. As it squeezed past, a female voice called on the bearers to halt. A woman with a long nose and close-set eyes pulled back the hangings and raked her gaze over Jergan. Her smile made him feel unclean.

"Agrippina, look." The woman beckoned to a companion. Another woman leaned forward and peered at him. She must be nearsighted. Their features said clearly they were related.

"Oh, my!" the second woman exclaimed.

"My humble slave draws the attention of the imperial sisters. I am honored." His new owner's voice behind him was not obsequious, no matter these women's status. It held the faintest hint of sarcasm and more, contempt. "How good to meet you, Julia Lavilla, Julia Agrippina."

The sisters had the same first name? Ahhhh. They were

named for the first dictator of Rome, no doubt to display their lineage.

"We were on the way to the night market to see if there were any slaves left from the victory parade. The one we bought didn't last, and we have need of new fodder for our . . . attentions." They only glanced to his owner. Their eyes drifted back to his naked body.

"You have saved us the trouble of the market, Livia Quintus. This one suits our needs."

"I am desolated, exalted ones." Her voice was too sorrowful to be truly sorry. "He is not for sale."

"Nonsense," Julia Lavilla snorted. "Name your price."

"A thousand apologies," his new owner mourned. "I cannot think of a sum that would mean more to me than the anticipation breaking this slave raises in my breast."

Breaking. The second time she had spoken of it. He ground his teeth together. Whatever lay ahead, he would bear it. But that didn't mean he wasn't frightened, somewhere down inside.

"But Agrippina, how can she . . . ?" the other sister sputtered. She must be called Agrippina to distinguish her from her sister.

"Livia Quintus Lucellus withholds that pleasure from us, Julia. Well, perhaps we will see you and your slave at a victory banquet. Once you have been sated by him, you may be in the mood to share."

The curtain dropped and his owner gave the signal to move on.

He stared straight ahead and concentrated on not limping. The full horror of being a woman's slave in decadent Rome came home to him. He wondered if he could hold out without submitting to her. He'd at least make her work for it. No matter the tortures she employed. He swallowed, his mouth dry. He was a warrior. His troop had joined the rebelling Gauls to face the overwhelming Roman legions with valor.

He only hoped he could face what lay ahead.

"LEAVE US," LIVIA said to Lucius Lucellus, the freedman who ran her household, and the two maids who normally attended her. The three bowed themselves out of her chambers doubtfully, but there was no arguing with her tone. Livia turned to the barbarian, standing naked, his wrists chained behind him, in the middle of her chamber. The lamplight glowed on intricately woven tapestries in vibrant colors and marble busts on pedestals. A delicate bronze figure of Pan sat on a carved wooden sideboard. She could command the elegances of Roman culture, next to which the giant naked barbarian seemed even more out of place. The wound in his shoulder stood out lividly, and he had fading bruises over his ribs and his right hip. But these wounds were not his first taste of combat. Old scars on thigh and chest gave tribute to his history as a soldier. He stood, green eyes glaring at her, not like a slave at all in spite of the chains.

Perhaps Titus was right. This might be difficult. What had she been thinking to buy a slave like this? He would be nothing but trouble. She should have Lucius take him right back down to the market and dispose of him for whatever price he would bring.

But somehow, she had no intention of doing that.

She tapped a finger to her chin, studying him. "How well do you speak Latin?"

"Well enough," he grunted, not bothering with any term of respect. Not promising. She could compel the slave of course. The Companion in her blood gave her control over human minds if she called up its power. But one couldn't compel a human constantly. It took effort and energy. She must sleep. Her attention would inevitably wander. Then, of course, using the power of her Companion in public would reveal that her eyes went red. So she needed this barbarian willing, or at least inured to being a slave, if he was to be of any use as a pretense of a bodyguard. It was time to see if he was intelligent. She had a theory about slaves and she meant to test it. Romans considered that slaves were not truly men, that they had no animus or spirit, and therefore no honor. But Livia didn't believe it.

"Let us come to an understanding, then." She paused. "How did you become slave?" She knew what must have happened.

He swallowed. "I was given into slavery by the general of the Gauls when his army was defeated." The man's eyes were hard.

"So you are not of the Gauls?" That was strange.

"I had a troop of two hundred Cantiaci only. We crossed the channel from Centii, our homeland, to scout out the Roman numbers. We expected the Romans to attack Britannia. I joined my troop with the Gauls who were rebelling against the Romans when we were cut off from our ship."

So he was Celt. No wonder he looked so fierce. "And in defeat that general gave your men to the Romans as part of the truce." It was the way of the Romans. They decimated their enemy's army at the same time they filled the city with slaves, among other tribute. She wished his own commander had given him as a slave, though. That would have been a stronger obligation.

"He gave only me and my two lieutenants to the Romans. My men were spared by agreement. He was an honorable man."

Unlike the Romans. That's what he wanted to say. It didn't matter. She had what she wanted. This man spoke easily of honor. He valued it. He had made an agreement with the Gaulish general that spared his men. He had given his word. Her ability to keep him depended on his having a good portion of honor himself.

"And what happens if you try to escape? I mean besides the fact that you will be hunted down and crucified?"

He took a breath. "I will have dishonored my people and myself by breaking both my troth to the general who spared my men slavery and his promise to the Roman general."

"So, let us be clear. Your choices are to be sold to a brothel for men where you will be drugged, beaten, and raped routinely, or possibly to Agrippina and her sister Julia, where I assure you, the result would be much the same. Or to try to escape, thus dishonoring your pledge and guaranteeing your death by crucifixion. Or to serve me. Does that sum it up?"

He glared at her. A muscle in his jaw worked. Then he nodded, once.

"You will want to know what I require, so you may measure your choice. After all, you might still choose the brothel or Caesar's sisters. If you do, I will return you to the market, without punishment for your choice."

Now he was wary. He nodded again.

"You will address me as Mistress. You will speak civilly when spoken to. Which has not been the case thus far," she noted. "I expect obedience, honesty, and ungrudging service." She cleared her throat. "And one more thing." How did one ask for this? "I will use you as a bodyguard. You will be given a weapon and I expect you to protect my person at the cost of your own." He was examining her, his judgment reserved. "Not so different from serving in the army." Would he see it as similar? Or did protecting a woman who was his people's enemy seem a betrayal of his honor? "Do you . . . do you have questions? You may ask them now."

He looked her up and down. She waited. At last he said, "Are you a harsh master?"

He had a right to ask that. "I . . . I consider myself exacting but not harsh."

"If you find me wanting, what punishments will you employ?"

She drew herself up. "I want no slave who must be whipped to obedience. If you are sullen, disobedient, or dishonest, I shall simply sell you. Take your chances in the market."

He frowned. He didn't like that prospect. Good. "Do you expect me to pleasure you?"

She flushed. She hadn't expected him to be bold enough for that question. Was he taunting her, or was his curiosity genuine? Still, she had given him permission to ask. "I . . . I have no need to order slaves to my bed. I have my pick of Roman citizens." That was true, yet she had not taken a lover in years. She was too busy trying to put Rome to rights, and she didn't want entanglements. Still, some part of her whispered, *Yes! I want my pleasure of you, and your pleasure, too.* The thought of those strong thighs and that pretty rod stiff and eager to plunge inside her was making her wet. That was only the influence of her Companion, whose urge toward life made vampire kind easily aroused. She thought those urges had faded from lack of use. Apparently not. This barbarian's constant presence might actually be a torment. "You are forbidden to rut among my servants, male or female, though. That will result in immediate sale."

She thought he might be smirking, but his lips did not quite turn up. Curse her blush. He knew he had discomposed her. He probably knew she wanted him. His hot gaze roved over her. She felt more naked than he was. A man like this no doubt always had his way with women. More than anything she wanted to wipe that smirk off his face. So it was time to tell him exactly what was at stake and seal the bargain between them. "If you serve me faithfully, I will allow you to earn your freedom."

His gaze snapped back to her face, questioning. She saw a spark of hope bloom there and be suppressed. "How long?"

"That will depend on your behavior."

"How do I know that you will do this thing?" he growled.

"Ask Lucius Lucellus. I freed him."

His brows drew together. "Yet he still serves you."

"But now he does so by choice, for a salary. A good one."

They stood there, staring at each other. She had to tilt her head back since he towered over her. "Choose, barbarian. Do you serve me, or do I give Graccus and his friends, or Agrippina and Julia, another opportunity to buy you?"

He looked away and stared at the ground. She watched his chest rise and fall for three breaths. Finally he turned back to her. His green eyes bored into hers. "I will serve you." He said it as though it was a vow.

"A wise choice. Then kneel." His first test.

She saw him struggle with himself. But the combination of his honor, the possibility of freedom, and fear of the brothel would win out. He bowed his head and sank slowly to his knees.

She took out the key to his shackles and walked around him. Her eyes widened. His back, buttocks, and thighs were laced with stripes in various states of healing. She bit her lip and bent to his shackles. "Who whipped you?"

"Who did not?" he answered grimly.

She could imagine the expression of defiance he wore even in defeat attracting the wrath of his captors. He must have been naked when he'd been whipped, and the blows had occurred over time. "They took your clothing?"

"The wool was fine, the cuirass well-wrought. The boots were tooled leather." He had contempt for those who had stolen from him. She had thought all Celts fought in the nude. At least he wasn't that barbaric.

"So they marched you all the way from the shores of Gaul without clothing or boots." She glanced to the soles of his feet and saw that they were bruised and cut. She wasn't proud of the Roman army at this moment. "And whipped you into the bargain."

As she released the shackles, he shrugged and began rubbing the circulation back into his hands. "They wanted the other captives to despair as their leaders were humbled."

"How did you get over the mountains?"

"I wrapped my feet with the leather jerkin of a captive who died. When it got cold some peasants along the way took pity on me and tied some animal skins about my body."

But his spirit had not been broken. She had a tenuous truce with him, no more. Romans thought slaves had a need to submit their will to another's, that they did not appreciate freedom. Not this slave. He might submit because his honor required it or because it was the lesser of two evils. But that was all.

"Come," she ordered. "I want the stink of the slave market washed from you." She clapped her hands. Catia, her maid, appeared. "Assemble a basket of astringent and unguents, Catia, and see if you can find a tunic for him. Oh, and make up a poultice of *acetum* and garlic."

He rose gingerly. How had she not noticed he was footsore? Or was he too proud to limp through the city of his captors, no matter the pain? She turned her back on him and walked into the gardens. The *thermae* was out near the back wall. She had taken two steps before she heard him follow. She avoided the graveled paths because of his feet and kept to the flagstone walk among the olive trees.

As she passed the wall that held back the hill, covered with a gnarled wisteria vine, she paused. A feeling of uneasiness wound up her spine. She should know something, or do something. She had been feeling strange all night, full somehow, urgent.

She shook herself and pushed the feeling down. Nonsense.

Her purpose now was clear. She must establish her dominance over this slave so he could pose as her bodyguard and deflect any attention another attack might bring on. She strode to the marble building that sat among the olive trees. Though in the heart of the city near the crown of the Capitoline Hill, her property had enough land to support a spacious house, private baths, outbuildings for a kitchen and the domicile of the servants, as well as a garden, all within secure stone walls. Her kind just seemed to attract riches. And they had all the time in the world to acquire wealth and watch it grow. Her lands on the other side of the Tiber provided enough wheat to make bread for a tenth of the city. It was her wealth that gave her power, at least partly.

She trotted up the shallow stairs between the columns of the pediment to the four rooms of the bath. The *frigidarium* was lined with benches. Stone niches on one wall held the bather's toga or *palla* and *stola,* sandals. It was cool, made cooler by the January air outside and the deep water of the cold plunge pool in the center. He had no clothing to discard, but he needed protection for his feet from the heated floor beyond.

"Put on a pair of those wooden sandals." He looked at

her through narrowed eyes. She raised her brows and waited. Reluctantly he selected the biggest pair and slid them on. They barely fit his feet. She motioned him into the *calidarium* through a wall of heat. The slaves kept the fires stoked at all times. The round pits in the center of the floor gave up waves of heat from their banked coals. The air was moist from the tanks of water above the coals and, beyond, the heated pool. The place smelled of sage and salt and olive oil.

"Sit on that bench while I see if they have found what I require." She watched him sit carefully on the warm marble bench against the wall. The welts and scabs on his backside must make sitting difficult.

"What is this room?" he rumbled in that deep baritone.

"Your term of respectful address?"

He glowered. There was a long pause. "What is this room, Mistress?" He almost choked on the word.

"It is the first of the cleansing rooms."

"All this will do is make me sweat the more."

"Exactly." She left him and headed back to the house. Let him feel that there was really no escape. Though his shackles were gone, his honor held him in wait for her.

The household had been unable to find a tunic big enough for the huge barbarian, but Lucius produced a flaxen cloth to wrap around his loins, and a wide leather belt to hold it in place. At least it was clean and bigger than the scrap he had worn in the trader's stall. Her maid-servant held out a basket filled with small colored-glass bottles. She told Lucius to send for a barber. She would pay dearly for dragging one out at this hour.

By the time she headed back to the bath it had been nearly half an hour. In the cool changing room, she un-wrapped her *palla,* removed her *stola,* and wound a large linen bath towel around herself, tucking it securely in over her breasts. She slid on her personal wooden clogs and took a breath. What she was about to do would be torture for her, plain and simple. Big as he was, he couldn't hurt her. She was a vampire, after all. But his nearness would exacerbate the sensual cravings he had already started. Why were they so sharp? She had no trouble ignoring the Roman men who set their lures for her.

But she had no choice but to enter the bath. She would spend much time with this slave. And he must see that even when he was alone in a bath with her, their relative positions did not change. He was a slave. He did her bidding. If he did not, it was back to the market and the block with his honor lost and his bond, to his people and the general who saved his men, broken.

She entered the *calidarium* and saw that he had eased himself against the wall. His eyes were closed and he gleamed with sweat in the light of the coals. For anyone else, this room would be dim, but, as a vampire, she saw well in the dark. She noticed how drawn he looked. Dark half-circles hung under his eyes. Marching, wounded, from Gaul to Rome at the tail of a cart had been an ordeal.

"Relaxing, isn't it?"

He sat forward and shrugged, unwilling to admit even so simple a truth if she suggested it.

"Hold out your hands." She reached for an amphora set on a low table along with a tray of salt and several curved, ivory-handled *strigils*. She poured some oil scented with sage from her gardens into his cupped hands. His right palm was calloused from long contact with the pommel of a sword. Both wrists were raw. "Rub this in your hair."

He looked up at her, incredulous.

"How else am I going to drag a comb through it?"

He glared at her and set his lips. But he smoothed the oil over the tangled ends, then reached up and untied the

leather strip that held the sides of his hair back. She poured
more oil on his scalp, and he worked it into his hair. The
bulge of his biceps and the revelation of dark hair under his
arms were intimate and frankly arousing.

She cleared her throat. "Now, more for your body." He
held out his hands and she poured them full of oil again.
It smelled like summer.

"Do you Romans not even know of soap?"

"Soap? What is this?" She watched as he rubbed his
chest and belly. This was definitely torture. It was dis-
tracting her so that she had forgotten to demand he be respectful.

"A way of cleaning. Much better than oil. How can one
be clean with oil?"

"Well, what is your 'soap' made of?"

"Sheep's tallow and charcoal." He was rubbing his
thighs. "It creates a lather."

"Sheep's tallow and charcoal? *That* sounds clean. I
prefer olive oil and salt."

He glanced up at her, as if he had not realized before
how absolutely insane rubbing sheep's tallow on your
body sounded. Then he returned to smoothing oil over his
arms.

"You forgot your . . . your genitals."

This time his glance had all the disgust of a glare in it,
but he rubbed the oil over his private parts. They weren't
private now. They belonged to her. That thought was dan-
gerously exciting. She mustn't be seduced by her reaction
to him, or by the insidious lure of slavery. She bit her lips
and throbbed between her legs.

"Turn round." She stood on the bench and poured the
oil over his back and rubbed it in. The touch of his flesh
was hot, but that didn't explain the jolt it gave her. She
vowed to ignore her reaction, but both her body and her

mind seemed disobedient tonight. "Now use the rock salt in that tray to scrub yourself. The salt will hurt the open sores, but it helps prevent infection."

He shrugged. "No matter." He scooped up the salt and rubbed it over his body, even into the wounds at his wrists and ankles. He didn't make a sound other than a sharp intake of breath as it seared him. The man was practically a Stoic. She took up a handful of salt herself and climbed up on the bench again. She spread it carefully, focusing only on the fact that he must be cleaned, not on the fact that she was hurting him.

He didn't even flinch.

"Now," she said. "Hand me one of the *strigils*. You take the other."

"What?"

"The ivory-handled scrapers." She had to remember that he was a barbarian and knew nothing of the civilized world. Sheep's tallow, for Jupiter's sake! "You scrape the effluvium from your body." They scraped in silence. She concentrated on avoiding the welts.

"There." She stepped down, feeling like she had passed an ordeal herself. "Into the pool."

He rose and stepped down into the steaming pool. At this end the water came to his knees. He looked around. "How is this done? A volcanic spring?"

A slave should not be allowed such questions. But there were limits to how much slavelike behavior she wanted. If she was successful in taming him, she would be around him for much of her night, every night, at least for a while. A totally silent and submissive companion would be boring. What she wanted from him was an acknowledgment of his slavery, not cowering submission. In other slaves, achieving that balance was easy, because they were already broken to their slavery. She had only to allow them certain freedoms and they were grateful. But this one—in this one, that balance might be elusive.

"Our spring is cold. The pool is heated with pipes and fires, the same as the house."

He looked at her as though she were mad.

"I should think you would appreciate it in January. Now duck yourself."

He waded into the center where the steaming water was almost up to his nipples and submerged, then came up streaming water. She motioned him to duck himself twice more before she waved him out. "Into the next room."

She followed him into the *frigidarium*. A mosaic of Neptune rising curled around the dark circle of water. He turned and looked his question at her. Even in the dim light she could see his nipples had tightened with the cool air. "It is the cold plunge." She motioned to the pool. He clenched his jaw. Was that resistance? "Just jump in. It's deep enough to take even a big brute like you."

He stalked forward into the pool and sank immediately over his head. He came up sputtering. "Belatucadros's horn," he swore. "That's like to freeze a man's bollocks."

"Out." As he climbed out, she saw that the cold water had indeed tightened his genitals and brought gooseflesh out across his body. Her own body still burned.

She pointed to a bench. He sat, dripping. She knelt in front of him with her basket and chose several vials. She dribbled liquid from the first over his right ankle. He sucked in air. "I know," she apologized. "It stings. But this, too, will prevent festering." She repeated the action on the other ankle. This time the pain did not surprise him and he made no sound. She cupped her hands and took the same astringent and rubbed it over his feet.

When she was done, she busied herself with opening the unguent.

She could feel his eyes on her and glanced up. "You have a question?"

"Why do you abase yourself before me? I am your slave."

She chuffed a laugh. "With ownership comes responsibility. I am responsible for the health of your body."

"You could send others to do this."

"I could. But I want you to know you belong to me. It is I who feed you and see to your wounds. I clothe you as protection against the elements, and give you boots that your feet may not be bruised by stones in the streets." She rubbed his feet and ankles with the healing unguent as she talked. "Because I forbid you to engage in sexual activity, you will achieve release by your own hand weekly under my eye. It is unhealthy for a male to be pent up."

She looked up again as he blinked in surprise, then glowered at her. *That* would make it clear just what belonging to another really meant. He was not his own person anymore, not a single part of him, and he must realize and submit to that idea.

"Now rise. I wish to apply these medicines to your welts." She climbed up on the bench to do it. She pulled his wet hair off his back and laid it over his shoulder. The feel of his damp skin under her fingers was probably as much torture for her as it was for him. She worked down his back toward his buttocks.

"You have a gentle touch." This was said in almost a puzzled tone.

"Thank you, slave." This couldn't go on. "What is your name?"

"Roman slaves have no names of their own." His voice

was harsh. "My name is whatever you call me." He glanced back in suspicion, as though he thought she was trying to trap him into saying the wrong thing.

"It is too much effort to think of a name for you. What is the name you bear now?"

There was a long pause. He knew that by saying his name he was giving up something of himself. "Jergan. My name is Jergan."

"Jergan?" Surprising. "That is not the name of one from a Celtic tribe."

"My father traded in far lands in his youth. My name is from the Goths." His mouth had drawn into a hard line. His name had caused him trouble.

"Jergan will do." She liked it. It seemed . . . familiar. She couldn't have guessed what he would say before he said it, but now that he had, it seemed she had always known it. "And when you are asked, you will say you are the slave of Livia Quintus Lucellus."

A tiny, wizened man poked his head in at the doorway. "My lady called for a barber?"

"I did," she said, stepping off the bench. "Put this slave on your regular list. He should be shaved every three or four days."

The little barber nodded, his bright eyes surveying the barbarian terrain as he opened his bundle of blades and scissors. "His face, of course, but his body should be shaved as well."

Julius Caesar was to thank for the fashion that led Roman men to have much or all of their bodily hair plucked or shaven. "No, just his face. I rather like him natural."

"Sit, slave," the barber said, as he took out a gleaming blade. "And be still."

"You would shave me like a woman?" Jergan growled. His look was so menacing the barber flinched away.

"You are in Rome, Jergan, not some backwater of the empire. Romans shave. Even their slaves shave. It is not effeminate. In fact, Romans would think your long hair womanly."

Oh, dear. That made him glare even more fiercely.

"Do you want it cut off, Lady Lucellus?" The barber enjoyed Jergan's discomfiture.

Jergan mastered himself and relaxed his shoulders. Had he realized that it was not up to him anymore whether he was shaved or had his precious hair cut short? That deserved a reward.

"No. The contrast between his masculinity and his long hair is exotic, don't you think?"

"That is one way to name it, my lady." The barber made his face blank.

Livia tilted Jergan's head back, baring his throat to the barber's razor. That would demonstrate just who was in charge here. She watched the barber ply his trade until Jergan was pink-cheeked and smooth, then sent the barber in to Lucius for payment. As she turned back, she stopped and stared. Her slave had a cleft chin under that beard. And his lips were full. She hadn't noticed that before. He was really a fine figure of a man. And she was not the only one who had noticed it. Caesar's sisters had noticed him. She'd have to be careful of those two vipers.

He rubbed his chin, looking so thoroughly disgusted with himself she had to smile. "You'll get used to it. And to being clean. Romans bathe every day, even slaves, though most must use the public baths. You will bathe here."

He shot her a speculating look.

"Yes, with me. I require protection even in my bath. The emperor frequently sends his guard to take his enemies prisoner at their bath. Now let me see that wound of yours. Javelin?"

"Short sword."

She poured astringent in it. He couldn't help but flinch. The wound had been deep, but it was healing well in spite of the fact that it had probably had no treatment at all. The flesh had drawn together into a jagged, shallow trough, though it still seeped a little clear fluid. Too bad it had not been stitched. The scar would be more pronounced as a consequence. She poured again.

"Why does a woman have enemies?" His voice was tight. He was trying to take his mind off the pain.

"My enemies realize I am working behind the scenes to depose those in power. They would rather I stop, and they mean to see that I do, even if it means killing me." Did Gaius Caesar really know who was behind the Senate's plot against him? He had tortured several senators' slaves to find out. But not, she thought, anyone who actually knew. Had one of her fellow conspirators leaked her name? But then why hadn't Caesar just sent the Praetorian Guard to arrest her? Or them?

"A woman depose a man in power?" Jergan snorted, drawing her attention back to him. "Not possible."

She took the poultice from the basket. "Then you do not know any women with spines."

"What can a woman do? She is weaker than a man."

She looked up at him as she bound the poultice in place. She was vampire, and he would never believe how strong she was. But she couldn't tell him that. "You are stronger than I am. Why are you my slave?"

He clenched his jaw and said nothing.

"A woman can work through men to see her will imposed. She can create circumstances where men choose to do her will. We have been doing it since the beginning of time."

She stood back. The only thing left was his hair. She

took a large ivory comb from a niche in the wall and walked around behind him. She began pulling the comb through his hair, starting at the bottom. The oil had made it slick. If she couldn't comb it out, she might have no choice but to cut it off or leave it in the tangled ropes that lay against his back. He said nothing and she worked in silence. The pulsing between her legs seemed to have gotten into her ears. She was throbbing all over now. When she was done, she worked astringent into his hair to cut the oil, and then bade him bend over so she could ladle water over his head. When he sat up she came round to the front and saw that he was more than half-erect and rising still. He had found his bath as erotic as she had.

She ignored both the erection and the heat in his eyes, though it caused her almost physical pain to do so, and tossed him the flaxen cloth and the belt. "Cover yourself." He stood, his impressive cock swollen, and belted the cloth around his hips. Gods, was she going to have a man around who left her constantly aroused?

She could order him to her bed. It didn't look like it would be a trial to him. And yet . . . She had never had a male body slave precisely because it felt wrong to order a slave to service you. Sexual pleasure should be mutual and carried out between consenting parties. That was what was wrong with pedophiles and rapists. And a slave could not really consent because he could not refuse.

"Keep the wooden sandals. They will protect your feet." She wanted a bodyguard only, she reminded herself. Not to defend her, but to avoid the discovery of what she was if she defended herself.

Which meant she had to give him a weapon.

4

JERGAN LIMPED ACROSS the garden after the petite woman who owned him body and soul, glowering. His flesh was still warm from the bath. The damp wee hours of the night in the month the Romans called January were a shock against his skin. He smelled of oils and herbs. Were they mad to clean their bodies thus? Apparently they did it every day. Still, he had to admit he felt clean. And it was good to have the stink of the horrible journey removed. The astringent still stung in his wounds and the unguents she had applied had a strange tingle to them, but she had been efficient at her treatments and he would be willing to wager that he would heal faster now. He rubbed his chin. He missed his beard.

This night had brought more twists of fate than his mind could quite compass. First there was the clamor of the slave market, the shame of being evaluated by these effete Romans, men of short stature who somehow had produced a war machine that decimated the Gauls and would probably decimate Britannia if they ever crossed the channel. Worse, there had been the prospect of prostitution in a brothel for men, to be raped and beaten at their sick whim. It was everything he had imagined of Rome on the long journey over the mountains. He had been deeply ashamed that those vile beasts had been able to rouse his cock. The trip from the slave market to this amazing house had been pure torture. And then there was this enigmatic woman who owned him. . . .

Hateful. She was beautiful and she knew it. He watched her walk ahead of him. Her winter clothes only hinted at the curves beneath them, but his imagination supplied the rest. Her bare shoulders over the bath cloth she had wound about her body had been delicate and smooth. He pressed down the feelings that thought evoked. She lorded it over him as no woman should be allowed to do. Still, she was unlike any of the simpering Roman women who had come to goggle at him in the market. She had the courage to buy him. Her scent was exotic. Did she bathe in cinnamon? That spice brought fifteen times the price of silver for an equal weight. She must be very rich. She had an energy about her that was nothing less than exciting. She knew he'd been excited by her tonight, in spite of his revulsion at being her slave. He'd be glad to plunge his cock inside her, if only to hear her screams of helpless passion. That would teach her who was truly master here.

His mind skittered over her incongruities. Her touch had been gentle. She had knelt before him, yet had never given over her mastery of him. Puzzling.

She seemed to have no man. And this woman needed a man to teach her a woman's place. Was her husband dead? In his country such a woman would be claimed by another man before the corpse of her husband was in the ground. Yet she talked of power and needed a bodyguard, not because she was afraid of ravishment but because she thought her political enemies would assassinate her. What kind of woman was that?

He followed her into the house, if one could call such a clean and spacious place a house. More like a fortress, only built of stone, not wooden palisades, and open to the elements at the rear. Heat emanated from the floors. The engineering wonders he had seen tonight . . . whole pools of hot water, for instance, when there was no volcanic spring . . .

But back to the woman. He vowed to be the worst purchase she had ever made. She was crafty; he had to admit that. She had baited him to make him remember he was a commander of men who owed a debt that could only be fulfilled by his slavery. She had made the terms of owning him quite clear, and the alternatives.

So he would serve her. Not willingly but because he must, at least for now. And best she keep her promise of freedom. When he was free, he would have his revenge for the submission she had required, if it was achieved with the last breath in his body. And then he would go home to Centii in the southeast corner of Britannia, back to the land and his place as first son.

However, freedom was not to be a gift. She had said he could buy it. But in what coin? Who knew what the price might be and whether he could bring himself to pay it?

THE NIGHT WAS paling. Livia could feel the sun pushing up toward the horizon. It would be dawn in a little more than an hour. Her vampire nature required protection from the sun.

"Lucius," she called. The man raised his head from where he was setting out bowls on a table. She didn't have to give the command.

He looked conscious. "I had not realized it was so late." He bustled about closing the great wooden doors against the coming light. He paid no attention to the huge barbarian slave just now hesitating in the middle of the room. "Your repast is laid out in your chambers, my lady. I shall send in Catia to serve you."

Livia's vampire hearing took in the growl of the slave's stomach at the mention of food. "Not necessary. I will serve myself. But you can find me a short sword and a scabbard." She motioned the slave to follow her. Her chamber had a great bed covered in goose down mattresses and laid with embroidered bedding. A small table sat next to a carved chest that held her grooming utensils and cosmetics. Three more tall chests held clothing. The carpets were of bold red and blue woven in intricate detail from her native Dacia. Romans did not care much for carpets, preferring their warm floors bare, but carpets reminded her of her roots. On a long table to one side were laid several dishes of simple food: bread still warm from the oven, smelling yeasty, roasted root vegetables from her land beyond the city walls, spicy Lucan sausages, an amphora of wine, olives and their fruity oil, and, for the after-course, some sweet cheese made into a cake.

"What have you been given to eat lately?" she asked her slave.

"Not enough."

She set her lips. "This is *not* a promising start."

He looked puzzled at her reaction.

Really, didn't the man understand the basic tenets of being a slave? "You use no term of respectful address, and your response is surly and not to the point." That muscle was clenching in his jaw again. She sighed. They must rub along together somehow. "If you can't bring yourself to call me 'Mistress,' 'my lady' will do. And the *reason* I ask what you've been fed is so I do not give you food to which you are not accustomed. I won't have you vomiting all over my carpets." She raised her brows.

His fists clenched, as though it was all he could do to respond. "I was fed gruel when I was lucky, *my lady*, and whatever moldy bread or vegetables were left from what the Roman army foraged in the countryside. My belly will hold whatever you deign to give me."

She went to the table that held the array of food and picked up a pottery bowl. He was probably right, since she avoided rich sauces. She used a large silver serving spoon to scoop vegetables into the bowl and forked several sausages into it as well, then tore off a sizable hunk of bread. How much did such a large man eat? She handed it to him. "Start with this. You can have more if you like."

He began to pick out the sausages with his fingers immediately, wolfing them down as though he was afraid she would take the food away at any moment.

"Wait." She handed him a round silver spoon from the table. "Go and sit on the carpet next to the table, or kneel, whichever is most comfortable." His backside might be too sore to confront the pile of the carpet. She poured two goblets of wine and picked out some olives, some cheese and vegetables, for herself. She sat at the table and pushed one goblet over to the side nearest him. He had chosen to kneel. He was still going through his food at a furious pace, chewing and swallowing with a single-minded fervor, though now he used the spoon. She picked at her own food as she studied him. He was indeed a little lean. But he would fill out nicely with proper care and nutrition. She would have to make time to take him to the gymnasium at the Field of Mars. A man like this needed to be active. He scraped up the last juices from his bowl with his bread.

"Would you like more?"

He had that wary look again, as though he didn't believe she'd keep her word.

"I said you could have more and you can."

"Yes," he said, holding out the bowl, then added, grudgingly, "my lady."

She handed him the goblet of wine before she rose and

filled his bowl again, giving him more meat and cheese this time. "How is it that you speak Latin? Your vocabulary and your grammar are remarkably good." She was growing used to his accent as well.

There was no answer. She turned with the bowl and cocked her head in question.

"You will not like the answer, my lady." His eyes met hers. He set down the goblet.

"I did not ask you whether I would like the answer or not." She handed him the bowl.

"I learned it from Roman slaves my father kept." His gaze was steady as he gauged her response.

"Well . . . well, that is interesting. And how did your father come to have Roman slaves?"

"Romans do not always win. The Goths took thousands of Roman soldiers as prisoners after the battle of the Teutoburg Forest thirty years ago." His expression was blank, but she sensed the satisfaction there. "My father brought them back from one of his trading expeditions."

"Your father bought slaves to teach you Latin? Why?"

"They were bought to till the fields. Strong backs, though the men were small. They taught me Latin in the evenings because my father thought it would be good to know the language of the people we were born to conquer."

She drew herself up and was about to warn him that she would not tolerate such insolence when she realized that turnabout was in some sense fair play. Victors and the vanquished changed places time and again over centuries. She sipped her wine in a semblance of nonchalance while she regrouped. "Then I expect you know how slaves are to comport themselves, and will act accordingly, since the situation is now reversed."

Anger flashed in his eyes before he got control. Perhaps he, too, realized that turnabout was fair play. "As you say, my lady."

They ate in silence. He went through his second bowl of food at a more reasonable pace. As he was finishing, Lucius appeared in the open doorway and bowed.

"My lady?" He held out a Roman short sword and a leather scabbard on a wide leather belt. Lucius could procure anything at a moment's notice. The sword was perhaps thirty inches in length, squat and lethal looking, not elegant but serviceable. This one had a pommel bound with leather strips to improve the grip. Livia rose and took it from Lucius. Would she really give this barbarian a weapon? Decapitation was the one way a vampire could be killed. He wouldn't know that. But other wounds could cause her pain, and her swift healing would have to be concealed. And she'd have to have the slave killed for attacking her. She didn't want that.

She took a breath. A sense of inevitability washed over her. She would give him the weapon. It felt as though she had already done so. That strange feeling of having done all this before washed over her again, along with a sense of urgency that there was something she must do. *Remember your purpose,* she admonished herself. She needed a bodyguard to at least look as though he could vanquish her enemies. And she knew with a certainty that had no reasonable explanation that he would not use it against her. She took another deep breath.

"Thank you, Lucius. You may go."

Her majordomo glowered in the direction of the slave. "My lady . . ."

"That will be all, Lucius."

Lucius bowed, a shade reluctantly. "Shall I send Catia to you?"

"Not necessary tonight."

Lucius backed from the room. Livia turned with the sword and the scabbard and saw the barbarian staring at it, eyes almost glowing. That was not reassuring.

"If you are to be a bodyguard, you must have a weapon." She had to make him understand the consequences of her trust. "If you misuse it, you will be crucified. That is a painful death."

"I saw the men on crosses that line the road into the city. A barbaric practice, *my lady*."

She blinked. Rome, barbarous? It was the city of light, casting the beams of civilization into the dark corners of the known world. Well, this barbarian couldn't be expected to understand Rome. "Then we are clear." She swallowed and held out the sword.

He put down his bowl and reached for the weapon reverently. He grabbed the hilt, hefted the weight of it, and then slashed the air, once, twice. He held it up, thumbed the edge of the blade, and smiled.

It was the first time she had seen him smile. Not a pleasant smile on the whole.

"A fine weapon, my lady," he almost whispered, his eyes still caressing the blade.

"I'm glad you like it."

"Short, fit for close work only, of course."

"But effective. Such a weapon wounded your shoulder, did it not?" she asked with raised brows.

He did not acknowledge her point but held a hand out for the scabbard. "You wish me to wear this at all times."

"Yes." At least she thought so.

He strapped the belt low across his hips and thrust the sword into the scabbard. His back straightened, his shoulders squared. He felt like a warrior again, though a slave.

She understood that. She counted on it. It would remind him of his honor.

"I wish to retire. You will sleep at the side of my bed, on that small carpet there." Could she bear to have all that male animal so close? Would she get any sleep at all?

He cast her a smoldering look that hinted at rebellion. But he knelt on the carpet beside the bed and lay down on his side, one arm crooked under his head as a pillow. She'd have Lucius find a real pillow for him tomorrow. His other hand rested possessively on the hilt of his sword.

"Do you require a cover?"

He shook his head. "This room is warm."

She made a mental note to have Lucius find at least a light blanket for him. That might help her as well, since it would cover that muscle. She watched the blood beat in the hollow of his throat. The feeling of anxiety that had haunted her all evening came over her again, as though there was something she should do. Feed? But she never fed from her own household. Twin bites on her servants' necks would soon cause talk, and that she could not afford. Still . . . there was something niggling at her.

Oh, dear. She was still dressed. She couldn't go to bed fully clothed. Maybe that was what was bothering her. Normally she wore exotic embroidered night robes from Constantinople. But she had no intention of disrobing before this barbarian. She would simply sleep in her *stola* tonight. And tomorrow she would have Lucius install a screen in the corner so that she might change in privacy.

She thought about how blithely she had told the slave that he would attend her in her bath. That would be expected of a bodyguard. But she couldn't imagine letting that incendiary gaze rove over her naked body. What a coil she had gotten herself into. Why had she bought *this* slave?

But it was right, somehow. Indeed, it felt as though she had been searching just for him. Something inside her made her feel that someone, maybe everyone, knew things she didn't. The whole thing was . . . disconcerting. Even now he watched her as she unwrapped her *palla* and folded it, then laid it across the bench of her dressing table. Feeling the thinness of the fabric in her *stola,* she walked to the lamps and extinguished them one by one. The fabric, fine as it was, scraped across her sensitive nipples. The creature had her aroused again. She felt full to overflowing, and throbbing with desire. In short, not like herself at all. When the room was dark, she went to her bed and crawled under the richly embroidered wool coverlet. She could see the slave still watching her.

HE HAD AN erection for the third time tonight. Gods, could she raise his prick even as exhausted as he was? But the floor was warm through the thick red carpet, and his belly was full of better food than he had eaten in half a year, and rich red wine. She had fed him from her own table, not with scraps or rotten leftovers. The room was suffused with her scent, spicy and exotic. She probably didn't know that he could see her form clearly through the thin fabric of her tunic as she moved in front of the lamps. Her breasts were full, as were her hips, her waist narrow. The outline of her nipples, taut against the fabric, was almost enough to make him spill his juices.

Fingering the hilt of the short sword, he watched her take to her bed. It was a simple weapon, the hilt bound with leather to absorb sweat from his palms. Practical. Good in tight places like a city. It made him feel like a man again.

Why did she trust him with a weapon? For all her brave talk, she must realize he could run her through and leave her bleeding her life out onto that red carpet. She had no way of knowing it was against the creed of his people to use a weapon against the one who had given it as a gift. What did Romans care for the beliefs of those they conquered? Yet she trusted he would keep his bargain to save his men because he had told her he would. It wasn't because she was naïve. This woman was clever, perhaps ruthless. No. It was because she believed in his honor. . . . That was a burden in some ways.

Would he defend her? The fact that he'd be put to death on one of those crosses if she died did not weigh with him. It would be worse if he landed back in the slave market, fair game for filth like Graccus or those foul imperial sisters. He didn't like to risk that. But letting her enemies have their way with her would certainly be satisfying.

Would it?

She'd cared for his wounds, fed him, given him a weapon. Her touch had been gentle even when her words were not. His thoughts were growing muddled. She was a puzzle. But she'd dared to own him, curse her. The only service she'd earned was the service of his cock. Once she'd tasted his skill, she'd beg for more. Then who would be master? He smiled in satisfaction at the thought as the warmth of sleep took him.

A feeling of pressure built inside her. She was too full, as though she were a ripe pomegranate ready to burst in the sun and spill red juices that soaked into the earth. And there was something she should do. About the slave. Where was he? She looked around and saw only writhing bodies lusting after one another. In the

*center of the room, a fountain spurted water from an
artful series of nymphs and randy cupids. Where was
she? She didn't recognize the house, but she recognized
the feeling of danger. It lurked here somewhere.*

*She began stepping over kissing couples, groping for
each other's genitals. Men and women, women and
women, men and men. Her search grew more frantic.
She couldn't have lost him, could she? But there! He
stood in a niche behind a statue of Venus, and Julia
Lavilla was running her hands over his body. That was
bad. She had to get him away from Gaius's sister. Or
Gaius's mistress, whichever you chose to believe. Jergan
was holding himself in check. Like a wild beast, every
muscle was tight, coiled for the spring. He mustn't offer
the sisters an insult or he'd end on the cross. Now
Agrippina ran her hand up under his tunic. Keep your
head, Jergan, Livia pleaded silently as she saw a sneer
cross his face.*

*She must get to them before his restraint burst, be-
fore Agrippina went too far, but Livia couldn't find a
path through the writhing couples on the floor. . . .*

Livia sat bolt upright in her bed, gasping. Beside her,
Jergan rose to a crouch with a snarl, sword drawn. She
couldn't get her breath.

They both looked around the dim room, the doors and
windows outlined in lines of sunlight from the day outside.

Nothing.

"It . . . it was a dream," Livia choked. But was it? It felt
more real than any dream.

Jergan looked disgusted.

She swallowed. "Put up your weapon and go back to
sleep."

"It is daylight out," he observed, sheathing his sword. "Do you not rise?"

"I am sensitive to sunlight. I sleep during the day and rise at night. Therefore, so will you."

His eyes narrowed as he examined her. Finally, he grunted and lay back down.

Livia lay back, too. But she couldn't shake that silly dream. It wasn't really frightening in the same way the horrors she'd lived through frightened her—the wars, the earthquakes, the torture of innocents. It was just so . . . *real*—almost like a memory. She saw every splash of the fountain, the sweat on the lovers' bodies. She smelled their perfume, and underneath, the scent of musky desire in the air. The sense of impending disaster had been overwhelming. She'd been afraid for her slave, as though he were the most precious thing in the world.

Jupiter and Juno, but she was getting to be an old woman about dreams. She lay back down. But sleep was long in coming. Finally she heard the soft buzz of her slave, returned to slumber. He must be exhausted. The sound was vaguely comforting, as though she had heard that gentle snore for decades, not just for a few hours. She closed her eyes, sighing, and let his rhythmic breathing carry her to sleep.

5

LIVIA LAY THERE, half-asleep, feeling full, her thoughts lazily coming round to consciousness. Something was happening today. Something exciting. Was today the day she and her friends could finally act against Caesar? No, it wasn't that. Other steps must still be taken before the plot could come to fruition. Was it . . . ?

Diana the Huntress save her, she was filled with anticipation because she had a new slave.

Her eyes popped open. He lay beside her bed on the carpet, still asleep. The muscles in his shoulders, chest, biceps, were smooth, quiescent. But he looked powerful nonetheless. The bandage on his shoulder only accentuated his latent strength. Yet his eyelashes were as long and as thick as a girl's. They made him look vulnerable. His hair had dried into a heavy mass of midnight waves that flowed down his back and matched the curling hair on his chest and belly. His hand still caressed the pommel of his precious sword. She felt a . . . a longing when she looked at him that she could not explain. It wasn't just sexual, though certainly he roused her.

It was that feeling that she knew him, had always known him. Ridiculous, of course. How could one feel like that about someone one had met only last night?

But she did. He was honorable. Courageous. He would

be a fine leader. But he also had softness inside him that would make him a tender lover, a good father. He was protective. He would be a staunch provider.

Where was all this coming from? She couldn't know these things about him.

He must have felt her watching him, for his eyes blinked twice and opened. She saw the realization of where he was come into them. He jerked up on one elbow, breathing hard. Perhaps his nightmare wasn't one experienced while sleeping. He looked around the room, dim with the dusk outside, and slowly mastered his breathing. His gaze, steadier now, came back to her.

"Are you feeling stronger?" She cleared her throat. Why should she feel nervous?

He nodded brusquely. He seemed to have forgotten the lessons of last night. He set his lips, apparently determined not to give her the satisfaction of polite address.

She sighed. She would need him for a few days at most, until the plot was brought to fruition. Then she'd free him and send him on his way back to his homeland. She couldn't let him serve in her house as a freedman like her other servants. Not this man. A few days. But these few days looked to be long ones.

"Come," she said, rising.

Jergan slipped the wooden clogs onto his feet. The soles were still bruised and swollen.

Catia heard her stirring and opened the door. She had a pair of sandals at the ready. Livia stopped to let Catia tie them and thanked her. Then Livia motioned to Jergan and went out through the evening to the little house beside the *thermae* with water sluicing through it in a stone-lined trough. She used the facilities first, then emerged and motioned for Jergan to do the same.

He looked uncertain as he poked his head inside the door.

"Go on," she said. "Relieve yourself."

He shot her a look of surprise. Roman plumbing was apparently an innovation. "It's amazing what a little civilization can do," she muttered.

When he was done he ducked outside again, looking perplexed. "How is this done?"

She raised her brows.

He ground his teeth, then took a breath. "How is this done, my lady?"

"We are on a hill," she said, turning back to the house. "If we were not fortunate enough to have a spring with sufficient water volume on the property, we would need a series of pumps run by slaves."

She would have callers soon. There was no time for a bath. "See Lucius Lucellus," she ordered as she went to dress. "Just off the kitchen. He will no doubt have procured a tunic of sufficient size for you."

JERGAN WAS EAGER to talk to her majordomo. The man had been freed. Jergan found him sitting at a small wooden table off the kitchen. He pored over an unfurled scroll by lamplight.

Lucius looked almost guilty as Jergan surprised him. "My owner told me to see if you have procured clothing."

Lucius nodded as he hastily rolled the scroll. It looked very old. The edges were torn and crumbling. "Come this way."

In a storeroom of some kind, Lucius held up a blue tunic and a strip of white flax. "Use this strip to tie your loincloth, and buckle the leather belt outside the tunic." He measured the tunic against Jergan's frame with his eye. "This had better be big enough. It was the only one

I could find. I'll have to have others sewn specially for you."

"It looks to fit," Jergan muttered. He unbuckled his belt and took the strip of cloth. Now to ask his questions. "You are a freed slave?"

Lucius nodded. He was past middle age, with eyes that drooped in a perpetual look of sorrow, and graying locks. "She freed me."

"How is it that your name is the same as hers?"

"When a slave is freed he takes his master's name. All her freedmen are named Lucellus."

She had freed others. This boded well. Jergan pulled the tunic over his head. It was sleeveless and came almost to his knees. Now for what he really wanted to know. "Why do you still serve her?" When belted, the tunic reached mid-thigh. It was made of thin wool fabric, dyed dark blue and coarse. But these southern winters could not hold a candle to the ones he was used to. It would be enough to protect his body from the cold.

"A master who frees a slave may command his services still, but she does not. I stay because I want to serve her."

Jergan would want to set a thousand leagues between him and his slavery if ever he could. "You have nowhere to go?" The man spoke with only a slight accent Jergan didn't recognize. But he had to have a home.

"I have been in Rome for thirty years. I understand it. The only family I have is here. My sister. Her son. I have bought their freedom with what I earn from Livia Quintus Lucellus."

He didn't seem happy about it. Indeed, something seemed to be making him nervous. His gaze stole to the scroll laid out upon the table. He stared, distracted. Coming to himself, he ripped his gaze from the scroll, took a breath, and held out two leather wrist guards. Jergan slipped them around his forearms. Lucius jerked the leather thongs tight in the lacings.

Jergan started to ask what he had done to earn his freedom, but Lucius interrupted him. "Enough questions," he snapped. "You are still a slave. Remember that." He handed Jergan his sword, its belt, and some boots and motioned him from the room.

At the door, Jergan glanced back and saw Lucius return to his scroll, a look of great perturbation on his face. Could household accounts mean so much to him?

Jergan strapped on his weapon, but he carried the boots. He couldn't imagine putting them on his bruised feet.

As he came through the house, he saw that the door to his owner's bedroom was open. She had her back to him. Her maid was winding a dusky green wrap shot through with iridescent threads around her. A *palla,* they called it. Her tunic left one shoulder bare. The whiteness of her skin was remarkable. It was almost translucent. And the delicate bones in her shoulder, the graceful curve of her neck, made her look incredibly . . . feminine. He paused, transfixed.

The maid snuffled. That caught his owner's attention. "What is it, Catia?"

"I'm sorry, my lady. I did not mean to . . ."

She lifted her maid's chin. "No, tell me, Catia, what makes you cry?"

Jergan slipped to one side. He could still see the two through the crack between the door and the doorjamb.

"It is my mother, my lady." The maid spoke hesitantly. "Her master beats her." The floodgates broke and the maid rushed on. "But she is too old to scrub floors. She has many talents. She bakes wonderful bread. She sews with tiny, elegant stitches. But that awful man who runs her master's house makes her work on her hands and knees, and says she isn't fast enough."

"Oh, Catia," her mistress said, holding the girl's shoulders. Livia's voice was drenched with sympathy. Jergan wished he could see her face. "I thought you were buying her freedom."

"I am," Catia managed, as sobs began to take her. "But he has set her price high, and . . . and I haven't enough. I . . . I went to see him yesterday. And that's when I saw my mother. . . ."

"How much do you need?" His owner's voice was calm, sure. "Stop crying now and tell me. Did he quote a price?"

Catia snuffled. "Fifty. Fifty dinars for an old woman."

"Ridiculous. But go to Lucius now. Tell him to make up whatever you still need of the fifty dinars. I have need of a seamstress. She can work in my household until she decides what she wishes to do with herself. Lucius will go with you and arrange the whole."

There was a stunned silence. Jergan craned his head around the doorjamb. Catia seemed frozen. Finally she took a quick sharp breath, blinked twice, and raced from the room, calling, "Thank you, thank you so much, my lady," over her shoulder. "I'll send Helena to help you with your jewels."

The maid passed Jergan in a blur. He heard his owner mutter, "Brute."

Oh, this woman was puzzling, all right. Was she the same one who had said only last night that she would require him to spill his seed under her eyes? Then she had seemed so heartless it was easy to hate her. Today she had done a kind and generous thing. Hating was not so easy.

He cleared his throat and stepped into the room.

She looked up and surveyed him. He had never felt so much like property. "Will you be warm enough? It is January after all."

"I would hardly call this a winter," he said by way of answer. Then he remembered and added, "My lady."

"You will tell me if you require a cloak."

He would rather die.

An older woman bowed her way into the room. "Helena," his owner said, "can you get me some bandages?" The woman nodded and hurried off. Livia motioned to the bed. "Sit, Jergan."

At least she hadn't yet ordered him to put on the boots. What she did was turn to the delicate table that held hairbrushes and inlaid and silver boxes and many little glass jars with cork or glass stoppers. She picked up a tiny blue glass bottle in the shape of an amphora and upended it in her hand. Again she knelt in front of him and rubbed the contents into his feet. The feeling of confusion had found its way into his belly, and below.

"Your feet are better today," she remarked. "Though I expect the prospect of wearing boots is a bit daunting. Still, the cobblestones will only make your cuts and bruises worse."

Helena entered with several rolls of gauze. "Excellent," his owner said. Jergan watched her as she wrapped his feet with them. "This should make the boots less onerous."

It did. When he shoved his feet into the boots, he had to admit the gauze padding helped. He laced them as she watched him. They came up over his calf. She seemed to be waiting for something.

Ahhhh. "Thank you." He didn't mean it to come out so much a growl. "My lady."

"You're welcome, Jergan." She turned and picked up some dangling earrings from the little table and put loops of wire through her ears. She had pierced them like the barbarians from the south. "Now, we have some senators to entertain."

"**Send your slave** away, Lady Lucellus," the old man said, "that we may talk freely."

Jergan stood behind his owner, hands clasped behind his back.

"I wish my slave to stay by me," she said to the three old men who stood about her as she reclined on a chaise covered in intricately embroidered fabric. One of the men was the one who had attended her at the slave market last night, the one she had called Titus.

"Do you not trust us?" one of the others asked. "You are safe with us."

She turned a glowing smile his way. "Of course I trust you, Marcus Belius. But who knows but that the Praetorians might not burst through the portico at any moment?"

"I wonder you trust him." This was from Titus. "If he's tortured, he could betray us all."

"But I do trust him, strangely." She glanced back at him and he saw a kind of wonder in her eyes, a confusion. "He must know what is at stake so he can value the trust placed in him."

"He is a slave," one of the others muttered. "I understand your . . . interest in him, my lady, but slaves have no honor. He will betray you at the first touch of a hot iron."

"I beg to differ, citizens. And really you have no choice. If you wish me to continue in our quest, he comes with the bargain, since I intend not to let him leave my side."

They would refuse. Why did they need a woman?

But Jergan saw them look chagrined. Was it that feeling of life and vitality that buzzed around her that put them in her thrall? Titus said, "You have owned him less than twenty-four hours, Livia. How can you be sure of him?"

She smiled, and looked supremely confident. "I am sure."

Why? Why was she sure of him? She wasn't stupid. Why would she think he would stand torture to defend her secrets and those of these old men?

But her confidence seemed to sway them.

"There will be little time for him to betray us anyway," Titus said. "We must strike now. The recent attacks on you are certain proof, Livia."

"Not yet," she said, shaking her head. "Our tool is ready when we are. Gaius Caesar's death is assured. But what comes after? It is easy to bring down a despot, but not so easy to put up a stable government in his place that gives the people a voice and preserves them from abuse of power. We must not supplant our problem with one worse. We need a republic, citizens."

"If Gaius dies without issue, isn't a republic ensured? I thought that was the point."

"If he dies without issue, Marcus Belius, the Senate can anoint another emperor. Would you have his grandmother put the laurel wreath on Agrippina's spawn? No, we must be certain we have the Senate behind us before the deed is done."

"And how do we do that, pray?" This one's bald pate gleamed in the lamplight. Outside, the dusk was deepening into night. "We can be certain of only perhaps twenty. . . ."

"Gaius Caesar is expensive, Flavio Antellus. Very expensive. Think how much there would be for public projects if Rome did not find it necessary to support his excesses."

That made them look thoughtful. "That would sway another ten," Titus observed. "But . . ."

"Perhaps some would support more money for foreign conquests?" she asked sweetly.

"Fifteen, perhaps twenty at a stretch . . ." Marcus Belius said slowly.

"And then there is the theory that without Gaius there is simply more for the rest of us."

"I don't know. . . ." This from Flavio Antellus.

"I'm not sure any one of those buys us enough votes for a republic." Titus looked sorry he had to tell her that.

"And who said we would use only one approach?" She smiled and watched her proposal sink in. The woman was devious; Jergan would give her that. "Titus, your reputation dictates that you contact the ones who would be in favor of public works. Marcus Belius, you have been a hawk in your day. Contact your fellow predators and argue for war. And Flavio . . ."

"By the gods, you don't think my reputation is for selfishness!"

"Of course not," she soothed. "You pretend to be outraged that if Caesar were overthrown and there were no new emperor . . . if there were a republic . . . there would be those who would take advantage of all that loose money saved. And, well, you see my point. They will think they thought of the idea themselves."

"Brilliant." It was Marcus Belius who expressed what they all were thinking. Including Jergan. The woman had a head for scheming, which he supposed all women did. But to see it applied to the politics of the Roman Empire was . . . a little shocking.

"What happens when the alliance built for avoiding an emperor accomplishes its goal and a republic is established? The alliance will not stand if all want something different from the outcome." Titus said what Jergan was thinking.

"All alliances are temporary. Once we have a republic, we form new alliances. I can think of a dozen permutations possible."

"I cannot." Flavio Antellus pulled his toga over his shoulder. "But I believe you can."

"Enough to stake your life on it?" Marcus Belius asked, and looked around at the aging conspirators. There was a moment of long silence. Then nods, some more grudging than others.

"Go to your work, gentlemen," she said, rising. "The people deserve better than Gaius Caesar. And we are just the ones to help them to it."

"And you . . . you should stay within doors, my lady, until we can bring this thing off," Titus said, coming to take her shoulders and look into her eyes. The old man cared for her; it was obvious. "These attacks may well continue."

"And bring suspicion down on my head by looking fearful? No, my friends, I must be seen at banquets and celebrations of the empire's victory. I stay only to bathe and dress."

Titus had worry writ in the myriad lines of his old face. She patted his hand. "Courage, old friend, just a little longer."

"You put us to shame, my dear," he said, low, and squeezed her hand in return. The men bowed themselves out.

She turned to Jergan. "Come; I must bathe."

A shiver of anticipation rustled through him. Would she expect . . . ? He imagined her body, nude as he had been in the bath last night, covered with oil. He felt his loins tighten. Belatucadros's horn! How long since he'd had a woman? How would he keep himself from grabbing her shoulders and pulling her to his body to feel the soft press of her breasts against his chest, her desire and her fear trembling through her? Best he resist his impulse, or she'd have him on the auction block by midnight, if not hanging on one of those gruesome crosses.

He followed her out to the bathhouse the Romans called a *thermae,* trying to make his cock behave. He wasn't winning the battle. A maid was just leaving. Once Jergan would have thought the maid a tidy plum, ripe for plucking, but she was nothing compared to her mistress.

The girl bowed. "Would my mistress like attendance at her bath?"

"No need for you to trouble yourself. Jergan will do." His owner's voice was husky.

She said he would not be required to pleasure her. He didn't want to be bidden to her bed like some obedient animal. The very thought was degrading. But his body wouldn't object. Even the dried old husks who conspired with her wanted her. He could see it in their eyes. She made them feel alive.

He thought about that. In some ways, she made him feel alive, too. Even now she buzzed with energy. Or was that desire? Did she desire him? Was that why she invited him to her bath?

He hoped so. And he despised himself for that.

6

LIVIA COULD FEEL him at her back. She was already wet between her thighs. How would she bear his touch, scraping her naked body in the bath? She regretted now that she had told him she would not use him for her pleasure, and hated herself for thinking that. What kind of a civilized woman was she? She was no better than Agrippina and Julia.

And yet Livia enjoyed the Roman attitude toward sex. It was so much more open than her homeland. Whatever one did was acceptable in Rome as long as it was consensual. The exception to the need for consensus was sex with a slave. Romans thought there was nothing wrong with compelling slaves because slaves were less than real men and women. If you did not believe someone was as good as you were, was it long before cruelty was acceptable? That was a problem for some vampires, too. They thought of humans as lesser beings, and therefore fair game for cruelty. Julia and Agrippina bought and tortured slaves. It was rumored that they both slept with their brother, too. An open attitude was good, but surely some things must be wrong. And that was the problem with Rome under Gaius Caesar. It had lost the idea that anything was wrong, if you had enough power to enforce your will.

Livia, on the other hand, knew very well it was wrong

to take advantage of a slave. So she was going to deny the strange attraction she had to her new bodyguard.

As she passed the vine-covered rock wall in the back of the garden, she felt a strange frisson of the urgency she had experienced of late race up her spine. She stopped for a moment and looked around. The garden wall nearly shut out the sounds of the city beyond. The scent of sage and rosemary filled the garden even in winter. From behind her in the outbuilding that was the kitchen, the scent of her servants baking bread wafted out. The air was sweet and clean, unusual for Rome. Everything was just as it had been for many Januaries past.

And yet . . . there was this *feeling*.

Maybe it was the feeling of the slave standing behind her. She trotted up the steps to the *thermae*. Why did it seem as though she had known him forever, instead of less than twenty-four hours? She lusted after him. She must get through the next hour without abandoning her morals. Her back could do without scraping tonight.

Stranger than her attraction to him was the fact that she had trusted him with the secret of her conspiracy. She could *tell* herself that as her bodyguard, he would know all sooner or later anyway. But that was not strictly true. She could have concealed it from him.

Yet she trusted him. With her life. With the lives of her friends.

It made no sense. Hadn't a long life taught her better?

She found herself in the *frigidarium* and looked around as though she'd never been there. He was close behind her. She could feel his heat.

"Shall I remove my tunic, my lady?" he said, his voice hoarse.

"No," she said quickly. "No, you will remain clothed. You are here to guard me." Keeping his role to one of bodyguard was her only chance of resisting her needs. "You will turn your back and stand ready with your sword in case of intruders."

She turned to face him. He looked . . . disappointed. He nodded once, brusquely, and turned to face the door.

She slipped the *palla* from her shoulders, unwound it, and folded it upon the bench. She slid a glance behind her to make certain Jergan was not looking, then pulled her *stola* over her head, then her chemise, and hurried into the *calidarium* beyond. The humidity and heat assaulted her. She sat on the bench in the corner. "You may stand at the inner door with your back to me." She felt so vulnerable, naked, with Jergan standing not ten feet from her. It was impossible to relax and enjoy a good sweat. After ten torturous minutes, she poured out the oil and rubbed it over her body. He stood with legs set wide, arms folded. His form blocked the doorway entirely. By the fires of Vulcan, but he was a massive man. In all ways.

She wouldn't think of that.

"I am going to several celebrations tonight. People may wish to look at you." How could they not? "You must not give offense."

She saw him stiffen. She must make him understand. "I cannot afford to attract attention to myself just now. And if you were to be surly or rebellious, that would attract attention. People would expect me to punish you. If I do not, then *that* attracts attention."

There was a long silence as she rubbed the salt over her skin. "Well, do you agree?"

"I will be a model slave." His disgust was plain.

She wondered if he even knew what that meant. She grabbed a *strigil* and scraped what skin she could reach. Too bad Catia was not here to scrub her back. Or maybe it

was better after all. It surprised her to realize that she
didn't want to share her time with Jergan. What she
wanted was to call him over and command him to scrape
her, then take his tunic from him. . . .

Why couldn't she seem to banish these thoughts?

She rose and waded into the hot pool, rinsing her body
to open her pores. Really, bathing was nearly the most
civilized thing about Rome. She sighed and splashed hot
water over her shoulders. She would need her wits about
her in the next few days. A week at most, and then it was
done and she could tend to the fledgling republic. In a republic, men of honor in the Senate could plan a better
world in which people's lives were easier. Education
could be offered even to the humble classes. There would
be no starvation to fill Caesar's coffers. Perhaps someday
no slaves would be needed to fuel the Roman economy.
She could return Rome to what was best about it, and forget what it had come to in the last years.

She stepped out of the water and took up the large linen
towel to rub her ruddy skin. "Stand at the outer door again
so I can use the cold plunge." He stalked away. She had no
time to dry her hair in front of the fires tonight. So instead
of jumping in, she eased herself quickly down to her neck.
The water wasn't really icy—it just seemed so after the
hot pool. Still she gasped and pulled herself up to sit on
the edge.

She realized that at her gasp Jergan had turned, poised
for some kind of action. She hastily crossed her arms over
her breasts. "How . . . how dare you?" she chattered. "I
t-told you not to turn around."

Clenching his jaw, he swiveled back, but not before his
eyes lit with appreciation. "My mistake, my lady."

Hardly, she fumed to herself. She'd wager he planned

to catch her out. She reached for her bath cloth and dried herself briskly. Time to end this torture.

SHE STALKED PAST him. He grinned as he fell in behind her. Had she noticed that his cock strained against the cloth about his loins underneath his tunic? If she did, she gave no sign. The last half hour, imagining her rubbing herself with oil and salt, listening to the sluicing of water over her body, knowing she was naked and practically within reach, had been painful. And then, when he had turned round, thinking she had seen an intruder, the glimpse he had gotten of her body confirmed all his imaginings. Pale, lush, the nipples pink, the dark triangle of hair enticing. Was she so immune to the charge between them? Perhaps not. It might be resisting that pull that irritated her so. He hoped so, because then she would not resist for long.

He shook himself. What was he thinking? Did he want to degrade himself by performing to her order?

No. Deliberately, he imagined her writhing under him, spreading her legs to him. That was what he wanted: her abject submission to her desire for him. The moment her desire mastered her, she would be in thrall to him. And he would have had a kind of revenge on her. He felt better. He could relax about her effect on him and put it to good use. Yes. All in all, their attraction was a good thing. It would deliver her submission to him.

He stood outside her chamber as her maid dressed her. When she emerged, she was clothed in a tunic of nearly transparent rust-colored fabric—they called it a *stola.* Her wrap, equally transparent, was embroidered richly with gold. The only reason she did not look naked was that there were so many turns of the stuff about her. She was a tantalizing prospect. She wore gold chains looped and braided in her hair. Gold drops hung from her ears.

As he handed her into her litter, she glanced at him as though she felt the shock of flesh to flesh as strongly as he did.

This time he was not chained to her litter as they wended their way through the streets. He had a tunic, a weapon, and a task. That felt better. He scanned the crowd for anyone who might try to accost the small procession. Already she needed him. That felt good, too.

But they made it to the huge villa that was their first destination without event. He handed her out. She sailed into the noise and the laughter like a ship pushed by a high wind. At the door, a slave motioned him to give up his sword. He gripped the pommel, loath to let it go.

"You'll get it back when we leave," she whispered to him. "It's rude to wear a weapon in another man's house."

He handed it over with a frown, already feeling naked again.

Inside the villa, the sights that met his eyes were almost overwhelming. Men and women lounged on chaises, eating and drinking from vessels of silver or gold. Slaves picked their way among the guests, pouring wine, bringing platters with new delicacies. In the corner, musicians played on lute and flute and drum, while in the center of the room, dancers clothed only in wisps of fabric that concealed nothing writhed in artistic ecstasy.

They were hardly more erotic than the guests themselves. Some talked. He heard snatches of gossip. But others fondled each other openly, kissing, squeezing. Not only men and women, but three in both combinations lounged on chaises as big as beds and touched one another in the most private places. No one seemed to notice or to care, except when a couple beckoned a third to join, or a woman broke off with one man to embrace another. Barbaric!

And yet the flesh exposed, the flushed, inward expression of the revelers, was . . . intoxicating. He glanced to his owner. She seemed to take no notice of the outrageous behavior. Did she behave this way? He felt a surge of . . . something he couldn't name. She bent to kiss one man, and it was a lingering embrace. The brute was attractive in a feminine sort of way, Jergan supposed, with his shaved face and short hair. Jergan itched to send the fellow packing until she moved on with a smile and a few gracious words.

"Have you eaten, Livia Quintus Lucellus?" A large, florid-faced man, whose toga looked more like a tent, descended upon them. "Here, take this chaise." He handed her to lounge across an upholstered bench provided with many pillows. She curled like a cat, her curves obvious beneath her translucent robes. How had Jergan not noticed that her toenails, revealed by her dainty sandals, were painted with gilt? The ruddy man clapped his hands and slaves appeared with plates of food. Jergan went to stand behind her as she selected tidbits from the offered plates. His stomach rumbled. He had not eaten yet tonight.

"Is this a new slave?" the host asked, eyeing Jergan frankly.

"Yes. One of the spoils from the northern front."

The man chuckled. "I'll wager you're having a jolly time breaking this one in."

"Yes," she said shortly. She glanced up at Jergan. Did he imagine her blush?

The man took Jergan's chin to turn his face to the light. He had to reach to do it. It was all Jergan could do to allow it. *Don't cause trouble,* he recited to himself. *Don't attract attention. She doesn't want a scene.* A scene would endanger her.

"Exotic, but on the whole, attractive. I take it he is as well built everywhere?"

"Oh yes." Her lashes brushed her cheeks. It was almost demure—an act, of course.

The florid man smirked. "You always had a taste for the outrageous, Livia Quintus." A slave came up and murmured to him. He bowed to Jergan's owner. "I must attend to the wine." And he departed.

Several couples approached to invite her to join them. She politely declined, saying she had not yet eaten. Both men and women eyed not only his owner, but Jergan, too. He noticed that some male or female slaves were entirely naked except perhaps for gold rings piercing their flesh, or gilded nipples and elaborate braided girdles at their hips that shook with bells or metal disks. Several were openly copulating with guests in dim, secluded niches. His eyes widened.

"Shocked, Jergan?" his owner asked. "The Celts, I understand, are not so open about satisfying their sexual needs." She beckoned to him. He crouched beside her on his haunches. She handed him a drumstick from her plate. He hated to admit it, but that was thoughtful of her.

"I expect no more of Romans," he growled under his breath so only she could hear him over the chatter.

She laughed. "I suppose I deserved that." She eyed him, curious as he devoured the duck. "Some would say your attitude indicates that you are ashamed of the sexual act."

He looked at her, speculating. She was dressed far more modestly, if just as richly as the creatures around her. And she had not indulged in what she chided him for denigrating. It occurred to him that the other slaves in the room, whether serving food and drink, or copulating, did not look their masters in the eye. She had not demanded this most intimate subservience from him. Indeed, she handed him a breast of duck. "I reserve my enjoyment of the sexual act for the privacy of the bedchamber, my lady, where I can show my partner sufficient respect and attention." He had no intention of granting Livia respect when at last he bedded her. Still, that would put her Roman debauchery in perspective for her.

It was a victory that she looked away. "Do you?" she said, trying to make her tone careless. But that was speculation underneath her attempt. "Well, perhaps there is something to be said for that. Still, I find Romans' joy in sex, their playfulness, refreshing."

He tossed the denuded bones onto a tray carried by a passing slave. So she had an outsider's perspective on Rome. "My lady is not Roman by birth?"

She tore off a hunk of bread and handed it to him. "I was born in Dacia. You would not know it."

"My father had a map of the world. He used to tell me we were bound to rule it. Your land has a great river, and mountains almost impenetrable."

She stared at him. "Latin and geography? What next, barbarian? Poetry, sculpture? You are practically Roman."

He set his lips. She thought being Roman was a good thing? "And what is that, 'practically Roman'?"

"Rome is the light of civilization," she replied, suddenly serious. "It is all that stands between the world and darkness. And yes, it is sculpture and poetry, religion, laws and roads and aqueducts. And peace in which to enjoy those things."

"Pax Romana?" he asked, snorting. "Achieved only when Rome has laid waste to the land and conquered its people."

"Granted," she said after a pause. He admired her for that. "But once that is done, the petty squabbling that eats away at the world is done, too, and finer things can flourish."

"*Roman* things? Hardly. You borrow your religion and your sculpture from Greece, and your geometry and mathematics. Rome has contributed nothing original in all its years."

She looked away. He had won. But then she turned back to him. Her eyes were wise beyond their years. "What Rome contributes is more practical, but nonetheless necessary. Call it efficiency. People need water and commerce to make their lives better. Commerce needs roads. When people have leisure they can appreciate all those Greek things that enlarge their souls."

"Leisure? Rome's leisure is achieved on the backs of slave labor."

"See here, I am not proud of slavery. But one can't build the Rome that Rome *can* be in a day." She glanced around and lowered her voice. "One thing at a time. Besides, you said yourself that your people hold slaves. Slavery is universal."

Sounds of passion issuing from a dim niche claimed their attention. A woman was on her hands and knees being penetrated by two men, one below in her vagina and one above in her anus. She was obviously enjoying the experience.

The moment lengthened. Jergan felt his owner's discomfort. Was she imagining, as he was, what it would be like to couple? His cock, which seemed to have been aching ever since she bought him, tightened. Her attention jerked abruptly to the entry.

"Julia Lavilla, Julia Agrippina, what a wonderful surprise," their host called, hurrying over to the newcomers.

"Vulcan's hammer," Jergan's owner swore. "Not those two."

Jergan looked up to see the emperor's sisters bearing down on them.

"LIVIA QUINTUS," JULIA simpered. "How lovely to see you here. And your new slave."

This was bad, Livia thought. Had they been sent by their brother to spy on her? Or were they only interested in Jergan? Either way, she did not care for their attentions. Jergan, who had been crouching beside her, rose to his full height.

"My, my, but you were percipient in your purchase, Livia Quintus." Agrippina could not take her eyes off Jergan. "He cleans up nicely. And I rather like that you left all that barbarian hair." Livia was glad he was fully clothed. Let them not notice what she had: that he had been aroused by the love play so much in evidence around them.

But that was too much to ask.

"Oh, ho," Agrippina chortled. "He is ready. What a randy beast he is." She moved in and ran her hands over the coarse cloth of his slave's tunic, paying special attention to his nipples and the bulge at his groin. "Do you not think he wears too much clothing? A slave like this ought to be naked, as you had him last night when he was chained to your litter."

Jergan was scowling, his fists clenched at his sides. Livia shot him a warning look. *Keep your composure,* she willed him. "It is January, Agrippina," she said. "A tunic is only merciful."

"Nonsense," Julia Lavilla snorted. She moved up to join her sister in moving her hands over Jergan's body. Julia's hands smoothed his tunic over his buttocks, gripping the muscle. "What does a slave's comfort matter? His purpose is to please."

Livia gritted her teeth. She wasn't sure she could speak.

Agrippina ran her hand up under his tunic. Jergan stiffened. He was barely holding himself in check. "You allow him a loincloth as well? Livia Quintus," she chided. "That is merely an obstacle. He should be ready to give pleasure at a moment's notice."

"He . . . his performance has been most satisfactory," she managed. These women were the most powerful in the empire. She must give their brother no excuse to notice her, to arrest her. She was vampire. He couldn't hold her, but she would have to translocate, and everyone would see her disappear in mid-air. She'd have to leave Rome. That would probably stop the plot. Her fellow conspirators would lose their courage.

"We shall judge his performance," Julia purred. "Oh, what fun we could have."

"If he fails to please us we'll have him whipped and then his member rubbed with that crushed beetle from Hispania so he might try again to satisfy us." Agrippina was practically drooling as she breathed up at Jergan.

Livia felt a rising tide of revulsion and . . . fear. They could have their brother confiscate Jergan.

Julia pulled Jergan toward one of the shadowed niches, not even asking Livia's permission. He shot Livia a look, half threat, half command. If she did not rescue him, he was prepared to make a scene. Panic rose in Livia's breast. She couldn't let these two spiders abuse Jergan, or let him incur the consequence of refusing them.

She felt full, full to overflowing. Something inside her was scratching to get out. She must get Jergan away from Caesar's sisters. Julia was drawing him toward a niche.

Agrippina trailed in their wake. They were approaching the statue of Venus. Water tinkled from a fountain.

Livia's eyes darted to the nymphs and randy cupids spilling water.

Time slowed. It was her dream! The same fountain, the same feeling of panic. She had dreamed this exactly as it was happening. And now something was trying to come to the top of her mind and she didn't know what it was.

She jerked herself forcibly back to the present. How to get Jergan away from them?

"How . . . how is your brother?" Livia called, hurrying after them. Best they were reminded that they were powerful, but not in comparison to their unstable brother. Would he suffer his sisters, to whom he was only too close, to cavort in public with another, even a slave? He was notoriously jealous.

A trumpet was heard in the courtyard. The sisters looked at each other, frozen like the statues of them that stood near the Temple of Jupiter. Julia dropped Jergan's arm.

"Ask him yourself," Agrippina said. Something like fear slid through her eyes.

Livia sucked in a breath. She heard the gasp of reaction from around the room and murmurs of "Caligula." No one would dare call the emperor by his nickname, which meant "little sandal," in his hearing. What brought him to Melanus Devenus's humble banquet when there were state-sanctioned celebrations of the returning armies to attend? At least the emperor's presence had stopped his sisters' pursuit of Jergan. Still the solution seemed like killing two scorpions by letting a cobra loose.

The man who entered the room was not handsome. He had not inherited a jot of his grandfather Augustus's rough good looks. Caligula's face was pinched, with narrow eyes. He was tall, but rumor had it that his legs were spindly. His servants said his hirsute body more than made up for the thin hair and balding head, though he shaved to conceal it. Caligula had decreed that no reference to goats could be made in his presence, upon pain of death. First of the Claudian line to inherit the title of Emperor, he had come to the throne at only twenty-five. Four years had not matured him. His predecessors had had the grace to mask their authoritarian power. He made no pretense. He could do anything. And he did.

At first he had won the favor of the people by pardoning the many prisoners his uncle Tiberius had taken for imagined treason. Caligula had staged elaborate games in the arena, in some of which he fought himself, though his opponents were wounded by the Guard before they were allowed to step onto the sand with him.

But then his mask had slipped. Paranoid, his sense of humor vicious, his elaborate jokes often resulted in death. Now he held Rome in a nightmare of dread.

He arrived at the head of his retinue—among them Decimus Valerius Asiaticus, his chief counselor, and the head of his ever-present Praetorian Guard, Cassius Chaerea. Livia glanced to Chaerea's impassive face and quickly away. She dared not betray that she had ever spoken with him.

Caligula's gaze swept the room.

"Hail, Caesar." The murmured greeting swelled as all bowed. The slaves knelt. Livia elbowed Jergan and surreptitiously pointed to the marble floor. Did he not know the result of refusing to kneel to Caesar? After a hesitation, Jergan fell to his knees and bowed his head.

Gaius Caesar looked over the silent crowd with disdain.

"We wonder that so many tarry here tonight, Melanus. Did you not know there is an official celebration scheduled?"

"A thousand pardons, my emperor. I provide refuge only for those who did not merit a place at the official table." The ruddy host bowed lower. He apparently remembered Caesar's sisters. "Or those on their way to your own illustrious event."

Why was Caesar himself here, instead of at his palace? She glanced to his sisters. Fear lurked in their eyes.

Gaius pushed past Melanus and approached his sisters. "Slumming, Sisters, or on the hunt?" His eyes passed over Livia and came to rest on Jergan.

Livia was disconcerted. Caligula seemed genuinely not to notice her. Wouldn't he acknowledge in some way that he knew she was his enemy? Wouldn't some spark of hatred, or at least recognition, betray the fact that not two nights ago he had sent assassins after her, if indeed it was he behind the attacks?

"On the hunt, we see." His gaze roved over Jergan. "About to enjoy the spoils of our northern victory. Not unattractive. . . ."

Oh, dear. This was not an improvement. Caesar was known to like the services of both men and women. She could not compel him to leave Jergan alone in such a public venue without revealing the red eyes that came with her Companion's power. Livia racked her brain. She couldn't publicly refuse the emperor anything he might want. So he must be brought not to want Jergan. Very well. "I, too, thought him attractive, my emperor. But . . . but not being as brave as your sisters, I have not yet mustered the courage to make use of his body."

Gaius looked down his nose at her. "You have not the spirit to master a slave, Livia Quintus Lucellus?"

"Celt barbarians from Britannia are known to be af-

flicted with syphilis," she apologized. "I have only had
the courage to make him my bodyguard."

All three of the imperial family visibly shrank from
Jergan. He himself glared at her, but then something of an
appreciative crinkle emerged around his eyes. Not a smile
precisely, which was a good thing. More a hint of admiration.

"I . . . I thought you said he had been satisfactory,"
Agrippina managed.

"He has. He is quite skilled with a short sword."

Gaius Caesar, called Caligula behind his back, snorted.
"We wager you'll find your courage soon, Livia Quintus."
He stepped past her to his sisters, and gave each one a kiss
that was far from brotherly. "Perhaps you're right, my
pets. The official ceremonies are quite stultifying."

Livia sighed in relief as his attention passed on.

"May I offer you slaves, wine, food?" the host in-
quired, most humbly.

"Yes, we will take all you have. Asiaticus, see that his
goods are confiscated."

A hush fell over the room. Melanus's ruddy complexion drained of all color.

"We don't believe you provided a haven for those not
invited to our banquet, Melanus. We think you thought to
compete with us." The emperor's eyes were heavy lidded,
but that did not conceal the maniacal gleam in them.
"What?" he challenged, looking around the room. "Why
do you not continue your revels?"

The room burst into counterfeit gaiety. "To our emperor's victory!" someone shouted. Raucous applause ensued, lest the emperor think they were less than loyal for
being at Melanus's gathering and confiscate their worldly
goods as well.

Livia gestured for Jergan. He tried to make himself

unobtrusive as he slid to her side, which was almost laughable. He would never be inconspicuous among Romans.

"Let us go, my lady, before these vipers strike again," he whispered.

"Leaving before he does would be considered a slight. That would not be healthy for either of us." She led him to a corner by the door. "He will move on shortly. He must return to his own banquet."

They watched in morbid fascination as Gaius paid a lover's attention to both his sisters, fondling their breasts, even fingering their private parts as the wine continued to flow. They accepted his attentions with loud protestations of pleasure. Livia wondered if they were as enthusiastic as they made out. Did Julia care that her brother had had her husband killed? Did Agrippina resent that Gaius had forbidden her to remarry after her husband died? Or were they both so jealous of their dead sister, Drusilla, and the place she had in Caligula's heart that they would do anything to emulate it? Some said that Drusilla's death was what had snapped her brother's balance. He'd had her deified and mourned her like a lover. Not surprising. Livia thought all the rumors were true. He emulated the eastern potentates, who carried on their line by marrying their sisters. Caligula didn't actually marry them, but she would wager he wanted to get them with child. It was a miracle it hadn't happened already.

Caesar did not leave. Apparently the official celebrations would have to proceed without him. The evening stretched on, taut. Finally, Asiaticus leaned over and whispered in the emperor's ear. He frowned. But then his brow cleared, and without even a farewell, he swept from the room, leaving his retinue to scramble after him.

There was a distinct sigh of relief in the hall, after which everyone began to disperse. Livia touched Jergan's arm and nodded toward where Melanus had given way to gusty sobs. Jergan followed her, eyes hooded and watchful as she went to comfort Melanus, and offer him her support. Then Livia and Jergan slipped into the night.

Outside in the street Jergan took deep gulps of air as if he had been holding his breath all evening. But Livia's relief was tempered by niggling doubt. Why had Caesar materialized here? Was it only to spy on his sisters? Was it to frighten her? Did he have that much control that he could pretend not to recognize her and succeed in giving away not even so much as a flicker in his eyes? And why would he bother to conceal his enmity? What just happened to Melanus proved that Caesar had no fear of public action against the senatorial classes. Again she returned to the fact that if Caligula knew she was behind the plot, he wouldn't send anonymous attackers. He would send the Praetorian Guard.

So who was organizing the attacks upon her?

"Shall I call for your litter, my lady?" Jergan asked, bringing her back from her unanswered questions. Several of Melanus's slaves had scurried up, ready to do her bidding. Actually, they were probably Caesar's slaves now.

She shook her head, staring off into the dark streets. It had rained while they were inside, and the moist, cool air was refreshing. "Tell the Nubians to take the litter home. I need the breeze off the Tiber in my face."

Jergan looked concerned.

"I want to walk," she insisted.

He nodded to the slaves around them in silent command, and the slaves hustled away. He was born to lead, she thought, and the fact that he was a slave did not conceal that. As she started off down the street, he grabbed a torch from its bracket on the wall and stalked behind her, holding it high, his other hand on the pommel of his sword. The streets were deserted. Either everyone was still celebrating or the rumor that Caligula was abroad had everyone staying behind doors.

"I must free the city of him," she muttered. She couldn't kill him herself, though. It must be done by someone whose action would in itself create the possibility of a republic. She had to wait for her planning to bear fruit.

"He is a bad man. The whole world knows it," Jergan agreed from his place at her shoulder.

"You must not think all Romans are like him. Rome is the city of light." Now she was talking to herself as much as to him as she hurried through the shiny black streets. She shivered. "He can destroy it all, rot it from within. . . ."

Jergan started to say something. Probably he wanted to contradict her about Rome. She heard him clear his throat. But then he thought better of it. She took another breath and slowed her pace deliberately. She mustn't let the fiend rattle her. They were walking up the Capitoline Hill now. The villa was not far.

"The dream last night—the one that woke you—I had a premonition of tonight," she said. Perhaps that was what rattled her. She expected him to snort in derision.

"Are you a witch?" he asked. He sounded serious.

She laughed. "No. At least I don't think so. But that has never happed to me before. I imagined all of it—the fountain, the smell of lust in the air." *The need to rescue you from Caligula's sisters.* She didn't say that part. And what about the other part? The part where she felt full to bursting, and on edge about something, something she needed to do? She shook her head. This conspiracy was making her nerves raw. She brushed at her forehead as though she were brushing away cobwebs and picked up her pace again. "Let's get home. Your poultice needs changing."

7

JERGAN WATCHED HER slip behind the screen to remove her clothing in preparation for retiring. The sun had
risen. Lucius had closed up the house hours ago. She had
come back from that awful "banquet" and forced herself
to sit down at her desk. A servant girl had changed the
poultice on Jergan's healing wound. He had to admit he
wished Livias had done it herself. She had scribbled on
scrolls for several hours. She bade him eat from the food
laid out on the long table but did not touch any herself. Af-
terwards, he sat near her, drinking cool water with lemons
she said were from Amalfi, watching her as she drove herself to finish whatever task she had set for herself. When
the scrolls were sent off with her servants as messengers,
she seemed to deflate.

Now he watched her shadow on the changing screen.
He'd wager she didn't know how the lamplight outlined her
form as she moved behind it. As concealment it was almost
useless. Perhaps more than useless, since the shadows
made her form even more seductive for the pretense of being hidden. His testicles tightened. He seemed to be constantly in a state of arousal. Was it Rome, or was it her? He
was being corrupted.

But she was not corrupt.

What kind of a woman was this? *A woman of honor.*

That concept—that a Roman woman could possibly have honor—was so foreign, it struck him like a blow. The reason she could believe he was honorable was that she possessed honor herself. She emerged from behind the screen, attired in a shift of some fine fabric he did not recognize.

She could wear such light cloth only because the house was so miraculously warm. It had started to rain outside. He could hear water dripping from the eaves. The house was a strong shelter, more comfortable even than the wooden halls at home made of bound poles. He thought of the mud in winter, the smoky air, the rank smell of men and women who rarely washed. Maybe Rome *was* more civilized. . . .

He pushed that thought away. He wanted to get back to his home in Centii, however civilized Rome was. "What is that cloth? My lady," he added as an afterthought.

"Cotton. It comes from India. It is lighter than flax or even linen and smoother to the skin, though not so fine as silk from China." She moved about the room, turning down the lamps. Her dark hair hung down her back in loose waves from being braided.

He did not know these places. That brought home the fact that Rome was the trading hub of the world. His owner's life was complex. He had been shocked that she was the driver behind the conspirators who met in the audience room this evening. *She* was complex. Not what he expected at all. He could feel she was tired. The vibrant aura she always seemed to have about her hadn't lessened. But it had taken on a subtle sadness, as if she were a light that pulsed against an endless night, knowing it was useless.

She smiled at him. "Lay yourself down, Jergan. Rest." A shadow crossed her face. "I'm sorry those two creatures touched you so offensively tonight. I am grateful for your restraint."

"Are they so powerful that you must convince them I am diseased in order to keep their hands off your property?" He was her property, if not in his own eyes, surely in theirs.

"Yes. Their brother could confiscate my property just as he did with Melanus tonight. Including you." Her voice in the darkness turned thoughtful. She crawled into her bed. Jergan laid himself on the carpet. She had provided a small rolled pillow for his neck tonight.

"I'm not sure he knows about my plan," she whispered in the darkness. "And if Caligula did not arrange the attack on me three nights ago, who did? I cannot see my way."

"You must move quickly, my lady," Jergan said. "There are vipers everywhere."

"Yet I must let our little group do its work before any plan can do more than kill one viper and replace him with another." She sighed. Silence stretched. He heard her breathing grow more regular. "And I have this feeling that there is something else I must do," she murmured. "It's the oddest thing. Because the more I try to think what it is, the more it seems to elude me." More time elapsed. "Perhaps it will come to me. . . ."

She was asleep. But Jergan was not. She was playing a dangerous game. And she was drawing him into it with her.

Out of the darkness they lunged. Why hadn't she heard them? Metal glinted. Short swords and knives were wet with rain. So many! She pulled one off balance and broke his neck. Where was Jergan? There, his own sword drawn. He slashed, but they were on him. They thought to take him first, and leave her as easy prey. Another of them gripped her wrist. She twisted and jerked. He screamed as his arm broke. She plowed toward Jergan, but two others grabbed her, snarling like jackals. A sword raised high over Jergan. No! They mustn't kill him. Couldn't! Because she couldn't imagine life without him.

The sword came down.

She woke to a heavy weight on her left side, started to struggle, and quickly stilled herself. It was Jergan. With her vampire strength, she might have hurt him.

"Shush," he whispered, stroking her hair as she gasped for breath. "Another dream, no more."

The scent of human male surrounded her. His breath was warm on her face. He sat next to her and had pulled her against his body. The wool tunic was rough against her cheek. His heartbeat thundered in her ear as he held her against his chest. His hands moved over her back, and he made low soothing sounds deep in his chest. Slowly the tension drained out of her. She closed her eyes and deliberately slowed her breathing.

She'd had a dream. One that might be another premonition. Why did she have to wake before she knew how it ended? It had seemed sure that Jergan would be taken from her. She slid her arms around him. The muscles in his back bunched as he held her closer. This felt so right. She had known that he would feel like this, smell just like this.

He bent and kissed her hair, quite tenderly. She wanted to turn her face up. She knew just how his day-old beard would scratch across her face. She had always known. And his lips, so incongruously soft against hers . . .

And he would take that as a command.

She pushed herself away, a knot in her belly replacing the heat that had begun to bloom there. "Thank you," she said brusquely. "That will be all."

He reached for her in the darkness. "You needn't . . ."

"E . . . enough!" Her voice hardly shook. It could have been worse.

He straightened. She could feel his affront hanging in the air. "As you wish, my lady." He stood, looming over her bed in the dim room. Then he turned abruptly away and lay down on the carpet, his back toward her.

She ran her hand over her forehead, a feeling of hopelessness settling in her core. There was something she must do. But she didn't know what it was. And all she wanted to do was bed her unconscionably attractive slave, not just because he was handsome, but because she felt she knew him, and maybe something more. It didn't matter why. Even now she was tempted to order him to stand, remove his tunic and his loincloth. She had a feeling that when he did, she would see that he had been as aroused by their embrace as she was. She would study his chiseled body. Under her stare he would rise further, until his rod was straining to be sheathed in her. She would gesture to him to come and lie with her. And he would obey, eager. . . .

She shook herself. What was wrong with her? She'd had many male slaves. When first she came to Rome, she'd had a houseful of them before she'd grown uncomfortable with owning slaves. Some were quite attractive. She'd never once had trouble controlling herself around them. She'd never once imagined ordering them to her bed. In those days she had amused herself with Roman citizens to satisfy her twin needs for blood and sex. But she hadn't even done that in many years. It had all begun to seem the same, and as she denied her Companion's sexual urges, they had grown dimmer—a faint flutter that seemed a distraction from her work, no more.

Until she encountered Jergan, she had carved out a rough truce with her Companion.

And now? Apparently that truce was over. But she needed a bodyguard for a few days. One who could give a pretense of protection so that no one would know she could protect herself so well. If she was attacked, she would raise her Companion and compel Jergan to forget what he would have seen her do. He was a tool for a few days, no more. She must bear the effect he had on her. She turned on her side away from him.

Everything was very disconcerting just now. His effect on her, the fact that she felt as though she had known him forever, the dreams, the feeling of urgency, the panicky knowledge that she must do something immediately, but not what it was.

Her world seemed to be changing. What she had built here in Rome was precious. She had come here posing as royalty from the province of Dacia, which in a way she was. And of course she was rich beyond belief. Romans respected wealth. She had used their reverence for the exotic to carve out a life and influence, waiting for the time when she could use that influence to push the world ahead.

She couldn't afford to be distracted from her purpose. Not by dreams that seemed to foretell the future. Not by this strange feeling that she had done all this before. And certainly not by a slave who roused her sleeping vampire libido.

She could tell by his jerky breathing that he was not asleep.

It looked to be a long day for both of them.

JERGAN WASN'T QUITE sure when he slept again. But it was good to have slept. His mind sifted lazily through his senses, her scent, spicy and exotic, the warmth coming up through the floor. He had a morning erection. With all this stimulation lately and no relief, he was lucky he was not spilling his seed on her carpet in his sleep. He cracked open his eyes. It must be dusk, his new morning, for even the little light that had leaked in around the shuttered doors was gone. He couldn't quite see, but he sensed she was looking at him.

He snapped awake. She had quite clearly rejected his advances last night, when it would have been natural to let his comforting embrace turn into shared passion. He knew she desired him. He smelled her lust underneath her spicy scent. And yet she pushed him away. . . . Was she afraid of him? He had to admit that was a possibility. She was tiny in comparison to his six-foot, three-inch frame. And he was as far from these effete and hairless Roman men as she had likely ever seen. It crossed his mind that she might have seemed so severe that first night for just that reason. He didn't like the thought that she might fear him. He wanted to best her in the bedroom, but certainly not with violence.

Or maybe she knew that once she had bedded him, and once she wanted more (which he had no doubt she would), she would be as much in his thrall as he was in hers.

So be it. She did not intend to bed him. He almost let out a groan. He had been shocked when she had said she would supervise him spilling his own seed once a week. But now that seemed a mercy. Let him relieve his tightness and he might be able to stop reacting so to her.

Or maybe not. He grunted and sat up.

She rose, a darker blotch upon the night, and turned up a lamp, then went to the door. "Send Catia to me. I would bathe."

He wondered if he would survive guarding her through another bath.

"Go and relieve yourself," she murmured to him. Yesterday she had gone with him to the marvelous room adjacent to the *thermae*. Did she trust him to go alone today?

"My lady." He nodded and padded directly from the room on bare feet that were markedly improved. He hardly limped. When he returned, the servant girl had bathing items in her arms and was trailing after his owner.

"I shall not need you, Jergan. Catia can see to my needs. Bathe by yourself while she dresses my hair. One of the servant boys can scrape your back. See that you are thorough."

He was not to bathe with her then. That was good. An hour of torture evaded.

So why did he feel so disappointed?

SHE NEEDED BLOOD. That was all. In a small polished metal mirror she watched Catia dress her hair. It was only a week since she had last fed, but this feeling of irritation must certainly be because she needed blood. It didn't feel precisely like hunger in her veins. But what else could it be? She should be *doing* something. She just didn't know what it was. And she had to stay away from Jergan. She had nearly taken advantage of him last night.

But if he was to be her bodyguard, she couldn't stay away from him. Well, at least she could avoid bathing with him. She wouldn't think of his body sweating in the heat, him rubbing oil on his genitals. Would he rise? Perhaps he was thinking of her as well. Oh, dear. She really shouldn't torture herself like this. She'd find what she needed in a brothel tonight, and then perhaps everything would return to normal.

THIS WAS THE opportunity he'd been looking for. A young man led the way to the bathhouse. Jergan would question this slave about her. If Jergan couldn't be with her, he could at least make use of the situation. And perhaps one younger than Lucius would be more forthcoming.

They stopped in the cold room to shed their clothing. Apparently the boy was going to bathe as well. "What is your name?" Jergan asked, as he untied the poultice from his shoulder.

"Tufi."

They sat on opposite benches in the stifling heat of the *calidarium*. "How long have you been slave to her?" Jergan asked after a moment. He did not need to name her. Who else would they be talking about?

"I was slave only a few months before she freed me. Now I am called Tufi Lucellus."

"She freed you, too?"

Tufi looked incredulously at Jergan. "All in her house are freed. You are her only slave."

Jergan narrowed his eyes in disbelief.

Tufi laughed, a low chuckle deep in his throat. "She is very eccentric. A waste of money to free slaves, the Romans think. And they are right."

"Why does she not hire freedmen in the first place and save the cost of the slaves?" The woman puzzled Jergan at every turn.

"We have all asked ourselves this question," Tufi said slowly. "I think it is because our gratitude makes us more devoted than any hired servant. We keep her secrets even unto death."

"Does she have secrets?"

Tufi merely smiled. "Even a lummox like you must have noticed a few of them."

Jergan assumed Tufi was not talking about her conspiracy. Certainly she kept that secret close. She was stupid to have trusted even him with it. "If you mean the fact that she is sensitive to sunlight, everyone must know that."

"Well, it's early days for you. You'll see soon enough. Let us just say that what she is has other consequences, and she must bend to them." Tufi handed him an amphora of olive oil.

"What consequences?" Jergan poured oil over his chest and began to rub it in.

Tufi paused in rubbing his own lean body with oil, looking mulish.

"If I am surprised by them, I might offend her," Jergan reasoned. "And if I offend her, she will not free me. Better I know and can prepare myself."

Tufi thought about that. Jergan saw him wanting to relent. "But are you trustworthy?" he asked. "She has not yet freed you. You owe her nothing but the service of a slave."

Jergan pretended outrage. "Do you question my honor? I have sworn my loyalty to her. I served my king and the general who protected my men even unto submitting to slavery." He looked Tufi straight in the eye, unflinching. "I will not betray her." Was he lying? He was half-surprised to find that he was not.

Tufi took a breath. "She drinks blood."

Jergan frowned. "Do you think me gullible because I am not from Rome?"

"Oh, she'd love that reaction." Tufi chuckled again. "Don't say I didn't warn you."

Jergan thought about this while he rubbed oil over his thighs. "How do you know this?"

"Every two weeks or so, she goes to a specific brothel. They say she pays a fortune for an hour with some strong young buck. The prostitute comes out with no effect a few hours' rest won't cure. He doesn't even know what happened." Tufi lowered his voice. "But he has two wounds, just here." He pointed to his jugular. "And he is pale. Once, blood was seen on her lips."

Jergan frowned. "She wants reaming, that's all." He poured oil over Tufi's back.

"Then why, once, when she was burned by sunlight, did she send Lucius with orders to cut a prostitute and bring her a cup of his blood?" Tufi looked triumphant. "Catia heard him get his instructions. And the goblet definitely had blood in it. Shortly after drinking, she rose from her bed hale and hearty." Tufi poured oil over Jergan's back in turn.

"If she drinks blood, why do you serve such a monster?"

"But does she seem like a monster?" Tufi snorted, rubbing oil over his arms. "She freed us. We are paid well. She is a little haughty perhaps, but otherwise considerate. I am buying my sister out of slavery to a fat pig of a Roman with my salary. What is a little blood from a prostitute to match that? She never takes our blood. We have nothing to fear from her."

A ghost walked up Jergan's spine. Children told stories around the fires at night in Centii to frighten one another about monsters drinking human blood. Could this woman be such a monster?

Of course not. The servants were just making up wild stories about her. He rubbed oil over his private parts. The one fact in all this blather was that she did free her slaves. That boded well for his future. Yet . . .

"How does she set the price a slave must pay to buy his freedom?" He thought of Catia's mother, whose price was so high she could never be free without help from Livia Quintus.

"I think she bases it on what we can earn. Lucius's price was much higher than mine. He could keep accounts for one of her friends. I raise a flock of ducks and sell their eggs. I saved seven dinars. That was my price."

"How long did it take you?"

"Three years."

Three years? An eternity. Jergan had thought to be a slave his whole life, set to an oar or breaking marble in a quarry. But suddenly he could not bear to be *her* slave for even three years. What would his price be and how would he be expected to earn it? Tufi wouldn't know those answers. Jergan felt a kind of despair settle into his belly. The meaning of slavery was brought home to him as it had not been before. Three years as slave to Livia Quintus Lucellus. Three years before he could go home. Three years before he was a real man again. . . . And it might be longer. Who knows how long she would keep him?

Tufi handed him a tray of salt.

"**WHERE IS HE?** Is he not finished yet?" Livia groused. She put a wide golden bracelet around her upper arm.

"I am here, my lady." His voice sounded . . . dull somehow.

She turned and saw him, hair still wet, clothed in a clean tunic colored like sage leaves. It matched his eyes. He smelled like sage, too, and underneath that, like a human man. "Good. I would be off."

He turned and retrieved his sword from beside her bed. Two red stripes soaked through his tunic. "Why are you bleeding?" she barked.

He shrugged. "Tufi was zealous with the salt. It is nothing."

"It is *not* nothing. How are you to heal if the idiot boy scrapes away the scabs?" She turned to her maid. "Catia, get the unguents. Jergan, remove your tunic. Now the welts must be treated all over again."

He unbuckled the wide leather belt and drew his tunic over his head as Catia scurried away. He seemed . . . resigned. The ribbed muscles on his belly moved and caught the lamplight. Livia swallowed. At least he still wore his loincloth. But as she stalked around him, she saw some blood spotting there as well. "Your loincloth, too." After all the trouble she had gone to avoid his bath, here she was with his body naked before her, making her feel exactly the way she didn't want to feel.

Catia hurried in with the basket. "Why for God's sake was he not more careful?" Livia asked, trying not to look at the round muscles of Jergan's buttocks. Anger rose inside her to see him laced again with red.

"I relayed your message that he was to be thorough."

"Not at the cost of blood! Does no one have any sense? Must I do everything myself?" She didn't know why she was railing at Jergan, except that he was sending shocks of feeling down between her legs. "I should give him welts so that he might see how they feel." She opened the jar and filled a finger full of the sticky, translucent goo. "And no poultice for your shoulder. Catia, go prepare a poultice. Must I think of everything?" Catia ran from the room.

"This will hurt." Livia laid the unguent along a welt that had opened.

"Not as much as the salt," he muttered.

She sniffed and kept to her work, trying not to let the feeling of his flesh shake her resolve to be absolutely in control around him. "And now I am late."

Catia entered with Lucius as protection. "I have sent word ahead to expect you at your leisure, my lady," he said. "There is no cause for haste. Would you prefer Catia tend your slave?"

Livia glanced to the comely girl. "No, I would not. I've had enough incompetence this evening." She sighed as the girl flushed. "I'm sorry. I'm sure you would be most effective, Catia. I am sharp because I feel responsible for his condition."

Lucius glanced to Jergan and repressed a smile. Dear Juno, was he . . . ? She turned around. Took a breath. Let it out. He was. Erect. And blushing for it.

"I canceled your audience for tonight," Lucius continued, covering her blush in response. "I hope that was acceptable." He knew she needed blood.

"Yes. The ones I care to see are busy. I must make myself available tomorrow, however." She finished her job in haste. "Bind your loins, Jergan. Lucius, a clean tunic for him."

Lucius nodded. "Catia?" When the girl had gone for the tunic, he came closer. "Be careful tonight, my lady." He turned to Jergan. "And you, slave, guard her well."

8

JERGAN STALKED BESIDE the litter, senses on edge. He scanned the passersby. The streets of Rome were wide here. Channels cut at the stone edges carried the rainwater away toward the Tiber. Even at night the avenues were busy. Citizens and slaves, rich palanquins and poor men, all jostled one another. At one point a phalanx of soldiers marched past them. Black square shields with the symbol of Rome picked out in imperial purple, black brushes on their shining black helmets, they were like no soldiers he had seen. The veil of Livia Quintus Lucellus's litter parted, and she watched them pass. The captain seemed to glare especially hard at her.

"Who are they, my lady?" Jergan asked under his breath.

"Praetorian Guard—the emperor's personal bodyguard. They are the only soldiers allowed inside the city," she murmured.

"They look like guards to the gates of hell."

She chuckled ruefully. "You may be right. But even Pluto is divine. Perhaps the Guard will surprise us one day and prove they have souls, too." Her head disappeared inside as the veils fell down around her.

Their destination was a large and lavish house off a narrow street. As the bearers laid down their burden, a chubby man wrapped in a voluminous toga stepped out on the portico. "My dear Livia Quintus, how good to see you again so soon." He gathered her out of the litter and protectively into one arm and led her up the steps. She wore blue tonight. Her garments were more colorful than those of Roman women. "I have just the slave for you tonight, well muscled, eager."

This was a brothel. Jergan was stunned. She wouldn't take her pleasure of him but would buy it from some prostitute? But no . . . Tufi said she took more than sexual pleasure at a brothel. She drank blood. Jergan sucked in a breath. Best he was on his guard tonight for many reasons.

"Excellent, Drusus Lucellus. You may settle with Lucius on his price tomorrow."

"I warn you, my lady, he was expensive."

She laughed. "I'll pay your full cost for him, Drusus. Don't give me discounts."

The owner was her freed slave as well. Was the city littered with them? No wonder he kept her secrets. Perhaps the secret was that she meant to kill the prostitute. Why else would she pay Drusus the slave's cost but that she would kill him? Tufi had said she didn't hurt the ones she drank from, but what did Tufi really know?

Jergan swallowed. She *was* a monster. All the legends of blood-suckers, soul-stealers, shape-shifters that decimated entire populations, everything his people talked about in whispers, came to sit in his mind.

He shook himself mentally as he followed her up the shallow stairs. Jergan's father had taught his sons not to believe in those tales. He heard his father's rational voice admonishing his brood to believe in what they could see and what they could do with their own two hands. There. That was better. He had hold of himself now. She was just going to let this sex slave sate her.

That was bad enough.

"And who is your glowering companion?" the man called Drusus asked, glancing back.

Livia smiled. "My new slave. He is fresh from Britannia and still rough around the edges."

Jergan clenched his jaw.

"I wonder that you frequent our small establishment when you have such fodder at home."

"Don't tease me. You know why, my friend."

Before they could enter, a man strode up the shallow stairs from the street, wrapped in a fine toga. Two companions, obviously drunk, wavered on their feet in the street below. "Drusus, we require women," the one who had bounded up the steps slurred.

The portly man frowned briefly, then pasted on a smile and bowed. "I regret that my establishment is not able to serve you, citizens."

"Our money is as good as anyone else's," the leader said, drawing himself up.

"Ahhhh. Regrettably, it is not. I will not have my slaves injured."

"An accident. I paid."

"I cannot afford accidents. My property is my livelihood, citizens." He nodded to the two tall Nubians wearing loincloths and little else except great golden pendants that stood out against their smooth, black chests. They opened wide the door and then closed it pointedly on the sputtering would-be patrons. Inside, Jergan expected the crowded scenes of drunken orgy he had seen last night at the "banquet." Instead, music was being performed by a quartet in the corner. A woman danced among three or four groups being served food and wine. She was draped in sinuous fabric, but she was fully clothed. No sexual activity was in evidence, though private rooms opened off the central area. The prostitution probably took place there. His owner remained behind a screen, concealed. Drusus guided her directly to one of the private rooms.

"Guard the door," she whispered to Jergan as she entered. Jergan caught a glimpse of a well-built young man, naked and ready for her. His muscles were smooth and hard. His body was hairless except for a patch at his groin. His features were almost girlish in their ripe vulnerability. He held an amphora and a goblet of wine.

Jergan turned his back on the curtain that swung into place and crossed his arms over his chest, frowning. Drusus sailed off to take care of his other guests. Murmuring voices could be heard inside the room. Jergan couldn't quite make out the words. She was going to take her pleasure of that creature. Jergan found that distasteful in the extreme.

He felt her in the room. The vitality that always hummed around her ensured that he would always know exactly where she was. Her presence was that imprinted on his brain. Or on his cock. The very thought that she was . . .

He gritted his teeth and stared ahead, not really seeing the patrons before him choosing their companions for the evening. *Keep your mind off what she is doing in there. With him. And not with you.*

He felt her energy quicken and expand even through the curtain. It was sliding up some scale like a flute, until it seemed to feather his spine with tingling energy. What was happening in there? Was she letting that young buck suckle at her breasts?

He heard a moan of pleasure. It sounded male. Brid and her handmaidens! The creature was no doubt filling her with his cock.

If she *were* drinking the prostitute's blood, he wouldn't moan in pleasure. Jergan fidgeted. He had rejected that accusation. It couldn't be true. Could it? The choice was clear. Monster, or a woman who took her pleasure from prostitutes instead of from him. He chewed his lip. The energy emanating from inside the room had reached a fever pitch. Either way, she would be distracted. She wouldn't notice if someone was to . . .

He turned and eased the edge of the curtain away from the door frame. The young slave lay across a large bed. His muscled limbs arched against her. She was fully clothed. She lay against his side. She'd turned his face toward her to expose his neck and she was sucking there. The slave was moaning in pleasure, his prick rock hard.

Jergan could hardly believe his eyes. It was true.

Even as he watched, she pulled away. Her eyes opened.

They were a deep red.

Jergan sucked in a breath.

"My fine young slave," she murmured, "you will remember only that we made exquisite love tonight. You were masterful. I was nearly insensible with pleasure." The slave smiled up at her, knowing, sure of himself. He didn't seem to notice the twin drooling rivulets of blood that wound down his neck. "And tomorrow Lucius will buy your freedom. Tell him what you would most like to do and he will help you do it," she continued. "Do you know what you want to do?"

"My father was a potter."

Livia Quintus Lucellus smiled at the young man. "Then a free potter you shall be. Make me a graceful amphora in remembrance of this evening."

She kissed him once, quite tenderly, and rose. Her eyes slowly faded to the fine dark brown with which Jergan was familiar. The slave was already heavy-lidded, half-asleep. Jergan let the curtain slide back into place as quickly as he could without attracting her attention, and turned, crossing his arms. She had never even undressed herself. His brain vibrated with questions, not the least of which was whether he should be horrified.

She pushed out of the room. The whole thing had taken less than half an hour. She was flushed, her energy more pronounced. She looked like a woman sated with sex.

But she wasn't. She hadn't coupled with the young man. She drank his blood with eyes that went red as no human's could, just before she freed him. Emotions churned inside Jergan. His thoughts caromed from one extreme to another. She had been incredibly generous to the slave. But she was a monster. At least she hadn't taken her pleasure. Because Jergan wanted to be the only one who pleasured her.

He was going mad to think that.

LIVIA GLANCED UP to Jergan as she came out. Wondering horror sat in his eyes.

Jupiter and Juno, no! Could the man not follow orders? She set her lips. Now she would have to use her powers of compulsion to erase the memory of what he had just seen.

"Come," she said, and gestured to another room that had the drapery pulled back against the door frame, indicating that it was empty. "We must talk."

As she walked into the room, her intentions to erase his memory crumbled. A certainty pounded at her from somewhere deep inside. She *wanted* him to know what she was. It was unbelievably important that he know.

What was she thinking? She could not trust a slave she had owned for less than two days with this most precious of secrets. Not even Lucius knew the whole. Yet she did trust Jergan. And it was the most important thing in her life that he know what she was. All of it.

Ridiculous! She was *not* going to tell him she was a vampire. She was going to compel him to forget what he had seen. He was horrified and would tell anyone and everyone what he had discovered about her.

She turned to face him as he let the curtain fall behind them. He was wary, but he was not afraid. He looked . . . confused.

"You spied on me."

"Yes," he answered thoughtfully. He wasn't embarrassed or repentant. More important, he didn't look so entirely appalled as he had a moment ago.

She paused, searching his face. The feeling that she must tell him what she was almost overwhelmed her. She wavered there, resisting. Secrecy was her only protection. It was forbidden to tell humans about their kind. Their lives depended upon it. Sweat broke out on her forehead. The urge to tell him seemed irresistible. Her breath came in labored gasps. Perhaps she could appease whatever it was inside her that wanted her to tell him with a partial truth. If she didn't find some way out of her dilemma, she might just stand here, quivering, until she rotted.

"I have a . . . condition," she blurted.

"You are ill?" His eyes narrowed.

"In a way. I am. . . ." She cleared her throat, pushing down the urge to utter the word "vampire" and be done with it. "I have an illness. I was born with it. You cannot catch it," she hastened to add. How to say this? She must tread some line. "I . . . grow weak if I do not drink . . . what you have seen . . . every fortnight or so. I . . . I do not harm them. He will be healthy as well as free in the morning. And he won't remember what happened."

Jergan chewed his lip. "And this . . . illness is why you cannot stand the sun?"

She nodded. She wanted to tell him the rest. But she couldn't. But she must. Everything depended on it. It was all tied up with the feeling that she had to *do* something.

"Your servants told me about the blood. But not about the eyes, and why the slave will not remember." He paused and gathered himself. "Are you a witch?"

She sighed, half-chuckling under her breath. That at least she could answer truly. "No." How to explain *without* telling him all? "Do you know the snakes called cobras from the east?"

He shook his head.

"They stare at their prey, willing it not to move. Or . . . or perhaps it is like the shepherd dogs that stare at their sheep and the sheep obey. You know such dogs. Only my eyes change color. Not sinister, I swear. And I used it only for the slave's comfort."

"And your convenience."

"True."

"What else?"

Words rose in her throat as if they were whispered by someone else inside her.

Say it! "*I am vampire. I have lived seven hundred years already. I am stronger than you by many times. I can hear things you can't hear, see things you can't see, and I can raise the power of the thing that courses in my veins and wink out of space to appear somewhere else. . . .*" You must tell him. It is the first step on the path to righting what went wrong.

But she didn't say it. She wanted to groan with the urges battling inside her. She had to say something. "I smell of cinnamon from the east and ambergris from the leviathans of the far north. It is not perfume but my condition. And I seem . . . energetic to others."

He nodded slowly. "You feel more alive than anyone I have known."

She smiled, not daring to say more, much as she wanted to. So she just shrugged. He rubbed his chin. After a moment she felt more in control. "Are you afraid of me?"

He shook his head and looked surprised that she would think one of his courage, one who had faced the Roman war machine and slavery, could be afraid of her. "No. You may still be a witch." He considered her. "But that does not mean you are evil."

"Well," she chuckled. "If I must be a witch, I'd like to think I am a good witch."

"Do you want my blood? Is that part of serving you?"

"No. I will never take your blood unless you want me to."

He recoiled almost imperceptibly. "Why would I want you to suck my blood?"

It was distasteful to him. What else could she expect? She gathered her courage. "Some think it is a sensual experience." Why had she admitted that? It was as if some part of her was not quite under her command.

He paused, considering. "You do this during the sexual act?"

"When my partner wishes it." Though she hadn't done it in a hundred years.

His eyes glowed. "And why did you not have sex with that slave tonight?"

Breath seemed hard to get. Best that she remember why she hadn't used that slave. "It would not have been an equal exchange. Slaves cannot say no."

He came forward, uncoiling like that cobra she had described. His eyes were hot. "And what if one says yes, even before you ask?"

The voice inside her was practically shouting at her to

take him up on what was obviously an offer. She managed to push it down. "I . . . I would say he wanted to curry favor with his mistress." Now that was the hardest thing she'd said in a long while. "Come. We must return home." She pushed past him and out into the main room of the brothel.

SHE HAD TURNED him down again. He could hardly credit it. Or himself. Why was he accepting what she was? Why did he not think her a monster? He turned to follow her, his cock swelling against the fabric of his loincloth. Because she had been kind to the slave. Because she thought that forcing slaves to her bed was not honorable.

Damn her honor.

In spite of what he had seen tonight, he wanted her. Maybe because of it. She was dangerous. And the thrill of danger about her was almost as attractive as her vibrant energy or her beauty.

He stalked out to stand behind her as she thanked Drusus, the slave she had freed to found his own business, even if it was a brothel. At least it was a brothel with standards for its patrons and slaves who were well cared for and could earn their freedom. Better than the brothels in Jergan's own country. He remembered hollow-eyed women, dirty, beaten. He had never spilled his seed there. Pleasure could not exist side by side with cruelty. Taking them was not an achievement, something valuable to be earned. Because they could not say no? He understood Livia Quintus Lucellus because there was something they had in common.

That was a dangerous thought.

He followed her into the night, conscious only of the fact that the enigma of her made her even more attractive to him. She was like no woman he had known. A witch? She acted almost like a man, assuming equality as her right, demanding it in her sexual partner.

And she did not deem him an equal.

He sucked in a breath as though he had been struck. He wasn't her equal. He was her slave, and that stood between them.

If he were not . . .

If he were not her slave he would have pulled her into his chest and ravished her mouth with kisses just now until she was weak and breathless, and then he would have pulled her down on the bed in that room and pleasured her until she moaned in his embrace, and then, only when she was gasping and wet with desire, would he have swived her well and fully, feeling her cling to him as their ecstasy overtook them and he spilled his seed into her.

Jergan took a ragged breath. It had been raining while they were inside. The streets were wet and shiny black. The Nubian bearers brought her litter up. He handed her into it. His fingers burned where she touched them for support.

"Home," she ordered the bearers. The curtains fell between them as he walked beside the litter. His mind was so filled with wanting her, he could attend to almost nothing else.

Movement took his eye. His hand leaped to his sword hilt. Out of the darkness to his left, three men came rushing, crouched low. A glint of steel in the moonlight told him they had knives. He spread his legs for stability and drew his sword with a metallic slither against the metal fittings of the scabbard. He glimpsed two other shadows in the background. The first three were on him even as he felt the litter rock against his back. Others were attacking from the far side. She would be helpless against them. He slashed and cut an arm, raised a knee to throw off a thrust, and parried another with the hardened leather at his wrist.

"My lady," he shouted as the three drew back before another charge. One of the two who had hung back ran round to help the ones attacking Livia. "Are you well?" There was no answer, only the sounds of scuffling. Jergan thought he heard a male voice grunting in pain. The Nubians dropped the litter with a crash and backed away. He did not blame them. They had no weapons. The three attackers charged in again, now joined by the remaining one from the shadows. This time Jergan's sword was waiting. He slashed to his right, kicked another in the groin. Did the others have her yet? Rage maddened him.

One of his attackers fell, his shoulder cleaved to the bone and beyond. Jergan hacked low, at a thigh, and another collapsed. Jergan turned on the others and saw a Nubian come up to help. "Go to your mistress," Jergan yelled as he cut at an attacker's neck. The man toppled even as his fellow turned tail. The Nubian scrambled around to the other side of the litter. Jergan would have pursued his adversary, but he had other priorities. He whirled around the litter to see Livia standing, the breeze ruffling her *palla,* among a heap of bodies with limbs askew. The Nubian stood there, stunned, staring at the carnage.

"Are you all right?" Jergan growled, not sure how she lived.

She looked up, her eyes clear, and nodded. Then her eyes got big. "Jergan!" she shouted. "Behind you." She lunged toward him as he turned. Another assailant from who knew where had raised a short sword. It was descending, inches from Jergan's neck. The sword moved slowly, as things will when death is imminent. And he seemed to move even more slowly as he ducked to the right and rolled his shoulder so that he fell in a ball. The clatter of the sword against the frame of the litter echoed. He rolled to his feet and cut off the arm that held the sword extended, then thrust into the belly. The man folded over Jergan's sword. Jergan yanked it out and the man collapsed onto the paving stones.

Jergan scanned the street for a second before he took Livia's shoulders and examined her for wounds. There was a cut along her bare arm. She seemed about to wilt in his arms, now that the danger was past.

"Are you all right?" she asked breathlessly before he could ask the same.

He nodded. "You?" He turned her arm so he could see the cut. Not deep, but it needed attention. He examined her face. She would have a bruised cheekbone and chin.

"I thought they would kill you." She sounded dazed. "I saw it in my dream last night."

"I don't see why you aren't dead," he said, looking at the bodies that surrounded her. One's neck was obviously broken. One's throat was slit. There were five of them. She had killed four. She held a bloody knife she must have gotten off of one of them. "How . . . ?"

"I'm strong. I forgot to mention that," she whispered, shaken.

"And you know how to fight," he muttered, scanning the street. It was empty. That was strange. The streets on previous nights had been busy at this hour. Did everyone know they should not be abroad on this street just now? Or had someone blocked it off? He turned to the litter. Only one Nubian had stayed to help. "We'll have to walk home."

He took her upper arm and pulled her along. The loyal Nubian trailed in their wake. Why had she bought Jergan as a bodyguard? What did a woman who could kill five men need with him?

"Thank you," she was saying to the Nubian.

"Others were afraid, my lady," he said.

"I know. I don't blame them."

"Which way?" Jergan growled.

She pointed up a hill crowned with majestic stone buildings. "Over the next hill." She looked back. "We can't just leave them."

"Yes, we can." He pulled her along. He had to get her back to the protection of her house before someone came along to see whether the attack had been successful. She might have been able to kill five men, but perhaps she couldn't have dispatched nine.

LIVIA STUMBLED UP her street behind Jergan, who stalked ahead with his sword ready in one hand and her hand clutched in his other. The Nubian trailed them, glancing around fearfully. She was shaken by the death she'd caused tonight, the boldness of the attack, the fact that no one was about. Someone, if not Caligula, knew that she was behind the plot. The attacks proved that if nothing else. Who had leaked the information? Had she slipped up somewhere? Everything seemed to be closing in around her. She was not afraid for herself, of course. But there was so little time to accomplish what she must before the chance to make a difference was gone forever.

And then there was the fact that Jergan had nearly been killed in her service. If she lost him . . . What? Had he become so important to her in only two days? That was nonsense. Things didn't happen like that. She had a fear in her belly, though. It must be because another of her dreams had just come true. That was nonsense, too, but how could she not call it real?

As they approached the house she saw the telltale black shields and horsehair crests standing at the portico. The Guard. Her steps slowed. She pushed down panic. It would do no good to run. She could not leave Lucius, Jergan, and the others to face the wrath of Caesar and his Guard. She felt Jergan go quiet beside her. She glanced over to see him fingering his sword.

"Do nothing," she said as she started forward. "They will cut you down without a thought." She glanced to the Nubian, who was visibly shaking. "Be calm, Edo. They will not hurt you." That might well be a lie.

As she approached, the six soldiers parted for her. One removed his helmet as he stepped forward, and held it under his arm. He was a cherub-faced creature perhaps no older than his Caesar. He bowed.

"Lady Lucellus," he said. "Your slave must give up his weapon."

"In my own house?" she asked sweetly.

"Consul Tiberius Claudius Drusus Nero Germanicus honors your house with a visit."

Ahhh. Surprising. But thanks be to the gods that's why the Guard was here. They protected the Claudian line ferociously. Even Claudius. She nodded to Jergan, who reluctantly handed over his sword. The young guard took it and opened the door for them.

Lucius met them in the foyer, his eyes round. He had probably never seen a member of the imperial family this close, let alone had to entertain one.

Livia peered beyond his shoulder. "Where is he?"

"Your audience room."

"Thank you, Lucius.

"Come with me," she said over her shoulder to Jergan. She didn't want to let him out of her sight.

Entering, she saw that Lucius had provided the consul with wine and a selection of cheeses and nuts. Claudius lounged on a chaise picking through the plate. He was not an unattractive man, like his cousin. He was perhaps fifty, with regular features and well-opened eyes. His body gave no evidence of his infirmity. But all of Rome knew he had been born defective. His limbs were weak and sometimes gave out on him. His hand shook, and occasionally his head as well. He was the shame of the Claudian line. "To what do I owe this honor, Consul Tiberius Claudius Drusus Nero Germanicus?"

"L-Livia Q-Quintus Lucellus." And then there was his stutter. It made them all think he was stupid. His cousin had made him consul as a joke. Caligula was a great one for joking. And now he made such fun of his cousin in public places like the Senate, berating him, asking him to speak on ridiculous topics, that the poor man looked positively haggard. "A-are you w-well?"

At his words she looked down and saw that her *palla* and *stola* were torn and muddied. "A slight misunderstanding in the streets."

Claudius put aside his plate hastily and rose. "J-just what I had h-hoped to p-prevent."

What did he know of this? Maybe he knew about it because he had arranged it. She did not share Rome's view that he was stupid. He might be just the one to work in secret to support his cousin. Would Claudius try to prevent the assassination that would free him of a persecutor? Blood was still thicker than water. Did that mean he might be an ally? She couldn't make out her way here. Now that the adrenaline of the attack had subsided, she was left feeling dislocated and stupid. "We were attacked by brigands. How could you have prevented that?"

He chuckled and looked down for a moment before he peered into her face. His expression had none of its usual vacuity. "L-let us not d-dissemble, good lady. You were attacked b-because you are a c-catalyst." He glanced to Jergan.

Claudius knew! She managed not to blink an eye. "My bodyguard is privy to all my affairs, Consul. It seems I must keep him by my side constantly." She motioned Claudius to sit. "Take no offense at that, I pray you."

Claudius settled himself gratefully. "I do not. You m-must have a b-bevy of bodyguards to have survived the n-night."

"Just the one." She took her seat on an adjacent chaise, trying to compose herself. He *knew.* Then why was he not talking to his cousin, instead of here tonight?

"R-r-really?" Claudius examined Jergan more closely. "If w-word of that r-reaches my cousin's ears, he w-will have him in t-the arena."

Livia hadn't thought that she might be putting Jergan in danger by making him her excuse for surviving, but that had been brought home to her twice tonight. She should take him and run from the city. But she couldn't. Not before her plot had been consummated.

You can't leave the city. There is something here, something you need.

It was as if a voice inside her shouted at her. An unwelcome, anxious feeling settled in her breast. What could she not leave? She shook her head to clear it. She needed her wits about her when dealing with Claudius.

Claudius might be enemy or friend. Even if he was her enemy, she might be able to hold him off long enough to execute his cousin. If Claudius was her friend, he might be able to tell her the answer to what puzzled her. Because he was dismissed as negligible, he was privy to the innermost chambers of the palaces. But first she must see where he stood.

"Rome is rather thin of company these days," she remarked. "They retreat to their county estates even in winter to escape the arrests, the disappearances, the confiscation of property. Did you know the phrase 'summoned to Rome' has become synonymous with death? People say of a dead man that he has been summoned to Rome."

"My c-cousin has c-created a . . . t-tense atmosphere."

"Yes. For you, too. How do you bear it? Don't play stupid with me, since we are not dissembling tonight."

"Have you ever n-noticed how f-few of my astute and ambitious r-relatives are alive?"

She could not help but smile. "A disguise then?"

"M-made easier by the c-cursed infirmity of my b-body." He gulped his wine.

"So the question is, Consul, are you here representing yourself, or the imperial family?"

He did not answer. "I think my c-cousin has done R-Rome a favor. J-Julius and Augustus c-cloaked their absolute p-power in b-benevolence, so Rome would forget the v-value of what it had l-lost. But Gaius r-reminds us why giving absolute p-power to anyone is f-foolish."

That still might mean Claudius was using her future actions or her future death by brigands in some deep intrigue of his own to garner power. It didn't prove he hadn't ordered the attack.

He saw he hadn't convinced her. "T-There are w-whispers in the Senate today. W-whispers of the advantages of a r-republic. You p-play a bold game. T-too bold."

Ahhhh. He might want his cousin dead, but Claudius didn't want a republic. Perhaps he wanted a chance to cloak his power in honey like Julius and Augustus.

Claudius must have seen her wary expression. "N-n-no, no," he sputtered hastily. "N-no p-power for me. Th-that's why I came. T-to assure you of my s-support." He realized what he'd said and looked around as though his cousin might leap out of some vestibule and skewer him. He reminded her of nothing so much as a hunted hare.

If it was an act, it was a good one. Of course, this man had been putting on an act for years, at least since puberty. "Who do you think is behind the attack, then? It isn't your cousin."

"If it w-was, you'd be d-dead."

"Yes." Well, no, not dead. But her plot ruined, her servants tortured or dead. She raised her brows to repeat the question.

"I d-don't know who it is." Claudius looked thoughtful. "Or how l-long whoever it is will w-wait to tell Caesar a-about you. I w-would move q-quickly for m-many reasons, Livia Q-Quintus." He looked around again. "I m-must go." He rose and she rose with him. "I would s-say stay indoors, b-but that will do you no g-good if my c-cousin finds out about your p-plot."

With that, Claudius hurried away, limping slightly, without a backward glance.

Now the question was, how had Claudius found out about her little plan? Had one of her trusted conspirators leaked her role? By the gods, everyone seemed to know. Or maybe only one person knew and Claudius was the one who had arranged the attacks on her.

Livia let the air from her lungs, close to collapse.

Jergan was at her side in an instant. "Lucius," he called.

The majordomo appeared, looking surprised at who had summoned him.

"My lady requires wine."

Lucius swallowed once at being given orders by a slave. Livia nodded to confirm them. Lucius hurried away. Jergan glowered. He was used to being obeyed in another life. How hard for a man like this to be a slave.

He pushed her gently onto the chaise again. "Rest."

"Thank you for tonight. I hadn't realized the danger into which I put you."

He chuffed a laugh. "You didn't seem to need me. Why did you buy a bodyguard?"

"For appearance's sake. If I had to defend myself, I wanted someone else to get the credit." She ran her hand over her forehead, then looked up at him. "But I *did* need you tonight. I'm not sure I could have taken—what were there? Eight? Nine? Someone wasn't taking any chances." She couldn't have died unless they knew to decapitate her. But she could have been wounded, taken prisoner when she was weak. Then she would have had to escape and leave her household at the mercy of her enemies, and Rome at the mercy of its emperor.

"You should leave the city," Jergan said in a most unslavelike manner.

"I can't. Titus and the others will lose their nerve if I am not here to prod them. And . . ." The anxious feeling rose up and almost closed her throat. "And I've been having the strongest feelings that there is something here I cannot leave, and something I must do."

"What?" he asked, frowning.

She shrugged helplessly. "I don't know." A thought occurred. "Maybe it has to do with these dreams. The attack tonight occurred exactly as I dreamed it. It's as though I've lived this all before." She looked up and saw the doubt in his eyes. "I know it sounds mad."

9

JERGAN LOOKED DOWN at her, her brown eyes big with doubt, and wanted to protect her from the danger that was so clear around her. "You are not mad. Just tired."

He hadn't been sure she needed protection before tonight. He thought she'd bought him just to make him suffer. But he believed it now. And in spite of her strength, in spite of the things he had learned about her tonight and the fact that she was a witch, he wanted to protect her. Her honor demanded she free her people from the capricious evil of the emperor. Rome was worse than Jergan had imagined.

Or perhaps it was much better. It held women such as Livia Quintus Lucellus and the men of honor who plotted with her.

At that moment Lucius announced another visitor. "Titus Delanus Andronicus." Lucius hardly got the name out before the man himself pushed past him.

"Livia Quintus, are you well? I came as soon as I heard."

Jergan stepped behind her, making his face a mask.

"Yes, Titus." She waved a dismissive hand. "I am fine. Jergan here fought like one of those Pictish berserkers our spies tell us about."

Titus looked up at him, surprised. "Nine bodies were found in the Via Apollonia."

"And there was no one in the streets at all to witness the attack. It was very strange."

"Not when you know that the Praetorian Guard had blocked the side streets for the passage of Caligula."

Jergan frowned. If the emperor didn't know of Livia's plotting, why was his Guard involved in the attack, even if peripherally? Or maybe someone took advantage of the situation, someone who knew the emperor's route in advance.

"Never mind that now. How goes your effort with the Senate?" Livia asked.

"We need more time. They waffle. They delay. No one wants to commit."

"Just tell them. We don't need commitment, good friend. Plant the seeds. When you are done, the deed itself will water them."

To Jergan's surprise, the old man knelt at her feet. "You are wise, Livia Quintus, beyond your years and your sex. If we could be ruled by an empress, you would have my full support."

"Never say that, friend," she said. Jergan swore there were tears in her eyes. "Only free men of goodwill can give Rome the governance she requires. Now go, before you are seen here without the protection of a general audience. Send a slave to let me know when you and the others have talked to all the senators. Then it will be time."

He rose. "We will be quick. Two days . . . three, and we will have managed to see everyone." He took her hand. "Stay well until then."

He turned and was gone.

Livia's shoulders sagged. "I feel old, Jergan," she

whispered. "What if the tool I have selected for the deed fails in his task? All the talk of a republic will be linked to the attempt. Caesar will hunt out those who spread the rumors and kill all my friends."

Jergan came around from behind the chaise and lifted her chin, not caring that it was not slavelike behavior. "And you of course. He would kill you." That would be the greatest tragedy.

"The world moves forward," she said, examining his face as if she could read salvation there. "No matter what you think of Rome, it brought all those Greek ideas to the world. Rome actually achieved men governing themselves in a republic." She sighed. "But then the world takes three steps back into despotism and cruelty. I must try, at least, to preserve the light."

"You have great courage." He meant that.

"I don't feel up to it. Not tonight."

"You were attacked and hurt tonight. That's all." He looked at her face. There were no traces of the bruises he thought would bloom there. "Speaking of which, we should tend to your arm." He glanced to the smear of dried blood across her fine, fair skin.

"Oh. That. It was not my blood. I wasn't cut."

And now that he looked closely at it in the light, he saw that there was no wound, just the dried blood. He could have sworn . . . "Perhaps a bath would refresh you, my lady."

"Yes," she sighed. "A bath. And one for you as well."

"Yes, my lady." A heat started to glow somewhere below his belt.

She made as if to call her maid.

"No, my lady." He stayed her hand. "I will attend you in your bath. After what happened this night, you will not dismiss me again and leave yourself unprotected."

"But . . ."

He frowned at her. He knew now just how much protection she required. Who knew how many they might send against her? He would not back down, whether he angered her or not.

She sighed. "Very well. I am too dispirited to argue with you. If you will permit me to have Catia bring us towels and bath supplies?" She raised her brows at him, mocking.

It felt strange to have her ask him for permission, yet natural. They had progressed to some new understanding that was barely related to her stern speeches of just the night before last. He could hardly repress a smile. He hoped his nod was gracious.

It must have been because she smiled at his audacity. He liked her smile. It was the smile of a generous woman, a passionate woman. He wondered if she had ever been a carefree girl, if she had ever loved anyone, if she had married and lost her husband to war or assassination.

When Catia had disappeared to get their supplies, Livia rose, gathering the torn blue fabric around her. She looked like an empress in spite of the dirt and the blood that smeared her. Her black hair hung in heavy waves down her back, intermingled with the small braids now, the pins of its intricate arrangement having deserted their posts.

He had never seen a woman he thought more desirable. It wasn't just her beautiful, delicate body. It was her courage and her honor, her self-doubt. All monsters should be that noble in spirit. In fact, it didn't matter that she was probably a witch. If this was what it felt like to be bewitched, he only wished he had discovered it years ago. He followed her outside. She did not hurry, in spite of the light rain. The breeze off the Tiber cleared out the aromas of a city of a million people from among the olive trees that dotted the garden. Instead, it smelled like growing things. Different smells from those of his Centii. Sage, rosemary, olives. But still the scents reminded him of mown hay and wet grass. Outside the grotesque marble city was this land so different from his own?

She paused once before a vine-covered rock wall and peered around her as though searching for something. Tension sprang into her shoulders. He fingered the pommel of his sword and glanced around.

"What is it, my lady?" he whispered. Did she sense something he could not?

She shook herself. "Nothing," she said. "A feeling I have. It is just nonsense." She gathered her skirts and moved on.

Inside the bathhouse, she turned her back on him and began unwinding her *palla*.

"Let me remove your sandals, my lady," he said, and knelt. She lifted her tunic to allow him to untie the delicate leather strips painted in gold at her calves. The curve just at the back of her knee made his breath catch and his fingers clumsy. Above him, her breasts would be pressed against the light fabric of her tunic—the one that was almost invisible beneath the windings of her *palla*. Would he be able to see her nipples, their erection a sure sign of growing desire? She slipped out of the delicate sandal and he turned his attention to the other one. A pin from her hair dropped to the mosaic of the floor.

He rose with one small gilt sandal in each hand, their leather laces dangling, and placed them in a niche. She put the folded fabric of her *palla* in another. Her nipples were indeed outlined clearly against the fine fabric of her midnight blue tunic.

He knew what he wanted to have happen here, in the heat of the bath with the rain pattering on the flagstones outside the door and against the tiles of the roof. She had refused to indulge her own attraction for three days because he was her slave. He wasn't going to allow that to get in the way tonight. He'd find a way around it.

"Disrobe, Jergan." Her voice was husky. In the dim light cast by the lamps she seemed exotic as well as beautiful.

He unbuckled his belt and pulled his tunic over his head. She surprised him by kneeling before him to unlace his boots in reciprocation. He sat and pulled them off. She unwound the linen from his feet and examined his soles.

"The unguent helped."

"Thank you for your care."

"My responsibility." She set his boots aside and bundled up the linen strips.

"Would other Roman women have bothered?"

"Many would," she said, and looked away. She must know that wasn't true. She gently untied the bandage that bound the poultice to the wound in his shoulder. He peered to look. The wound had sealed itself even further in the last days. It no longer seeped fluid. It was only a jagged, rough line of pink flesh.

"The astringent leached out the fluid," she said with a satisfied smile.

"Is that why it burned so?"

She nodded.

He stood, dressed only in his loincloth, and watched her pull off her own tunic and chemise. She was naked. The lamplight of the changing room flickered on her breasts, the flare of her hips. She looked at him and did not cover herself. Brid and her handmaidens—he had a chance. He saw it in Livia's eyes. She moved past him

into the hot room. His erection was almost painful. He
kept his loincloth. He didn't want to frighten her with his
too-obvious desire.

She sat on a bench against a wall and closed her eyes.
He took the bench on the opposite wall. But he had no desire to close his eyes. He watched as her breathing slowed
and her skin began to glow with perspiration. She had
delicate ankles and wrists. He liked that in a woman. Her
breasts were perfectly formed. The way they rose and fell
with her breathing was torture. They didn't look like they
had been suckled by children. Too bad. Wise, generous,
caring, she would raise strong sons with a moral core as
deep as her own.

Catia came in and quietly left bath supplies—the tray
of salt and herbs, giant linen towels. She glanced to Jergan as she left and smiled. It was not a smile of desire
but . . . but of . . . gratitude? Oh, the story of him saving
Livia had gotten about. They were grateful she had not
been hurt. Little as it had been due to him. They must not
know exactly how strong she was. Still, could she have
vanquished all nine? He wasn't certain. She must have lim-
itations. He couldn't bear to think of a sword cleaving that
lovely flesh. The question was not why she had bought him,
but why she didn't have a dozen bodyguards.

It was perhaps half an hour before Livia opened her
eyes. She looked more herself. He rose and hefted the
amphora of oil over his elbow. She lifted her hair. He
poured it in a thin stream and she rubbed it with one hand
over her shoulders and arms, across her breasts, her belly,
Brid help him.

"Can you do my back?" she whispered, half-turning.

His hands seemed coarse as he rubbed oil across the
ridge of her spine, the delicate wings of her shoulder
blades. Touching her sent fire straight to his loins. She

twisted her hair into a knot to keep it out of the oil. He set down the amphora and knelt to offer her the tray of salt and crumbled sage. She took a handful in silence and rubbed it over her body. He bowed his head. He couldn't watch her rub her thighs or he would spill his seed right here and now. But he couldn't master his eyes for long. They glanced back to her and were held transfixed.

She didn't look at him, but she felt him watching her, he could tell. She was only doing a ritual she had probably done a thousand times. Yet it was so much more to him. She could not help but know she roused him. He could smell her woman's musk beneath the scent of oil, salt, and sage. Was this more than a ritual to her as well?

His hand could not be called steady as he rubbed the salt over her back and down over the swell of her hips and buttocks. He wanted to turn her around, spread her thighs wide, and bury himself inside her. But one must go carefully with a woman like this. A woman who still owned him. He couldn't quite hate her for that anymore. Perhaps he never had, no matter what he told himself. She'd saved him from a brothel and treated him kindly. He still wanted to repay her in the next hours in a coin that only he could deliver, make her open herself to him, moan with her desire, and acknowledge him as a man. Not exactly revenge. Somehow revenge was not as important as it had been. But he wanted . . . he wanted, in some sense, the same power over her she had over him.

A dangerous mission, not only to his body but likely to his soul.

LIVIA FELT WEAK. Not physically. Physically she felt fine. Her wounds had healed almost immediately, as was the habit of her kind. She'd been a bit disoriented by the whole attack, or perhaps it was by the feelings of urgency and familiarity that plagued her, but she was better now. Still, the feel of Jergan's hands on her naked body had made her weak with desire for him.

Jergan was reaching for a *strigil* to scrape away the salt and oil. She must have the strength not to command the use of his body.

He was aroused. That was why she had not asked him to remove his loincloth. What if he offered himself? What if he *chose* to make love to her? Would she have the strength to refuse?

He scraped in silence, her back, her shoulders. She did not take the *strigil* from him, but leaned back against the wall so he could do the same for the front side of her. He swallowed and continued without instruction. He held out her wrists and ran the ivory-handled blade along her arms. Then he did her chest, slid the tool seductively along the curves of her breast, lifted it gently with his other hand to scrape her ribs. Was it an accident that he brushed her nipple? Sensation jolted toward her loins. Venus, be merciful. She hadn't felt this much desire for a man for . . . for forever.

What was it about him? (The *strigil* was moving over her belly.) She trusted him with her life and the lives of her friends and servants. He would not betray her plot to assassinate Caligula. She didn't know how she knew that. But she did. She had trusted Jergan with at least part of her secret. He thought her a witch. Some part of her whispered that she should tell him that she was called vampire and that she had what amounted to immortality. She should tell him about translocation, and all the secrets of her state, including the fact that he could become vampire, too. The thrill of unease that accompanied that thought coursed through her and was carried away by the heat and the sensation of his hands on her thighs. Of course she couldn't make him vampire. That was against the cardinal Rule of her kind. The very thought of telling him anything frightened her. Not allowed. Not allowed!

She pushed that thought away. She had been on edge lately, what with the dreams and the feeling of urgency. She let fear gush out of her along with the sweat. This moment was heat, and oil and the scent of a man and a woman together. All else could wait.

She opened her eyes. He crouched before her, his knees touching hers, his body all hard planes and the bulge of heavy muscle. His eyes were hotter than the *calidarium*. "Your turn," she breathed. "Remove your loincloth."

He swallowed. "I . . . I would not offend you, my lady."

She smiled. "How could I be offended?"

He stood, and untied the simple cloth strip that bound his loincloth in place. His erection, freed, was as impressive as she remembered it. Thick and straight. He was a lucky man.

She stood. "Sit, so I can reach to pour the oil."

He sat on the bench in her place.

"Pull up your hair." How she loved the bulge of the muscle in his upper arm when he reached behind his neck. She poured the oil over his back and chest. He rubbed it across his belly with one hand. "Let me." She smoothed the oil across his thighs, his knees, around his calves, his feet, carefully ignoring the organ that strained between his legs. There was certainly no question that he was willing. She retrieved the tray of salt and slipped behind him. "I promise not to open any welts with this."

"Do as you will," he growled.

Carefully she rubbed the salt between his welts, over his hips. Men were so wonderfully constructed. So hard, with so many corded places, and yet their skin was smooth and fine. He took handfuls of salt and rubbed it over his chest and belly, his thighs, as though he was in a terrible hurry. That didn't offend her, either. She knew why.

Would she do this? She knew she did not have the will to resist the pull inside her that told her it was right to make love with this man, in spite of the fact that he was her slave. She was so wet between her legs that the throbbing seemed to have gotten into her blood. He handed her a *strigil* and took one himself. Again, she worked carefully, he quickly. He stood. She worked the *strigil* over his buttocks. They clenched in response. Livia felt faint with desire. How those buttocks would clench as they drove his rod into a woman! Into her.

"Let us to the pool," she whispered, taking his hand. Touching his hand was almost as intimate as rubbing salt over his body. Lovers held hands. Lovers.

They waded into the hot water of the steaming pool. The rain drummed harder outside, but here all was heat and steam, inside their bodies and out. The lamps flickered. The water sluiced the last remnants of tonight's attack from them. She was glad she could afford to indulge herself with chest-high water. She smoothed the water up over his shoulders as he stood, eyes glowing with want. She touched the scar of an old battle on his chest. Her breasts brushed his ribbed abdomen through the water. He did not touch her, just submitted to her touch. But he was like one of the leopards Caligula so liked to kill in the arena, all coiled muscle, ready to spring. His eyes glowed with his desire. They both ducked themselves into the water and rinsed the sweat from neck and face. Water streamed from them.

"I want you, my lady," he said, his voice husky. "Of my own free will."

"I want you, too, Jergan." She thought she had tired of

lust a long time ago. Apparently not. Doubt assailed her. Lust was enough between two mature people. But this seemed more than simple lust. It was almost mystical in its intensity. How could one resist this feeling that she was meant to make love to him? She should free him first. But she could not sign his name in the registry until tomorrow. That didn't solve tonight. It didn't solve tomorrow, either. There was no guarantee he wouldn't make love to her only out of gratitude for his freedom. Their stations were too unequal. So she should not make love to him ever. And yet . . . his body confirmed that he would do it of his own free will. What to do?

He saw the doubt in her eyes and gripped her shoulders. "There is only one way I can satisfy the need I see in your eyes tonight, Livia Quintus Lucellus, and the need I feel in return, and that is equal partner to equal partner, just as we fought together tonight. No constraints, no orders, regardless of what we are to each other in the eyes of Rome. Those are my terms."

It did not feel unnatural that a slave should dictate terms. It was only surprising that they were exactly the terms that would free her to act. He seemed to know her so well. But no, nothing could surprise her about Jergan. She had known him forever.

And he would make her whole. She felt it. That was why this was more than lust.

She turned her face up. He was more than a foot taller than she was. "I accept your terms."

The water swirled around them. Now that she had accepted, she expected the leopard to pounce upon her and ravage her. She wouldn't mind that. But he didn't. He took her shoulders gently and drew her in to him, then bent to kiss her. His lips glided against hers, just touching. It made her shiver. Her breasts brushed his chest again through the water. Her nipples bathed her in sensation. His tongue slid between her lips and she opened to him as he deepened the kiss. Kissing was the surest sign that this was not a master/slave liaison. Masters never allowed their slaves the intimacy of kissing. He probably didn't know that. As he wrapped his arms around her, she slid her hands up under his hair, around his neck. His erection lay against her belly and she moved against it, loving the moan that elicited. She had loved men for centuries. She knew what pleased them, even if she was a little rusty. And she wanted to give Jergan pleasure.

One of his hands moved lower, cradling her buttocks. She probed his mouth with her tongue. He tasted sweet. His other hand had found her breast. She pressed herself into his palm, and his thumb rubbed her nipple gently. She lost herself in sensation. Somehow his hand had descended to her mound; he was asking her to spread her legs. She was happy to oblige, pulling him down as she widened her stance. She thought he would lift her onto his cock. But his finger split her nether lips, letting in the hot water. It wasn't as hot as her flesh. His finger caressed her swollen membranes, wet not only with water but also with the thick slickness her need produced. Most men didn't know that the tiny nub hidden in a woman's folds was a secret to her pleasure, or didn't bother to use that knowledge if they did. Her bud of womanhood strained under his fingers as they slid back and forth. How long had it been? She moaned into his mouth. He deepened his kiss even further, and began to rub her in earnest. She could hardly get her breath. She banged her hips against him, feeling the hard length of his cock between them. It didn't take long before the sensation ramped up until her head was singing with it, like a glass tapped with a spoon. Then the glass shattered. She leaned back, his arm supporting her, and shrieked her ecstasy, on and on, until her hips jerked from his hand of their own accord and she collapsed against him.

It had been so long. This was like the pleasure she had remembered, and yet not like.

All at once, he lifted her into his arms and sloshed out of the pool. "There is a lounge in the *tepidarium*," she whispered, in case he did not remember. Not quite a bed, it would still be far more comfortable than the hard stone benches of the *calidarium*. And they had much left to do tonight. He swept her through the doorway—he had to duck his head—and laid her on the red upholstery in the cooler room. She scooted closer to the wall so he could join her. God, but he was an impressive specimen of a man. The water droplets on his body gleamed in the lamplight. He lay next to her.

She could not help but smile. "You know something of women," she whispered.

He smiled in return. She had not seen him smile just so before. "Something."

"I feel obligated to reciprocate with what I know of men." She slid her hand along his cock and licked his nipple. It contracted under her tongue. She nibbled as she stroked him lightly. His breathing hissed in and out. His cock throbbed against her.

As she continued, he writhed under her touch, groaning, straining his hips against her. Abruptly he pulled back, gasping, then gently put her hand from his cock. "Have mercy, my lady. I will not last until you are ready again."

"I'm ready now."

His green eyes smiled at her. "Are you?" He dipped his head to her breast and suckled.

"Juno and Venus," she muttered as his skillful tongue

drew sensation from her nipple she didn't know it was capable of giving. When he turned to the other breast, she thrust up to make it available. His hands moved over her hips. She felt small in his embrace. She'd never had such a big man before, big all over. It was her turn to writhe under him. He raised his head and kissed her mouth again, deeply, as his fingers slid between her legs once more.

"*Now* you are ready."

She chuckled and spread her thighs as he rolled between them. He held himself over her, propped on his elbows. She lifted her hips to slide her wet channel along his cock. He was having a hard time breathing. When he could hold back no more, he pushed at the entrance to her. Most men closed their eyes to turn all their attention to the sensation building inside them, but he kept his burning green gaze fastened to her face, drinking her in. She smiled encouragement, and he eased inside her, slowly, so slowly. She was filled with him. She opened her hips even more. She had not quite gotten all of him in, for she didn't feel his pelvis flat against her. He eased himself out, trying to breathe, and pushed in again. She sighed as she felt him press against the upper reaches of her womb. His breath hissed out. Now she had all of him. He began thrusting. She arched to meet him. Ahhhh, how long had it been?

They met in counterpoint, each of his strong thrusts met with her equal force. She made certain it was only equal. She only matched his strength, though hers was so much more. It would not take long for him to peak and she was rising fast as well, but that didn't matter. She would raise him yet again tonight. And they had the long day together. The edge approached. She gasped and fought for breath. The friction of his pelvis grinding against her loins sent frissons of sensation across her nub of pleasure. Inside her, his rod rubbed against that most secret of places in her womb, and the edge of the cliff rushed up. She was falling over, her insides contracting in spasms of pleasure. But he was contracting, too, and they were free-falling together into darkness, full, together, whole . . .

BEWITCHED, INDEED. HE had never met a woman so open to a man, so passionate. Her womb, contracting, had milked him of his seed until he was like to have lost his mind. He lowered himself to her side, so as not to crush her with his bulk. He was still full inside her. She rolled a little with him to keep them together. He had half-expected her eyes to go witch-red, but they hadn't. It had been sexual congress like any other, and yet like no other in his busy past. None of the big-boned women of his homeland who gave themselves so lustily to a comely man could hold a candle to this little Roman witch. Gently he brushed his lips across the salty silk of her neck. That reminded him of what she had done to the slave prostitute earlier tonight. Or had that been weeks ago? She had said that sometimes her partners wanted her to take their blood. He couldn't imagine it at the time, but now . . . Would it not be just another form of sharing? And giving her what she needed to survive. He felt an overwhelming urge to take care of her, as useless as that was.

He kissed her lips, softly. She smiled up at him, her lids heavy with satiation.

That part hurt, the part about how strong she was, how wise. Could a woman who was a witch, who was strong enough to kill four men, apparently with her bare hands— could a woman like that need a man the way other women did? But she *did* need him. He had killed the other five. And then there had been the doubt in her eyes tonight, with the weight of a plot to free Rome from the snake that entwined it on her slender shoulders alone. He could soothe that doubt.

And he knew he had pleasured her tonight. No matter that she probably took pleasure almost every night. She had said she didn't need a slave for sex because she could have any Roman citizen she liked. He did not doubt that. Who could resist her? Perhaps tonight was ordinary for her. . . . He almost couldn't bear the thought.

He moved out of her. His cock was still full, if not erect. She curled in his arms like a cat. He held her, and stroked her wet hair. "We need another bath," he said roughly, because he could not ask whether this had been an ordinary night.

She chuckled against his chest. "Not yet. It might be a waste, don't you think?" Her hand moved over his hip. Brid's breasts, but Livia could raise him with just a touch.

"Then let us wait," he said. He was glad she wanted more of him.

She snuggled closer. "The sun is rising even now. We have all day."

It was still raining. The sky outside was lighter, but there was no sign of sun. "How do you know the sun rises?"

"I always know the exact moment," she murmured.

Because it burned her. Because she was a witch. He didn't care. She had promised him a day of making love. "Will your servants not come to check on you?"

"Perhaps. They may bring us refreshments. It won't matter."

It wouldn't matter because no one would dare question the mistress of the house. They would expect her to be using him. His owner. He must not forget that. With a start he remembered that he had wanted this sexual act to be some kind of revenge on her for owning him. He had believed that if she wanted him, she was in some sense in thrall to him.

How differently it had worked out. He was now doubly in thrall to her.

10

By NOON THEY had bathed again. After making love, and dozing and making love again. Now Livia lay with her head on Jergan's thighs, drowsing, with the doors closed against the gray day. Lamps flickered against the stone of the bathhouse, warm and sensual. He brushed her temple lightly with one calloused finger. How she had loved being cradled in Jergan's big arms all morning. How complete she felt. She'd never thought herself lonely. But she was. And Jergan made her feel as though she would never be alone again. She wanted that, yearned for it with some part of her that had been growing stronger each day she had owned him.

Except he lived only a human life span.

And she did not. She would live on long after he was dead.

Sadness and that strange sense of urgency she'd had lately intermingled in her breast. She must do something about that. She sat up, restless, making him stare at her.

But what could she do? To make him vampire was an abomination—against the cardinal Rule of her kind. And he would abhor her for it. Unthinkable when she couldn't even bring herself to tell him that the name of her kind was vampire, and that she lived forever. He didn't want to stay with her anyway. He stayed only because of his vow to his general. He made love to her because making love tied her to him and gave him more control of his situation. He was a slave. He could do nothing else.

The differences between them would always make it impossible for their relationship to be more than an interlude of sexual pleasure. She couldn't do anything about that. But she could at least make certain he had a choice of whether to engage in such an interlude or not.

She had to free him. Today.

"What is it, my lady?" His brows had drawn together.

And when she did, he would return to Britannia. Centii was his home. Why would he not?

It was all so hopeless. She had an impulse to tell him about the eternal life. That was the important part of what she was, which he *must* understand. Why? What could that possibly do but drive him away faster?

What did it matter? He would go anyway. Because she was going to free him.

"There's something I must do today." She had control of her voice, if nothing else about her life, at the moment.

He looked taken aback. "In daylight?"

She nodded and rose, pulling a towel about her. "Lucius," she called. He would be waiting outside with refreshments in case she called for them, guarding against intrusion.

Jergan's expression registered shock as Lucius opened the door and poked his head in.

"Refreshments, my lady?" He did not look at Jergan, still naked on the chaise.

"I will go out today, Lucius."

He looked surprised but nodded. "I have a blanket to cover you on your way into the house, and a clean loincloth and tunic for your slave. I will make ready."

"Thank you, Lucius."

Lucius left the two piles of clothes and walked away. He would hang her litter with the heavy draperies to keep out the sun. No matter what she did, this would be painful. But the registry of names was only open during daylight hours. The discomfort she must suffer each time she freed a slave was a penance somehow for Rome's practice of enslaving. A third of the population of Rome were slaves. She turned to Jergan and handed him the tunic and loincloth. "Dress yourself," she said. It sounded like a command, perhaps among the last she would give him. She shrugged her apology. "Today I make you a free man."

THE LITTER STOPPED before an imposing stone building. Columns supported a pediment carved with a frieze that showed some battle. Jergan stood beside the palanquin. The sun was bright after the rain. Or maybe it only seemed so bright and clear white because he had been sleeping through the days and had known only night. The steps up to the building were busy with people coming in and out. The marble gleamed in the sun.

Beside him, he heard the hangings being drawn aside and a little gasp. He turned and saw her jerk her hand back out of the sunlight. "Let me," he growled. He pulled back the heavy woolen hangings. He should be happy. She had told him that when she listed his name in the registry, he would be a free man. "Cover yourself more carefully, my lady."

She pulled the heavy woolen *palla* up over her head and forward to shade her face. She had bound her feet with cloth inside her sandals, and now she put her hands inside the folds of the loosely wrapped *palla*. He noticed that the hand that had pulled aside the hangings was red. Was she as sensitive to sunlight as that? He reached in and bundled her out into the light. She was breathing quickly.

He was not happy. Did she think the love they made was just a way for him to bribe her to free him? Did she think him that calculating? Did their lovemaking mean so little to her?

She darted up the broad marble stairs and he trotted after her. She stumbled and he took her arm, supporting her. She was trembling.

If he was free, he could go home. How often had he wished for that on the long and painful journey to Rome as the soldiers whipped him and the elements tore at his nearly naked body? That prospect, so near at hand, no longer filled him with undiluted joy.

They ducked in between the columns and through the open doors.

"Are you all right, my lady?" he whispered to her.

"Fine," she said, a quaver in her voice. She cleared her throat. "Fine." But she didn't put back her *stola*. The great building was open to the day. Channels of light from the doors that had been opened all along both sides made the room as bright as the steps outside. "Come with me," she managed, and started off among the many Roman men crisscrossing the wide hall.

He followed her as she made her way to a side room, its floor covered in a black-and-white mosaic of grape leaves and some figures of Roman gods he didn't recognize. An old man in the traditional white wool toga sat behind a large wooden table on which lay a huge scroll. A line of perhaps twenty men and one other woman stood before him. Each citizen had a slave beside him. Was it as simple as writing a name on a scroll? Apparently.

Livia stood, trying to get her breath as the others in line noticed them and began to stare at her, all bundled up as she was. An open pediment sent a ray of light cutting in a channel through the room to illuminate the great scroll.

He could feel her holding herself in check as they got slowly nearer to the man who was murmuring to each citizen at the head of the line. At last it was their turn. Her head was bowed, to let the fold of *palla* over her head give her maximum protection from the light.

The wizened man looked up, his quill poised over the parchment lined with names. "Who have we here?" he queried. "Show yourself, woman, for only a citizen may free a slave."

Would she do this just to free him? He heard her take a long breath. Then her hands came out from under her cloak and put back her *palla*. She squinted against the light. "Livia Quintus Lucellus," she said, and this time there was no quaver in her voice. "I wish to free this slave."

"Ahhhh, Lady Lucellus, a frequent visitor," the man said, nodding. Could he not see that her face was reddening in the channel of light? "Sign the scroll," the old man ordered, and swiveled it across the desk.

Livia took the stylus and dipped it in the inkwell. Her hand was shaking, already red and beginning to blister. She scribbled her name and straightened. "What name do you give him?"

"Jergan Britannicus Lucellus," she said. Her voice was small.

"I suppose you cannot write it," the man said to Jergan. "She can write it for you."

"I can write," Jergan growled. He pulled the scroll toward him. He took up the stylus and wrote the name she had given him. When he had finished, the old man took the scroll, examined both signatures, and then looked up.

"Jergan Britannicus Lucellus, you are now a freedman with all the rights thereof. Obey the laws of the Eternal City upon punishment of death."

He stood there, holding the stylus, suddenly adrift. He was free.

Livia took the stylus from him gently and laid it on the table. Her hand was blistered. Her face was red. "Come, Jergan. You can stay at the house while you decide what to do next." Jergan could not stand it longer. He reached over and pulled her *palla* up over her head, then twitched it forward to cover her face better.

"Watch that you are not impertinent, slave, else she may change her mind about freeing you," the old man complained. He peered at Livia. "But you always free them, don't you? Impertinent or not." He heaved a sigh and turned to the next in line.

Jergan turned with her while the citizen behind them stepped up impatiently with the old man he intended to free. Jergan followed her from the building. She took a breath for courage before she hurried down the steps.

A large man with purple woven into the edge of his toga blocked her way. "Livia Quintus Lucellus," he greeted her. "I so rarely see you out and about. What is the occasion?" His hair was a gray, thick shock. How did he know her, bundled up as she was? Jergan recognized him from the retinue of Caesar at the banquet the other night. That meant he was dangerous.

"Decimus Valerius Asiaticus, you surprise me," she choked.

"It was your slave that betrayed your identity. Word has spread of his prowess. What was it," the man asked Jergan, "nine?"

Jergan grunted assent, wishing the sun would go behind the clouds that scattered across the sky and give Livia even a modicum of relief. He had a feeling that the light leaking in under her *palla* was continuing to burn her. The man had a crafty face with darting brown eyes that saw everything.

"You are fortunate in your selection. Many would give a high price for a slave like that. Would you consider selling?"

"Not possible. I have just registered his name. He is a free man."

The man was peering under Livia's *palla*. Of a sudden he grabbed her hand from among the folds of her *palla* and lifted it to his lips. The broken blisters sent little rivulets of fluid across her knuckles. How could the man torture her so? Didn't he realize what he was doing? "Are you well? The sun seems to have an unfortunate effect on you."

Livia snatched her hand away, unable to speak.

"I think Caesar should get to know such an extraordinary woman better. I will send a personal guard to escort you to his investiture of a new consul in the Senate tomorrow. We wouldn't want you set upon again."

"Thank you for your kindness," she choked, and Jergan took her elbow, hurrying her back to the litter. He opened the hangings and thrust her inside. Glancing back, he saw the counselor to Caesar watching them with narrowed eyes.

"To the house," Jergan ordered the Nubians, who lifted the poles. "And hurry."

LIVIA GASPED FOR breath inside her litter. So much sunlight! This had been worse than previous visits to the registrar. The angle of the sun in winter was unfortunate. She heard Jergan urging the Nubians forward. The litter swayed and rocked. She touched a finger to her face and winced. Her hands were blistered and swollen, her face probably only slightly less so. She hoped Jergan hadn't noticed how bad it was. The sun weakened her system. If she had any other wound, she'd have healed by the time she crossed her doorstep and Jergan would never know about the healing. As it was, she must conceal how bad the burns were. She laid her hands carefully on the cushions of the litter. The scraping of her *palla* hurt too much to hide them now.

She lay there, half-insensate. When the litter stopped swaying it was all she could do to rouse herself. The draperies were pulled back. She cringed away from the light. She must gather herself and get out. She had to face the sunlight just once more.

But big hands laid her own hands gently on her lap, then pulled her *palla* around her. Arms lifted her. She hissed as her hands rubbed against the fabric.

"I can walk. I'm fine," she protested faintly.

"Of course you can." But he didn't put her down.

She laid her head against his shoulder. He smelled familiar now. She would always know that scent, his alone. Her *palla* fell back to expose her face. Pain shot through her.

"Lucius, pull up her *palla*," Jergan ordered sharply. "Shield her face."

"Oh, my lady, what have you done?" The *palla* was adjusted.

Jergan carried her into the house as though she weighed nothing. The great doors clanged shut. She began to breathe again, limp against his chest. He carried her into her quarters and laid her down on her bed.

She huddled there inside her *palla,* afraid to move just yet. She'd be fine. She always was, no matter how bad the burn. But it would take some hours this time. "Leave me," she said, to whoever was in the room. Her voice was thick and strange.

She heard footsteps and the doors were shut. Now all she had to do was wait out the healing. She could bear the pain until then.

The bed creaked as a weight descended on it. "Can't you follow orders?" There was no question about who it was. His scent betrayed him.

"I'm not your slave anymore," he said softly. He moved the *palla* off her face.

She cracked open her eyes, swollen and crusty. She could barely see the grim expression on his face. She must look a sight. "It isn't as bad as it looks," she mumbled through cracked lips. "I react strongly, but it goes away." Just like he would, soon enough.

He pulled the edges of her *palla* carefully away from her hands. She didn't lift her head to look. Why bother? She knew what they looked like. She had been burned before.

"Does this happen every time you free a slave?" He laid her hands carefully on the bed.

"Not this badly. The shaft of sunlight . . ."

"A high price to pay for a generous deed."

She closed her eyes. "Uncomfortable for a while. It doesn't matter. Leave me now." Leave the room, leave the city—her heart contracted.

The weight lifted from the bed. She heard his steps moving around the room. No sound of the door closing after him. Sloshing. Scraping—was he opening a drawer? Then the weight was back. He lifted her shoulders.

"Drink." Cool water passed her lips. She had to admit it was welcome. He laid her back down. She watched through her cracked eyelids as he busied himself with something. He leaned over her and smoothed some of the unguent she had used on his welts across her lips. His touch hurt initially, but then the salve soothed the burning.

"Thank you." She was about to order him to leave again when she realized it would make no difference. He knew how bad the burns were. He would realize how much she healed. Her lame explanation that the reaction faded either would satisfy him or wouldn't.

"Would it help if I spread unguent on your hands and face?" he asked.

"The effect will pass. I can't imagine anyone touching my skin." Already she was speaking a little more clearly.

"Then rest." He removed her sandals and the wrappings on her feet.

She was already feeling sleepy as the Companion in her blood began to do its job and heal her. A thought crashed through her lethargy. "Will you wait to leave for Britannia until I wake?" She made it a question. She had no right to ask it of him. Not anymore.

"I won't leave."

Good. She would see him again. Once more. It was all she could expect. She closed her eyes, too tired to examine the confusion in her breast.

11

WHEN SHE OPENED her eyes again, she could feel that the sun had set. Lamps were turned low around the room. It felt like it was after midnight. She must have slept for many hours. Jergan sat on the end of the bed, his back to one of the bedposts that supported the curtains hung to keep out the bugs in summer.

"Better?" he asked.

She sat up. She felt fine. She would look fine. "Yes," she said warily. Had he grasped what the healing truly meant? Some part of her surged up inside her brain and hissed, *Tell him!* She couldn't do that. Their kind existed in secret. It was their only protection, that and the disbelief of humans, against mobs with torches. She could die in only one way. No prison could hold her. But she had learned long ago that her servants could be killed, her work undone. She couldn't tell anyone what she really was. She looked at her hands, once again smooth and white. The hands of a woman of thirty. Now he would ask what the healing meant. And she could never tell him.

A furrow created creases between his brows and he chewed his lower lip. He had been sitting there thinking for a long time. That was bad. But he surprised her.

"Why did you free me?" Lamplight flickered on the planes of his face. She couldn't read his expression.

"I always free my slaves. Tufi and Lucius must have told you that."

"They said a slave has to earn it. You made the others earn it. I did nothing to earn my freedom. Unless you count bedding you a service."

That struck her to the heart. He thought she freed him in payment for the sex? She managed a chuckle. "It would have taken more than one night to earn your price, barbarian. You were expensive."

"Then why?"

"Maybe I can't own slaves anymore. I haven't the stomach for it."

"I don't think that's it."

"You're certainly insistent about things now that you are a freedman."

"Are you going to tell me?"

No. She didn't want to tell him. What use? He was going to leave anyway. Why bare her feeble hopes? She hardly dared admit them to herself.

Take a chance, Livia. You'll regret it if you don't. And regret will poison you. I know.

The effect was so strong it almost startled her. It seemed like an actual voice inside was admonishing her. She had heard it now several times. A shudder ran down her spine. She wished she only had vague urges now. Jergan had folded his arms across his chest, the muscles in his upper arms bulging, his brow puckered as though in disapproval. He was waiting her out. She tried to focus and cleared her throat. Very well. She could tell him this. "I couldn't go on bedding you if you were a slave. In spite of the fact that you appeared willing."

A small smile softened his stern expression. "I didn't *appear* willing. I *was* willing. And it was more than last night. It was this morning, too." He cocked his head to look at her. "You want it to go on, so you freed me. Yet you are certain I will leave for Britannia now that I am free."

"I know. It is stupid." She fussed with her *stola,* embarrassed. Of course he would go. Romans had treated him abominably. He disapproved of everything about Rome.

Take a chance.

"I wanted you to have what you want most." There. She'd said it.

"And what about you? You need a bodyguard more than ever."

"I'll hire one."

She watched emotions flicker across his expression. Regret, something almost like anger. Then they faded, leaving . . . what? Resolve. The changes were so subtle and so fleeting that once she might not have recognized them, but now she knew his features and his guarded expression of emotion well.

"Good," he said, finally breaking the silence. "But since no one you hired would really care about whether you lived or died, it's a good thing that one man of good character who does care will apply for the job. Do I submit my application to Lucius?"

"You would stay?" She hardly dared form the words. She wanted him to stay so badly. But he longed for his home. She knew that. Those traces of emotion in his face just now had been the realization that his decision would cost him what he wanted most, at least for a while.

"Until your little plot is over. Depends upon the pay, of course."

"This is dangerous, Jergan. You know that now." She had to give him a way out.

"All the more reason you need a bodyguard. How much?"

"One dinar a day." That was likely ten times the going rate.

"I am probably being cheated." He shook his head, mock sorrowful. He had control of his expressions now. He seemed to consider. "With room and board thrown in?"

He was making light of a decision that must be truly difficult for him. She felt a smile light her eyes but managed to keep it from her mouth. "We are somewhat short of beds."

"Then you must share yours, my lady. Do we have a bargain?"

She held out a hand and realized that it no longer blistered. She almost snatched it back.

But he took it and clasped it firmly. "Done. I am your bodyguard until the plot is over, one way or another."

"Thank you," she said. She should make him go. It was safer. And yet to share the burden with another was such a relief, she could not say it to him. Was she selfish in allowing him to stay? Yes. But the attack last night had proved she needed him. And the plot still needed her. If she needed him in other ways as well, was that so bad?

He looked seriously at her. "If it goes wrong, do you have some escape route planned?"

Of course she did. She of course would just disappear, literally. "As the time approaches, I will send my household to my estates in the Tuscan hills. That is not far enough, of course. The Roman army has a long reach. But they can disperse from there to the far corners of the empire. If . . . if we are compromised, we will follow them." She frowned. "But we must provide for the other conspirators as well."

"How many are there?"

"Just the three, including Titus. Four if you count the actual perpetrator."

"You have never said who that was."

"Only I know who it is. It's safer that way for all concerned."

It was his turn to frown.

"What is it?"

But he shook his head. He appeared to be thinking. "The man on the steps, who stopped you in the sunlight—he was with Caesar the other night. Who is he?"

She nodded. Hmmm. Jergan was right. That was concerning. "Decimus Valerius Asiaticus, Caesar's closest advisor besides the captain of the Guard."

"He saw you burn. He will see you are healed when you attend the ceremony tomorrow."

"I will tell him it was a brief reaction. How can he say otherwise?"

Jergan kept his silence, but it was clear he didn't like someone so close to the emperor knowing her vulnerabilities.

She rose and called for food. Lucius must have had it waiting, for before she could even light all the lamps again, a line of servants brought in trays. Tufi grinned at Jergan, and Jergan grinned back. She had almost forgotten how Jergan must feel. This was his first day as a free man. His slavery had been but a short nightmare.

As the servants trooped out, she invited him to pull up a chair to the table. It felt companionable to sit here, dishing him food, talking of small things.

"Would you like to know one of the first things that shocked me about you, my lady?" he asked, around a mouthful of fresh, yeasty bread.

She grimaced. "I hardly dare guess."

"The fact that you fed me from your own table, not scraps or leavings, but the same food you ate. That, coupled with the care you took of my wounds, belied your harsh words."

She brushed away the inference. "I'm ashamed to think of what I said that first night."

"Why? You were right. I was feeling rebellious, even violent. You said the only things that could make me accept my lot."

"I lied to you." She glanced up from dishing up her own plate to find him questioning. "I said I would not use you for my pleasure." She flushed.

"I call what we did a partnership of equals."

"Equally lustful," she said, bemused. The fire was rising in her loins again with this talk.

"Something Romans should understand."

"It isn't just the senatorial class, Jergan. The general population of Rome is also less judgmental about the needs of their bodies, though less . . . orgiastic in satisfying them. On the whole, that attitude is much less constricting than that of my homeland."

"Dacia must be a hard land."

"Yes." He, of course, had no idea how hard. The Elders set the Rules by which relations between humans and vampires were controlled, though humans didn't know that. They punished transgressions, like making humans vampire. She'd heard stories of days in the sun, and long bouts of painful torture, until the vampire longed for death. The elders were right, too. What would happen if every vampire made another? Soon there would be no humans left to provide blood, for vampires could not draw sustenance from each other unless one very old took blood from one very newly made. That didn't last for long. When the vampires were of more equal strength, the two Companions warred, each with the other. Not only painful until one Companion triumphed, but the blood itself was destroyed in the process, providing no sustenance.

And then there was the fact that most made vampires

went insane when the enormity of what they had become became clear to them. The sense of being more than a single being, whole, created by the Companion that shared their veins did not counterbalance for them the need for blood, the loss of the sun, the temptation to see humans as lesser beings. Made vampires often ran amok and killed for their blood or used their powers of compulsion to victimize the humans around them.

Why was she thinking these things? What point? She raised her goblet. "To your freedom."

He raised his goblet and clicked with hers. "To your generosity."

They ate in companionable silence. The servants came to clear the table.

"Is the room warm enough for you?" Lucius asked, in the doorway. "I can have the boys stoke the hypocausts."

"It is fine, Lucius."

"Rest, my lady," he adjured her, as he closed the door.

But Livia wasn't ready for rest. It was still four hours until dawn. She got up and began to pace the room. And the itching in her veins wasn't hunger. It was as if something inside her was trying to get out. She couldn't help thinking that she couldn't leave Rome, or this house, even if something went wrong with their plan. She had to be here, not up in Tuscany. *Something* here was important. It must be these dreams of premonition that had her on edge. They were a new experience in a life that held nothing new anymore. And this feeling of being *too* full, more full than she felt with her Companion, was also disconcerting. She almost felt that there was something inside her trying to get out. Some knowledge? Something she had overlooked in plotting Caligula's assassination? Even as she thought it, she rejected that idea. But something inside knew what it was. Something knew all about her.

As she turned, she almost bumped into Jergan.

"My lady," he said, taking her shoulders. "Lucius was right. You should rest."

"I cannot rest. Every time I sleep, I dream of something that comes true, almost as though I had already lived what happened." She searched his face. "And I have this sense of urgency. That there is something I must do, and time is running out to do it. And I don't know what it *is*." She took a breath. "I sound insane, even to myself."

"Being able to say that is one sure sign of sanity." He smiled at her, a tender smile. The feel of his hands on her shoulders belatedly made its way into her senses, like realizing you'd been burned before you felt it.

Even as the sensation struck her, she saw it fill his eyes as well.

"I am a free man, Livia Quintus Lucellus." His voice was hoarse. "And I am going to make love to you until you have screamed away all your tension, and this talk of madness seems silly." With that, he leaned down and kissed her. His tongue searched her mouth. One hand moved from her shoulder to hold her neck. The other clasped her waist and held her to his groin, so she could feel his arousal. His beard of three days scratched her cheek and made him feel like a dangerous masculine animal that would ravish her without a second thought.

She wanted to be ravished.

He picked her up and carried her to the bed. Holding her with one arm, he swept away the *palla* that still lay across the embroidered coverlet and then laid her down. He did not bother to undress her. He took the neck of her *stola* and . . . and ripped the delicate peacock silk and the chemise below it down the front, leaving her naked.

He stepped back and unbuckled the wide belt that held his tunic. "Now I will pleasure you, my lady, as a free man." He pulled his tunic over his head and tossed it away, unlaced his boots and kicked them off, and unbound his loincloth. His rod was stiff and straining. As he approached the bed, his eyes grew predatory. He devoured her with his green gaze just like one of the leopards the legions brought back from the lands below the deserts behind Carthage. She liked that image of him. Kneeling on the bed, he bent to suckle at her nipples. Lord, there was no thinking at all when that sensation was jetting back and forth between her nipples and the place between her legs.

"Jergan," she murmured. "You will drive me insane if I am not mad already."

He chuckled. "That is a good kind of madness." And he applied himself assiduously to the other nipple. His hand was on her mound, pressing, as if there were not already enough pressure, what with her blood all coursing from her head to her loins until there was no thought left, only the pulsing of need. She needed him inside her.

"Jergan, I need you."

"Yes, you do, my lady. And I intend to see your need satisfied."

She expected him to lie between her legs. She was not wrong. She wanted . . . What was he doing? He was scooting down until his shoulders were even with her thighs. He parted them, a hand on each. She opened to him. What was toward? His thumbs opened her nether lips and . . . and he pressed his lips against her nub of pleasure and . . . and licked it.

She gasped, startled at the intensity of the sensation and the act itself.

"Jergan! What are you doing?" She got up on her elbows, trying to close her thighs.

"Pleasuring you with my mouth, my lady," he said, rising from between her legs. "An excellent way to avoid getting you with child."

"It is almost impossible for ... my kind ... to have children ... and ... and isn't that distasteful to you?"

"Of course not." He seemed surprised. "We bathed only this afternoon." He peered at her. "Has your lover never pleasured you with his mouth?"

"Romans ... Romans consider it ... unclean."

He barked a laugh. "There is something the Romans do *not* do? I thought they were open to everything."

"Not that." She flushed.

He pushed her gently back down. "Then prepare for a lesson in pleasure, my lady. I spent some time in my youth among the Gauls. It seems barbarians know a thing or two that Rome does not." He laid a hand on either thigh. She felt vulnerable as she had perhaps never felt. She could forbid him, or just close her legs. But he had issued a challenge. She could not acknowledge she was narrow or afraid. Besides, the forbidden exerted a strange attraction. Then, too, his tongue was ... was licking again, softly. Venus and Juno, but that was intense! His tongue slid up and down the moist folds of her flesh, spreading her own juices, adding to them. It glided over her point of pleasure until he had her moaning. And she forgot to be tense or appalled. She thrust her mound up, the better for him to lick her. Her thighs were splayed as far apart as she could open them. She wasn't sure just when she gave herself over to him, but she had, and now the flesh between her legs was so engorged that there was no blood in any other part of her body.

"Jergan," she moaned.

"Shall I stop?" he mumbled, raising his head. "You have but to command me."

"No. No, don't stop." She pulled his head back in

toward her needing, throbbing woman parts. "Don't ever stop."

So he rubbed her harder with his tongue, shaking his head quickly from time to time, holding up her hips, the better to lick her. Then he thrust inside her with two fingers all the while he licked. In and out he slid his fingers. He sucked on her engorged flesh, lightly.

She gave a little shriek, shocked at the intensity of hand and mouth, both focused on pleasuring her. "More," she whispered. And then she couldn't say anything, because sensation turned to something else entirely, overwhelming, engulfing. She gasped and cried and arched into him as he sucked and pulled at her. He might as well be drawing out her soul, or filling it. Her orgasm took her and shook her and wouldn't let her go. She couldn't see or hear. She couldn't even feel his lips. Blind and deaf, still she knew she screamed.

Slowly she came back from the place where she had gone. Air rushed into her lungs and out. He slid up beside her and wiped his mouth on the coverlet. She rolled into him moaning, still contracting in irregular spasms. "Jergan," she whispered as if that said it all.

He ran his hands through her hair. "Abhorrent?"

She looked up at him, unsure. "Not for me." Had he sacrificed to give her pleasure?

He grinned at her. "Not for me, either. Your musk is salty-sweet." He cradled her close against his chest, and she breathed in his scent. He bent. "Would you like to taste?"

She couldn't admit she was shocked. She raised her eyes. He kissed her, tenderly. And there it was, just faintly, a taste of . . . something. Not abhorrent. He was right—sweet, musky.

"Is that . . . me?"

He nodded. His eyes were so tender.

The sense of newness washed over her and she realized how long it had been since she had experienced the sweetness of surprise. It was a joy, a gift, and he had given it to her.

It required reciprocation.

For the first time in centuries, she felt ignorant. His need was apparent in the stiff rod she felt along her thigh. His generosity required an equal gift. But how? She sucked in a breath. "I . . . have heard that . . . it is possible to do the same for a man. Would it be pleasurable for you?"

His green eyes were laughing at her even though his mouth was serious. He nodded again. "Yes, my lady." She was glad the furrowed brow was gone. She had distracted him from whatever he might have asked her about the healing. She could distract him more.

Still, shyness almost overcame her. "I have no knowledge of this way of pleasing you." She raised her chin. "But I would like to try." Who would have guessed that she, who had lived so long, would ever say such a thing?

12

JERGAN FOUND HER tentative resolve endearing. Who would have thought that Romans, who were debauched in the extreme, would think this most basic of pleasures forbidden?

"Experiment freely," he said, rolling onto his back. He clasped his hands behind his neck, leaving himself vulnerable to her. She needed to feel she was in control. And he wanted to earn her trust, in preparation for the question he was resolved to ask when they were done. He wanted to show her that he accepted her in spite of what he was certain would be her answer to that question. *Why* he accepted her still puzzled him. But he did. What she said would change everything between them, likely. Whatever it was that was between them. But he had to know. And he wanted her to trust him for other reasons. Reasons he didn't want to examine closely.

"I am yours," he whispered before he was aware what he was saying. He wished he could catch his words back. He wasn't hers anymore. He was a free man.

And yet perhaps she held him more securely now than if she owned him. Had he not committed to stay with her, at least through the completion of her plot? He could not abandon her when she needed him. The answer to the question that was coming meant he should be running back to Centii as fast as he could go.

He wouldn't think of that. Now she needed to know how to please a man with her mouth, and in spite of what she was, she didn't know. He wondered if she would let him show her.

She sat up and drank him in with her eyes. Their brown was liquid heat. His cock strained against his belly, caressed by her hot gaze. She reached out a small, graceful hand and stroked it. His breathing faltered as she clasped it firmly with one hand and cradled his stones with the other, kneading gently. He was leaking a little clear fluid, a result of his restraint. Her breasts swayed as she bent and ran her tongue cautiously across the tip. She sat up, startled.

"Does it taste bad?" he asked, worried.

She ran the tip of her tongue over her upper lip, then raised her brows. "No," she said. "Just surprising. It tastes salty. A muskiness different from mine. It reminds me of . . . of you."

He smiled. "A good description."

She bent again, licked her lips, and this time took the head into her mouth. She did not use her teeth. He had been worried about that. He didn't want to have to correct her, but he didn't want to risk emasculation, either. Her tongue swabbed him. He bit his lip. She tried a little gentle sucking. He could not help but lift his hips to her.

"I like that," she said, sitting up.

"I also," he managed.

"Can you tell me other things you would like?" She caressed his stones.

"If . . . if you insist."

She smiled at him, and he saw mischief in her eyes. "It is your turn to give orders."

He swallowed, mouth suddenly dry. "Very well. Uh . . . clasp me firmly at the root." She did. "Rub your hand along my shaft as you put the tip in your mouth." She bent and went him one better. She sucked as she slid her hand up and down. His breathing grew ragged. "The . . . the underside is very . . . sensitive. I mean the . . . the upper side to you."

"That I know. Across this ridge here." She flicked her tongue across it.

"Ahhhh, yes." His hips began to move of their own accord. Her tongue swabbed the tip of his cock as she sucked.

"Do you have more instructions?" she paused to ask after a while. She returned to her task.

He writhed, his genitals fully controlled between her hands and her mouth.

She paused again.

"Jergan?"

"Don't . . . stop to talk."

He could feel her smile. She worked at him and he groaned. He was close to coming. With a great effort, he said, "Wait. I want to finish inside you." She'd said she couldn't be impregnated. He wanted to fill her. And he wanted to spare her his ejaculation, in case she found that distasteful. "Can you mount me?" He kept his hands behind his neck to make her feel safe. She grinned at him, knelt, and swung her white thigh over his hips. He was so close, so close. But he must stop the growing pressure from releasing. He tried to think of other things.

She made that difficult. She positioned his cock and sank down on it. Her slick softness surrounded him. They throbbed in unison. She raised herself and lowered, her palms on his chest. The curve under her breasts and the fact that her nipples were peaked with desire maddened him. He thrust up in counterpoint and saw the mounting urgency in her eyes. She sat back, still moving her hips over his cock, ran her hands lightly over her breasts, and then tangled them in her hair. She pounded against him now, gasping for air. He must wait. Wait for her.

Then he felt it, even as she shrieked. Her womb contracted, milking his cock, commanding it to spurt its all into her. He refrained through three contractions; then his own orgasm took him and he strained against her, spurting, spurting.

They collapsed in a heap. The light sweat gleaming on her body mingled with his. He unclasped his hands from behind his neck and hugged her to his chest. They were still joined, groin to throbbing groin. He ran a hand through her hair. She groaned.

"Distasteful?" he asked, suddenly as uncertain as she had been earlier.

She raised her head and smiled up at him. "Delightful. How could the Romans, who love sensation, have denied themselves this?" A worried look washed through her eyes. "Did I perform adequately? You didn't want to finish in my mouth."

He chuffed a laugh. "Oh, more than adequately. I wanted to plunge myself into you." Time enough for other ways in the lovemaking to come. He hoped to have many opportunities. "You were wonderful." He rolled them to the side, being certain not to lose connection.

She had let him give her orders. This was, perhaps, the final proof that she was a generous person, a generous lover.

Something was happening here. Something that made him nervous. He hardly knew himself at this moment. It wasn't that he'd chosen to stay for a few days when he could be on the road to Centii at this very moment. Delaying his own desires he understood. A palisade needed men to build it even though it was hot and the river called. A family needed the deer he'd brought down more than he and his friends did. It was always something. Nor was it that he put his life in danger for her. He'd chosen to be a soldier even though he was a firstborn son. No. It was something else. Something that made him feel as though he'd stepped into a bog concealed by marsh grass.

Weak. That's what he was. What business did he have with those kinds of thoughts? He should be thinking of what he wanted her to tell him. He had refrained from questioning her earlier, only to be certain she was properly prepared for openness. Well, if she didn't trust him now, with him still inside her body, she never would.

"Livia," he murmured into her hair. "It's time to tell me about the healing."

SHE JERKED HER gaze up to his face. She thought she had escaped his questions. And she felt betrayed. She pushed herself away from his chest. Their hips pulled apart and broke their union. "Is that the reason you came to my bed, so you could pounce upon me with your insinuations when I was so grateful to you for pleasuring me that I would . . . that I would just . . ." She sputtered to a stop, a confusion of emotions in her breast. She was a vampire with secrets she could trust to no one. He had ambushed her. But some part of her *did* trust him. Wholeheartedly.

"Nay, Livia," he protested. "I wanted you to know that you could trust me, that was all."

He was siding with that part of her that seemed to whisper in the corner of her mind, *Tell him. It is imperative that you tell him all.*

But why should she open herself to this man or any other? The part of her that whispered did not answer. Was it because she could not hear the answer, or because there was none?

Tell him.

He looked at her seriously. "Do you want me to guess? I had some hours to think about it while you were sleeping."

Fear flashed through her. Could he know? The two halves of her, arguing over what she should do, froze her lips.

"I think," he said firmly, looking her straight in the eye, "the healing could mean that you are very old. If you can heal burns and wounds like the one on your arm the other night, why not the ravages of time?"

He had guessed it. One part of her was horrified, the other part relieved. She chewed her lip. Finally she nodded. What use to deny it?

"How old?" He was holding his breath.

"More than seven . . . seven hundred years," she whispered.

His eyes widened. He swallowed. Twice. "Well, it's no wonder you are wise. Are you . . . immortal, like your gods?"

She couldn't let him think she was a goddess. "I can be killed." She saw him trying to digest that. She was a fool to tell him the next part.

Tell him.

"Decapitation. I can be killed by decapitation. I can heal anything else. Poisons are nothing to me, or sickness." There. She had told him her secrets. Now he would know how to kill her if he wanted to do that.

"So, unless you are decapitated, you will live forever."

"A gift with drawbacks. Some of us go mad from boredom. Some get drunk on immortality and do unspeakable things. At the very least one becomes a cynic, inured to the repetition of man's weakness and cruelty."

"You don't seem any of those things." His eyes were . . . tender? After what she had just told him? He seemed to actually accept what she said. He didn't pull away.

So she might as well tell him the rest. "It's something in our blood. We call it the Companion. It's another form of life, too small to see with the naked eye, that swims in our veins. It has power, Jergan. And we can use that power. The Companion rebuilds our bodies and we don't age. And of course it gives us all those things you know about, strength, acute senses. It makes us . . . easily aroused."

"I like that part," he said, and held her to him. But she could feel a sadness in his voice. He felt the differences between them now, as she did. "Strange to think you are invincible."

"Not invincible. Drugs suppress its power. Poppies and decapitation. Hardly invincible." In her desire to seem more like him, she had given him dangerous knowledge. How could she be so sure he wouldn't use it? But she was.

"Are there many of you?"

She shook her head against his chest. "Perhaps seven score. A hundred are at Mirso Monastery, a refuge for those too wearied or maddened by time. The Rules dictate that the rest live one to a city, so no one notices our presence. My city is Rome, though I cannot stay forever. People will begin to notice that I don't age."

"One to a city. . . . That must make it difficult to . . . marry."

She snorted. "We do not marry. Harder to take vows when they really mean forever. And then you wouldn't be allowed to live with your mate anyway."

"So . . . an endless string of lovers like me?" He was holding himself tightly in check.

"I haven't had a lover in many years," she whispered. "A hundred? Perhaps."

There was a long pause as he considered that. "It sounds lonely," he finally said.

She was just beginning to realize how lonely it was. "Do you have a wife, Jergan?" How had she never asked? Perhaps she didn't want to know that he had a life beyond being her slave.

"Nay. When I chose to be a soldier, I left getting heirs to my younger brother."

"But you don't need to be a soldier now. You could return to . . . to whomever you left behind." She couldn't believe she was practically convincing him to go. But she had to know if he was tied to another.

"I left no woman there."

Something in her dared to hope . . . She shook her head. It did not matter. She would live and he would grow old. Who could bear that? Still, a few years . . . when her task with the Roman emperor was over. If Jergan didn't go home immediately. If he was not appalled by what she was. She couldn't ask him about that. Men did not like commitments. He had told her he would stay until the plot was over. That would have to be enough. She raised her head and looked up at him. He didn't look appalled. He looked . . . sad. She lifted her lips to his. Her confession hadn't made either of them feel better, in spite of the fact that he seemed to accept her.

But living was not just for sweetness and light. He kissed her, tenderly. She put her hands on his chest and piqued his nipples with her thumbs. She felt him rise again. She had had her pleasure twice already this night, he only once. The sun rose outside the dim room. She must keep the dark of the future at bay, and live in the moment. It might be all they had.

She was dreaming. She knew it was a dream, but she couldn't wake herself. She didn't want to have another premonition. She was looking into a mirror. But no, there was no mirror. Another her stared back at her. "Let me out," the other her said. "I know what you must do."

"Who are you?"

"I am your future self."

That was absurd. Unless . . . "Is it you who give me premonitions?"

"I know your future." A shadow crossed the face that was her face. "But perhaps the future I know is changing even now. Perhaps I made a mistake in coming. I hadn't counted on us becoming one. Or that you would be the one in charge. We must hurry."

"Hurry and do what?"

"Let me out. Give me control. To do what you must do."

"What will happen to me if I let you out?" she asked. This whole conversation was ridiculous.

"I don't know," the other her said. She was receding, though she did not move in any way. The dream was fading.

Livia woke with a start to pounding on the door to her courtyard. Outside, metal and boots clattered in the street. Even Jergan could hear the noise. He jumped to his feet and grabbed his sword, crouching naked in a fighting stance. He looked over to her. But she couldn't reassure him. Caligula might have sent the Praetorian Guard for her at last. In which case, her only alternative was to go with them or transport herself away, leaving Jergan and the servants to bear the brunt of their wrath. She ran her fingers through her hair. She had been dreaming. It was a strange dream, important somehow, but she couldn't remember it now. It was about the sense of urgency she'd been feeling lately, but . . . the memory wafted away.

A single set of footsteps sounded outside the door, followed by a gentle tap. "Lucius, my lady," he called.

She pulled the sheet up around herself and stood. "Come in."

Lucius entered, bowing. He was becoming adept at ignoring Jergan's nudity.

"What is it?"

"Decimus Valerius Asiaticus has sent an escort to the Senate floor so you may watch the naming of a new consul, my lady."

Livia and Jergan both sighed in relief.

But their relief was short-lived. A man in full black armor pushed in, his hand on the pommel of his sword, his helmet clutched under the other arm. It was the captain of the Praetorian Guard, Cassius Chaerea. Behind her, Jergan growled. Livia pulled the sheet more tightly around her. She dared not let anyone know she had ever exchanged words with the captain. His gaze roved over the tangled bed, Jergan's nakedness, and his brandished sword.

"Put down your weapon, Jergan," she hissed. Even though it was Cassius, they could not afford to provoke the Guard. "Now," she insisted.

Looking disgusted, Jergan threw his short sword to the carpet.

"Sorry to interrupt." The captain bowed. "But we have little time before the ceremony."

She glanced behind Lucius to the open door. The sun slanted low. It was perhaps five in the afternoon. It would be dusk soon. She could do this. Why the Senate was meeting so late she didn't know. "It will take me a moment to ready myself." Jergan was already binding his loincloth around his hips.

"I shall wait. Order her litter," Cassius said to Lucius, and turned on his heel and was gone.

All three stared after him. Lucius nodded to Livia. "Well, I suppose I had better obey." He turned to go, then thought better of it. "Oh, and I have procured Jergan Britannicus Lucellus attire more appropriate to his current state."

"I'll not wear your damned togas," Jergan warned. "A man can't fight all wrapped up in a shroud, unless he wishes to need one."

Lucius smiled enigmatically before bowing himself out.

"And sandals are no protection . . ." Jergan called out after him.

"Do not think you are going with me." Livia wouldn't let Jergan face whatever danger this command performance might represent. She hurried to one of the three chests that held her favorite winter clothing. He did not argue with her, half to her surprise.

She would wear the deep red color of her homeland.

"Do you think this Decimus Valerius Asiaticus is behind the attacks on you?"

Jergan was astute for having lived less than forty years. "It is possible. But it makes no difference in what we must do tonight."

"And why would the captain of the Praetorian Guard come himself to escort you?"

She wouldn't tell Jergan that.

"I do not like this. Any of it," he muttered.

Actually, she didn't much like it, either, but it would do no good to rail against it. She pulled open a second drawer, having rummaged without luck through the contents of the first. Catia slipped through the door. "Catia, where on earth is my garnet-colored *stola*?"

"Let me," the girl said, and opened a third drawer where the offending *stola* lay smugly on top of the pile. "And which *palla*, Mistress?"

"The one with golden threads woven through it."

Lucius ducked back into the room. He carried a folded cloth with a snaking band of leather atop it. He offered it to Jergan. Livia smiled to see Jergan's scowl as he shook out the bleached white wool. Lucius had, as usual, out-done himself. It was a simple tunic, cut in one piece with loose sleeves that would hit Jergan's massive arms above the elbows. But the cloth was very fine. The hems were bound in embroidered bands of rich blue and red geometric figures. Catia's mother was indeed a fine seamstress.

Jergan grunted his acceptance and pulled it over his head. His long black hair, tangled after their lovemaking, hung down his back. The tunic hit him just at the knee. It would shorten when he put on the belt and bloused the fabric above it for easy movement. Livia herself was pulling her *stola* over her head. It bared one shoulder and was tight enough so that easy movement was not a consideration. Lucius handed Jergan the leather belt. No longer worn leather with a simple iron buckle, this belt was finely tooled and studded with brass. It boasted a brass buckle. Lucius produced boots that laced up the front, tooled to match the belt.

Livia saw Jergan nod in approval. He cleared his throat. "Thank you. You are generous," he said to Lucius.

"Livia Quintus Lucellus is generous," Lucius returned, his eyes filled with even more sadness than usual. He looked away. "It was her money that procured them."

What was wrong with Lucius?

Jergan cleared his throat again and turned to Livia.

"Thank you, my lady." He picked up his sword and strapped on the scabbard. The way it hung across his slim hips made Livia ache for him. Could she not get enough of this man, even with the Praetorian Guard in the courtyard?

Catia wrapped Livia in her *palla*. It was a technical and difficult task, though in a pinch Livia could do it herself, unlike most Roman women. Livia felt like she was being prepared for a sacrifice. Could the fact that Asiaticus wanted to draw her to the emperor's attention account for the feeling of itching urgency that scratched at her? *What* had she been dreaming? She couldn't remember. She watched Jergan pull his hair back from the sides of his face, plait it deftly twice, and tie it with a leather thong. Long hair had never looked so masculine.

Livia clasped a garnet necklace around her neck and fastened garnet drops in her ears, while Catia pulled her hair to her nape and knotted it simply. She was ready.

Jergan led the way into the outer room. The light was fading. Lucius threw open the main doors. "Will this light burn you?" Jergan asked, looking concerned.

She shook her head. "The sun has set." Still she pulled the translucent fabric of her *palla* up around her head and over her face. She marched ahead, Jergan at her shoulder, hand on the pommel of his sword. "You may accompany me to the courtyard, but no farther."

Outside, Cassius Chaerea stood at the head of a dozen of his black-clad troops. Their helmets revealed only their stony eyes. The ebony brushes of horsehair gleamed in the glow of sunset. The captain glanced to Jergan and jerked his head toward the litter.

Jergan started forward, pushing through the guards.

"You will stay here, Jergan," she snapped. The man seemed to ignore every order. Even now he made no move to obey her but only motioned her forward in his wake.

"His presence was requested also," Chaerea grunted. "But he leaves his sword."

Livia felt a sinking premonition, almost as strong as she had experienced in her dreams. Jergan stopped, surrounded by the guards. He unbuckled his scabbard, his lips a thin line. Chaerea took it and handed it to Lucius. Jergan pushed toward the litter. She knew how naked he must feel without his sword, surrounded by enemies. She took a breath and followed him.

Livia climbed into her litter. Jergan stalked beside it, flanked by the Guard. At least she was certain, with Cassius Chaerea in charge, they would not turn on her. But some part of her knew, with a terrible clarity, that she was heading into trouble and so was Jergan.

13

JERGAN GAZED UP at the amazing marble rotunda that was the Roman Senate. The floor was laid with intricately cut marble, a mosaic, but on an enormous scale. The domed roof was supported by dozens of marble columns that glowed in the sunset. Inside, half of the aristocracy of Rome milled and whispered. Jergan stayed close to Livia's shoulder as she moved through the crowd. But what could one do in these close quarters if someone lunged in for an attack on her just now? Titus Delanus Andronicus approached her.

"What are you doing here?" he asked, concerned. "Did I not tell you to stay home?"

"Command performance, Titus," she whispered in return. "By Asiaticus. And you should not approach me in public."

"Why? They all know I've been your friend for these ten years," he retorted.

"Then we had better disabuse them of that notion." She raised her voice. "I wonder that you dare to greet me, Titus Andronicus, after your perfidy." She thrust her chin in the air and pushed past the old man, who stared at her in surprise.

"Well, Titus, the scorpion stings at last," someone laughed, and clapped him on the shoulder.

Jergan left the scene behind as he strode after her. She was protecting her fellow conspirators as best she could. She found a place to stand near the edge of the crowd even as the trumpet fanfare announced the arrival of the emperor.

The crowd made way as his procession entered, led by a company of the Praetorian Guard, followed by the emperor himself, wearing a golden facsimile of a laurel wreath as a crown, his purple cloak trailing behind him like a train. His sisters followed, decked out with so much gold jewelry they looked to be weighed down by it. And then, astoundingly enough, a guardsman led in a black stallion. He had a purple embroidered robe thrown over his saddle, and his bridle was laid with small golden plates. His hooves were painted gold. They echoed against the marble floor. He was unnerved by the sound and tossed his head. The guard could barely contain the horse's prancing nervousness.

Caligula strode to the center of the rotunda and turned. "I give you Incitatus, the newest consul of your number." He smirked, and pointed toward the horse. "Incitatus, may you serve Rome as selflessly as you have served me."

There was a stunned silence in the hall. You could feel the tension in the room at the obvious insult. Caligula's smirk turned to a petulant glower.

One pair of hands began to clap somewhere. Claudius limped out of the crowd. He continued to clap. In front of him, Jergan heard Livia snort her derision and begin to clap as well. Someone else joined them and soon there was desultory clapping all around the great rotunda. *Well,* thought Jergan, *Claudius knows how to practice survival.* And Livia had just planted in many minds the idea that she was a supporter of the emperor.

"Claudius," the emperor called. He gave a very unimperial giggle. "Just the man. Perhaps you will read the new consul's acceptance speech."

Claudius closed his eyes for a single instant. His face suffused with color. His cousin was going to make him stutter through a speech in front of everyone. "Of . . . of c-course, m-my emperor." Someone handed Claudius a scroll.

The public setting and the obvious desire to humiliate him would make the stutter worse. Jergan stood, stoic, while Claudius tried to get through the speech. Laughter coursed around the rotunda. It was not funny when the emperor made game of them by confirming his horse as a senator, but it was apparently fine to laugh when he made game of another. Jergan could feel Livia's distress for Claudius.

The emperor grew impatient after the point had been made and snatched the scroll from Claudius's trembling hands. "Enough, my idiot cousin. This august body has no patience for your mewling." The horse began to rear and slip on the slick marble surface of the floor. "Even Incitatus has had enough of you." Caligula signaled to the trumpeters, who blew another fanfare. The emperor came directly past where Jergan and Livia stood. Caligula's cold eyes scanned the crowd and rested on them. Out of nowhere, Asiaticus appeared and whispered in the emperor's ear. The emperor nodded once, then raised his chin and strode out of the rotunda. Asiaticus spoke to Cassius Chaerea, who looked annoyed.

"Let us go," Livia murmured, turning. "While we can."

Chaerea was suddenly bowing in front of them, his spine stiff. "His Imperial Highness wishes you to attend the banquet he is giving in honor of the newest consul."

"I . . . I am feeling weary, Cassius Chaerea. Perhaps another time." Gods above, but she was bold to refuse such an invitation.

The man's face was impassive. "My guard will escort you to the banquet."

Well, that was clear enough. Livia glanced back to Jergan, a dilemma written on her face. "Surely a bodyguard is not required at the banquet, and with your good escort, I shall pass safely through the streets. I shall send mine home." She was trying to protect him? Jergan was about to protest her decision, but he needn't have bothered.

"Your bodyguard is requested as well."

"Very well," Livia said with all the composure of a brave woman facing a death sentence. "Then lead the way."

Jergan clenched his jaw and followed.

AT LEAST THE emperor and his sisters thought Jergan had syphilis. Livia tried to calm herself. With the maniacal gleam in Caligula's eyes, it would be a rough night for whoever attended the banquet. Their guard waited until the rotunda cleared before they started out. They wended their way to Caligula's palace. He had enlarged it from the one he inherited from his uncle, even expanding it until he encompassed the Temple of Jupiter as his vestibule. He wanted the Roman people to understand that he was as unstoppable as a god, as inevitable. Livia wondered if Gaius Caesar was actually mad, or whether he was just too young to inherit ultimate power. He might be twenty-nine, but making his horse a consul was the prank of an adolescent. Caligula could just be emotionally backward. Regardless, it was not safe for a twisted child to rule the most powerful empire in the world.

Jergan handed Livia out of the litter. They walked up the broad and shallow stairs among many others, flanked by the Guard. Some part of her knew that something bad would happen here tonight.

Chaerea left his helmet and sword at the door but was still dressed in full armor. Nervous guests filled the antechambers. Wine flowed, bloodred, from a fountain.

Slaves, dressed scantily if at all, offered goblets and guided guests to the main room. Huge doors of beaten gold were braced open, and music issued from beyond. Livia could feel Jergan hold himself tightly, disapproving. There was much to disapprove of. She wished with all her heart he were safe at home. But perhaps there was no safe place in Rome right now.

Incitatus was standing on a dais with his head in a golden bucket. He had apparently calmed down, and Livia wondered what was in the bucket. His bridle had been changed for a jeweled halter. In front of him Gaius Caesar reclined on a chaise lounge with Julia and Agrippina at his side. Julia wore no *stola* and her *palla* revealed one breast and much of her belly entirely. She was feeding Gaius bits of peacock tongue. A second chaise on his left, equal to Caesar's, was occupied by an older woman, still attractive. A very comely male slave knelt, serving her.

Chaerea moved forward to greet the emperor and congratulate Incitatus. Livia noticed that Chaerea glared at Asiaticus, who stood just behind the emperor in a place of honor.

"Who is that?" Jergan whispered. "What woman sits as equal to the emperor?"

"His wife, of course." She smiled at Jergan's look of shock. "Caesonia. She's his fourth."

"She . . . she permits all this?"

"For a while she was a moderating influence. But now he routinely threatens to kill her and her children in most inventive ways as a dinner joke. So she dares make no protest."

Livia saw Titus, looking unhappy, and several of the others. She couldn't take refuge in their company. A slave girl, who appeared to be Egyptian, naked except for golden rings in her nipples and a girdle of gold about her hips to match the little golden chains that bound her black hair, bowed her head and offered goblets. Livia took one. Jergan shook his head, glowering.

"Take it and smile, Jergan," Livia said softly.

He pressed his lips together and took a goblet. He was apparently incapable of smiling.

"May I escort the Master and Mistress to a chaise?" the girl asked.

"Yes, please do," Livia answered. The room was already crowded. "Someplace remote."

"A thousand pardons, Mistress, but those seats were the first taken."

Not surprising. They followed the slave girl. Livia noticed a definite dichotomy around the room. For the emperor's intimates, the celebration was already in full swing. They were eating, laughing, drinking. But most of the senators were not in a merry mood. They sat picking at their plates, talking quietly among themselves. Good. They had seen their fate if Caligula continued. It wasn't bad enough that he was accusing some of their number of treason to confiscate their estates. They were to be made a laughingstock. Worse than something that happened to someone else. Maybe now they would entertain the idea of a republic.

She saw Jergan's eyes get big as they passed a niche. The curtains were pulled back. One of the slaves who had Caligula's favor, a Greek named Helion, lounged inside. The man had pulled up his toga and bounced a tiny slave girl on his cock openly, as he lay drinking wine.

Jergan shot Livia a look of disgust. She put a hand on his arm and shook her head.

Their slave-girl guide was surveying the available places.

"Would the Mistress like one chaise or two?" She had correctly identified by her dress that Livia was the citizen.

"One," she said. She wanted Jergan close tonight. The girl nodded and selected a double chaise softly upholstered in deep green and strewn with exotically embroidered pillows.

"Thank you, girl," Livia said, and produced some coins. The slave bowed low, making the rings in her nipples swing, and withdrew. Livia settled herself on the chaise. Jergan looked too tense to sit. She took his hand and tugged him down.

"You're not smiling."

"How can one smile when it feels like we are in a giant serpent's den?"

"One smiles so the serpent will not notice us by our scowls."

"He keeps the city that rules the world trembling upon his next whim," Jergan said, his eyes examining her face. At least he kept his voice low. Musicians strolled nearby with their flutes and harps. She didn't think anyone would hear him.

"Yes." She pulled him close and kissed his ear, taking the opportunity to whisper into it, "But not for long." She straightened. A male slave brought a tray with a variety of tidbits on it and knelt beside them. He wore nothing but a small silk bag that held his genitals by a string around his waist and up between his buttocks. He was lithe and lean and submissive, no doubt just how the emperor liked them. She stabbed a preserved plum with the little metal spear provided and popped it into Jergan's mouth, then took one for herself. The slave would kneel here before them until he was dismissed. She knew, though Jergan probably didn't, that the slave would also obey any commands either of them might give as far as sexual service was concerned. Even now such activity had begun in darkened corners. Jergan's eyes narrowed in distaste.

She must take his mind off this.

"Tell me of Britannia," she said, skewering him a small, spicy sausage from the plate the slave held.

"An island of barbarians, you would say," Jergan said, chewing as he looked around. And she knew he was thinking that what he was seeing was far more barbaric than anything at home.

"Where do you live there?"

He turned his attention to her. That was better. "Centii is in the southwest."

"And what did you do there? Before you were a soldier?"

"I worked the land. My father had many hectares under cultivation."

"And you were the eldest son. So it would have come to you. Tell me of it."

"It is a rich land. On the eastern shore there are oyster beds. In the west there are forests for wood, and then there are the rich plains, fed by a broad river." His eyes got far away. "In the summer the grain nods in the sun. The sheep grow their wool. The trees bend with fruit."

"It sounds like a good place. You will soon be back there."

He sighed and nodded. His shoulders relaxed. He smiled at her. It was . . . tender. "Don't think I don't know what you are doing, Livia Quintus Lucellus." His tone was mock severe, unlike his eyes.

"Well, someone has to keep you from rending anyone you can reach limb from limb."

He took a skewer and stabbed her a slender morsel from the slave's plate. "What is this?"

"A peacock tongue." She popped it into her mouth.

A group of men got up from chaises just around Caligula and headed for a doorway.

Jergan was immediately alert. "Where are they going?"

"To vomit so they can eat more."

He turned back to her, incredulous. "Can Rome afford such waste?"

"No. Rome has so many wastrels. That is different. Our poor still go hungry." She turned toward the lithe slave. He would be well used before the night was over. "You may go. Send a slave with a tray of the heavier meats."

"Yes, Mistress," he said, bowing extremely low before he rose.

"He will never earn his freedom, will he?" Jergan asked.

"No. A slave's master must allow it. And I would guess freeing slaves is not the emperor's priority, though he has his favorites."

"Then why did you give that slave girl coins?"

She bit her lip. "Mistaken optimism, I suppose."

He saw her distress and reached to touch her hair. "You will never go mad from boredom or become a cynic."

The fact that he accepted her made her eyes fill. That and the fact that what she was would stand between them forever. Even if he stayed with her, it would break her heart to see him age and die. A frisson of urgency went down her spine.

It doesn't have to stand between you.

For Juno's sake, *why* was she having these thoughts that seemed to dart into her head?

Another slave boy knelt in front of them, carrying a

tray of meats. She shook her head to clear it and picked out a slab of beef for Jergan.

THE EVENING WORE on. Jergan found speaking more difficult, though Livia tried to keep the conversation going. As the Romans grew drunker, what little decorum they had was overcome. Caligula's cronies ordered slaves whipped for no apparent reason. Women kissed women. Men fondled men. Men and women caressed one another, eating and vomiting, sliding off to shadowed niches in groups of twos and threes. The slaves seemed to take it as their lot to service these decadent creatures sexually. It crossed Jergan's mind that perhaps Livia had tamed him to be like them. He served her body, almost worshipped it. Was he so far from their subservience? That prickled at him. Had he given his soul to Livia even though she freed him?

Caligula stood suddenly, shaking with fury. The whole room stopped in mid-breath. The musicians fell silent.

"Do you plot against us?" he shrieked, sounding almost girlish.

The man who had been whispering to his neighbor on the emperor's right was unfamiliar to Jergan. He rose, quaking. "No, my emperor! I am a loyal subject."

"Chaerea!" Caligula shouted. "Take this man away. Asiaticus, confiscate his property immediately."

The man began to blubber, bowing, apologizing for something he did not do.

"And bring his family to Rome."

That was a death sentence, according to Livia. Jergan grew grim.

Some of the senators moved to go. Livia said that was an insult. They must be very angry about the horse.

"You," Caligula shouted. "Sit down. Failure to honor Incitatus will be considered treason."

The senators sat.

"Musicians!" The flute began a fluttery, off-key trill and the other instruments joined in. The music stabilized and covered the silence of the guests.

"Celebrate," Caligula commanded, and sat, his face screwed into a petulant frown. He waved his hand and the guard took the blubbering senator away. Slowly the crowd forced themselves back to whatever they had been doing.

Chaerea materialized in front of their divan. "The emperor will accept congratulations now, Livia Quintus, from you and your freedman." He gave her a meaningful look that Jergan didn't understand. Was there something between these two? A beast growled inside his belly. He suppressed it. What was he doing? Feeling possessive of a Roman woman? Gods above, he had been *her* possession until yesterday.

Besides, Livia couldn't have given herself to this dark wolf. She had said it had been a hundred years. But . . . that seemed impossible, too.

"Jergan," she said, indicating he should follow her. "Stay close and be silent," she whispered. She had courage. They picked their way through couples now returned to open copulation. She made obeisance in front of the dais where the emperor again lolled with his sisters. The air was heavy with his mood. The dark Praetorian captain hovered at their backs.

"Livia Quintus Lucellus, Your Imperial Majesty," he intoned.

"Approach, Livia Quintus." The emperor and his sisters perked up, showing dangerous interest. Asiaticus stood just behind the emperor with his iron gray hair and air of wisdom. Jergan glanced over to Caesar's wife. She had turned her back to the group near her chaise and was speaking to some older women.

"Congratulations to you, Caesar, and to Incitatus." Livia bowed gracefully.

Jergan bent to one knee at a small signal from her, his eyes fixed on the ground in front of him. *Honor the damned horse and leave, Livia,* he willed her. From the corners of his eyes he saw the sisters' gazes rove over his body and grow hungry. How clever Livia had been to insinuate that he was diseased. Now if only Livia were as safe as he was. . . .

"You were invited especially to see Incitatus invested today, Livia Quintus." Caligula nodded graciously. *Why?* Jergan asked himself. Was it to accuse her, arrest her publicly?

"Thank you, Your Imperial Highness," Livia murmured.

"Decimus Valerius Asiaticus thought you might be of special interest to us." Asiaticus himself gave a tight smile and inclined his head.

Jergan swallowed. Had the emperor's counselor guessed Livia's secret? At the least, he knew how to harm her.

"I hardly dare hope that is true," Livia said. She was covering her concern well.

"Our sisters also wanted to see your progress in breaking your slave."

Jergan felt Livia grow even more wary beside him.

"We understand you have overcome your fear of disease." Caligula smirked.

"What can His Imperial Majesty mean?" Her voice was humble.

"Only that we heard you had been using your slave."

Jergan glanced up. Chaerea must have told Caesar

what he'd seen at Livia's house this afternoon. Caligula's sisters were really showing interest now. Julia Lavilla licked her lips.

Livia cleared her throat. "A momentary lapse I hope I shall not pay for."

"More than momentary. We heard you use him day and night."

This was bad. Only Livia's servants knew that.

"Hardly, my emperor," Livia said, deprecating.

"It would scarcely inconvenience you to loan him to us for a day or two. In the service of your emperor." Agrippina's voice was dulcet.

So much for protection, Jergan thought.

"Alas, he is no longer a slave. I cannot dispose of his services."

"What?" Julia sat up.

"I registered his name yesterday. He is a freed man."

Jergan could feel her willing him to silence. He wished he had his sword.

"Well, Sisters . . . We cannot confiscate him if he isn't property."

Agrippina tried again. "I knew she had freed him, dear brother. I had another aim. Your person is so precious to us after all. We want only to protect it."

"Protect us?" Fear had crept into the emperor's voice.

"We heard there was a plot against you among recently freed slaves. We thought to ferret out some intelligence about it."

Caligula sat up, sloshing wine onto his white toga. "And you think . . ."

"We think, dear brother," Julia soothed, "if he does not come willingly, you should arrest him and see what he knows."

"Jergan has nothing to do with any plot!" Livia said through gritted teeth.

"Give him to us to question." Julia Lavilla licked her lips again. "If we are not persuasive enough, we will give him over to the Guard."

"He's done nothing; I swear it," Livia hissed.

"Silence," Caligula shouted. The horse raised his head from his bucket, drooling red wine and oats. "Can't you see we have a headache? All these plots," he muttered, rubbing his temples.

Again there was silence. Jergan kept his head down. He did not want to provoke them. They could have him and welcome, if his imagined treachery was not blamed on Livia. She should not have defended him so.

"Arrest him, Chaerea. My sisters will question him." Caligula rose and placed a wet, mouth-to-mouth kiss on each sister's lips. "You always have our best interests at heart. Let us know if you need assistance."

Jergan set his lips as two guards each grabbed an arm and hauled him to his feet. He knew what was to come. Well, he'd stood worse. He hoped.

"If Livia Quintus is implicated in this plot, do let us know, Sisters. It is very strange that she should have freed him so soon."

A chill ran down Jergan's spine.

The emperor turned to Asiaticus. "Is this why you thought she would be of interest to us, Decimus? You, too, always have our best interest at heart."

"No," Asiaticus said thoughtfully, staring at first at Livia and then at Jergan. "I had something else in mind. But there is plenty of time to explore that, my emperor."

"Bring him," Julia ordered Chaerea. The captain of the Guard motioned his two men forward. Livia bit her lip.

Jergan saw blood bloom brightly. He smiled, willing her to let this go. Anything she did now would only endanger her further. She must know he would never betray her. Even as he watched, her lip healed. She was extraordinary. He was only ordinary. They could hurt her, arrest her, torture her, even if they couldn't kill her. He would do anything to spare her that, no matter the cost to him.

She stood abruptly and took his hand, pulling his head down. "Do not provoke them. I will find a way to come for you." She kissed him, lightly.

"No," he breathed into her mouth. "Let me handle this." If she tried to spare him whatever would happen here, she would bring the imperial vipers down on her own head.

"Ahhhh, he has bewitched her, this barbarian." Agrippina smiled. It was not a pleasant smile. "He must have extraordinary skills."

"We shall see." From Julia's smile one could see they were sisters.

They bowed before their brother and backed from the room.

14

LIVIA LOOKED AROUND wildly as Chaerea's guards hustled Jergan from the hall. Agrippina and Julia followed. What should she do? What *could* she do? She stilled herself, feeling her heart thump against her breast as though it were trying to free itself from her body altogether.

Quiet, the voice that had plagued her of late shushed inside her. *Draw no further attention to yourself. You'll make it worse.*

Livia took a breath, grateful for the counsel, regardless of its source. At least she was not imprisoned. Not that a prison could hold her, but waiting until she was left alone in her cell to disappear and escape would take too much time. They were taking him into the bowels of the palace. She'd promised she would come for him. But how? The place had hundreds of rooms. How could she know where he would be?

If she did find him, what would she do? Just appear out of nothing in front of Caligula's sisters and guards and then disappear with Jergan? That would reveal what she was to everyone. Strictly forbidden by the Rules laid down by the Elders. And her dreams of eliminating Caligula would disappear. She'd have to flee. Titus and the others would lose heart. Would her instrument still be willing to risk the deed? Probably not. And if he did, there would be no republic to follow. The Guard would be set upon her and Jergan. How would she get him out of the city?

You can't leave the city.

The thought wrenched her as though it were shouted in her ear. She squirmed. But there would be no choice.

You can't leave the house. Quieter this time, but just as insistent. She must ignore the voice. Because if she tried to save him, they must get as far away from Caligula as possible. India maybe, or the lower parts of the Dark Continent.

The thought of leaving made her physically nauseous.

And all those humans seeing what she was as she rescued him? Not allowed. She rubbed her throat as if she could swallow her anxiety.

Could she wait until the sisters tired of him and slept?

Their accusation was merely a ploy to get him alone and in their power. They couldn't know about the real plot. If he'd serve them sexually, he might avoid their other games.

But what if he couldn't? What if they meant to torture him no matter his innocence? What if they did know about the plot, and meant to torture him until he betrayed the conspirators?

Titus made his way across to her, and laid his hand on her arm. "Sit down, Livia."

She looked up at him, knowing her fear showed in her eyes.

He was nervous, too. He had much to lose if Jergan betrayed the plot to assassinate Gaius Caesar. "He is strong, and devoted to you." He was trying to convince himself that Jergan would be tortured, perhaps to death, without revealing the plot. Titus pushed her down on the nearest empty chaise and grabbed two goblets from the nearest passing tray. "And there is nothing you can do." He handed her one. "Drink this."

Livia clasped the stem so tightly she was in danger of bending the gold. Behind her, Caligula's petulant voice rose.

"Sit close to us, Livia Quintus. I want you near at hand in case your freedman implicates you. Don't think to slip away."

"I am honored by my emperor's company, Caesar. Why ever would I want to slip away?" She bowed and took an empty chaise just next to the emperor. Her heart sank. She couldn't go for Jergan, even if she knew where he was, if Caligula kept her by his side.

Titus had gone white about the mouth. But he sat next to her, and downed the contents of his goblet.

CHAEREA HUSTLED JERGAN through the vast palace. The two sisters led the way, hips swaying. Four guards accompanied them. Agrippina pushed open a door and the troop made its way into a large room, hung with heavy purple draperies. Heat rose from the marble floor and a brazier brimming with glowing coals. The room contained a wide bed covered in purple and gold cloth, several wooden cupboards, and, most ominously, several ornately carved posts. From each hung a pair of manacles. Jergan held himself still inside. The price of not involving Livia was either the bed or the posts. He would stand it. An elderly slave, apparently the attendant for this horrid room, bowed low.

Julia and Agrippina ran their hands up Jergan's arms under the sleeves of his tunic, caressing his biceps. Jergan gritted his teeth.

He glanced to Chaerea. The captain hovered, uncertain. What was the matter with him?

"In something so serious as a plot against the life of the emperor," he finally said, "I cannot allow such a dangerous man to threaten the sisters of the emperor as well. I shall remove him to the Guardhouse for questioning."

"Did you not hear Caesar's orders?" Agrippina sneered. "We are to question him."

"In the matter of the emperor's safety, my responsibility overrides obedience."

"Oh, don't be stupid, Chaerea," Julia returned, annoyed. "There was never any plot. Since he was free, how could we get him except if he was under arrest?"

Chaerea visibly relaxed. "Most clever. Questioning him about plots would be useless."

"We would have to supply the details ourselves," Agrippina tittered.

Chaerea glanced to his men. "Still, I will leave my men here for your protection. You have never minded an audience for your games."

"I think it adds titillation," Julia purred, glancing to the stoic men. "But he won't offer any resistance. Did you not see how he looked at Livia Quintus? He's in love with her. And he knows that if he resists, we will say she hatched this plot of the freedmen. My so-obliging brother will see she is brought to justice in a most painful way."

Chaerea turned on his heel but paused before the two guards stationed at the doorway. "Assist when needed. And since we know anything he says to save himself is a lie, you will ignore admissions of guilt—his own or others'. When they are done, bring what is left to the Guard's quarters."

Chaerea was gone. He was the only one who might have contained the sisters. Now Jergan was alone against them. The old attendant was there to assist them. The guards would only watch. Unless, of course, he resisted.

Julia ran her hands up around his neck, pressing her breasts against his chest. "First things first. Strip off these clothes. A barbarian should be naked in front of civilized women."

The guards stationed themselves at each corner of the room. Three were impassive; one looked . . . excited. Jergan bent to unlace his boots. There was no question of escape. He might be able to take four guards, if he could disarm one and get a weapon quickly. But the palace was huge and filled with Praetorians. He pulled off first one boot and then the other. His lot would be torture and crucifixion. More important, they would blame Livia for his deeds. Caligula was hysterical, and his sisters knew how to play upon his instability. Jergan unbuckled his belt.

They aren't even going to ask about Livia, so there's no danger you'll betray her, he told himself. *It's just a little humiliation, and probably some pain. Nothing you can't bear.*

"Your tunic," Julia hissed, impatient.

He pulled it over his head. They couldn't use him sexually if he couldn't be roused. Thank Brid for his long days with Livia.

"Oh yes," Julia breathed. "Just as I remembered." She touched the hair on his chest. "So barbaric," she murmured. She traced the line of the healing wound in his shoulder and almost shivered in delight. "Your loincloth," she prompted.

As he unbound his loincloth, he kept his mind on Livia, remembering how she had rebuffed them the first night, how she had kept the women in the streets from touching him. How she had bathed him and tended his wounds herself. She had pretended it was a form of dominance. And Belatucadros knew he had been determined to resist her then, so maybe it was. But it was also in her nature to be kind, to accept responsibility. Her touch had been gentle. He would think of that.

He stood before them, naked. He forced his hands to his sides. He wouldn't demean himself by covering his genitals. Julia stalked around him and ran her hands lightly over the scabbed welts that remained, lingering to cup his buttocks.

"Oooh, look, Agrippina. How well he looks with lashes."

Agrippina straightened. "They aren't fresh enough."

Julia giggled. "We can remedy that."

Very well. A whipping.

"Now, if only his rod was stiff," Julia continued. "What say you, barbarian? Are you not aroused by the honor of pleasing the emperor's sisters?"

"The prospect of being whipped tends to dampen ardor." He hoped he managed an air of casual disdain.

"Agrippina?" Julia called.

Agrippina took a blue glass jar from the old servant. "I have a cure for that."

What was this? Jergan scowled.

Agrippina uncorked the fat stopper and offered it. "Rub this on your organ."

He clenched his jaw and scooped a dollop of the cream. No telling what it was, but he could predict its effect. His fingers burned. He hesitated.

"Go on," Julia urged. "Your prick won't fall off. You'll just have a rather painful erection for a few hours."

There was no choice. He rubbed it on. Blood rushed from all parts of his body to his cock.

"Don't forget your testicles. I want them swollen and hard as the proverbial stones," Agrippina gloated. She offered the jar again.

He took a breath and scooped up another dollop. It wasn't a normal erection he was getting. It itched and burned. "What is this?" he growled as he rubbed his balls.

"Oh, oil of this and essence of that." Julia waved a hand airily. "The main ingredient is a beetle from Hispania ground up into powder. The court physician concocted it for us in a mild version, so it doesn't actually poison you."

Jergan's genitals hung, heavy and burning, between his legs. The sisters could do anything to him and he would be erect through it all. Out of the corner of his eye he saw the servant pulling several iron rods about eighteen inches long from the cupboard. They had wooden handles on one end. He stuck them in the coals that glowed in the brazier.

Jergan swallowed.

"His shaft is more than adequate," Agrippina remarked. "Splendid even." Both sisters removed their *pallas*. Julia wore no tunic, but she unfastened Agrippina's tunic and removed it They didn't seem to care that four Praetorians were witness to their nudity. It was the guards who flushed. Agrippina was square and raw-boned. Julia, over-plump, had a belly that showed she had borne children. Her breasts sagged. It wasn't their bodies that made them unattractive, though. He would love Livia even if children stretched the skin over her hips and breasts. It was the cruel glitter in the two sisters' eyes. The servant took two silken robes from a stand next to one of the other cupboards and helped the sisters into them. Only Jergan was naked now. He clenched his fists until his nails bit into his palms.

"Sex first, or punishment?" Agrippina asked.

"Sex, then punishment, then sex again, then punishment and sex together . . ." Julia laughed. "The night is long."

"You first, my dearest sister, then." Agrippina waved a magnanimous hand.

"Why, thank you, dearest sister." Julia turned to Jergan and her eyes went hard. "On the bed, barbarian. Let's see what you can do with that lovely, hard shaft."

LIVIA COULDN'T SIT still. It had been more than an hour. What was going on in the bowels of the palace? Livia had no fear that Jergan would betray the conspiracy. He had courage enough for ten men. Her fear was that he would be maimed or killed.

Chaerea had emerged and now attended Gaius Caesar. Thank the gods that Caesar was blathering on about Incitatus to him and Asiaticus.

She must find a way to free Jergan. Her gaze caromed around the hall. But how? Titus said something to her. She didn't attend. He might be adjuring her not to draw attention to herself.

"Livia Quintus Lucellus."

She froze. She took a breath and turned. "How may I serve Your Imperial Majesty?"

"You're imagining your slave with my sisters." Caligula licked his lips. "They'll have him hard and needing now, satisfying their hungry cunts." He examined her face and found something amusing there. "He needs a more submissive attitude. Did you have him reamed by your freedmen? That is an excellent way to subdue a prideful male body slave."

Livia bowed her head, willing herself not to show her shock. She did not correct Caligula's characterization of Jergan as her slave. That would only draw the emperor's ire and could serve no one. "No, my emperor. That did not occur to me."

"Regular reaming, mark my words, Livia Quintus. That's what a barbarian slave needs." He sipped his wine. "Once they know they can be raped a dozen times a day at a word from you, they become most submissive. That one would have benefited from hard and regular use."

"I'm sure you are right, Caesar," she murmured.

Caligula rubbed his own genitals absently as he sipped his wine. No one around him dared speak. Beside her, Titus had turned to stone. Livia noted with alarm that Caesar's own rod, small as it was, was quite erect. He glanced around. The banquet was in full swing, at least for half the crowd. The offended senators sat talking quietly among themselves. But Caesar's contingent was half-naked, kissing, fondling, openly thrusting. Underneath the music of flute and harp, groans and heavy breathing sounded.

"Livia Quintus," Caesar said, his roving glance returning to her. "You are an attractive woman. Why have we not married you to one of our inner circle?" His eyes fell on her breasts and did not stray. "Then you could play with us any time we chose."

She suppressed a shudder. He wanted fear. So she would not show it. "That would be an honor too great to bear."

"Nonsense, Livia Quintus. You would enjoy it. You could sample many lovers." What he left unspoken was that they could sample her.

"As Caesar says," she acquiesced. But she had to nip this idea in the bud. And, as with Jergan, it had to be Caesar's idea. She couldn't tell him she had syphilis. What else was there? The only ploy she could think of was dangerous. Anxiety for Jergan pushed her to the edge. She threw caution to the winds. "I . . . I admit I would truly enjoy comparing the organs available to me in the palace with that of my freedman, Jergan." She smiled brightly. "My experience has been narrow. Though I must say his size and stamina would be difficult to replicate."

Caesar frowned. Several people in the near vicinity drew back visibly in fear. Everyone knew Caesar was sensitive about the size of his penis. Had she gone too far? Caesar looked as though he would explode. He was actually speechless. To give in to his rage would be to admit her remark hit home, and thus to confirm that he had something to be insecure about. Did he have enough sense to know that?

Caligula rose without warning, his member just visible beneath his toga. "I would retire."

All around him stood and bowed, including Livia and Titus. Livia breathed again. He did have that much sense.

"See that everyone remains," he ordered Asiaticus. Then Caligula manufactured a smile and shone it around the room. "I want Incitatus to have a good time." He didn't want to spoil the evening for his horse? Was that insane? No, Caligula played this game with his horse to shove his absolute power down the senators' throats. And just when everyone thought he would order her death—he didn't. That kept them off balance, prolonged the game. She didn't care. However it had happened, she had dodged the javelin.

Caligula stalked from the room, followed by Chaerea and a dozen of the Guard. Asiaticus looked after them with a sour expression.

Titus gave a sigh of relief and sent a speaking glance at Livia. He thought they had won through.

Livia was not so certain. She might have escaped, but what about Jergan? And where exactly was Caligula going?

JERGAN LAY GASPING on the tangled coverlet as Julia shrieked her orgasm. The sisters let the cream soak in until he was rock-hard, then rinsed his organ of the residue so it would not irritate their tender flesh. They tied him, spread-eagled, to the bedposts with silken cords and took turns riding him to their release. The friction was exquisite torture. The cream that caused him to swell allowed him no release. He was left in a state of painful arousal.

As Julia moved off him, he saw that behind her, Agrippina held one of the metal rods, its tip glowing red. He held his breath, praying to Belatucadros for strength.

"Are we ready for some punishment?" she asked rhetorically.

"Oh yes," Julia sighed. "It's more than time."

With no preamble, no questions, Julia pressed the hot iron into his left hip, just in from the bone. He grunted and tried to twist away, biting his lip to keep from screaming.

The poker was withdrawn. He gasped for breath.

"Again," Julia crowed, clapping her hands. "His chest this time."

Agrippina handed her the iron. "You pick the place."

Julia held the rod aloft, its glow fading a little as she pondered. Then she placed it just above the right nipple. He arched and twisted and this time a bark of pain escaped his lips before the rod was withdrawn. The scent of singed hair hung in the air.

"It makes me wet when he writhes like that," Agrippina murmured.

"And see how he sweats? Lovely." Julia turned to the brazier and thrust the rod back into the coals. "Was there too much cream left on his organ for you, Sister?"

"Only enough to madden me a little," Agrippina answered.

Julia withdrew a fresh rod. "Then, Sister, do you ride him, and I will wield the poker."

"Generous of you, Julia Lavilla," Agrippina whispered. She touched the burn at Jergan's hip with one finger that then strayed across his swollen cock. She opened

her robe and straddled his hips. Then she pulled up his
cock and lowered herself upon it. How different from when
Livia made love to him in the same position. He throbbed
inside Agrippina, burning. As she raised and lowered herself, her palms pressed against his chest, the right one covering the burn her sister had just made, he felt the sear of
the hot poker across his inner thigh.

*Belatucadros, help a warrior who has fought in your
name,* he prayed. But what did he pray for? There was
no escape. They probably didn't intend to kill him, so it
wasn't for his life. Was it his pride he mourned? He had
been a slave until yesterday. What pride could a slave
have? Still he wanted to end this night without begging
them for mercy.

LIVIA WIPED THE perspiration from her forehead
with a handkerchief. The Guard prevented anyone from
leaving. She couldn't just translocate from the middle of
the room. It had been twenty minutes since Caligula left.
She grew certain he was on his way to join his sisters. All
that talk about how he would have made Jergan submit to
him . . . Whatever Julia and Agrippina had done to Jergan, Caligula was capable of worse.

Titus had given up trying to comfort Livia. He was getting quietly drunk. That was dangerous. One needed all
one's wits about one at an imperial gathering.

Asiaticus drifted up behind her. She whirled on him.
"Do not look so fierce, Livia Quintus," he said, raising his
hand, palm up, in mock surrender.

"You are responsible for me being here tonight. My
freedman is arrested and no doubt being tortured, and
Caesar is threatening to marry me off to one of his inner
circle. Should I be glad to see you?"

He gave a half chuckle. "I have the strangest feeling

you are not what you seem, Livia Quintus, and I would most like to know how I can turn that to my advantage."

Livia took a breath. Predictable. And one could use predictability. This man was Chaerea's enemy. They competed for Caesar's favor. That could be used as well. Turnabout was fair play, wasn't it? Asiaticus wanted to use her. She wanted to reciprocate. "And what do you think I am, Decimus Valerius Asiaticus?"

"That I do not know," he mused. "You were blistered yesterday, yet tonight you are unmarked. Is there an explanation for that?"

"Everyone in my household knows I am sensitive to the sun. I kept to my bed all yesterday while the reaction passed." True, in a technical sense.

"Hmmmm, yes. I see that. Still . . . I sense a secrecy about you. The question is how can those secrets be of use to me?"

"And why would I want to be of use to you?" she snapped.

"One never knows when one will require a friend close to the emperor, Livia Quintus. You may have escaped his attention with that slight of his physical endowments, but I can assure you he has not forgotten you. I will ensure that he has not."

The emperor could not hold her. And she would never submit to his foul attentions or those of anyone in his court. The problem was what he could do to Jergan.

THE MANACLES CLICKED shut. He got his feet under him and stood at the post, his hands fastened just above his head. Two of the guards had dragged him from the bed. He was burned in four or five places, and still his cock hung heavy between his legs, red and swollen.

"Pick out a whip, Julia," Agrippina suggested. "Not the

one with the metal tips, though. That would make him useless too soon."

He heard rummaging.

"How about a quirt?" Julia asked. "Just heavy enough to leave stripes." There was a rushing sound, no doubt as she cut the air with her find.

"Would my ladies like assistance in whipping the barbarian?" the guard who had been excited all evening asked.

"We want the pleasure first," Julia tittered.

"Perhaps we'd enjoy seeing you whip him later," Agrippina mused, "if you stripped to your loincloth to do it."

"Your wish is my command."

A rush of air was followed so quickly by the sear of pain, Jergan didn't have time to prepare. It wasn't a heavy whip. Not like the ones used on him on the long march from Gaul. He braced himself for the second blow.

Instead noisy footsteps sounded in the corridor. The door opened without knocking and Caligula entered the room. "Stay outside," he ordered his guard.

Julia and Agrippina hurried over to their brother. He took one in each arm and traded open-mouthed kisses with them. Jergan wasn't sure whether to be relieved that the sisters were distracted or dismayed at this new arrival.

Caligula's glance took in the braided quirt that Agrippina still held, and strayed to Jergan. "Has he confessed yet, or implicated others?"

"Silly brother," Julia chided. "There is plenty of time for more severe questioning. Why make him unusable too quickly?"

Caligula let them go and strolled forward, examining Jergan more closely. "We see the attraction. Barbarians are so uncivilized, one has the immediate urge to dominate them."

Jergan bit his lips and kept silent. He hoped his hatred of this brand of "civilization" and these twisted souls who embraced it did not glow in his eyes.

"You know, Sisters, chaining him to only one pole allows the pole to protect his chest and his most impressive organ." Caligula looked around. "Guards, unfasten him and chain him between these two." Caesar gestured to poles about four or five feet apart.

Two guards hurried over to unlock one of Jergan's shackles. They stretched him out and locked his wrist to the other pole's shackle. The wound at his shoulder tightened.

"Now his ankles. You'll need to pull his legs wider."

Jergan felt as he had in the slave market, totally vulnerable.

Caligula stalked slowly around him, tapping one finger to his lips. "We see you started with the irons." The light touch, when it came to Jergan's back, made him feel like an insect was crawling over him. The finger traced his newest welt. And then the hand moved down over his buttocks and slid between his cheeks. Jergan's breath came in gasps as he tried not to give the creature the satisfaction of trying to squirm away. A finger rubbed Jergan's anus gently.

"Have you reamed him yet?" Caligula asked. What did he mean?

"No, Brother." Agrippina grinned at Julia. "We hadn't yet gotten enough of his organ."

"Has he been cleansed?"

The sisters shook their heads. "We have a basin and a bladder for the purpose, though."

Jergan ground his teeth. *You will stand whatever they do,* he told himself. His eyes strayed to the brazier of coals and hot irons. Did they mean to . . . ? He realized fear was creeping into his heart. He steadied his breathing.

Caligula turned to the guards. "Would one of you like to dominate this barbarian for us?"

The one who had been excited all evening cracked a smile while the other three tried to remain so impassive they were invisible. "At your command, Caesar."

"Excellent," Caligula remarked, turning back to Jergan. "That will be entertaining." He stalked up to stand in front of Jergan, whose erection almost touched Caligula. How Jergan would like to spit in that cruel face. But he must maintain control. He had to think of Livia. "We've heard that barbarians sometimes stimulate their partners' genitals with their mouths." Caligula gave a mock shudder. "How horrible. Still . . . we feel it's an emperor's duty to experience all the sensations craved by our subjects. It's why we fight in the arena on occasion."

He meant Jergan to suck his cock? Not in this life or the next!

Livia. If he didn't, what would happen to Livia? He swallowed. "I am not your subject. Britannia is not part of your empire." He had little hope that would make a difference in the choices he was given here.

"No, not a subject," Caligula actually giggled. "We declare you slave again."

Jergan blinked. He could do that? Of course he could. He could do anything. And now Jergan would not be a slave to an honorable and generous woman, but to this viper.

"Oh, Brother," Agrippina said. "Excellent. Can he be our slave?"

Julia came and stroked the emperor's other arm. "Yes, Brother. Give him to us. Then we'll have all the time in the world to play with him."

Caligula laughed again. "Only if we may enjoy him, too."

"But of course," Julia murmured. She motioned to the servant. "Clean his anus."

More rummaging while the sisters and Caligula discussed Jergan's most immediate future.

"Let the guard have him first," Caligula was saying, "from the rear, while you, Sisters, use that quirt on his chest and belly. Then I'll command him to suckle me and you can either whip his backside or use the handle on his anus."

Jergan chewed his lip. The emperor was a fearful creature. Perhaps he could use that. "You should fear for your member," Jergan growled, "if you put it in my mouth."

Caligula giggled again. "We're not concerned. After all, your careful attention to pleasing us is the only way you can avoid some very unfortunate consequences to Livia Quintus Lucellus. We saw the way you looked at her tonight."

Jergan let out a grunt of anguish. They had him. He would do anything to keep Livia from being victimized by this sick bastard.

They laughed. By Belatucadros, they all laughed.

15

LIVIA COULDN'T BEAR it any longer. He could survive what the sisters might do to him, but a man like Jergan would be changed forever by what Caligula could do, even if he survived it.

Everyone in the room would see her use her powers. It was against every tenet of the Rules that had governed her kind for millennia.

Livia closed her eyes, once.

It was the Rules or Jergan.

She took one long breath. She had seen a slave once who had been tortured to death carried out the back door of the palace and thrown into a cart like so much garbage. The image of his broken body hovered in her brain and would not be banished.

There was no choice, really.

It didn't matter that her nature would be revealed, the Rules broken. It didn't even matter that her plot might be undone. She would do the best she could to avoid those eventualities, but in the end they didn't matter. She looked around.

She needed someone who was familiar with the palace. Slaves? But what slave would be allowed into the inner sanctum of the family? Not those who served at banquets, surely. Asiaticus would know. He had drifted over to talk to Helion. But Asiaticus would never aid her.

Her eyes fell on Claudius, looking distinctly uncomfortable in this cauldron of lust.

"Gather the other senators and go home, Titus," she murmured, rising. "The Guard won't dare stop you if you all go together."

"Don't do anything you will regret, Livia," he hissed.

But she was already moving off among the crowd. Several senators clustered together and pushed toward the door. Claudius had several cronies around him. That would not do.

"Claudius Drusus," she said, at her most dulcet. "We have hardly had a moment to speak."

He jerked around. "L-L-Livia Quintus L-Lucellus, I was s-surprised to s-see you on the Senate f-floor today."

"Asiaticus arranged a personal escort from the Guard to the event," she said. Let Claudius draw his own conclusions.

Claudius nodded, thoughtful. On the imperial dais, Caesonia had called for attendants to take Incitatus back to his stall. Livia had heard it was made of carved ivory and contained a golden manger. Caesonia was planning to leave. The Guards certainly wouldn't stop the empress. The Praetorian Guards at the entrances were confronted by a group of senators, Titus among them, who had found safety in numbers. Claudius saw his opportunity and rose.

Livia put on her most seductive smile. "Do not go. I would be desolate."

Claudius blinked at her warily. "P-perhaps another t-time."

She took his arm. "But who knows what the fates have in store for us? There may be no other time." She glanced to his friends. "Of course, your friends have other obligations, do they not?" He looked around as though for assistance. His friends were smirking.

"Don't let us interfere, old fellow," one said.

"If ever you want to speak to me, Livia Quintus, just say the word."

They melted away, one waving. Livia turned back to Claudius. He looked rather alarmed.

She leaned up to whisper in his ear, "I need your help." She made it look like a caress. "I have no one else to ask."

He relaxed. Apparently being asked for a favor was preferable to being invited to seduction. He glanced around and nodded to a curtain from which slaves emerged with trays of food. It didn't look secluded, but Claudius had not survived the constant assassinations in the imperial family by being stupid. She followed at a discreet distance.

Claudius slipped through the curtain. After a moment, Livia followed. He was nowhere in sight, but a door stood slightly ajar on her right.

She found herself in some kind of storage room, filled with platters and goblets, finger bowls and intricately embroidered cloths to wipe one's hands. It was lit with smoking lamps so the slaves could pick out what they needed from the stores. It smelled of the oil used on the platters to make them shine, and the underlying acrid smell of the metal itself. He turned on her. "Now, L-Livia Quintus, what is it y-you want?"

How to ask him? And why would he risk helping her? But there was no one else.

"The slave I freed has caught the attention of the imperial sisters."

"I n-noticed. C-can he keep his m-mouth closed?"

"He won't betray us." She took a breath. "That's why I can't allow him to be tortured."

"N-nothing you can d-do, I'm afraid."

"I think Caesar has joined his sisters." Claudius would know what that meant.

Claudius pursed his lips. "Then you'd b-better resign yourself."

"No," she hissed. "Jergan is an honorable man. He doesn't deserve what Caesar will do."

"R-Rome d-doesn't deserve what Caesar d-does," Claudius muttered. "That d-doesn't change fact."

"It does. I can get Jergan out."

"For an h-hour."

"No. I can free Rome from Caligula forever. You were right about me. And there are others with me. I'll accelerate our plans. But first, I must free Jergan."

"H-how?" Claudius examined her face. "I w-won't be a p-party to some d-doomed plan."

If he didn't believe she could succeed, he would never help her. Claudius, the pragmatist. That's how he'd stayed alive. Then she must show him her powers, since using them was the only way she could succeed. How much truth to tell him? *If* he would believe it. That was her kind's great protection—humans never believed that vampires lived among them.

Tell him, that voice that had grown inside her said. *It will be all right.*

No. She had to show him. She reached for a platter. It was thick, made of beaten copper. She bent it double, and then doubled it again like it was paper between her palms. Then she crumpled it into a ball with one dainty hand. Her hands *were* dainty.

She glanced to Claudius. He had gone white in the dim room.

"I am not like you." Would that be enough?

"Ob-obviously n-not." He gathered himself. "But s-strength alone m-may not w-win the d-day." His stutter was worse, just as it was when Caesar had forced him to read the proclamation.

"There are other things about me. You do not want to know them."

Fear reverberated behind his eyes. "W-what are y-you?"

"A woman. A woman who wants to save this man." Claudius looked wary. That explanation wasn't enough. She drew herself up. "I have been touched by the gods, Claudius. And what I am will help you free yourself from a cousin you hate, and Rome from a tyrant who makes her less than she can be." Livia softened. "It is a burden I bear, to be different. Some people would say different is evil, at the very least, worse. I don't believe that. I think differences can be used for good. Can you understand?" She knew he could. That's why she said it.

She saw him frown and pressed her advantage. "Help me. Tell me where they are."

"How will you get through the guards?"

He was back to being pragmatic, but now he was testing her plan. That was a victory of sorts. She dared not give vent to her relief.

"I can wrap darkness around myself. I can wrap darkness around Jergan, too."

"I believe you are strong, Livia Quintus, but no one can command the elements."

Livia ran her tongue over her lips. It was too late to draw back now. She called the power of her Companion and let the darkness whirl up to her waist. She saw his widening eyes. "Not evil, Claudius Drusus." She held up a hand as though to stop his thought. "Not evil, just different." She let the darkness seep away. "I am still Livia Quintus Lucellus. All I need to know is where Jergan is being held."

Claudius mastered himself. She admired him for that.

Claudius nodded, thoughtful. "I have l-lived in the c-corners of life, unobtrusive. Th-that was my p-protection." He was trying to decide.

"The center of the rotunda, speaking before the Senate, is not an unobtrusive corner." She took a chance in reminding him of that.

He flushed in shame. "A-an aberration I did not seek."

"It needn't be." She said it quietly. "You can be a force for progress." If he had aspirations to be more than a joke, now was the time to prove it.

"Y-you are a S-Sibyil at the l-least." He sucked air into his lungs. "What you n-need, Livia Q-Quintus, whatever you are, is a d-diversion."

He pushed past her, limping. She followed. They wended their way through kitchens where brawny, sweating, half-naked slaves turned giant spits of meat over the fires, and women took countless loaves of bread from brick ovens. The place smelled of every kind of food, and spice and wine. It wasn't surprising that the slaves and servants all bowed respectfully to Claudius. He was obviously patrician. But that he called many by name and thanked them as they opened doors was amazing. Claudius might be nobody to the royal family, but here he was valued. He knew his way here, where, she would wager, no other member of the imperial family had ever trod. Perhaps this was one of the corners where he had lived his life. They passed through storerooms and a steaming laundry. Everywhere slaves blessed him as he passed.

They emerged from a curtain back into the imperial section of the palace. Rustic tiled floors gave way to marble, iron straps on wooden doors to gold leaf and mosaics of lapis lazuli. Livia could not help but have faith that he knew where he was going.

He stopped abruptly and held up a hand.

They listened. Male voices, some rough laughter.

He limped to the wall and pressed his back against it. She slid up beside him. He leaned in and whispered in her ear, "The guards are in the next ch-chamber and your m-man and my cousins in the n-next after that."

"How far to the inside of the room where they have Jergan?"

"F-fifty feet? Yes. Fifty f-feet." He took her hand. "The guards know m-me. S-several have s-served as my b-body-guard. When they t-turn to l-look at me, w-wrap your d-darkness."

She nodded. "Thank you."

"Do n-not thank me. If anything g-goes wrong I will v-vow I do n-not know you."

She reached up to kiss his cheek. "You pretend to have no courage, but I know better."

He looked at her seriously. "W-whatever you s-see in that r-room, j-just take him and g-go. Go f-far."

She swallowed. The very thought of leaving Rome made her almost physically ill. She couldn't think of that now. She had to get Jergan out of here.

You can do this. You will do this. You have done this. The voice inside her was reassuring.

"Hurry," she adjured Claudius.

He turned and limped into the next room. "Am I l-late?"

There was a clack. Spears crossing over the door. Livia peered around the column.

"Consul Tiberius Claudius Drusus Nero Germanicus." It was the cherub-faced guard.

"Open th-the d-door, Gratus, or I'll m-miss every-thing."

"The emperor does not wish to be disturbed, Consul."

His voice held respect for Claudius. Kindness even. That was strange. Livia wondered whether Claudius's common touch extended to the Praetorians who guarded him.

"D-do you ch-challenge a m-member of the imp-perial f-family?" Claudius's stutter had gotten worse, but there was iron in his voice. Livia held her breath. What kind of a diversion could he make if they just turned him away at the door?

"No, Consul. I . . . I was just trying to save you the emperor's anger."

Claudius relented. "I know, boy. But there are things that must be done, anger or no anger."

The young guard pursed his lips. Then he shook his head. "I can respect that." He pointed to his fellows.

The spears clacked open.

"That's b-better."

"I tried to warn you, Consul. I beg you to remember that." Gratus sounded sorry.

Now was the time. *Companion!* she called. An answering shiver of power ran up her veins. A film of red dropped over the world.

"Gaius," she heard Claudius call. "Julia L-Lavilla. Have I m-missed the fun?"

More! Livia shouted silently. And a whirling blackness rose around her. *Fifty feet,* she thought. *Fifty feet.* All went black. The familiar pain arced through her, making her gasp.

Then she sucked in breath as a new room appeared around her. She was in the shadows near a great bed, whose coverlets were twisted in disarray. Claudius was coming in through the door. All turned toward him, even the three guards with swords drawn. Dimly she noted a brazier burning with hot irons in it. Jergan was chained to two ornately carved posts in the middle of the floor. She took in at a glance that he was sweating, and that there were welts across his chest and red weals on several places across his body. Julia stood in front of him, fondling his erect penis. A man Livia did not know was caught in the middle of removing his loincloth behind Jergan. He was erect as well. Was she too late? Caligula lay on a couch with Agrippina, watching, his own erection small but stiff.

"What do you mean by this, you drooling idiot?" Caesar said, rising on one elbow.

Get away from him, Julia. She couldn't steal Jergan with Julia so close.

"Everyone s-said the f-family was g-going to use L-Livia Quintus L-Lucellus's freedm-man. And a-after all, I'm f-family." Claudius's expectant look was comic, an effect Livia was sure he intended.

Julia tittered and took two steps away from Jergan. "Not you, Claudius. Why, I'm sure you've never tortured a slave in your life, let alone raped one."

Now all were turned toward Claudius, even the man who held his loincloth to cover his erection. Livia noted a pile of greaves and a breastplate on the floor. He must be one of the guards. And he was clearly planning on raping Jergan. Rage boiled up into her throat. She slid out of the shadows. *Companion!* The room went red.

Claudius looked from Caesar and Agrippina to Julia, disappointment on his face. Livia saw his eyes register her and move on. She glided up behind Julia and the naked guard.

More power! The blackness started at Livia's feet even as she closed on Jergan. His eyes grew big. She touched his mouth. The blackness was at her knees.

"Hey!" one of the guards cried.

She'd been seen. She threw her arms around Jergan, pressing her body to his.

"This will hurt," she whispered. The blackness engulfed him as well. It was at their chests. The others were turning back now. Chaerea saw her. She thought about her house, her bedroom.

As the blackness descended over all, Jergan bellowed in pain.

THEY COLLAPSED IN a heap, gasping for breath, Livia on top of Jergan. Slowly the sleeping quarters of the house on the Capitoline Hill settled around her. The colors of the carpets swirled before her eyes. The feel of Jergan's bare flesh against her, the dim sconces flickering, all registered slowly. They were free. But it might be brief.

She rolled off Jergan so he could catch his breath. Translocating was even harder on humans than it was for her. "I'm sorry. I know that was . . . painful."

His chest heaved. "How did you . . . do . . . that?"

She flushed. "Did I forget to tell you about that?"

His breathing steadied. "Apparently."

"Well . . . the power of the thing in my veins can be used to push me out of one place and into another. I . . . just held on to you." She touched him, here, there, her hands running lightly over his body. He was still violently erect. It could not be natural.

"Is there anything else I should know?"

"I . . . I think that's the last of it." The burns were ugly but not deep. They would heal. No wounds she could see. But . . . . "Did they . . . violate you?"

His eyes darkened. "Of course they did, the bitches." Rage warred with shame in his expression. "They used my cock with some kind of cream that made me hard.

They whipped me and burned me." He squeezed his eyes shut, breathing hard. Then he forced himself quiet. Deliberately, he opened his eyes. "But the guards had not yet gotten at me, or . . . or the emperor."

Who would come through such an experience unscathed? Not a proud warrior like Jergan. He could hardly acknowledge that he was a slave. "This is my fault," Livia lamented.

He put a finger to her lips. "You are the last person to be blamed." He reached up and brought her down to lie against his welted chest. "Without doubt I have you to thank for what shred of self-respect I have left."

"I should never have allowed them to drag you along today." Tears welled. They would drip salt into his welts. But she couldn't stop them.

"You had no choice." He stroked her hair.

She took a breath. She could not afford to give in to weakness now. She sat up, determined. "We have not much time. They will be wondering how you disappeared from among their midst. I think Chaerea and one of the guards saw me. They'll be at our door shortly."

"Will Claudius pay the price for his distraction?"

So, Jergan realized what the plan had been. "I think Claudius can take care of himself," she chuckled. "That man is more intelligent, more devious, than even I gave him credit for."

"Courageous, too," Jergan said, struggling to sit. "I hope I get a chance to thank him."

"No time for that," she said, standing. "I will engage the plan tonight. If they have not yet seen all the senators, so be it. We must to Tuscany with the servants. It is the only way I can keep you safe if the plan fails."

Pain stabbed through her head as the voice inside her shouted, *You cannot leave Rome.*

"Livia?" Jergan staggered to his feet and took her by the shoulders. "What is wrong?"

She took several ragged breaths. "I . . . I don't know. The feeling that we shouldn't leave was so . . . strong . . . it was like a needle in my brain."

"It is these dreams you have been having."

He was right. This voice inside her was tied up with the premonitions and the feeling she had done all this before. The dream that told her so flashed into her memory. How had she forgotten that dream? Or had she suppressed it? It did not matter that the whole thing was incredible. She herself was incredible to people like Jergan and Claudius. She could not deny there was *something* she should do. She didn't know what it was. But the voice knew.

"Tell me . . ." she whispered, to whom she did not know. "Tell me what to do."

Let me out. Give me control.

She couldn't do that. That might be giving in to madness. And they couldn't stay in Rome, disappearing every time the Guard recaptured them. Jergan might be killed the next time. She straightened. "It doesn't matter. We have to go." Again the stabbing pain.

NO!!

She moaned a little, her knees going weak. Jergan caught her about the waist.

"Just start the plot in motion," he whispered. "If it succeeds, there is no need to leave."

She nodded, rubbing her temples as if that would make the pain go away. "Yes. Yes. Dress yourself." She gestured toward the trunk for Jergan's new clothes. "Wait. . . . I will send for a cooling astringent to ease your arousal and some unguents for the burns—"

"No time." He guided her to the desk and sat her down.

He pushed the stylus and the inkwell toward her, before turning to the chest to dress.

Livia pulled out a parchment with shaking hands. She could do this. Caligula must die if she and Jergan were ever to be safe. She would convince him to go to Tuscany without her. She could stay and see it through. She didn't seem to have much choice. The voice would not let her go.

She scratched the stylus across the parchment. "Now is the time, my friend," she wrote. She melted tallow from the candle and pushed her signet ring into the wax. After dusting sand across the ink, she rolled the parchment and tied it with a red ribbon. She went to the door. "Lucius."

He appeared as he always did, almost instantly, as though he had foreseen her wish.

"Have Tufi take this to the statue of Drusilla. He must place it in the basket of flowers she carries. No one must see him do it. Do you understand?"

Lucius nodded. He hesitated. "And if there is no opportunity?"

"Pray to the gods there is an opportunity, Lucius. Then he must return here immediately."

Lucius nodded, turned on his heel, and left. It was done.

"Will your instrument know to look there?"

She nodded. "He looks there every night." The preparations needed for the household to relocate to safety were complex and immediate. She hoped Tuscany would provide safety long enough for them to disperse to places where the Roman army wouldn't find them.

Jergan pressed. "This plan must go forward quickly. What if he doesn't look tonight?"

"He will look tonight of all nights, after what he saw. He'll know I can't stay long."

Jergan took her arm and turned her toward him, his

eyes searching her face. "Chaerea is your instrument, isn't he?"

She saw Jergan's disbelief, his sudden doubt. "Who is closer to Caligula?"

"Why would he do this thing?"

"Because he, of anyone, knows what Caligula is." She sighed, and turned. "And he is the perfect choice. Only the Praetorian Guard could protect those who killed an emperor. Only they can ensure a republic is viable." She cupped Jergan's jaw with her hand. "A republic is a tenuous thing, Jergan. It cannot stand against armies without an army of its own, and the Praetorian Guard is the only army allowed anywhere near Rome. It cannot stand against chaos and bickering. Free men must be granted the luxury of time to establish their fragile rules and policies, until those laws live on their own. So yes, it must be the Guard that kills Gaius, and the Guard that supports the republic that will follow. Chaerea is the only choice."

She took a breath. "Now, prepare to escort the servants to Tuscany. I will not rest easy until they, and you, are out of harm's way." Again the headache stabbed her.

He cannot go, either.

"I'm not leaving you here." His voice was hard. He took her arms. "I'm staying if you stay. The voice, it tells you that is right, doesn't it?" Jergan clutched her to his chest. "Livia, listen to this voice. It must be from the gods."

"If you stay and the plot fails or is delayed, you will be back in the palace chained to two posts before morning." Her vision was swimming. "What if I cannot rescue you again? Do not worry for me. They cannot hold me."

"We will leave the house, but not Rome. Is there not somewhere we can hide?"

She couldn't think. "I . . . Where would he not think to look?"

"The brothel?" Jergan asked, lifting her chin.

She blinked. The pain receded. The brothel. Not an unacceptable idea. "But Drusus Lucellus must not pay the price of harboring us."

"We are enjoying his facilities. He can disclaim all knowledge."

"Yes . . ." But they would torture him anyway. She was putting him in danger. But what choice was there? He would be suspect anyway, just because he shared her name. She straightened. "Yes." At least her next course was certain. And there was no stabbing pain in her head to tell her no. Did that mean this was right? She felt unmistakably, as she had so often in the last days, that she had done all this before. "There is much to do." Her mind raced. Lucius would need money for the journey. The household had only minutes to pack. They must be roused.

"What can I do to help?" Jergan asked, as though girding himself for battle.

16

JERGAN TOOK LIVIA'S hand and led her behind a pillar of the portico at the brothel owned by Drusus Lucellus. Dawn was near now. The night had taken its toll. Jergan was exhausted. His other palm caressed the pommel of his short sword. There had been no litter, no bearers, no escort. He and Livia had hurried through the wet night streets of Rome like the refugees they were. Tufi had returned, victorious. The message had been delivered. The household was dispatched like thieves in the night, practically as the Guard appeared in the street. Jergan and Livia slid out through the garden past the baths that held such bittersweet meaning for him.

A vengeful emperor would have mobilized all Rome against them. Jergan had no faith that the captain of the Praetorians would find Livia's note and a way to kill the emperor all in one night. Jergan listened for pursuers. Cats screeched in mock battle. Drunken revelers wended their way home. But there was no tramp of soldiers' boots, no hiss of metal withdrawn from a scabbard.

Livia moved to the knocker on the brothel door.

"Let me." He pressed her into the shadows, then raised the heavy round iron ring and let it fall. The hollow thunk sounded like a call to any guards who might be looking for them. It seemed forever until the door cracked open.

"You are late, citizens," the fat man said as he opened the door. He froze as he registered who it was, and peered past Jergan into the night. Had the word spread already?

Livia stepped into the light of the sconces hung at either side of the great door. "We come only to purchase a room, Drusus." Jergan had never heard her sound so humble, even to the emperor.

The man she had freed and whose business she had staked swallowed once and opened the door wide. "Your patronage is always welcome, Lady Lucellus." He ushered them into the anteroom. But this time he did not take them into the main room where patrons usually waited for their choice of partners, and dancers undulated in sinuous provocation. He opened a side door, a worried frown creasing his forehead. "Will you need a slave today?"

"No," she said gratefully. "Just a room."

"And perhaps some refreshment for my lady," Jergan added. "It has been a long night."

The brothel owner's face softened. "Of course. I will send both food and drink." He guided them to a chamber with a heavy door, rather than the usual curtain. It was sumptuous, but it also looked lived in. Heavy shutters blocked out the dawn. Parchments were scattered across a writing table along with two plates strewn with bread, cheese, and a half-eaten bunch of grapes. These were his private quarters.

Jergan sat Livia at the table and cleared away the plates. She seemed almost in a trance. In truth, the worry eating at him had so many sides, he could not focus on it. The emperor would be looking for them even though he did not know about her plot. She had thwarted his will, and he was a petulant child who would not tolerate that. Her plot might fail. Rome was not big enough to hide her in that case. Jergan had no faith that the old men who had been lobbying for a republic would not be taken by the emperor and questioned. They would reveal her role at the first flash of a hot iron. Jergan had no faith in this Chaerea, and he couldn't see why she did. And he could not forget that someone knew she was the lynchpin of the plot and had made attempts on her life. Everything seemed to be closing in around her.

And yet she would not leave.

The pain she had experienced when she even thought about leaving was disturbing in itself. The gods had marked her. That was certain. The dreams, the premonitions, the voices in her head . . . these were as disturbing as her other qualities, because she, who was so mysterious and wise, did not understand them.

A male slave appeared in the doorway wearing a discreet loincloth. He proved to be the head of a procession of slave girls clad in short *stolas,* carrying amphorae of wine, plates of food.

Jergan directed them to lay their burdens on the table while Livia watched, remote. "Thank you," he said when they were done. "You may go."

The door thunked behind them.

He turned to Livia. Why did he accept her? Why was he not horrified? She had disappeared into thin air tonight. That would have condemned her as a witch in any country.

Was it because she had explained it so matter-of-factly? Or was it because she had used that power to save him?

He thought of the frogs the bully in his village had captured when he was a child. The pig-faced boy had slipped them into a cauldron of warm water where they swam happily. But the cauldron was over a fire, and the heat of the water slowly increased and increased until the frogs were boiled alive without even trying to get out of the cauldron.

Was he a frog in boiling water? Perhaps where Livia was concerned. He had slowly become so enthralled by her that he accepted anything. That would likely have consequences.

She came to herself and smiled at him, registering him for the first time, he thought. "Are . . . are you well?"

He deliberately softened his demeanor in case his anxiety was writ on his face. He nodded and sat, his knees rebelling. The violent erection had subsided. The welts were unimportant. But the burns had sapped his strength. The whole experience left him nauseous.

"Yes. I am well enough." She knew he lied. She served him roasted lamb and stewed apples. He somehow managed to eat. She must know his hands shook as he cut his meat.

The world closed down to just these walls. Caligula was outside, and Chaerea, and her mysterious attacker. Outside, Rome was puzzling and despicable. Livia might not be able to save it from itself. But here the floor was warm, the wine pungent and relaxing. The food tasted of the earth, which was the same whether in Centii or in the valley of the Tiber. This place, this time, might be just the atmosphere to boil a frog.

Jergan didn't care.

He had survived tonight. He felt on the edge of some discovery, whether the discovery of his own mortality or of transcendence he couldn't tell. But he would boil in the heady brew and know its essence. And it would damn him or save him. Of that he was sure.

LIVIA FELT HERSELF jerk into the present. It was as if she had been dreaming somewhere and wakened suddenly.

She breathed in, slowly, and smiled. Jergan, across from her, took tidbits from the bowls and plates, placed them in his lovely mouth. The movement of the muscles in his jaw as he chewed was riveting. He was due for a shave he would not get. He sipped his wine. All hung on a fulcrum, balanced, neither bad nor good, failure nor victory, sanity nor insanity. There was only the moment. How strange for someone who had fought through so many years to feel those years drop away and know that one lived, at this moment, only in the moment.

Two slave girls came and took the plates away, bowing. Livia asked them to bring medical supplies. Jergan wasn't well. She saw his hand shaking. Every time she thought of what he had borne, she got angry all over again and felt ashamed into the bargain.

"See that we are not disturbed," she ordered when a girl returned with the small pots and jars Livia had requested. She turned to Jergan. Those green eyes studied her as though she were a puzzle. His forearms corded as he clenched and unclenched his fists. She felt herself grow wet with desire.

His eyes never left her face as he unbuckled the wide belt that held his short tunic. He pulled the tunic over his head and unwrapped his loincloth. The unnatural erection had subsided, thank the gods. He was still full, though. His chest and belly were laced with welts, not bloody, as the ones on his back once were, but angry red. He turned and put his foot on one of the stools at the table to unlace his boot. The bend of his back and the muscles that moved under the skin were riveting. She saw several burns, one on his thigh, one on his buttocks, one on his chest and at his hip. The sisters were animals.

He glanced up and caught her staring. She busied herself with the jars. Salve of rosemary. And aloe cream. That was good for burns.

Neither spoke. She took the aloe cream and scooped some on her fingers. It was cool to the touch. Touch.

That's what she was going to do. Touch him. She knew where that could lead. But not tonight. He was injured.

She spread the cream on the burn on his chest. He made his breathing even to cover the small gasp. And then the one on his hip, his buttocks. He smelled like rosemary and aloe now. It covered the smell of the sex the sisters had forced on him. She bent to put the cream on his thigh. Her crotch was slick. She stood up and surveyed her work.

"I'll do." He smiled. He must have seen her doubt. "The Cantiaci are a hardy lot."

"Jergan, I am so sorry." Guilt washed over her again. She pushed it down. "Come to bed. You must rest."

He nodded. His face looked almost gray. He lay down. She doused the lamps, checked the shutters, and lay down beside him, careful not to touch his burns. He was asleep within minutes.

SHE WOKE SOMETIME mid-day. The room was comfortingly dim. He had turned in toward her and thrown an arm across her belly. She had been too exhausted to dream. She saw his eyes flutter open. He reached over and kissed her shoulder. His hand ran over her belly. He shouldn't do that. But he didn't stop and she didn't tell him to stop. He pulled her closer and kissed her, long and slowly. She felt his rod growing stiff. Gods, but she was tempted. Her breasts grew sensitive even as he moved his hand to squeeze them gently under her tunic.

"You're injured," she protested, into his mouth, just before she kissed him back.

"Then make me forget last night." He moved in to her. "Make me feel like a man."

How could she not, when he put it so? He must have

known it. The man was a better manipulator than she was. She felt herself melting. "You'll tell me if I hurt you."

Her answer was a growl as he took her in his arms. He kissed her, almost ruthlessly now, opening her mouth with his tongue and probing it. His stiff rod prodded her belly. She put her hands around his neck and ran them through his hair. At least there she wouldn't be touching abraded flesh. He pulled at the neck of her tunic. "Wait," she protested.

"You brought others," he growled, and the fabric ripped.

The feel of her naked breasts, pressed against his chest where he clutched her to his body, was engrossing. He kneaded her buttocks as he kissed her again, fiercely. There would be no gentle foreplay today. He needed to feel his own power. She wanted that, too.

He ravished her mouth. She spread her thighs to him immediately. He stopped himself long enough to wonder if she was ready. She could see the question in his eyes. She nodded. He knelt on the bed, his erection straining with need. She opened her thighs even wider, split herself, inviting him to plunge inside her.

He did not need a second invitation. He positioned his rod. She wrapped her legs around his hips and met his thrust by drawing herself against him. Filled, she gasped in satisfaction. His first thrusts were fierce. But when the initial need for friction was eased, he slowed, and lowered himself to cover her entirely. One hand kneaded her breast as he kissed her. She opened her mouth to his thrusting tongue even as she opened her legs to him. Let him ravish her. Let him feel his power, his control. Let that heal him.

He slowed his thrusting to give her time to catch her pleasure. There was no need. The feeling of opening herself to him was so arousing she was afraid she would reach her pinnacle before he did. "Just take me," she whispered into his mouth.

He grunted, freed himself and thrust, inside her, faster now. Still he lasted a long time. She had thought he would just spill himself immediately. He must be holding back. And then she couldn't think anything, because the friction was raising her sensation to heights that might be unbearable, or might be transcendent. And he was whispering forceful barbarian words into her mouth and her ear as he thrust inside her. She felt him begin to spurt, and that satisfaction seemed to put her over her own edge. She heard herself shrieking from far away. She had only enough presence of mind to ball her hands into fists so that her nails dug into her own palms and not into his back as he banged away at her. His own shout of release seemed torn from his gut.

She sucked in air as though she couldn't get enough as the room swam into view around her. And she began to laugh.

He rolled to one side, cradling her. "What is it?" His voice was tender.

"I'll wager no one in this brothel last night had more pleasure than I just did."

He smiled. His eyes were soft. "Did you have pleasure? I only thought about me."

"You did *not* think only about you," she accused. "You waited for me."

"Not for very long."

"Good thing I was quick, then."

"I hope you were satisfied."

He must be truly worried. Ahhh . . . it was his approach that concerned him. She looked up into his eyes. "I never knew being ravished could be so deeply enjoyable." She saw his brow relax.

"You didn't have to pay for your pleasure, as the other patrons did." He kissed her hair. "Surely that is satisfying."

"Did I not? You were very expensive." She adjusted herself in his arms. "I wonder how I ever had the courage to buy you, you looked so fierce."

"You wanted a fierce-looking bodyguard," he reminded her. "Besides, you tamed me."

"I used your honor against you," she said, looking up, contrite. "I am sorry for that."

"I thought it very clever. It was the only way to keep me from strangling you, with all your arrogant speeches ordering me to spill my seed by my own hand under your supervision."

She could not help a chuckle. "That was a little much, wasn't it? But I had to act confident when you were frightening me out of my wits." How could she remind him of his slavery when she wanted to heal his raw emotions tonight? "That is behind us. I should not have mentioned it."

"I am not certain it is behind us, Livia. Caesar declared that I am a slave again tonight. Can he do that?"

"What can he not do? However, it makes little difference to our outcome, unfortunately. You can forget about it."

"Like you just helped me forget what happened with Caesar's sisters. That was generous."

She might have helped. But it would be long before he forgot the feeling of being helpless, she knew. She could still see the clouded memory of it lurking in his green eyes. What would she not do to spare him pain? Somewhere in the last days something had happened to her. And it wasn't only the dreams that came true or the voice inside that spoke so urgently. This man had come to mean everything to her. It wasn't that his body attracted her as none had before. That was minor in the scheme of things.

What was important was that his courage, his honor, and his intelligence spoke to her. No wonder his people had given him the important task of spying on the Roman army's advance. He was a born leader. She admired that.

But what she felt was more than admiration.

She loved him.

The realization made her suck in a breath of air. She felt about him as she had never felt about anyone in her long life.

"What is it, my love?" he asked as he felt her stiffen.

She looked up. Concern was writ across his bold barbarian features. He couldn't feel the same for her in return, no matter that he used the word as an endearment. She was vampire, for Vulcan's sake. And acceptance wasn't love.

Tell him. Tell him how you feel.

The damned voice inside her was getting more than annoying. What did it know? She couldn't tell him. Not when the gulf between them was so huge, when he didn't feel the same. The feeling of being uncomfortable in her own skin returned.

She rubbed the bridge of her nose. "Nothing," she murmured. "Nothing but our situation. And there is nothing to be done about that at the moment."

"Sleep now, my Livia. By tomorrow, it may all be over."

She shut her eyes, trying to enjoy how right his arms about her felt. But she didn't go to sleep again. The outside was creeping into the room again. By tomorrow all might have gone horribly wrong. He might be in prison, or in the sisters' clutches. And she might have lost all chance to affect the course of the empire. But whatever happened, it wouldn't cure the gulf between her and Jergan. And the feeling of urgency, of being full to bursting with something that couldn't get out, would not have disappeared, either.

And that was more frightening than all the Roman legions.

JERGAN LOOKED DOWN at her. She wasn't asleep. He could tell by her breathing and the tension that had come into her spine. He felt so helpless. The forces of the empire were ranged against her. There was nothing a barbarian freedman could do for someone like Livia. He loved her. Of course he did. Who would not? Everyone around her was at least half in love with her. But she wanted to fix what was wrong with empires. She had no room left over to love any of her worshippers. She was generous to a fault, courageous, as sharp as he kept his sword. And that was besides her strength, her red eyes, her ability to do something she called translocation.

She had given her body to him in ecstatic lovemaking—a deeper, richer experience than he had ever had. But she did not give her soul. That was saved for saving the world.

And why not? She was something larger in spirit than just human. Old, wise, powerful. She was closer to the gods than he was, whether his Celtic gods, her Roman gods, or some god even stranger, he did not know. She would never give her soul to a barbarian who until yesterday had been her slave, who lived but a blink of time, who had no powers other than those of a very human male.

Desolation crept into his heart. Worse than when he had been chained to a Roman supply wagon. Loving Livia might turn out to be worse torture than the emperor's sisters could ever devise. She owned him now more completely than before his name was written in the book.

"Let me out! You never listen to me."

The woman with her face stood with her hands on her hips next to a vine-covered rock wall in the garden near the thermae.

"Why should I listen to you?" she asked. "You're probably a symptom of madness."

"I am your future self. I know what's best for you."

"That's not possible. Perhaps you are a demon come to haunt my dreams or trick me into doing exactly the wrong thing."

"Just listen to me. I know what it is you must do to avoid a lifetime of unhappiness." The figure straightened. "I hold the key."

"What is it?"

A knock sounded on the door. Livia roused herself from Jergan's arms and reached for her *stola*. It would hardly cover her. Jergan wrapped her instead in the woolen blanket he had drawn over their bodies sometime during the day.

"Who is it?" she said. Her voice was calm. The Praetorian Guard did not knock. She pulled the wool around her shoulders. It was dark outside. How long had they slept?

"Drusus Lucellus."

Jergan reached for his own tunic.

"Come in, my friend." The door opened before Jergan could don his tunic, so he held it to his loins as he stood. She could not help but admire his strong form. His muscles moved under his skin. His tangle of black hair hung down his back, the leather thong still holding the sides away from his face. Only the burns and the welts, which still stood out lividly against his flesh, marred his image.

Drusus almost shrank away from him, he looked so powerful. "My . . . my lady," Drusus said. "It is reported that Caligula has his Guard looking everywhere for you and your slave."

"Jergan is no longer a slave, Drusus. He is a freedman." She would ignore the fact that Caligula had declared him a slave again.

The fat man glanced to Jergan and nodded. "Congratulations. I hope your freedom lasts."

"Is there no word of a struggle at the palace?" Livia asked. Chaerea must have had opportunity to act by now.

"No. They say Caesar is raging and calling you a witch. The Guard has orders to bring you both to him personally when you are found."

"They have not come here yet." She touched a finger to her chin. "But since you bear my last name, they will. We must leave."

"I will lie and say you are not here," Drusus declared, puffing out his chest.

"We will be gone. And you will say, dear friend, that we used one of your rooms and paid you well like any other patron, and that you know nothing of our whereabouts at the moment." She racked her brain. Where could they go? She thought it would all have been over by now.

"You must leave the city, my lady." Jergan took one arm firmly under the woolen blanket and glared at her.

The panic rose inside her. It washed up from her belly and splashed inside her head. She blinked. "You know I can't do that." She didn't like that the panic showed in her voice.

Jergan set his lips. "They will have already searched the house and found it empty." He glanced to Drusus.

"Yes, yes." The fat man nodded. "They destroyed everything. The place is nothing but a ruin. . . . All your lovely things, Lady Lucellus."

"Then that is where we will go. But we cannot stay

long, my lady," Jergan said. "Another day, perhaps. Then either the deed is done, or we must be gone."

She looked up at him. Again, his idea was a good one. She nodded. Now the problem was how to get to the Capitoline Hill without discovery.

Jergan glanced down at the floor. "We will have need of this carpet, Drusus."

JERGAN LET THE rolled carpet gently down from his shoulder to the cracked marble of the floor in Livia's sleeping quarters and kicked away the shards from the broken busts that had once graced the room. The fine wooden furniture was fit only for firewood. The tapestries hung in shreds. It would break Livia's heart to see it so. The only things intact were the great wooden shutters that covered the windows to the garden. Which made this room her only sanctuary from the coming sun outside. He set down the lantern he had carried.

"Are you well, my lady?" He whispered by instinct in this mausoleum of a house. He heard a muffled wheeze that might have been an affirmative. "I'll get you out." He pushed at Drusus's carpet and watched it roll away, disgorging a rumpled, gasping Livia. He helped her sit, and watched her look around. "I'm sorry."

"They are only things, Jergan, in a long line of things that pass through one's life."

That brought home to him what a barrier of experience rose between them.

"Did anyone remark a huge barbarian carrying a rug through the streets?" She managed a crooked smile.

"The hour was early. Few were about. Besides, there are many barbarian slaves in your city. I am not the only one who is tall."

"Well, I suppose that's good then." Her brows knit together as she peered around.

"What is it?"

"It feels right to be back here. Almost too right. Whatever it is I can't leave, it is here, Jergan. I feel it."

"Then perhaps it is a safe place." He drew her up and sat her on the bed. Its posts were gone, but the frame was intact. "Stay here. I'll see if the Guard left anything in the larder."

"Don't let anyone see you." She was whispering, too.

"The walls around your house still stand, my lady," he chuckled. "Their stone will protect me from prying eyes."

He came back sobered. There had been a single unbroken amphora of wine. Under the rubble of shattered pottery and broken crates he had found one miraculous basket of eggs and some olives, and inside a wooden cupboard that hung open, a half round of cheese and a heel of bread. The rest of the bread, the meat, poultry, was gone, looted no doubt. The vegetables had been trodden on and spoiled. Well, they could get by on what they had. For one day. And he was determined that that was all that they would stay. Livia couldn't risk being in the city longer. The emperor might not be able to kill her, but he could hurt her. Her wounds healed, but they were wounds nonetheless. Jergan couldn't imagine seeing Livia stabbed or cut, or whipped or . . .

He was driving himself crazy with these thoughts. He set his lips and balanced the cracked platter in the hand that held the amphora while he opened the door with the arm that clasped two goblets to his side. He had to start taking control of this situation if he was going to protect her.

"I could smell you coming." Livia smiled, erasing an anxious look he had surprised there. She was worried, too. She rose to take some of his burden. "Hmmmm. Scrambled eggs and cheese and olives. Excellent. I could eat an ox."

"It was all that was left, my lady." He had called her Livia when they were making love, but since he realized how much stood between them, that familiarity seemed either an imposition or a refusal to acknowledge reality. "My lady" was safer. He poured her a goblet of wine while she sat on the bed with the platter next to her. She used the bread to scoop up some eggs. He hadn't found spoons.

"Good eggs. And you cook, too," she said around a full mouth.

"May I ask a question, my lady?" He handed her a goblet and sat beside her, one leg under himself.

"Of course. You don't have to ask permission anymore."

"I have been thinking about these attacks on you. If someone knows about your plot, why not just tell the emperor about it, and let the rest take its course? The emperor couldn't hold you, but no one knows that, do they?"

She swallowed, and took a deliberate drink of the wine to settle herself. "I have been asking myself that for a week." It seemed to upset her that she didn't know the answer. "If Asiaticus is behind the attacks, it could be because he wants to quell the plot before he reveals it. Otherwise the emperor will be mad with paranoia and a danger to everyone around him. You know the old saying, 'Don't raise a question you can't answer.' He'd make Asiaticus's life a living hell until the conspirators were captured."

Jergan nodded. That could be true. Or there could be another answer. He looked up at her.

"What?" she challenged. Then she took another sip of wine, thinking.

He chewed his way methodically through some cheese and waited.

"Or . . . it could be Chaerea himself, couldn't it?"

He nodded. She'd gotten it. That possibility was, in fact, what he was most worried about.

"I'm the only one who knows his role in the conspiracy. If he was going to reveal it to increase Caligula's dependency upon him and the Guard, he might want me dead first, so I could make no accusations. But he doesn't know who the others are."

"Has he ever asked?"

"Yes," she said slowly. "Yes. He wanted to know the quality of men he was in league with, he said. I always refused."

"And yet he may know through other ways. Could he not have had your house watched?"

"But most of the Senate come to my audiences. Titus and the others' presence wouldn't be remarked."

"Except perhaps by its frequency?" Jergan asked.

She shook her head. "It doesn't matter now. Chaerea must know who has been asking around the Senate about what would happen in case of a republic. He might miss Flavio's ploy, but Marcus and Titus would be obvious." She leaped up from the bed. "I brought Chaerea into it. I thought he was the perfect tool, uniquely placed to do the job, uniquely placed to survive it and make certain the republic survived its infancy as well. I thought he was a believer." She turned on Jergan. "It could still be Asiaticus. He said he wants to pry my secrets out of me and turn them to his advantage."

Jergan rose and took her goblet gently from her. "But if it is Chaerea, then there will be no assassination attempt. We wait in Rome for nothing, when you could be on your way to safety."

He saw the anxiety at the mere mention of leaving engulf her. She whirled, rubbing her temples. "I can't think. If it isn't Chaerea . . . then there's still a chance. He just hasn't found an opportunity. It can still work out. And I can't leave. I can't."

"Come, sit and finish eating." Jergan wouldn't press her now. At least not about that. He poured her more wine. She gulped convulsively and calmed.

"Perhaps we might profitably use our time here to discover what it is you cannot leave."

She sighed. "I've thought and thought. Clarity always seems to be just beyond the reach of my poor brain. I get this feeling of . . . of urgency. I can't explain it any other way."

"Is there a pattern to it?" he asked.

"A pattern?" Her eyes were big with fear. She was afraid of this feeling she had.

"Is it after a dream? One of *those* dreams?"

"Yes." Now she was thinking hard. "Actually, there are two separate kinds of feelings. There's the feeling that there's something I must do." She rushed on. "And then there's another feeling that something is here I cannot leave. That's different." She paused. "And of course, there's the feeling I've been having of being too . . . too *full*. Like something inside me was trying to get out. That might be the voice. It . . . it wants to control me."

The thought that she might be possessed by some kind of demon crossed his mind. If she was a witch, and more, almost something some would call a demon, could she not be possessed by some worse spirit? He closed his eyes. He didn't believe that. He didn't. The gods would not make her so perfect, so imperfectly human, so wonderful, only to let a demon possess her. He heard his father's practical voice adjuring him not to believe in the supernatural.

"You know," she was saying as he opened his eyes. Her own eyes were fixed on the remains of the small bronze statue of Pan. It lay on the floor, Pan's flute bent, his hooves crushed. "I've gotten the feeling about something I shouldn't leave most often in the garden on the way to the bath." She ripped her gaze from the statue and let it drift back to Jergan. "Near the rock wall with the vine."

He looked at her for a long moment. "As soon as it grows dark, we will examine this place and see what it is you feel is so important."

"And the last time I dreamed . . ." Her eyes grew round. "The woman, the woman that is me that I dream about . . . she was standing just there, in the garden. . . ."

"My lady?"

They heard the call together. They both knew the voice. "Lucius?" Livia breathed. "What are you doing here?"

17

LIVIA COULDN'T BELIEVE her eyes. Lucius should be well on his way to Tuscany and safety with the rest of her staff. Had something happened to them? The small man hurried into Livia's chambers, wringing his hands and moaning as he glanced first to one precious object destroyed and then to another. "My lady, I knew . . . I knew I should never have left your house."

"You would only have been killed, and lives are more precious than any of these silly things." She sat him down on the bed. "Now, tell me, are the others well?" There had been twenty on her staff, including the old man who tended the gardens and his two helpers.

"Yes, yes. They are probably outside Ostia by now."

"But why have you left them? They depend on your leadership."

He waved a hand dismissively, his eyes still darting around the room in distress. "Catia and old Nara know the way. I left Tufi in charge. The gardener's boys have their short swords. They will get to Montalcino safely."

"But I gave express orders that you accompany them," she said gently. It was not like Lucius to disobey a direct command.

"How could I leave you in such distress?" His eyes grew sad. His breathing calmed. "One cannot abandon those one loves, no matter the cost." He looked away. "No matter the cost." This last was almost a whisper.

"You can do nothing, old friend. Now go from here before anyone finds you've returned." He might have brought the Guard down on them already, if he had been seen. She glanced to Jergan and saw his hard eyes and a muscle working in his jaw. He thought the same. She put a hand on Lucius's arm to guide him to the door, but he pulled away.

"I can take care of your wants, my lady. You need to eat."

"Jergan cooked eggs for me." She smiled. "I am sated."

"I'll wager he didn't make you tea. What does a barbarian know of a fine Roman lady's needs?" Lucius's tone was almost pleading. He must truly be frightened to be so overset.

She looked again to Jergan and shrugged. The damage was already done. Sending Lucius off again just provided another chance for someone to notice him. Jergan nodded, once.

Lucius saw the exchange. He let out a breath. "I'll go to the kitchens."

"You won't find much there," Jergan called. Lucius acted as though he didn't hear.

"Excellent," she sighed. "Now I am responsible for putting him in danger as well as you."

Jergan came and put his arm around her. "I am responsible for myself. Remember, you freed me. Therefore, the choice is mine to stay or go. His, too." He nodded after Lucius.

"I wish the sun would go down." Livia began to pace. She must find out what was so important that she couldn't leave this house.

"I can go look," Jergan said. He propped his big frame on one elbow on the bed.

She stopped in her tracks. "I'm not sure you would recognize whatever it is when you see it. But I will."

"As you wish. I might mention that there is no way to hurry the sun by pacing."

She sighed. "It is only to make me feel like I am doing something."

He shrugged, a smile lurking at the corners of his mouth. "In that case, please continue."

Lucius returned with a pot of hot water and some pungent-smelling leaves. "I found a pot for steeping that wasn't broken," he said, looking around for some place to set it. He settled on a chest, now without drawers, that still stood in the corner. His hand shook as he took a small oil-skin of leaves and poured them into the water. What was that smell? Her tea usually didn't smell like that. But beggars could not choose.

"I am eternally grateful for your kindness, my lady," Lucius was saying. His voice drifted back over his shoulder, drenched with too much emotion. "I'm only sorry I can't repay you more suitably." He turned. The tea steamed in a goblet with a crack in the lip. His eyes were filled with tears, no doubt a reaction to stress.

She took the cup. It felt warm and soothing in her hands. She sipped.

The bitter taste was a shock. She looked up to Lucius. His tears were spilling now. They should. How could he think she wouldn't recognize the taste of hemlock? She lifted her brows. "Why, Lucius?" The betrayal felt like a knife in her heart. She had bought this man, owned him, freed him, and employed him for ten years. She depended on him to run her household, trusted him. He knew more of her secrets than anyone else alive, except Jergan.

"The Guard took my sister and her boy," Lucius choked. "If I don't do this, they will die in the arena."

He had bought their freedom, Livia knew.

Jergan stepped up and grabbed a fistful of his toga. "Who told you to poison her, Chaerea or Asiaticus, you little worm?"

"Neither. Neither," Lucius panted, looking frightened. "Just the soldiers who came to tell me my family had been taken."

"Did they tell you to use hemlock?" Livia asked. It was an odd choice for poisoning. One couldn't miss the bitter taste.

Lucius deflated as though all the blood had been drained from him. "That was my idea, my lady," he said. His voice was dry as dust.

The hemlock wouldn't kill her, deadly as it had been to Socrates. Perhaps a moment of stomach cramps. "Well, then, you can go and tell them you delivered the dose and claim your reward." She upended the cup and drank the whole, then handed him the cup.

"Livia!" Jergan shouted, dropping Lucius like a stone. He knocked the cup from her hand. "Are you mad?"

"It won't kill me," she assured him. She turned to the man who had betrayed her. She understood his dilemma. He did not look happy about what he'd done. But he didn't look relieved that the dose she'd taken wouldn't kill her. He might not win his family's release if Livia wasn't dead. "I have some pressing business at sunset. Then tell the Guard you've done what they asked. I hope they release your family." But she wasn't sure they would.

Her stomach cramped and she doubled over, trying to breathe. Hemlock was a forceful poison. Jergan grabbed for her and swung her onto the bed. She took a breath and relaxed. "Better now. I told you."

He leaned over her. That was odd. He looked . . . blurry. His green eyes swam as though they were underwater.

"Jergan?" The whole room seemed to float. And now there was a noise somewhere. Many feet. Shouts. Were they far away?

"What . . . what have you done, Lucius?" she managed. "That wasn't hemlock."

Jergan lifted her in his arms, his face a rippling mask of concern.

Lucius stood at the end of the bed. "Yes, it was, my lady. I needed the strong taste of hemlock to cover the essence of poppy."

"Nooooo," she wailed. "How did you know?" Had Jergan told him? The room was running together. Her limbs felt like water, too.

"When I realized you were a vampire I searched out ancient texts that told me of your kind. They were most informative. So when it came down to betraying you or letting my kin be killed, I knew what to do. I didn't tell them about decapitation. And they can't keep you drugged forever. You still have a chance to win through."

The darkness burst apart. Men clattered into the room. Jergan dropped her on the bed. He would be drawing his sword. She couldn't quite see. Lucius must have given her an incredible dose of the drug to subdue her Companion.

The room was filled with boiling movement. She couldn't make out what was happening. Her limbs felt limp and heavy. Her eyelids closed in spite of her best intentions. She must help Jergan. But she couldn't.

She was powerless for the first time in her life.

JERGAN WHIRLED, SWORD slashing. One guard went down, fingers grabbing at the blood spurting from his neck. The bastards were well armored. They could be brought down by a thrust only at the neck, the jointure at the waist, or sideways into the groin under the protective flaps of hardened leather. He tried each way in turn. Three lay at his feet. He felt a sword point find his hip and jerked back. There were too many. He had to protect Livia. The flash of steel made him think about decapitation. Fear shot through him. Lucius said he hadn't told them, but he had lied before. Or they might happen on it accidentally.

"Halt! All of you!" a voice yelled through the throng. The attack ebbed. Chaerea himself pushed his way through his men. He looked like a carrion crow come to pick their bones with his gleaming black armor and the stiff black crest on his helmet. A black cape with a border embroidered in gold swirled around him.

Jergan crouched, panting, waiting.

"Look behind you, barbarian."

Jergan felt a cold hand on his heart. He chanced a glance to the bed. A soldier held an insensible Livia by the hair, his sword lifting her chin.

"He'll slit her throat."

Or worse. Jergan let his sword clatter to the floor.

"Bind him," Chaerea ordered. Two of his minions pulled Jergan's wrists behind his back, while another confiscated the abandoned weapon.

"And you, you have done well." Chaerea clapped Lucius on the back. Lucius looked ready to cut his own throat. "What is it you gave the witch to take her powers?"

"Distilled essence of the poppy," Lucius whispered. "It takes a massive dose."

"Then you have served your purpose." Chaerea's sword slithered from its scabbard and buried itself in Lucius's belly. The man doubled over with a groan, his hands scrabbling at his abdomen and the fount of blood that gushed there.

"My sister . . ." he gasped. "Her boy . . ."

"Good fodder for the arena," Chaerea grunted. He turned to watch the guards wrap Jergan's wrists together with strips of leather. His hands would soon be numb.

Behind Chaerea, Lucius fell to his knees and toppled over. His eyes glazed. Chaerea had saved Lucius the trouble of suicide. And the man hadn't even rescued his family. Rome had ground him under her heel, as she did so many. Jergan looked to Livia. She seemed only half-conscious, though he could hear her low moaning. They had found her Achilles' heel. Even if they didn't kill her, they could make her suffer. He gritted his teeth, feeling helpless to protect her. And that was what he had sworn to do.

"Bring both of them," Chaerea barked. "Caesar awaits."

THE ENDLESS MARBLE halls of Caligula's palace were gloomy at night, in spite of the lamps and braziers that burned everywhere. Jergan looked up and saw that the ceiling had been painted with animals in exotic array, probably cheerfully gilt, now dim with smoky lamp oil and menacing. He was being marched, limping from the wound in his hip, into the bowels of the palace by the group of a dozen Praetorians. Cassius Chaerea stalked in the lead and one soldier carried a limp Livia, her head lolling so that her hair hung over his arm in a heavy black curtain. Jergan was in some pain from his hip, but he could still walk, so the ligaments hadn't been cut. If he could but get a sword . . .

Fruitless thoughts. A sword would do him no good against these odds, with an unconscious Livia to carry through endless corridors and halls. He must bide his time. He swallowed his fear, but still it churned somewhere in his gut.

Two golden doors guarded by two immense Nubian slaves with feathered spears blocked their way. Chaerea gave the Praetorian salute, but before he could announce himself, the slaves pulled open the doors. They were expected.

Inside, the echoing room was all black and green marble with huge porphyry vases and white marble busts on pedestals everywhere. Caligula looked strangely insignificant in these surroundings meant to aggrandize him. Asiaticus stood at his side, looking more imperial than the emperor himself. At the sight of the Guard and their quarry, the emperor hurried over, rubbing his hands like a child anxious for a treat.

"At last, Cassius," he said, with relish. "How ever did you subdue her?" He gave an elaborate shudder. "Did she try to disappear?"

"One of her freedmen showed us how to negate her powers."

"Well," Caesar asked sharply, "how?"

"Essence of the poppy, Caesar. We must keep her plied with it in order to hold her."

"And she was behind the plot to kill us?"

"She was," Asiaticus's voice broke in, as though to remind everyone that he was there. "Though she had compatriots. If we keep her drugged, she can't tell us who they were." He shot a sharp glance to Chaerea, and Jergan realized that these two competed for Caesar's favor as though their lives depended on it. They probably did.

"No need to question her," Chaerea countered smoothly. "I've had her confidant, Titus Delanus Andronicus, picked up today, as well as Marcus Belius and several others. They've been spreading talk of a republic in the Senate. Presumably the plan was to reestablish the republic after you had been assassinated."

"The bitch!" Caligula shrieked. "Even crucifixion is too good for her." He turned and paced to a marble bust of a regal-looking man. In a fit of pique, he pushed it over. The pristine white marble broke in several pieces. A brass plate skittered across the floor. It said "Augustus Caesar" on it. The current Caesar, so much smaller in every way than Augustus, whirled. "How can we punish her if she's too drugged to feel pain?"

Livia being drugged had a positive aspect. Jergan could be made to suffer, but Caligula was right. Livia couldn't.

"I have an idea, great Caesar," Asiaticus said. "If you reduce the drug a bit, she can suffer as much as you want."

Jergan found it hard to get breath. He twisted his hands against his bindings.

"And what if she disappears and escapes us?" Chaerea growled.

"A risk, true. But you can't have it both ways. She is drugged but cannot suffer. Or we reduce the drugs a little and chance her escape in order to torture her."

"Well." Caesar frowned. "We want to torture her. I suppose there is no choice." He walked over to the guard who held Livia and squeezed her breast through her tunic. "We should like to have her before she is tortured. But really, it isn't amusing if she sleeps through the whole." He turned to Jergan, and his look grew sly. "You haven't told me what role this slave played in the plot."

"He is a freedman, great Caesar," Asiaticus murmured.

"Did you not know that Caesar decreed him slave again?" Chaerea asked in all innocence. "Oh, that's right: you were not privileged to be there at the time."

They were like children arguing. Well, perhaps Jergan could turn that to advantage. He took a breath. "You should ask not what role I played, but what role the captain of your Guard played, great Caesar."

Caligula perked up. Chaerea stepped over to Jergan and struck him with his fist. Jergan's head snapped to the side. "The slave seeks to poison your ears with lies, Caesar."

"I think we should hear him out." Asiaticus smiled.

"Speak, slave," Caligula agreed. "It will prevent us torturing the information out of you."

"Your captain was to be the instrument of your destruction, Caesar."

"Interesting," Asiaticus murmured.

Caligula frowned and turned to Chaerea. Jergan had to give the man credit. Chaerea didn't flinch and he didn't hesitate. "Of course I engaged with her. How else was I to uncover the plot? But why would I want a republic? The Guard would surely be disbanded in a republic, since any man they backed could declare himself emperor."

How clever to remind Caesar that it was the Praetorian Guard that provided the power base on which he relied. The emperor grew thoughtful. He had not missed the point. How could Livia have been so wrong about this Chaerea? But of course, he had told her that serving Caesar soiled his honor, and Livia had believed him because she had honor, and would never serve a vile worm like the emperor. The only problem for Livia was that Chaerea lied. He had no honor.

"Whatever you are, Cassius, you are not eager to give power away." Caligula's glance slid between his advisors. "It is one of the most reliable things about you."

Jergan had to try again. "He had Livia Quintus Lucellus attacked. He wanted to prevent her telling you that he was part of the whole."

Chaerea snorted. "Do you speak of that attack by street scum some nights ago? If I wanted Livia Quintus killed, I would simply send the Guard."

Jergan watched Asiaticus. With luck, he would be scheming on how to turn this against Chaerea.

"Not if you did not want anyone to know who was behind it. The Guard uniforms are so conspicuous. . . ." Asiaticus sounded almost apologetic.

Caesar screwed up his face in disapproval as he glanced between his two most trusted advisors and wondered what to think.

"I take it you did not order her attacked, Imperial Master?" Jergan asked softly.

That startled Caesar. "No. . . . No, we did not." He wouldn't like the fact that his advisors acted on their own, without his knowledge. Let that feed his paranoia.

"Enough!" Chaerea barked. "Caesar remembers, of course, that it was I who discovered the plot, and revealed it, as part of my job of protecting his person."

"Perhaps Caesar would like to be informed earlier in the process." Asiaticus shrugged. "I could have helped you make that decision, if I, his most senior and trusted advisor, had known."

Chaerea did a most surprising thing. He bowed his head. "Forgive me, Imperial Highness. I meant only to keep one care from your shoulders. It was my mistake, and my mistake alone."

The man was clever. Jergan would give him that.

Caligula came over and patted Chaerea on the shoulder. "You always think only of our welfare, dear Captain. We are grateful to you. You have our forgiveness."

Jergan glanced to Asiaticus. He knew Chaerea had just won the bout.

"So, we will torture the woman tomorrow," the emperor continued. "And what for this slave?" He walked around Jergan. Jergan felt a palm on his buttocks that made him want to shudder in revulsion. He forced himself to stand still. It slid around his injured hip. The emperor rubbed a finger in Jergan's bloodied tunic and put the finger into his mouth. He sucked noisily. "Is he too injured for the arena? I'd like to see such a strapping creature fight for his life. In the nude, of course."

"He'd do well in the arena, Imperial Highness," Asiaticus prompted. "Barbarians are used to fighting wounded."

"Then he can be part of tomorrow's festivities. In the meantime, strip him and bring him to my private chambers, Cassius, with six of your Guard."

Jergan swallowed, his stomach going hollow. The man apparently had sex with women or with men equally. And he didn't care who knew of his proclivities. When you were emperor, who could say you nay?

"Of course," Chaerea answered. He cleared his throat. "But if I may offer a suggestion?"

Caligula frowned. "Yes?"

"Use him as you like, but spare him torture, so he may give you good sport in the arena."

Caesar's brow cleared. "Good thought, Chaerea." He turned to his political advisor. "And I was going to have you invite my sisters to join me, Decimus. But really, they have no self-restraint. They'd whine when I refused to let them torture him. They can be quite tiresome." He frowned again. This snake would turn soon on his fellow snakes. "No, I'll see him alone."

"I advise against it," Asiaticus said quietly. "The man is too dangerous, even with six of the Guard."

"You question his orders?" Chaerea challenged.

"I, too, care for his safety."

"Or perhaps you doubt my ability to control the brute,

Decimus. Remember, I have fought in the arena myself. Chaerea, see to it." And with that, Caligula waved a hand vaguely and left the room by another door. Asiaticus turned on his heel and strode after his emperor.

"Take her to a cell," Chaerea ordered. "That old crank who tends to the emperor's imagined illnesses must have some essence of poppy. I want her dosed every hour. At dawn, stop the drug entirely."

He turned to Jergan. "And give this one over to the slave handlers to be cleaned for Caesar's use." He gestured to six of his men. "Tell the attendants to be quick about their work. Then deliver him to Caesar's chambers and stay as long as the cat cares to toy with his mouse. But the slave must be in the arena when the sun reaches ten tomorrow morning. Is that clear?"

"Yes, Captain," the six said in eerie unison.

Chaerea grinned at Jergan. But the smile never reached those flat, hard eyes. "Have an entertaining evening. It will be your last."

JERGAN'S HAIR WAS still damp as he stalked, naked and limping, escorted by his fully armored guard. His skin was flushed from scrubbing. He'd been purged and his wound stitched while he hung from chains. The attendants had been impersonal and efficient. The ritual left him feeling empty and more than a little disconcerted. They'd treated him like an animal. He was a sacrifice to Caesar, self-proclaimed god of the Roman Empire. Now he was being marched to Caesar's private quarters to complete the sacrifice.

By Belatucadros's horn, he would *not* feel like a victim here. That's what they wanted. The ritual of cleansing had given him time to think. He had a plan. Asiaticus had shown him the way. The emperor was vain about his fighting prowess. Jergan's biggest problem was that he didn't know where Livia was. So the Guard would have to show him.

He straightened his back. He had once vowed to be the worst slave Livia had ever encountered. He hadn't kept that vow. He almost smiled, even here in the belly of the beast that was Rome, to think of that vow . . . and Livia. So it was time to redeem himself.

The great golden doors behind this set of Nubian giants were set with lapis lazuli and exotic corals. They opened on a vast room that looked out through columns over the city of Rome and the Fora. Jergan slid his eyes around the room. The floor was heated, of course. There was a pool from which steam rose. A giant cushioned bed with a frame holding up elaborate curtained hangings occupied the center of the room. The usual marble busts stood on pedestals scattered about the fringes. On the far wall hung some ceremonial weapons: a sword, a lance, an ax. Possibilities. Plates of meat and cheeses, fruits, and wine stood on a sideboard—an embarrassment of waste for just one man, and a scrawny one at that. The food looked as though it had hardly been touched.

Sitting in a wooden U-shaped chair was the petulant ruler himself, two nearly naked slave girls massaging his neck and shoulders.

At the entry of Jergan's contingent, the emperor jumped up, pulling his toga over his right arm. His eyes were covetous as they roved over Jergan's naked body. Apparently Caligula did have hungers. They just weren't for food.

"They have cleaned you well." He snapped his fingers at the slave girls. "You can go." They hurried from the room, their relief obvious.

The leader of Jergan's guards bowed. "How may we assist you?"

"Stand away," Caligula ordered. "But be prepared to subdue him. No swords. We want him fit for the arena tomorrow."

The guards drifted into the shadowed corners of the room, twenty, maybe thirty feet away. Jergan clenched his jaw.

"Where did we leave off when your witch-mistress spirited you away?" Caligula approached Jergan, moving sinuously. Jergan half-expected the creature to have the vertically slitted eyes of a snake. "She won't be able to help you tonight."

Jergan thought of Livia. Her image might keep him sane no matter what happened.

"We seem to remember that you were going to suck the imperial organ until it spurted into your mouth."

"I would bite off your cock before I'd suck it." Jergan stared straight ahead.

"But you know you will obey, just to spare your mistress pain."

Jergan managed a smile. "You will make her suffer no matter what I do."

Caesar looked taken aback. "We can make *you* suffer, slave."

"If you torture me, you lose the pleasure of watching me die in the arena."

"We can make your mistress's death long or short." The creature's voice was rising. He wasn't used to anyone refusing him.

"It wouldn't matter what you promised. Chaerea promised to spare Lucius Lucellus and his family. Then he killed Lucius and sent his family to the arena. Rome doesn't keep promises, so yours are worthless." Caligula's face grew redder. Jergan took some small pleasure in that.

"I might as well take your manhood if I get the chance."
Caligula would never have the courage to demand he service the imperial prick now. One threat gone. Could he
avoid the next?

"It will take you *days* to die." Caesar was trembling in
anger.

"I accept that." Jergan was hoping to deny the worm
that pleasure, too.

"Guards!" the emperor cried. They plunged out of the
shadows. "Put him on his knees."

Guards each took an arm and kicked Jergan's feet out
from under him. "Frightened of me, Emperor?" he panted
as his knees hit the marble floor. "Can't take me yourself?"

"I've fought against better than you, barbarian." Caesar
was so angry he'd dropped the imperial "we." He grabbed
a sword from one of the guards and put the point at the
back of Jergan's neck. The creature was as vain as Jergan
had hoped. "Stand away," Caligula ordered the guards.
They stepped back.

Jergan breathed. Calm descended upon him. He glanced
to the guards. Thirty feet might be enough. The weapons
hanging on the far wall were too remote to be of practical
use. But one weapon was only too near. Its point pricked
his skin at his nape.

"Spread your buttocks," the emperor hissed.

Instead, Jergan rolled out from under the sword and
landed on his feet. The guards charged forward, shouting.
Caligula's eyes were wide as Jergan plunged in, wresting
the sword from the emperor's grip by the crosspiece of
the hilt. Jergan whirled the sword into the air to grasp it
by its hilt even as he grabbed a fistful of the emperor's
toga and slammed the imperial head against the nearest

marble bust. A dull thud sounded. Jergan pulled the emperor back to his feet and laid the blade against his throat.

The guards practically skidded to a halt and stood, frozen.

"The tables are turned," Jergan panted. He couldn't escape the palace. And inside there were so many guards he couldn't hold them off. Except if the cost for capturing him was the emperor's life.

"I'll have you chopped up piece by piece," Caligula wailed.

Doors on all sides of the chamber burst open. Both Chaerea and Asiaticus charged in, in response to the guards' shouts. Apparently both had been hovering just outside. But when they saw the situation, they, too, stopped stock-still.

"You fool," Asiaticus muttered. Footsteps thundered toward the room from far away.

"Let him go," Chaerea commanded Jergan.

"Take me to Livia Quintus Lucellus. I want her freed," Jergan growled.

"You'll be dead before you reach the street." Chaerea drew himself up, trying to maintain some semblance of calm.

"Then so will your precious emperor."

It was then that Jergan saw it. A flicker of satisfaction in Chaerea's eyes. The man *wanted* him to kill the emperor. It was the worst possible outcome. It meant the emperor was of no value to him. And Chaerea could kill Jergan afterward and proclaim himself a hero. Perhaps even declare himself the next emperor. Who would stand in his way? The frightened Senate, who had to be fooled into taking power?

Jergan knew he was beaten. He'd failed Livia.

"I wonder at you, Chaerea."

Chaerea turned to that calm and cultured voice. Asiaticus stepped forward. "How could you put His Imperial Majesty in such danger?" He shook his head as if in sorrow. "To let such a barbarian alone with him. I warned you."

"He wasn't alone," Chaerea bit out. "He had six of my finest."

"You are not careful enough of our emperor's person. Strange, that."

The subject of their conversation was openly crying in Jergan's hold. Jergan could feel his silent sobs.

"It makes me question your explanation of the assassination plot." Asiaticus did not give Chaerea a chance to answer but turned to Jergan. "We have a difficult situation. You don't believe in promises. So anything I tell you will be suspect. But you cannot hold him forever. And Chaerea here won't take you to her."

"Then bring Lady Lucellus here." Jergan was grasping at straws and he knew it. He could not force them if they didn't care about their emperor. And Chaerea, at least, did not care. It might be that Asiaticus was Jergan's only ally in the room. Could Asiaticus stop Chaerea from provoking the emperor's death? Once Caligula was killed, nothing would save Jergan, or Livia, for that matter.

"I think not." Asiaticus's tone said he was truly sorry. "But we will make a more practical bargain. Caesar." This was said sharply to focus the attention of the sobbing emperor. The creature snuffled in Jergan's hold and turned his head, as much as Jergan's sword would allow, toward his advisor. "I have a delicious game for you tomorrow in the arena with this slave and Livia Quintus. He must be allowed to live, though, to perform it for you." He spoke as to a child. "Do you understand me?"

With another snuffle, Caesar nodded.

"Let him go, slave."

"What prevents you from killing me as soon as I let him go?" Jergan asked.

"The fact that your death tomorrow will be spectacular. I have a unique idea."

Jergan barked a laugh. Strangely, it might work. He would join Livia in the arena. At least he knew where she was. His own death was inevitable now. But he might be able to save her. And Asiaticus had hit upon the only believable reason Caligula would let him live.

There was still Chaerea. He stood glowering at the tableau.

Asiaticus saw Jergan staring at Chaerea. "Oh, Chaerea would not dare deprive the emperor of the game I shall propose."

Chaerea threw up his hands in disgust.

Asiaticus had won. Jergan thrust the emperor away. Caligula stumbled to his knees, then scrambled up, sniffing and adjusting his toga as though that could return his dignity.

"I-I-I-'ll . . . I-I-I-'ll . . ." Caligula seemed to be affected by his cousin's stuttering disease.

"Your sword," Asiaticus ordered.

Jergan fingered the hilt. Giving up the weapon would leave him entirely naked again. But it was of no use to him. Now only Asiaticus could prevent his immediate death. He let it clatter to the floor.

The guards started forward. Asiaticus held up a hand.

"I'll have him . . ." Caesar sputtered.

"Wait until you hear what's in my mind," Asiaticus soothed. He took the emperor's arm to steady him. The front of Caesar's tunic was damp. The sniveling creature had wet himself. "Take him to the arena," Asiaticus said conversationally to Chaerea, "and see that he's in shape to give us a good show tomorrow." He led the emperor from the room, whispering in his ear.

Chaerea glowered at Jergan. A few guards grabbed Jergan's arms while one shackled his wrists. Asiaticus must have something in mind he was sure would entertain Caligula and give him supremacy over Chaerea. And that meant that Jergan was not going to like it.

18

LIVIA WAS CHAINED. Normally that wouldn't bother her. Chains couldn't hold her. But now, now the room was swirling and there was a buzzing sound in her head and she couldn't call her Companion. She felt sick and weak, and that was so unnatural, it made her want to retch. Stone. She was surrounded by stone. The place smelled of damp earth and urine and old blood. She lifted one of her wrists, marveling at the waves of light that action sent through her field of vision. A horrible clanking sound ensued and echoed in her mind. Where was she? It was dark. The stones were damp. Underground?

She remembered someone coming, forcing her to drink. Several times. Drugs. But it had been a while now. She was feeling slightly less muddled. Were her eyes open? No. Yes.

Yes, she could see her hand in the darkness, glowing white.

Whose hand was that?

Mine.

It was the voice again. Stronger. Louder than the buzzing noise of the drugs.

"Mine, too," she said aloud. But the sound of her voice cascaded sickeningly. "Who are you?" she whispered. That was better.

I told you. I am you but from a future time. I am called Donnatella then. But once I was Livia Quintus Lucellus.

"Why are you here?" Livia whispered. Was that a stupid question? She couldn't think.

Because you made a terrible mistake. I made a mistake, and I want to rectify it.

"Can you do that?" That wasn't what she should be asking, but she couldn't think right now. She was so muddled.

I'm not sure anymore. Already things are different from the first time.

"What things?"

Little things. Big things. Chaerea didn't kill Lucius the first time.

Tears sprang to Livia's eyes. "Poor Lucius," she whispered.

I didn't forgive him then, as you have.

Livia blinked. The wavering feeling of being underwater was fading. She knew now what she must ask. "What was the mistake?"

But Donnatella didn't answer directly. She seemed caught in her own thoughts. *I've lived a life of regret. I should have broken the Rules. I almost did, or you almost do, when you see how wounded he is after he fights in the arena.*

"Jergan lives?" Hope sprang up in Livia's heart. She put her hands to her temples as the room wavered again.

Yes. You'll bury him in Montalcino. The slow failing of his body broke both our hearts.

"But how do we get away from Caligula?"

There was a pause before the voice said, *Caligula was assassinated by Chaerea when I lived your experience.*

"But Chaerea won't kill Caligula. He betrayed our plot in order to curry favor with the emperor."

I know. That's one of the little things that are different.

"Then what am I to do?"

Let me control the body we both inhabit. I'll do what's right. Trust me.

"I don't know that. I might be going insane. You might be the drugs."

In your heart you know that's not true. The drugs let me reach you through that iron will of yours. Let me in. Let down your guard.

Livia rolled her head. The room swirled. Her stomach rebelled, along with some shuddering resistance in her soul. She had always been alone. It was just she and her Companion. And now the thought that something or someone was inside her trying to get control was horrifying. "No!" she shrieked, and clutched her temples. The push inside her relented.

If Caligula lives, there will be no time to do what you must to right my mistake. So you have to escape into my time. Go to the cave in your garden. The voice receded. *Use what you find there. And hurry. There is not much time.*

Something clanked in the metal of the door. The door creaked open. "Why? Why is there not much time?"

The voice was very faint. *The machine is fading. I can feel it. . . .*

"There's not much time because the emperor has decreed your death in the arena, woman. And the death of the barbarian slave." Chaerea stood in the doorway.

"Livia," Jergan's voice cried, hoarse, behind him. "Are you all right?"

"Yes," she said, though the room still wavered and her words seemed to echo in her head. Jergan was near. He was well enough to shout to her.

"Not for long." Chaerea came into the room and bent

over her, peeling up her eyelids and staring at her pupils. "Good," he said, standing upright. "Still drugged, but conscious." He turned to Jergan. Now she could see him in the doorway, heavily chained and naked. Would they make him fight without armor, without even clothing? The voice had said he lived through this experience. She had to believe that, though the voice also had said things were not turning out as they once did. Jergan's life couldn't be part of what changed, could it?

"Asiaticus has thought up a good entertainment, I'll give him that," Chaerea muttered. "You're going to suffer, Livia Quintus."

"You are the barbarian, Chaerea. Let her go." Jergan struggled against the guards who held him. "I'll fight whatever enemy you choose."

"You'll fight anyway," Chaerea said.

"I won't give you good sport. I'll just let them kill me. The emperor will blame you for spoiling his entertainment." Jergan sounded desperate.

Chaerea laughed. "Asiaticus has ensured that you'll fight." Livia couldn't see Jergan, but she could hear his growl of frustration and the clanking of chains as they dragged him away.

"Livia," she heard him call.

"Don't hurt him," she moaned.

"Worry about yourself. Strip her," Chaerea ordered. "Wrap her in a toga and take her up to the arena." The guards stepped up and tore her clothing from her body. The buzzing sound she had been hearing resolved itself into the distant roar of a crowd.

THE GUARDS SHOVED Jergan out into the searing sunlight, bright and clear for January. He stumbled, nearly blind after the darkness of the warren below the

arena. At least Livia was safe below. But for how long? He
had never seen so many people in one place. Row upon
row of them layered up into the blue sky until they were
but dots of white and color. In such massive numbers, people did not sound human. Their voices overlapped into a
constant roar.

His nakedness should have bothered him. But he had
other fears. He looked around. He was alone in the arena.
There was a post to one side of the center with manacles
hanging from it. And to the other side of center was a
marble block like a pedestal. That was all. Did they mean
to chain him to the post and let animals tear at him? Was
the marble square a chopping block for cutting off hands?
He couldn't see his way.

Between the post and the low pedestal lay a small
round shield and a sword. He limped over to pick them
up. He must live through what would happen here today,
that he might have a chance to help Livia. He did not
know how to get her out of the dungeons under the arena
unless she could get free of the drugs and transport away.

He had to think of something. Asiaticus knew Livia
could burn.

Jergan noticed for the first time that the post and the
pedestal were positioned in front of a purple awning.
Hanging down the stone wall in front of the awning was a
white cloth with the imperial insignia of a laurel wreath
in gold thread. And in the shadows under the awning sat
Caesar and his sisters with various slaves and attendants
pouring wine, presenting plates of food. Jergan thought
he could pick out Asiaticus standing by Caesar's side.
Was that Chaerea making his way into the imperial box?

Doors on either side of the arena opened at once. The
crowd went wild in anticipation. The roar was deafening.
From one side poured what must be gladiators. Each was

a muscled professional warrior, dressed in leather armor and greaves, and carrying the same small shield Jergan wielded. But each wore an outlandish leather mask that made him look like a grotesque animal, and each carried a weapon—an ax, a trident, a mace, a pair of knives, or a lance.

Jergan quieted his breathing. At least now he knew. There were eight of them. They split into two streams as they poured in. Four ran toward the post, and four to the pedestal.

From the other door marched another contingent of the Praetorian Guard looking, as usual, like black insects with shiny carapaces. They carried a bundle wrapped in white.

Jergan froze. Livia. The purpose of the post with manacles snapped to clarity. He glanced up. The sun suddenly seemed relentless. A shiver of dread shot through him as he remembered her face and her hands the day she had freed him. Curse Asiaticus to the Underworld. Jergan hoped to Brid that Livia was still drugged.

The warrior creatures ranged themselves in front of the pedestal and the post. One of Livia's guards broke away from the group. He carried a cup, careful not to spill the contents, and placed it on the pedestal. What was in that cup?

The Praetorians took their bundle, straightened it, and fumbled under the white cloth. To Jergan's horror, they produced two small hands they clapped in the manacles. The bundle hung forlornly. Then Livia's guard marched back to the opening in the far wall through which they had come, leaving only a single soldier and the four fierce warriors crouched in front of her, their weapons bristling.

Jergan knew then. The cup held more of the drug that could give Livia surcease from pain. Asiaticus stood at the edge of the emperor's box, shouting to explain the game. They were to see a witch fry to death in the sunlight. Her champion, a slave chosen especially by the emperor, could win her life only by besting the four gladiators who surrounded her. But he could only save her pain by also besting the four who guarded the cup that held the drug. By the actions of her champion would her guilt be judged. If her champion failed, she was evil, and would be left in the sun to fry. If her champion prevailed, then she was declared a force of good, and would be spared further torture.

Jergan hefted the sword in his hand, feeling its grip. He stilled the thumping of his heart. Fear for Livia would not save her. He put away his hatred of Chaerea and Asiaticus for later. There was room only for the sword, the shield, the moves his body knew better than he knew his name.

He watched the guard tear off the cloth and drop it to the ground. The crowd gasped as they realized she was naked. Her white body, so perfectly formed, hung in her chains, her dark hair a curtain shading her face and breasts. The dark thatch at her crotch only emphasized her pallor. Shrieking applause broke out around the arena. Roman beasts. Livia began to twist in her bonds. Already that lovely skin began to redden. She did not have enough drugs in her system to forestall the pain.

He'd take the four in front of Livia first. He could get the toga and stop the burning. Then he could fight the four for the drug that would stop the pain.

Time to go on the attack. He raced to the warrior on the far right. The man had a mace. Jergan wouldn't think about what was happening to Livia. The roar of the crowd faded. All depended on what the rules of the game were. If the gladiators all descended on him at once, it might be over quickly, and there was probably nothing he could do about it.

But he was willing to bet that no one wanted this over quickly.

Sure enough, when he engaged the creature with the mace, the others hung back. They were going to let Jergan struggle on, wounded by progressive adversaries, until he finally collapsed. All the while Livia burned.

He slashed at the shield of the mace wielder, even as Livia's first moans cycled up and struck to his heart. He steeled himself. The mace thumped his shield and the spikes of the mace stuck. He braced himself and jerked. Even before he knew whether the creature had lost his grip on his weapon, Jergan thrust in, under his adversary's shield. The mace spun free. The man dropped to his knees as Jergan whirled, slashing, on the creature next to him. Jergan's blow was parried by a trident, so he spun again and slashed for the groin. His sword felt flesh, then bone, and he was away, thrusting his shield up to parry the ax of the next brute, slashing low for the thigh and, as the gladiator fell, pushing through to the fourth of his foes.

The sword that pierced his side surprised him. But it didn't stop him. As the man drew out his weapon, Jergan slashed up. Livia was screaming now. He couldn't listen. He couldn't listen to his hip or his side. He thrust backward into the neck of the man with the ax, who had gotten up and attacked from behind. Apparently, once Jergan had engaged each of them, they could attack together if he hadn't finished them. His sword seemed to swing of his own volition into the neck of the creature that held the short sword.

Four lay around him. But he was leaking blood. He braced himself and turned to Livia. His eyes told him her pristine body was red and blistering, almost as though she was melting in the sun. Her shrieks were coming from low in her belly like an animal. His senses were shocked. He was glad her hair hid her face. He scooped up the toga and threw it over her. The crowd booed. Let them.

He turned his back on her. Four to go. He could feel the blood, slick and running down his thigh. He limped across the empty space toward the four who guarded the cup. They were shaky, these gladiators. They might wear the masks of invincible beasts, but they had just seen four of their number cut down by a naked man with only a short sword and a small round shield.

Jergan breathed deep. *Forget the wound in your hip, in your side. Forget exhaustion. You are for Livia.*

Jergan wasn't certain exactly what happened next. His body acted even when his mind was dazed. He remembered the prong of the trident in his shoulder, opening the old wound. He remembered the look on the face of the young man whose mask rattled away at Jergan's blow when he realized his throat was gurgling blood and he would die in the next minute. But the details of glinting sword and arcing ax and the jarring crunch of mace all ran together.

All Jergan knew was that he stood, every muscle trembling, alone in the arena, except for the roar around him and the moans he could hear from under the toga he had thrown over the post. He threw away the sword, the shield. They clattered to the sand. He staggered to the cup on its low pedestal. It was brimming with a liquid. He staggered to his knees and reached out.

The arena seemed silent. Perhaps his hearing was going. He felt far away from himself. He clasped the cup in both hands. Some of the liquid sloshed into the sand. His chest was heaving. He mustn't spill a precious drop. Somehow he got to his feet. He turned.

He'd have to uncover Livia to feed her the elixir that would bring her relief. Oh, gods, could he do that?

The world contracted to the sand beneath his feet and the post in front of him. He staggered toward Livia.

Doors opened in the walls of the arena. Praetorian Guard rushed in from all sides, swords drawn. They circled him and Livia. They weren't going to let him give her solace. They'd kill him now. He would have failed her. He fell to his knees. Precious liquid sloshed from his cup.

Chaerea. Chaerea strode to the center of the phalanx that surrounded Jergan.

"I didn't think you could do it, barbarian. Wounded, too."

Jergan looked up. Chaerea had his sword drawn. The captain looked up toward the imperial box. Jergan followed his gaze. The sign of life or death. If the emperor put his thumb down, Chaerea would kill Jergan, and Livia would be left to face her fate alone. The whole empire knew that sign.

Caligula stood.

Around the arena the crowd began to roar. The roar took on the rhythm of a chant. Jergan couldn't make it out. He looked toward Livia, writhing in pain under the shroud of the toga.

"Kill me if you will," he yelled to Chaerea over the chanting crowd. "But not until I have given her this cup." He was begging. It was all he had left.

Fruitless, his mind whispered. *They'll never let her go. You'll die and they'll torture her, even if they cannot kill her. She will not even have the respite of death to sustain her.*

Chaerea dropped his sword.

Jergan looked up; blood was running in his eyes. Had he taken a blow to the head?

"The crowd has saved you, slave. Even an emperor cannot deny it. Give her the drug, if you have the strength."

Jergan looked around. The soldiers of the Praetorian Guard took one step back.

Jergan clasped the cup. His head felt light. The arena's sand seemed to roll like the deck of a ship. He struggled to his feet. The crowd was chanting. He staggered toward Livia. The cup was sloshing. Was he failing, even now?

He leaned against her through the cloth for balance. Her moans were low now. He took a breath and straightened. He pulled the cloth off.

Somewhere from far away he registered that her body was blistered and the blisters had broken, weeping pain. He lifted her chin. Her face was relatively untouched, protected by the curtain of her hair. He lifted the cup to her lips.

"Drink," he whispered. He slid the liquid surcease down her throat. Her eyes looked up at him, her expression soft.

"Donnatella says I should tell you that I love you."

And then her eyes swam.

Who was this Donnatella? Had Livia just said she loved him? He wasn't certain. Jergan felt himself falling. He knew his knees hit the sand. The roar of the crowd swirled around him.

And then nothing.

"NO MORE. THAT cup he gave her in the arena should keep her helpless. What if too much kills her?"

She heard the voices from far away, through a haze of pain.

"Looks to me like she's a dead woman already. Makes my stomach turn."

"Well, cover her up, then."

A sheet of some kind was shaken out over her. The

cloth tore at her burned flesh. She rolled her head. She was in a cell with bars across the entire front.

"The emperor wants to see her after the banquet. Tomorrow, if she's still alive, he'll let in the crowds for a look." The barred doors clanged shut.

"That was something, wasn't it? The way she burned? I've never seen a witch before."

"Emperor didn't like that the barbarian saved her." The voices were retreating. "But what could he do? The law of the crowd."

"The barbarian fought like a demon to save a witch." Rough laughter echoed against the stone.

"Think we should leave him in there with her?"

"Chaerea wants them each to know the other suffers."

Another clanging door.

Jergan? She rolled her head the other way. He lay across the cell from her, sprawled on one hip on the rough stones, one knee drawn up. She blinked, trying to banish the cobwebs from her brain. Was it the juice of the poppy or the pain that caused that haze before her eyes?

"It's Jergan," she whispered, trying to focus. "Good." Was he alive? She could smell the blood. It made the Companion that ran in her veins pound weakly at her consciousness for attention through the haze of drugs and pain.

He didn't answer. The voice had said he would live. She remembered that. He couldn't be dying, could he? She had the strongest feeling there was something she should do. Right here. Right now. This was the moment—for what, she didn't know.

And then she wasn't sure.

Maybe it was the wrong time.

For what? For *what*?

How long had she before the emperor or his guard returned? If she could heal enough . . . If the drugs faded . . .

SHE WAITED. THE minutes seemed like hours. But she was fairly certain even so that hours passed. The drug *was* fading. She could tell because the pain ramped up almost past endurance. She bit her lip to keep from moaning. Any sound might bring the guards down on her. She *wanted* the drug to fade. Only when her Companion was freed from the drug could the healing reach full strength. She needed to heal as fast as possible. Until she did, all her Companion's power would be diverted to healing, with none left over for translocation, even for herself, let alone to take Jergan with her. Could she heal enough to get them out of here before those dreadful men returned and killed Jergan? If he wasn't dead already. . . .

She lay with her head turned toward him, waiting for some sign of life. It all meant nothing unless he lived.

Where was Donnatella? Perhaps the pain left no room for voices in her head. Livia must know what the mistake was, besides the enigmatic "following the Rules." And what would she find behind the wall in the garden?

If she ever got back there.

If Jergan lived and it was worth getting back there.

Her thoughts tumbled over and over in the same round.

Jergan groaned.

Livia had never been so relieved in her long life. With a massive effort, she rolled to her side, then dragged herself, her body screaming with pain inside the shroud of a sheet, toward him. Already she must have healed a bit.

He raised his head, a groan escaping him.

"Jergan," she whispered. Tears filled her eyes. How did she have enough moisture left in her body to support tears?

He blinked at her. "Are you all right?" he rumbled, hoarse. A sticky trail of blood snaked down his temple and into his eyes.

"I will be." She managed a smile. Things were looking up. "You?" She could see now that his shoulder had been wounded again in the same place as before. His side was pierced. Blood was everywhere on his belly and into his groin and over his thigh.

He looked down at himself. "Looks worse than it is."

He was probably lying to her.

With a grunt of pain he pushed himself up to sitting and eased himself back to lean against the rough stone wall. She could see his senses swim. His eyes refocused. He reached out for a corner of the sheet. "Don't look," she advised.

"Those bastards."

"You're alive."

"I'm sure they will correct that soon." He gave her a worried squint. "When they find you can heal, they may just do it all over again."

"Cheerful thought."

"Thank the gods Lucius didn't tell them about decapitation." Jergan frowned.

"Don't hate him." She gasped with the effort to talk. But talking took her mind off the pain. "Asiaticus told them about the sunlight. Don't hate him, either. He may still be of use."

Jergan bent down and took her head in his lap. "I know not how to feel about that man. He is the reason I am still alive. But he told them about the sunlight."

She focused on his lips. It was all she could do. "Keep talking to me. If . . . if you can. Tell me what happened last night."

He swallowed as if to gather himself. "Caesar wanted a

night of sport with me before the games. I wasn't in the mood to be raped." He took a ragged breath. "I got a sword to his throat to keep the Guard at bay. But Chaerea wanted me to kill the worm, probably to set himself upon the throne. So I had no leverage." Talking was difficult for him as well. He continued haltingly. "Asiaticus proposed that Caesar spare me if I let him go so I could perform our little ritual in the arena. And I just needed to live until I could get to you. We made a bargain." He looked down at her ruefully. "I didn't stop you suffering."

"I would have suffered more if you'd been killed." Let him take that how he would. Even if he lived, it wasn't for long in the scheme of things. Donnatella said he would be buried in the village near her estates in Tuscany. Her heart contracted.

"Who is Donnatella?" he asked after a moment.

She started back. "How do you know Donnatella?"

"You . . . spoke of her when you were drugged."

"Oh." She swallowed. She did not want to explain this, in pain as she was. But it was Jergan asking. And secretive as she had been all her long life, she knew she could have no secrets from him. "She is probably . . . the . . . symbol of my insanity." It was difficult to say it. "Hers is the voice I hear inside my head . . . or so she says."

"Really?" He didn't sound dismayed. "Who is she?"

She sighed. "She says she is me. . . ." She gathered herself. "But as I will be ages hence."

"Do you remember what she told you to tell me?" He looked expectant.

She shook her head.

The expectancy faded from his eyes. "Just as well. You were not yourself."

Livia was relieved. She didn't want to know what Donnatella had told her to say.

"Livia," Jergan whispered. "You need strength to heal. Last time you were burned, you took blood."

"Yes," she gritted out.

"Then take blood from me."

She squinted her eyes shut. "You've lost too much already."

"These wounds? Nothing. I've fought all afternoon with wounds worse than these. And with the way you've been feeding me, I'm strong as a bull."

She smiled at him. "I'll give you that. I never saw . . . anyone fight like . . . you did today."

"I don't think you saw much of it." He pushed some hair from her forehead.

"The guards called . . . you a demon."

He shrugged a little, nodding. "Perhaps we are well matched."

"Both nearly useless." She managed another smile.

He grew serious. "That's why you must take my blood. You must get back your strength. Only you can get us out of here."

He was right about that. Even a little blood would speed the process. "But I need power to draw my canine teeth. I . . . I have to wait until I'm healed."

He chewed his lip. "They'll return."

"Not until after the banquet. I don't know . . . how long that is." Here, in the entrails of the arena, all was dark and torchlight. "But the sun has set. I feel it's late."

"Then we can't wait. You don't need your power to take blood." He hefted her into his arms, cradling her against his chest. The rasp of the fabric that swaddled her almost made her cry out. The smell of his blood was overwhelming. He . . . he was holding her head to the wound in his shoulder. Blood trickled down his chest. Her breathing grew heavy. The Companion inside her shrieked in anticipation.

"No," she murmured. "I can't."

"Yes, you can," he soothed, stroking the back of her head. He brought her closer. Her lips were almost touching the place where the blood still welled just beneath the collarbone.

"Gods, no," she protested weakly. It occurred to her that he would hold her here until her Companion got the better of her. Even now it thrilled faintly inside her. Could she withstand temptation? Even now her tongue reached out and touched the blood, almost against her will.

Copper, tangy life! Her Companion sang a tremulous chorus. Rich, thick, luxurious blood.

She was lost.

She fastened her lips to his shoulder and kissed his wound. Blood welled into her mouth and she suckled there. He rocked back and forth, holding her there, giving her the one thing she most needed. So generous. So tender, he was.

Her Companion's song swelled inside her in response to the blood. She could feel the vibrations of its energy ramping up. Already the pain seemed to be less. Or was she just distracted by the feeling of life coursing down her veins? She was *alive*.

More! She sucked harder. *The blood is the life.* And oh, she wanted life.

No! She mustn't drain Jergan. And yet the seductive song of blood hummed in her veins.

She wrenched away, panting. Jergan gently drew her back. "No," she gasped. "I have enough." It was all she could do to turn away.

He examined her face, nodded once, and let her settle into his embrace. She could feel the healing speed. Pain mingled with a furious tingle. She looked into his face. He was pale underneath the smudges of dirt and the blood. And there was an expression on his face she wasn't certain she had ever seen there. It was unmixed with puzzlement or doubt. It seemed soft but . . . sure. Could it be . . . ?

It couldn't. She couldn't think that. "All you all right? I . . . I hope I didn't take too much."

"I'm fine." He swallowed. He was lying. But it was a beloved lie because he said it for her. She dozed. She didn't know how long.

When her eyelids fluttered open, her thoughts were clearer. Her Companion sang once more in her veins in a steady chorus. Jergan, above her, was dozing fitfully. Good. He needed strength. She felt guilty for taking blood from a wounded man. He had given her blood so they might escape. She knew that. But he had done it without fear. He had trusted her to take only what she needed. He had made himself vulnerable to her.

She wanted to spend the rest of her life with this man. All the centuries. It was a crime against nature that he wasn't vampire. If he were, she would break the Rule of one to a city. Regret seeped into her.

It felt familiar, as though she had always known regret.

What had the voice inside her said? Donnatella. Already she thought of the voice as Donnatella. Her and yet not her. She racked her brain. She had been so woozy from the drugs. The voice said she lived a life of regret because of the mistake. And the mistake occurred when she saw how wounded he was from the arena and didn't break the Rules. *I almost do, or you almost do, when you see how wounded he is after he fights in the arena.*

What could it mean? He was wounded, but it was clear he would live, if she could get his wounds stitched and, of course, if they managed to escape Caesar's wrath. It . . . it had something to do with breaking the Rules, but he wasn't vampire. She needn't worry about living more than one to a city.

The regret was that he wasn't vampire.

The realization hit her like a blow. Breaking the Rules meant breaking the *cardinal* Rule of her kind. Donnatella wished she had made Jergan vampire.

It made Livia gasp in dismay. One couldn't make vampires. If one made vampires every time one fell in love and those one made did the same, the world would be littered with vampires and the tenuous balance her kind had with humans would be lost.

She would be outcast from the vampire world.

Aren't you outcast now? When was it you last saw one of them?

Was that Donnatella? Or was it just her inner self, arguing for what she wanted more than anything to do?

It didn't matter what she wanted. Jergan had never said he would stay with her longer than to see her plot through to its end. She couldn't let a single soft expression on his face lure her into thinking anything else. Even if he did feel something for her, it wouldn't last. It wasn't as though she hadn't had human lovers before. But she kept her secrets from them. She had learned that early. If they found out what she was, either they were horrified or slowly the differences between human and vampire weighed on the relationship until it collapsed in on itself.

Jergan knew. And he accepted her. There was no reason she couldn't have an interlude with him. But she didn't want just an interlude. That was why Donnatella had come back. Donnatella wanted forever.

She couldn't have forever. Jergan accepted her, but he would never agree to become vampire himself. To lose the sun, and drink human blood? To risk the madness of eternity?

If he wouldn't agree, the only recourse was subterfuge. She could infect him with the Companion without telling him. Just bite her lip and kiss his wound, and it was done.

Hardly honorable. And he would hate her for it. The only conceivable reason to make him vampire without telling him would be if he were dying. In that case she would endure his subsequent hatred in order to save him.

But he wasn't dying. He would recover from these wounds, if he could get care. She couldn't make him vampire without telling him.

But something inside her was vibrating like a plucked lute string with anxiety. Was this the moment Donnatella had warned her of? How could it be? It took three days to make a vampire after the human had been infected with the Companion. Three torturous days filled with fever during which a human must get the immunity to the parasite from constant infusions of a vampire's blood. She couldn't have him sick and weak for three days, unable to escape Caligula.

In Donnatella's experience, Chaerea had killed Caligula. Things were turning out differently this time. Jergan wasn't wounded unto death, and Caligula wasn't dead at all. He was a viper still ready to take Jergan from her. Some tiny part of her was relieved that this couldn't be the moment when she had to choose between living a lifetime of regret and breaking the cardinal Rule, only to risk Jergan's hatred of her for violating him in order to save him.

Above her, Jergan opened his eyes. He blinked twice, looked at her. Then she felt his body tense.

"What's wrong?" he asked, suddenly alert.

Was he that attuned to her moods? She shook her head. "Only that the plot will never come to fruition. Caligula is still in power. I'm not sure there is anywhere beyond his reach, even if we get out of this cell."

Yes, there is.

That was definitely not her thought. Had the pain subsided enough to let Donnatella back? She could use some advice, even the cryptic kind. *Donnatella?* But there was no answer.

Actually, even the tingling was subsiding. She slid a hand out of her makeshift shroud. The skin was red and tender, but there were no blisters.

Jergan reached for her hand, examined it. He smiled and kissed the palm. Then he lifted the sheet. He nodded, grinning. "I don't think I will ever get over my amazement at the healing. I wish I could do the same."

"Believe me, I wish you could, too." She pushed herself up to stand above him.

"Your feeling of life has returned."

She nodded and offered her hand. He took it and she pulled him up. "Now let's see if I have enough power to translocate us out of here."

He loomed over her, wavering, as she pulled the sheet under her arm and tucked it securely in around her breasts. Then she slid an arm around his waist, pulling his naked body against her. "I probably cannot take us very far. Can you walk?"

He set his mouth grimly. "Yes. They will search the city when they find us gone, and probably the road north to Tuscany, too. Maybe all roads. Where can we go to ground?"

You know. I told you where.

Donnatella. "We have unfinished business at the villa. We must see what's behind that garden wall."

Something large and iron clanked.

They looked at each other.

Many voices echoed down the stone hallway outside their cell.

"If you can do this thing, now might be a good time," Jergan whispered into her hair.

"Brace yourself for the pain."

She held him firmly to her side. *Companion!* she thought. *Give me power.*

The familiar throb of instantaneous power did not answer. There was a sluggish surge up her veins. The cell went red, but it was not a deep, powerful burgundy. It was cerise at best. A wave of panic flooded her.

"You say she is truly horrible to look at?" The voice was Caesar's. It held a small boy's relish for the grotesque, cast through a muddle of wine and excess from his banquet.

"Yes, my imperial lord, so the guards say." Chaerea.

"Then by all means, let us have a look at her."

The crowd approached. The tramp of many boots on stone echoed.

"Companion!" now she called aloud. *Please.*

The turgid power pushed up. She chanced a glance down. Blackness swirled slowly at their knees. She would need more than that to take them both out of here. She set up a little song of wanting in her mind. *Power, please, Companion. Power. We are one. Dig deep. Power, power, please. Please!*

The blackness was at their hips. Just a little more.

"He fought well, did he not, Cassius? I was surprised. If we let him heal, perhaps he can fight again. I'd like to see him have regular service in the arena."

Livia pushed the panic down. She could not listen. She could not look at the faces that were even now appearing outside the cell door. Caligula, petulant and smug, Chaerea, impassive, and Asiaticus, with his usual remote silver serenity.

In another moment it would be too late. She created an image in her mind of reaching down, into the pit of her stomach, and grabbing everything she had, everything she was. "Companion!" she shrieked.

The world snapped to scarlet. Blackness snaked up around them and the cell disappeared even as she heard Jergan's shout of pain.

19

SHE'D BEEN TRYING for her villa. It was perhaps a mile, maybe less, from the stone arena that Stratius Taurus had built seventy years ago. But she was lucky to get them outside the arena walls. They popped into space in the darkness cast by the triumphal arch. Jergan sagged against the stone, cradling his side. She glanced around. The moon was a sliver setting low in the sky. Caesar had come to the arena this late just to see a badly burned woman. The man was not human, at least not a sane human.

A pang of regret that she could not rid the empire of him flashed through her. Her plans lay in a shambles. Her fellow conspirators and friends were in prison. All would soon be dead if they were not already. Lucius was dead. She could only hope her servants would make it to Tuscany. She and Jergan would be hunted.

All her hopes were lost.

Except one. She glanced up to Jergan. She couldn't put him through another translocation.

Besides, you need to save your power.

Donnatella's voice was getting stronger again. She was probably waiting inside Livia just to control her. But Livia was getting stronger, too. She pulled Jergan upright. "We must go."

He straightened, though it was obviously painful. He

held his side. But he nodded with some semblance of crispness and looked around.

This area of public buildings near the arena was almost deserted this late at night. Good thing. A naked, bleeding man would attract attention. Caligula and company would be coming out of the arena shortly. They'd try to guess which way she and Jergan had gone.

They would expect her to avoid the Palatine Hill, crowned with the palaces of emperors and senators because the air was better there. Caligula's palace was there next to the Temple of Jupiter. He had incorporated a vestibule of the temple into its structure. He was that sure he was a god himself. No one would expect her to go right by his palace.

She started up the hill, keeping to the side under the line of cypress trees that lined the street, her arm around Jergan's waist for support. She pulled his arm over her shoulders, as though they were just a pair of lovers wending their way home after a tryst among the temples. They were at the top of the hill when she heard the distant commotion behind them at the arena. She dared not turn to look. But even Jergan must have heard it, for he quickened his pace.

They struggled by Caligula's palace, and the house where Augustus had been born. By the time she and Jergan got to the ruins of her villa, she was half-supporting him. Good thing it was not daylight, or their pursuers would be able to simply follow the trail of blood. Would they ever believe that Livia and Jergan would return to the very place they had been captured?

Venus and Vulcan, she hoped not.

Her strength had been increasing all the way home, along with the full feeling she'd had since the night she bought Jergan. Soon she would be back to nearly normal strength, thanks to Jergan's offering. She'd need blood again tomorrow, from someone besides Jergan, but that could wait. First there had to be a tomorrow worth living for.

"Stay here," she said, laying him on a chaise in the audience room of her villa. "I'm going to see what's behind that garden wall."

Take him with you! Donnatella apparently felt ready to make another appearance. *And take a lantern.*

"Not without me," Jergan panted as though he could hear Donnatella. He pushed himself upright. The man had courage to spare.

"Wait while I get a lantern." She hurried away, hoping it had not been broken in the fight. In her bedroom, the lantern stood on the floor in the corner where they had left it. She saw well in the dark, but Donnatella apparently knew she would need more. Dared she trust something or someone that was trying to control her?

"Steady yourself," she muttered. "It's only a lantern. What harm can that do?"

Quickly! Can't you hurry?

"I'm doing the best I can," she said as she ran back into the audience room.

"What?" Jergan muttered.

"It's Donnatella. As I get stronger, she does, too." Livia waited for him to call her crazy, but he didn't. He set his jaw and she pulled him up. Together they staggered to the back of the villa.

The pungent scent of olive trees hung in the cool January air, along with the smell of the rosemary and sage bushes. The fall of vine over the rock wall ahead seemed to draw her.

"This is the place," she said to Jergan as they stood in front of it.

Yes! Donnatella hissed inside her. Whatever Donnatella wanted her to do, it lay behind this vine and this wall. And whatever it was, Donnatella thought it could save her from Caesar.

Livia pulled the vines aside. They were thick with years of growth, green still in January, but without a sign yet of the purple cascade of flowers that would come in the next month or so.

She was hardly surprised to see the great metal strap that acted as a handle on a door barely visible because it, too, was made of stone. She glanced to Jergan.

Hurry, fool! Donnatella hissed at her. *It's fading even now. I feel it.*

Jergan nodded. What was there to say? The whole thing had a feeling of inevitability.

Livia jerked the door handle with all her strength. It creaked open slowly. Inside there was a pit of blackness and a smell of decay.

Jergan held his nose. "Smells like a battlefield where no one bothered to bury the dead."

She knew what it was. "It's a Christian catacomb." She had been here before, in some life, in some time. "They like to set their dead on shelves and let them turn to dust." She felt Donnatella hovering inside her. The full feeling was approaching unbearable. Had she been here, or had Donnatella? It seemed almost as if they were one and the same. She couldn't trust anyone who wanted control of her mind, especially one who had the same iron will and determination that she herself did.

"On your property?" Jergan asked.

She raised her lamp. "It probably has another entrance down at the bottom of the hill on the other side." Stairs cut into the rock headed downward.

"Hard to believe this is what you couldn't bear to leave."

"It isn't the burial ground. It's something else." It was just on the tip of her mind. "But it's down there." She started down holding the lamp high. Jergan leaned against the stone wall and staggered after her.

At the bottom of the stairs the smell was worse. Rats skittered away. But the corridor led ahead. She had been down this corridor before. In the dark. "This is going to be gruesome," she murmured.

"I've seen death in my time." His voice was grim.

They started ahead. Livia kept her eyes on the corridor ahead and not on the rotting corpses that lay in the rectangular niches on each side. The shadows from the lamp swung wildly, as it illuminated flesh moving and alive with maggots or already stretched and dry behind curtains of spiderwebs.

"Just the place to spend some time," Jergan muttered.

The corridor ended in an archway. As they approached, she caught glimpses of gleaming gold beyond in the light from the swinging lamp. Was it a treasure of some kind? A feeling of unbearable urgency twisted inside her. She was approaching a crisis, both inside and out. She'd have a decision to make in a moment. It would change the rest of her life.

Livia walked forward into a large room. Jergan ducked his head to enter just behind her.

They gasped in unison.

A huge . . . something . . . made entirely of bronze loomed above them in the light. It was set with impossibly large jewels that sparkled in the lamplight. Wheels of every size with teeth around the outside interlocked in fascinating complexity. In the front was a long golden rod topped with an immense diamond. Livia had no eyes for the dusty niches that rose behind it. The gleaming metal seemed to bang at her consciousness. Was this what Donnatella thought would save them?

"What is it?" Jergan whispered.

"I . . . I don't know." She rubbed her temples. Pain shot through her head.

Let me in! Donnatella was shrieking. *You must let me in.*

"It looks like a mill of some kind." He glanced to Livia. "What's wrong?"

She couldn't answer. The fullness and the shrieking inside her were too much.

Then, as they watched, the entire huge contraption faded. It was as though she was seeing it through a light mist.

Then it popped back into clarity.

The headache stopped. The shrieking stopped. She could feel Jergan holding her shoulders. He was staring at the giant machine, too.

I can tell you. I can save you. Donnatella's voice was calm. *But you have to let me in.*

"I won't let you control me," she said. She was looking at Jergan, though she was talking to Donnatella.

Was I really this stubborn? No choice, Livia. Your chance is fading even now. His chance.

"I don't want to control you, Livia," Jergan said, puzzled.

The mist rose again. The machine faded. Livia held her breath. It seemed forever until it again flickered back to clarity.

Do you love him?

And that decided her.

She did love him. And this crazy part of her that may or may not have lived through this whole thing before thought it knew how to save him. So she would let Donnatella in.

Jergan's head snapped to the side, listening.

How had she missed it? There were people in the garden above them.

Jergan looked at her. They both knew who it probably was. Praetorian Guard.

Now or never.

She took a breath and closed her eyes. "Very well," she said out loud. "Do as you will."

She wasn't sure what she expected to feel, but the comfortable thunk of realization wasn't it. She had a flash of a grave, on a hilltop in Montalcino. Sorrow washed over her, more sorrow and regret than she thought she could bear. Then a flash of a man, an incredibly handsome man with his father's green eyes and dark hair. Gian. She knew with a certainty that she was already pregnant with Gian from her days and nights of making love with Jergan. A baby! So rare for their kind. Pride and love flashed through her. Other pictures, other flashes of emotion, sang in her memory, with strange houses and strange carts and strange people. Faster and faster they whirled. She was panting so hard she thought she might faint.

"Livia. Livia!" A voice cut through the whirl. Jergan was shaking her. "What's wrong?"

She took a breath and held it. The carousel of images and emotions stilled. She knew what a carousel was. That was surprising.

She glanced to the machine, blinking. "It's a time machine. A man named Leonardo made it. In the future, I am called Donnatella. And it brought me back from a long time in the future to rectify a terrible mistake I made. The machine can take us forward to that time. But we don't have long to use it. It's fading."

There were shouts in the garden above them. Jergan looked to the machine glowing there in the dusty catacomb. He frowned. "Are you sure?"

"For the first time, yes. Two versions of me can't exist in the same time. So when Donnatella came back, she merged into me. That's why I feel so overflowing and why there seems to be a part of me that talks to me, and knows what will happen. She's been able to come out only in dreams or when I was drugged, because I wouldn't let her take me over." She saw his look. "I know how it sounds. But for the first time, I am absolutely sure I'm not crazy."

He glanced again to the machine, then back to her. "I guess there has to be some explanation for this thing, and what has been happening to you. That is as good as any."

She smiled. He was better at trusting than she was. Who would have thought it from a barbarian? "I had to acknowledge her and yield her a place."

"Does she still talk to you?"

Livia raised her brows. *Donnatella?* she called. There was no answer. "I don't know. But I know everything she experienced, everything she would have thought about what is happening. She thinks we can escape Caligula with this machine."

"Now why would you want to escape us when we've had so much fun together?"

Both she and Jergan snapped their heads to the doorway. The emperor lounged on a staff, his head cocked, gazing up at the machine behind them. "We had to insist that this house be searched. You thought she was at Drusus Lucellus's brothel." This was directed at Chaerea and Asiaticus, directly behind him. "We would have missed her entirely. Luckily, your emperor is more astute than you are." He strolled into the room, followed by his advisors. A host of Praetorian Guard thundered into the passage behind them. Several could be seen in the arch of the entrance. "A machine, you say, that allows one to go back and forth in time? Interesting. How does it work?" Light increased as another lantern was passed forward to Chaerea. Livia saw Jergan glance around the corners of the room for another exit. There wasn't one. At least not from this room.

"I . . . I don't know," she said. Could she pull the lever, draw her power, and escape with all these people in the room? It had taken some time for the machine to work the last time.

"Then you are clearly lying about its purpose." Caligula fingered a great ruby winking in the largest gear. "A fortune, though, if it were dismantled." He turned around, avarice gleaming in his eyes. "Decimus, we claim this thing for the Roman Imperial Treasury."

Asiaticus bowed. "Yes, Caesar." He couldn't keep his eyes off the machine, though. Neither could Chaerea.

Livia thought frantically. There had to be a way to use the machine.

The emperor turned and surveyed Livia. "You have healed, Livia Quintus Lucellus, just as Decimus thought you could. We might use you for entertainment in the arena again, but we don't have any drugs to hand. Therefore, you are useless to us. We wonder you haven't disappeared already, witch." He put a mocking finger to his lips. "Ah, but of course, you don't want to leave this device, or this slave, behind." He paused in thought. "If disappearing is your power, though, you can do no harm." He made a sweeping movement with his hands. "So we will take your slave and your machine. Disappear now; go."

Livia wet her lips. "You have no idea what you have

until I show you. Taking the jewels and melting the bronze would realize only a millionth of its value to you."

"Really?"

Now she had his interest. "The future is richer than your poor imagination can conceive. There are whole continents full of gold, west beyond the gates of Gibraltar. Ships come home with treasure as ballast. And slaves? Oh, my dear emperor, slaves abound. Still, they are hardly enough to work the rich lands. These continents are called the Americas."

"You are making this up." But he wanted to believe. Even Chaerea and Asiaticus were at least speculating.

"I could not make up so wild a story. Did you know that the cult who buries their dead here someday rules the spiritual lives of most of the known world from Rome?"

"The Christ cult?" His eyes were wide.

She nodded. "The very same. They build a church across the river Tiber richer than anything you have ever seen."

"But we have plans to wipe them out." Chaerea sounded puzzled, as though if he planned it, a scheme could not possibly fail.

"You will only make martyrs and more believers, Chaerea." She said it kindly, as though it came from experience. Which it did.

"A larger world to rule. . . ." Caligula rubbed his chin. "We would see a demonstration of this machine." This was clearly an order.

Livia managed not to smile. She glanced to Jergan. Their son would be so much like him. She might get him out of this yet. It all depended on the machine. "Yes, Caesar."

She turned to the machine just as it misted over again.

"What was that?" Caligula yelled. The guards and

Chaerea pulled out their swords. Asiaticus stepped back a pace.

Livia held her breath. She could feel Jergan doing the same.

The machine snapped back to clarity. She took a breath. It had taken longer this time. "There is not much time to make use of this machine, Caesar, else it will disappear forever. And only I can use it. It takes a witch's power."

"Then do so," he screeched. The fact that the machine had almost disappeared apparently had convinced him her wild story was true.

She glanced to Jergan, silently telling him to be ready, and turned to the rod with the diamond on it. She knew what to do. If she had enough power to run it. If the machine stayed in place long enough to try.

Livia called to her Companion, "Power!" She said it aloud, so they could hear it. Much more impressive. Her Companion had been strengthening minute by minute on the way home. Was it enough? The familiar feeling of power surging up her veins came over her. They would feel the vibrations in the room ramping up, just as she did. Thank Jergan for his precious blood, given when he had little to spare. She pressed down the whirling blackness at her feet. But she could hear gasps behind her as they saw it. Her hair began to float around her head. It was time.

She grasped the diamond knob of the lever and pulled. The huge gear above her began to grind, sending all the other gears into frantic motion. "Companion, more!" she shouted into the charged atmosphere. The feeling of life and power surged again. The gears spun faster.

She tried to concentrate only on the whirling machine. She would need even more power to bring on the glow. It would take everything she had.

It occurred to her, as she watched the gears whir faster, that maybe the fact that Donnatella came back had caused the changes between what was happening now and what Donnatella had experienced. Lucius dying. Caligula living.

"Power," she screamed, and the word was torn from her belly. The surge was almost painful. She began to glow. "I need your strength, Jergan," she shouted. He took her hand through the white corona of light and squeezed it. It did give her strength, even if she had said it only to get him into position to be flung forward in time with her.

They would go forward into time and skip the intervening centuries.

She and Jergan would not be here. Gian would not be born here. So everything he had done in the centuries between now and Donnatella's time would not be done. Everything she had done. Would there be no Renaissance without her? That was unthinkable. And how would Leonardo know to make the machine? It was all too confusing.

Her body was taut inside the glow. The machine was a blur of movement. Things seemed to be moving faster.

Then everything slowed. She saw herself and Jergan, Caligula and the others, as from a distance through the glow in the room. Chaerea and Asiaticus were afraid. Caligula was laughing and laughing and couldn't stop. This was the moment for action, and she wasn't sure.

And then she was.

With a cry, she jerked backward, pulling Jergan with her.

She watched Caligula run forward, a maniacal gleam in his eyes. Chaerea grabbed for him. "I'll rule a larger world," the emperor yelled, losing his balance.

Livia and Jergan fell to the ground.

But power still hummed in the air. The machine stopped entirely. Caligula fell past them, stumbling into the machine. Time stretched and snapped forward. Everyone in the room screamed, including Livia and Jergan, as the air seemed to tear itself apart.

Darkness fell. There was no glow. Even the lanterns were out.

Livia struggled up, groping for Jergan. Outside the room, she could hear the soldiers yelling, asking what had happened. Only a few had seen the machine or that it had disappeared. Boots scraped into the room. A lantern flickered. Livia looked up and saw a cherub-faced young man in a guard's uniform hold it high and look around, eyes wide. It was the soldier who had been the head of Claudius's guard.

The room was empty, except for the nichelike crypts that lined it, and those trying to gather their wits and rise from the dusty floor. The machine was gone.

As was their only chance to escape to the future.

What had she done? Jergan looked at her with big eyes. She crawled into his arms. "It wasn't right," she whispered. "It wasn't right to go."

"Where is the emperor?" Asiaticus coughed, getting to his feet.

Everyone looked around.

But Caligula had disappeared. Did he go back to the crypt under the Basilica of the Duomo? The machine had been fading. Who knew whether it could actually return all the way to the place and time from which it came?

"You've killed him," Chaerea accused, pointing at Livia. But there was a secret smile of satisfaction gleaming in his eyes. Now they would run Jergan through, and she'd have lost the one thing she had lived for, traveled through time for. She would have lost everything.

Unless . . .

She glanced to Asiaticus. He was confused. She willed

him to raise his eyes to hers. His gaze drifted up and she held it. He must see what she was about to give him as the incredible opportunity it was. "You pushed Caesar into the machine, Chaerea." She let her voice carry. "You killed the emperor." Several of the Guard positioned in the doorway turned startled eyes toward their captain.

"N-nonsense," Chaerea sputtered.

Asiaticus rose to his full height. His silver hair gleamed in the lamplight. The man was really amazingly calm. "Arrest this man!" His voice was that of a born orator. It carried through the catacombs. The Guard hovered, uncertain.

"Touch me and I'll have you crucified," Chaerea growled.

"My dear Chaerea, the captain of the Guard serves at the whim of the emperor, at least ostensibly." Asiaticus sighed in mock resignation. "And as of one minute ago, we have no emperor, directly through your act." He grabbed the cherub-faced soldier. "You are the new captain of the Praetorian Guard. The Guard will be essential to keeping order in the next days, and protecting the new emperor until he can be voted on by the Senate and installed."

"Me, sir?" the lad asked, incredulous.

"If you show your mettle, you'll keep the job." Asiaticus patted him on the back. "Now give the order."

The cherub's eyes sifted through the possibilities, and he liked his chances. "Take him," he said to the others. "A tribunal will sort it out." The Guard surged forward. Several had doubt in their eyes at handling their commander, but they had a direct order from the man who had just been named the new captain. And they were shaken by the fact that their old captain was being accused of murdering the emperor.

They'll do it, she thought.

The cherub glanced to Asiaticus as Chaerea was hustled out, fuming. "I will have your full support?"

"What is your name, boy?" Ambition flashed through the advisor's eyes.

"Priaus Anticus Gratus, sir."

"Well, now I know how to name the new captain of the Praetorian Guard. Take Chaerea to the cells below the arena, Gratus. They are closest. Then bring a contingent to the palace. The new emperor will need protection."

"And . . . and who might that be, sir?" The cherub frowned.

"Who better than me?" Asiaticus asked, as though the thought had just occurred. "I have been the only one who cared about the empire for some time now, one way or another."

Gratus nodded, thoughtful. But no "Hail, Caesar" spilled from his lips. "The Guard has always supported the Claudian line."

Asiaticus waved a deprecating hand. "The only one left of that line—"

"Is Tiberius Claudius Drusus Nero Germanicus," Gratus interrupted.

Asiaticus narrowed his eyes. "You can be replaced as easily as you were promoted."

Gratus blinked twice. "If you think replacing me would have a different result, then by all means do so." He cocked his head and studied Asiaticus. "However, the emperor would need an advisor."

Asiaticus sighed and stared at the ceiling of the crypt. He could not do it without the Guard's support. And the Guard stood for Claudius, wonder of wonders. Livia realized that she was seeing an empire negotiated between a canny realist and a boy soldier.

"I suppose chief advisor is almost as good as emperor."

Gratus nodded. "You shall have the Guard's full support, sir, as advisor, as long as Claudius has yours." Gratus turned on his heel and left.

The corridor cleared. But Asiaticus made no move to leave. Livia sat, clutching Jergan. His breath came in ragged gasps. He'd lost much blood, more than warranted, thanks to her. She must get him to safety and stitch his wounds. Could he stand another bout of transporting? Did she have enough power left to transport? And where would they go? She considered using compulsion to force Asiaticus to let them go. But perhaps it wasn't necessary. If Asiaticus had wanted to imprison them, he would have ordered the Guard to take them as well as Chaerea.

"So what will you do with us?"

"What does one do with a witch who disappears and heals impossible injuries and seems to command even time? If that's really what just happened." Asiaticus tapped his lips with one finger. "I hardly think I can imprison you. I'm not sure I can kill you. But you plotted to kill Caesar and fomented all this talk about the republic. Did you really think those bickering fools in the Senate could hold together an empire this complex?" Now he seemed truly curious.

"A younger self did." She sighed. "The one who planned the assassination."

"And you aren't a younger self?"

"Not entirely. Now I'm mixed with the me who came back with that machine." She looked at him steadily, daring him to contradict her, with what he had just seen.

He shook his head. "A republic could never hold."

"It did once before." This, surprisingly, came from Jergan. The history of the empire was known even as far as

Britannia. In some ways he was defending her and her naïveté.

"Simpler times, my barbarian, simpler times." Asiaticus shook his head. "The empire was much smaller, the problems smaller, too."

"Maybe the empire should fall," Jergan said through gritted teeth.

"Maybe." Asiaticus smiled. "But for all its faults, it spreads roads and rule of law, learning, and . . . efficiency. The world runs better when it is run by Rome, in spite of the debauchery in the city itself." He looked to Livia. Curiosity flitted through his eyes. "Does it fall?"

He believed her. "Not for three hundred–some years."

"How?"

"Sacked by the Goths."

"I'm glad I shan't be here to see it. And after?"

"Darkness. For almost a thousand years. It takes me three hundred years to get all the elements in place for the Renaissance, once I see my way clear."

"I notice you didn't protest Claudius."

"It turns out he's a good emperor, in his way, a capable administrator."

Asiaticus blew out the breath he'd been holding. "So we win through. Now he can admit his cunning."

"You knew?"

Asiaticus chuffed a weary laugh. "It took me a while. He is that clever."

"We could do worse. Advise him well."

"Anything in particular you'd like him to accomplish?"

A strange tribute from a strange man. "More aqueducts should be built to provide more arable land so the city doesn't starve in winter. He'll expand the empire, too." She wouldn't say his primary conquest would be

Britannia. That would only hurt Jergan. And there was no use telling Asiaticus that ultimately Claudius would execute him.

Asiaticus nodded and turned on his heel.

"Wait," she called. "Free Titus and the others."

He paused. "Titus is already in Elysium," he said with his back still turned. "His heart gave out when Chaerea arrested him. I'll free the others. They're nothing without your leadership." Still he paused. "I don't have to tell you that neither of you will be welcome in Rome?"

Poor Titus. Had he died that way in Donnatella's experience? She couldn't quite remember. "I was thinking of going north, to Tuscany."

"And the slave?"

She glanced up to Jergan. "There is no slave here, only a free citizen of Centii on the island of Britannia. He goes where he will."

"He would be advised to leave as soon as he is able."

Asiaticus was gone. She heard his sandals on the stone stairs.

She stood and reached a hand to Jergan, who was looking very pale. "Come. Let's get you stitched up."

"The house is a shambles," he muttered, staggering to his feet as she pulled him up.

"Nothing money can't cure." She put her arm around him. They had made it through. And everyone thought Chaerea killed Caligula. History seemed to be reverting to the river channel it had already cut in time. Did that mean that all Donnatella's effort to come back and change the fact that Jergan did not live as long as she did was in vain?

She took a breath and they started up the stairs toward fresh air and a new start. But maybe it was an old start. He would stay with her, if history had its way. He wouldn't go back to Britannia. They would have a few years of love tinged with regret. They would have Gian. That at least. But now she knew she wanted more.

20

LIVIA GLANCED UP from where she sat on the side of the bed. The clatter in the street outside was even louder than the racket that had been going on all afternoon. The city was celebrating. Apparently, the Senate had finally confirmed Claudius as emperor. All this noise might wake Jergan, and he had just gotten to sleep. But he did not stir. His long hair tangled on the pillow. His skin was a rich color against the white linen of the bed. The only times she had left his side in the past week were once to attend the funeral of Titus and once to augment her strength with two cups of blood at Drusus Lucellus's place of business.

The thud of many boots stopped outside her door. Livia rose quickly. That could only mean trouble. Jergan was getting his strength back, but it was slow going. He needed at least another week before she would risk starting for Tuscany. So there was no avoiding whatever stopped outside their door.

Maybe it isn't trouble. She had grown used to Donnatella's voice. The full feeling of two of herself inside had come to seem almost natural. Sometimes she couldn't tell Donnatella apart from her own thoughts. They were in new territory together, never quite knowing whether what Donnatella had experienced would be exactly what happened in Livia's new experience. What did not seem natural was the confusion she felt about questions like destiny, and whether one could change the world at all. Donnatella had come back to change things. But maybe that wasn't possible.

Someone pounded on the street door. Livia hurried out of her bedroom. The house was almost bare but clean and livable again. The rubble of broken furniture had been cleared away. The larder was again stocked. She stopped in the front courtyard. One of the servants who had been sent by Drusus Lucellus hovered near the door. It reverberated with a pounding demand for entrance. She smiled reassurance to him, and nodded to him to open it.

Gratus, the new captain of the Praetorian Guard, stood in the doorway. His cherub face had taken on a new gravity. It was rumored he had whisked Claudius to the Guard's camp for safekeeping while the Senate wrangled over whether to confirm him. Livia's dream of a republic had never had a chance. A depressed feeling of being totally ineffectual had hung around her all week.

"What do you want, Gratus?" she asked. If he thought to betray Asiaticus's promise and try to take her or Jergan prisoner again, he would have a fight on his hands. He did not know the half of her powers.

"It is not what I want, Livia Quintus. It is what the new emperor wants." Gratus stood aside, and Claudius limped through the door into the courtyard, followed by a cadre of guards and Caligula's sisters, Julia Lavilla and Agrippina. "I present Tiberius Claudius Caesar Augustus Germanicus."

What was toward? Why would Claudius bring those two here? "Emperor." Livia smiled as she bowed. "I see you have adopted the name of your grandfather, Augustus. A wise tribute." It reminded everyone that he was the only male left in the line of Augustus. Claudius would need the gravitas of his grandfather to overcome the impression, still held by some, that he was not fit to be emperor. "January 24 will be hailed as a propitious day for Rome in days to come."

He looked amused and sighed. "I n-never wanted this. I hope y-you know that."

"Sometimes history cannot be denied." That thought made her wince.

"I h-hope I am up to this task."

"You will be." Of that she was sure, if of nothing else.

"Decimus says you are a witch who knows the f-future."

"I think I know very little, even about the present."

"I w-want to ask you questions, but it may be b-better not to know."

"You are wiser than Asiaticus." Claudius's stutter was much improved. She glanced to Julia and Agrippina. They were obviously frightened. They had never treated Claudius well, and now he was the emperor. They looked as though they had no idea why they were here, either.

"May I offer the emperor whatever my poor house can provide in hospitality?" Livia asked.

Claudius shook his head. "We do not wish to d-disturb you. But we have need of your wisdom. It will take but a m-moment of your time." The emperor had slipped into the imperial "we," but he didn't use it naturally.

Behind her, Livia felt Jergan's presence. She turned. He stood, pale but still imposing, in the doorway to the inner house. His hand rested on the pommel of his sword in its scabbard. He had donned a white tunic, and his sandals were hastily tied. He glanced from Gratus and the Guard to Julia and Agrippina and his face hardened into a scowl.

Claudius motioned him forward. "You may assist in this matter, Jergan Britannicus Lucellus, if you feel up to it."

Livia saw Jergan grow wary. "I am well. What do you wish, Caesar?" Of course Jergan wasn't well yet. His eyes had dark half-circles smudged under them.

"The first duties of a new emperor are judicial. I have pardoned those senators who were involved in the plot against my cousin."

Livia let out a breath of relief. If only Titus could have lived to be among them.

"However, Cassius Chaerea is another story." Caesar frowned. "He came before us this afternoon with a wild story of golden wheels and jewels the size of your fist and said my cousin had been thrown forward in time, not killed." He shook his head and shrugged. "Did he think to gain clemency with such a ridiculous lie?"

The cherub-faced Gratus remained impassive. He could have testified for his former commander. Gratus had seen the machine. But then he would not have retained his new rank.

"What will happen to him?" Livia asked.

"It has already h-happened. His head is d-displayed outside the Temple of Jupiter by now." Claudius raised his brows. "It would n-not do to let him linger and attract d-dissidents to foment rebellion."

History had righted itself.

"And what of the imperial funeral?" Jergan came up to stand just behind her. By the gods, how had she not seen it? There was no body to carry through the streets. Surely that would have bolstered Chaerea's story.

But she had reckoned without Gratus. "The crowd for the funeral procession was disappointed, but the corpse of the emperor was too disfigured to allow anything but a shrouded litter to feed their grief." And he gave a cherub's smile.

Livia wondered whose body was inside that litter.

"And n-now, there is another judgment n-necessary."
Claudius glanced to Julia and Agrippina. "We're afraid
where it c-comes to our own family, we might not b-be ob-
jective. What does one do with our c-cousins? They were
our dead emperor's m-most loyal supporters. Should they
be k-killed before they can intrigue against me? I . . . I
m-mean *we* are afraid we n-need your assistance. I might
be tempted to l-leniency. But they have w-wronged you as
well. What should become of them?"

Julia burst into tears. Agrippina chewed her lip. "Great
Caesar, spare us," Julia blubbered. "We meant no harm to
you. We just poked fun. We thought you liked it."

Claudius stilled all speech with a frown. "We leave
your f-fate to Livia Quintus and Jergan Britannicus.
B-beg for mercy from them."

Julia didn't hesitate. She threw herself on her knees
and actually wrung her hands. "Please, please be merciful
with us. You don't know what it was like to be his sister."

Agrippina took a breath and sank slowly to the tiles of
the courtyard. She did not supplicate but bowed her head.

Livia looked up at Jergan. He was the one who had felt
their irons sear his flesh. If he needed revenge to put that
incident behind him, then this was his chance. "I cannot
judge them, Caesar. I leave that to Jergan Britannicus."

The courtyard was silent except for Julia's sobs. Livia
could see a muscle working in Jergan's jaw. The Guard
stood impassive. Claudius merely waited.

Jergan blinked slowly. "Their brother made them fear
for their lives if they did not obey him. Yet they craved
what that obedience brought—power and privilege. They
used their position to inflict pain on others." He took a
breath, trying to decide. She saw his face harden. He was
going to order them to their death. He was a man, a warrior. Of course he would kill them.

They were banished, Donnatella said.

Livia licked her lips. The important thing was Jergan. The way forward for him was not killing. Yet he needed to put their crimes behind him.

"I can think of punishments worse than death," she blurted. "At least for these two."

He turned toward her and his expression softened. "Say them, Livia."

"Banish them from Rome to a remote place, with no slaves. Their lives should be ordered by a eunuch, who will direct an ascetic life for them, that they may contemplate the spiritual side of man, which they have so neglected."

Jergan glanced to the sisters. The look of horror on their faces was almost comic. He nodded slowly. "A more devious solution, my lady, worthy of a female." He looked to Claudius. "I concur with Livia Quintus Lucellus."

Claudius smiled, relieved. "A fit judgment. We shall see it carried out." He looked at Gratus, who gestured to the guards.

Two soldiers hauled the women to their feet. Julia began to wail again. "I can't live like that," she shrieked. The soldiers hustled them out into the street.

"You two are well m-matched," Claudius said to Jergan and Livia. He looked almost regal in his snow-white toga, bordered with the imperial purple. "As long as I r-reign, you will be undisturbed."

"Then we have more than a decade of peace ahead of us," Livia said.

"That long?" Claudius mused. "I would not have thought it. Time enough to set a n-new tone for Rome." He looked at her sharply. "Will you be content without meddling in p-politics?"

"My meddling apparently does no good." Livia sighed. "The world does what it will do."

Claudius nodded several times, thinking about that. Then he turned and limped out the door. The Guard hustled to surround him. The new emperor might not be impressive to some, but he would rule Rome for more than thirteen years, at times ruthlessly, but always with the intent of making Rome stronger for the common people.

Livia took Jergan's arm and turned him into the house. "Rest now. The crisis is over."

But that didn't change what stood between her and Jergan. She didn't care about the cardinal Rule. She would make him vampire in a minute in order to avoid the regret that she knew would haunt her all her days if she did not. Let the vampire Elders do what they would. That was Donnatella's influence.

But it seemed history reverted to its true course, even if the channel it took was different. She had been unwilling this past week to offer to make Jergan vampire for fear he would refuse her. If he did, knowing the years of regret ahead of her would crush her soul.

She let him down onto the soft linens of the bed. His eyes were serious, uncertain.

And if he refused her, there was nothing to say that he would even stay with her. His staying a few years didn't have any cataclysmic consequences to the world. What if such a small thing could be changed easily, like Lucius dying? Then she had nothing, not even a few years of regret.

She hadn't even told Jergan she was pregnant. Why not?

Because if he stayed with her only for the sake of his son, then being together would slowly poison them both, and Livia's life would be less than Donnatella had experienced, not more.

"Sleep," she whispered, and closed his eyelids with her fingertips, gently. He let her have her way, but she knew he would not sleep.

Gods above, what was her way forward? Her heart was twisted in confusion.

But how could she not try to get what she had come across time to achieve? She had to offer to make him like her.

But not today. She turned from the room and shut the door quietly. She'd wait until he was stronger.

JERGAN SAT IN the back of the wagon, dozing as it rumbled along. How could such a day occur in February? At home the wind was bitter cold this time of year. The sun warmed him through the woolen tunic and the cloak that Livia had carefully tucked around him in the pre-dawn light. He'd told her he could ride today. It had been more than three weeks since the arena. Stubborn woman. Though she had brought a horse for him. Maybe tomorrow.

One should make use of this weather. One could probably grow two crops a year if one was careful, if the soil was rich, as it had been in Centii.

He opened one eye, just to make certain the enclosed wagon she used for herself was still behind them. There it was, lumbering behind a team of six horses. Such a vehicle would founder on the narrow tracks of Britannia. But it did well enough on the broad Roman roads. She said sunshine would help heal him, so she insisted he ride in the open wagon during daylight hours. What healed him was her care—the careful stitching, her gentle touch as she tended his wounds. Now if only she would relent on her vow not to drain his strength with making love, he would be a content man.

Would he? He pushed himself up. One thing had scratched at him through all these days.

She had never said she loved him.

He didn't count that drugged disclosure in the arena when she murmured that Donnatella told her to say she loved him. He didn't think she even remembered it. Maybe she didn't love him. Maybe Donnatella wanted her to tell him that just to secure his help or . . .

He realized he had been watching the verdant hills roll by without really seeing them. She said they would be red with poppies in the summer.

What could love mean to a woman who lived forever? An interlude of passion? If she had lived that long, perhaps she was beyond loving. And he was only human. He didn't even bring down empires or engineer their rise. No wonder she couldn't love him. He was just a man.

A man without even an occupation. What need had Livia for a soldier? What need had Livia for anything he was? Oh, she liked making love to him. Abstinence was making her as cranky as he was. But that was not enough. He might as well be her slave, his body to be used as she desired, if he could contribute no more to their relationship.

Even her attraction to him would fade. He would grow old, his body weak, while her needs would continue to be those of a vibrant young woman. Would she press a gray head to her breasts eagerly? Could he stand to see her seek her pleasure in the arms of a younger man as he grew incapable of satisfying her?

He twisted irritably in his cloak. That pulled at his wounds. He had never felt so mortal.

He wanted to be with Livia. How he longed for her touch. He could bid the driver of the cart halt and go back to join her in her wagon.

Yet he did not.

What use? She would soothe him and cosset him. It wasn't enough.

ON THE EVENING of the fourth day, the little caravan consisting of Jergan's cart, Livia's enclosed wagon, and the carts stacked with luggage and supplies finally trundled through the gates of the villa in the hills outside the little village of Montalcino. Servants rushed to greet them. Her entire household from Rome was there. Only Lucius was missing. Livia climbed out of her wagon. She had used the pretext of Jergan needing sunlight to separate them during the journey. The dread she felt at asking him to let her make him vampire warred inside with Donnatella's prodding to at least try. Yet Donnatella seemed to be fading. Livia could not remember the future as clearly as she had in the catacombs, or even as well as when Claudius had come to her a week ago.

She had missed her courses. Not unexpected, given that she was pregnant, but a pressing inevitability that tapped at her mind. If Jergan stayed, he would soon know that she was pregnant. Didn't she owe it to him to tell him before it became obvious? Not if he was intending to leave as soon as he felt up to the journey.

The runners she had sent ahead had done their work. Light shone from the windows. The floor would be warm, the hypocausts stoked. She could smell the food. So why did she feel so desolate?

Jergan dismounted, looking haggard. He had insisted on riding the last two days. He rode well. She had watched his broad shoulders and his muscled thighs from a sliding panel she cracked open in the evening light. He would be too tired tonight to talk about the future.

Relief washed over her. She couldn't propose it tonight.

The servants had a table laden with food prepared. She glanced to Jergan as he removed his cloak. There was a distance about him she couldn't fathom.

Or maybe she could. He was probably wondering what he had gotten himself into. Life with a woman who must drink blood? Maybe he was already wondering how soon he could return to Britannia. Maybe even the fifty years she had with Jergan and her son in Donnatella's experience would be denied her. She would raise Gian alone. And she would, rather than blackmail Jergan into staying with her using her unborn babe.

This way lay madness. And that might be her lot. Everything was so confusing. Could she change what had happened to Donnatella without changing everything? Maybe she couldn't change anything at all. Or maybe she couldn't even achieve what Donnatella had experienced.

The worst part was that she had lost the refuge of a conviction that she couldn't change destiny. She'd once been certain one could not break the cardinal Rule, that there was no way around her fate. That certainty was what made a life with Jergan as he aged and died bearable.

Donnatella had taken that from her. Donnatella told her she could change her lot. It might be a lie. But Donnatella had thought she had to try.

She sat to table, Jergan across from her. They hadn't said anything to each other for hours.

"Did . . . Did you get to see much of the countryside?" How inane. She watched him chew a piece of beef from the savory stew the servant had ladled.

Jergan nodded. "It looks like fertile land."

She nodded. "Yes." Even the one word seemed to choke her.

"Can you grow two crops a year here?"

"I . . . I don't know."

"If you rotated the fields so that one of four was fallow, resting, and the others planted with different crops spring and fall . . ." He spoke almost absently as he ate. "I saw a pair of oxen pulling a wooden plow. They're late in turning the earth. That should be done in October." He looked up. "But of course, your earth does not freeze here." He stabbed another piece of meat with his knife. "Still, a metal plowshare would make faster work of it."

"You know much about working the land." He was full of surprises. "I shall add the title of farmer to soldier and geographer."

He shrugged. "I was the eldest before I turned to soldiering."

"Why did you go? You could have stayed and worked your father's land."

"The Romans threatened. Someone had to go. The next eldest of the boys was born with a twisted hip."

And Jergan was the one with courage, with honor and a sense of duty. She could think of nothing else to say. Shouting out that she wanted to make him vampire didn't seem an option, even if the servants had not been present.

The dinner was finished in silence.

She rose and Jergan rose with her. "You have been spending your days awake. Perhaps you would like to sleep through the night. Tufi can show you to a room."

Jergan looked up at her as though she had betrayed him somehow. Then he looked away. "That would be fine," he muttered.

Tufi bowed and grinned and motioned Jergan to the back of the house. Jergan stalked out of the room. Livia watched with dead eyes.

She couldn't go on like this. *Do you remember it being this awful, Donnatella? Tell me it gets easier. Tell me we can find love for at least a few years even if he refuses me.*

I don't know. The voice was faint. *I . . . I don't remember. . . .*

Or maybe that was just herself, answering her own questions.

Then that was it.

Donnatella couldn't help her. But when had she relied on others for help? She was a woman of action. That's what she did. She took action. All this wondering and being torn between possibilities wasn't like her in the least. She shook herself mentally. She was only a woman. But hadn't she made herself a soldier in the fight to make a better world a dozen times? She'd been feeling tired and dispirited lately. But that was no excuse. If she could fight for the world, she could fight for herself. She had to make a push for what she wanted, and if she ruined everything and he left her entirely, or if he flat refused her, she . . . she would take the consequences and deal with them, too.

She strode after him.

THE ROOM WAS dark.

"Don't light the lamps," he growled at Tufi.

Darkness matched his mood. How could he be worthy of Livia? He should just go back to Centii. But how could he live without her? He felt as though he had been in a fog that lasted weeks as he recovered, floating without thought. Only in the last days had the impossibility of his situation become clear.

Tufi closed the door.

Jergan unstrapped the belt that held his sword and dropped it on the floor. If he stayed, he would have only a half-life, knowing he was useless to her. She had a large soul, a large life, and his was suddenly very small. She already grew tired of him. He hadn't realized that was why she kept her distance during the journey. But her ploy became clear now that she gave him a separate room, like he was some guest with whom she was barely acquainted, instead of his lover. He unlaced his boots and unbuckled the wide belt at his waist, then pulled his tunic over his head.

The door opened behind him. A channel of light cut across the room.

He turned, holding his tunic to his loins. Livia was outlined in the doorway.

She just stood there. She didn't enter. Her vibrations coruscated over him in the darkness. The scent of cinnamon and ambergris hovered in the air. He didn't know what to say to her. Perhaps she finally wanted his body. Maybe that was enough. He'd take what time he could for as long as she cared to dally with him. He dropped the tunic to the floor.

He saw her take a breath. Her silhouette moved into the room. She closed the door. Darkness enveloped them like some comforting old friend.

"I can't go on like this," she breathed.

She wanted his services.

"I want to ask you a question," she said. Her voice sounded small.

"Ask." He didn't mean it to come out so roughly. But he was standing here naked in front of her.

"I can give you eternal life, Jergan."

That wasn't a question, but he didn't say that. "I never wanted eternal life." She couldn't give him eternal life. Did she think to lure him to her bed with empty promises? They could never be on equal footing.

"Oh." Hurt suffused that one syllable. "Well, then . . ." She was actually turning to go.

"You needn't promise me anything," he said. He couldn't let her go. "I'll bed you for as long as you'll allow it."

"I don't want that," she cried. Her voice sank to a whisper. "Not only that." He could feel her distress.

"Oh, I love you, if that's what you're worried about." He couldn't help the bitterness that soaked his words. "You own me, body and soul. I'm more a slave to you than ever."

Silence. "You love me?"

"Brid help me, yes," he muttered. He had made himself entirely vulnerable to her.

"Then let me make you vampire, Jergan." She rushed forward and gripped his biceps. "We can live forever."

The proposal was shocking. "You can do that?"

"By giving you my blood. It will make you sick. But I will give you my blood many times, until you are able to live with the Companion in your blood as I do." She was pleading with him.

He should have been shocked, but he wasn't. He had accepted what she was long ago. And it was but a short step from that to accepting it for himself. She wasn't evil. And the revulsion to taking blood seemed only a superstition at this point. But he could imagine nothing more bleak than knowing you would live forever in this perpetual state of longing for someone who did not return your feeling.

"Why would you do that?"

She looked up at him. Her face glowed with distress in the dark. "Do you know why Donnatella came back?"

He didn't. In the fog of his weakness after the disappearance of the bronze machine, he had never even asked. A flame kindled inside him. He dared not feed it fuel. "I assumed it was to tell you how to make your plot successful." If he thought about it at all. Which he hadn't. He was thinking about it now, though.

She sucked in a breath. "She came back because she

lived with more than a thousand years of regret that she hadn't made you vampire."

"I'm just a soldier, Livia," he warned, fighting against the flame. "I don't bring down empires."

"Neither do I, apparently," she sighed. "But you have courage and honor. You figured out that it was Chaerea behind the attacks, not me. And you know how to make the land feed the people better than it does today. There are so many things you could do with time."

"You have seven hundred years of experience I do not." There were so many reasons why he was not worthy of her.

"And I need to look at the world with fresh eyes. I'm tired, Jergan." She let him go and started to pace the dark room. "I'm weary of having to keep my secrets. I want someone to depend on. A partner." She turned on her heel.

"A partner." The words struck to his core. Her regret was for the things he could do for the world. It wasn't for what he could do for her. Donnatella had told her to admit love just to bind him to her purpose. It wasn't true. The thought echoed through an empty soul.

Not true. She didn't love him.

"Gods, man, does a woman have to say it?" She threw up her hands and stalked to the window. Her silhouette was a darker blot upon the night sky and the moving trees outside. The stars were thick and winking clear as they had not been in the noisy, lit city.

The flame of hope leaped up from the ashes in his soul. "Sometimes, yes, Livia."

He waited as though his life depended upon it. Which it did.

She heaved a sigh of resignation. "I loved you from the first instant I saw you. And maybe that was because

Donnatella was inside me and I had already loved you for more than a thousand years." She held up a finger of warning. "But don't go mad with wondering if I would have loved you without Donnatella coming back. It doesn't matter. By the time I'd owned you for a few hours, I trusted you with my life. By the third day I knew I couldn't live without you. The hardest thing I ever did was free you, thinking you would go back to Britannia."

The flame engulfed him, heart, soul. He could not breathe. Yet his eyes could fill. "I wish I were worthy of that."

"Don't you dare say you won't stay with me because you're not worthy." Her voice was imperious and cross. "I'm a woman. I've been lonely for centuries. And I need you. Not someone else. You."

That was the Livia he knew. Three strides and he could take her in his arms. She lifted her head and he kissed her, hard. He wanted to devour her, make her a part of him so she could never leave him.

She might leave him. Forever was a long time. But she had made a commitment. Without an equal commitment on his part, his life was over.

"Make me vampire," he breathed into her mouth. "Let us tempt the fates."

She held herself away from him. "How so?"

"Let them be jealous of our happiness."

SOMEHOW, ALL THAT possibility of happiness made her cry. She hadn't cried in five hundred years. She should be hard and strong and triumphant. She had what she wanted. There might be regrets, but there would never be the one soul-destroying regret.

Jergan put her head against the shoulder that wasn't wounded and she sobbed into the smell of his flesh.

"I'm sorry," she hiccupped at last. "I didn't mean to cry."

"I liked it," he rumbled, and kissed her hair. "It reminds me that you are just a woman." He looked down at her. "Do it now, Livia. Make me as you are."

"You will be sick for a while."

"But you will care for me as you always have."

"Yes."

"Then I am ready."

He didn't know what it meant to be vampire. But he was willing to take a leap of faith with her. Well, she would show him the way. And perhaps he could show her the way back to innocence. One of the gods had blessed her. She would raise a temple to whichever one it was. She'd think about just which god later. Perhaps Venus. Or maybe the Christ in whose catacombs the time machine had hidden. If Donnatella had not used the time machine to come back and give her courage, even the possibility of happiness would be denied her.

She thought about all that lay ahead of Jergan. "You will feel alive, my love. So alive. And strong. You will see and hear and smell and taste more acutely than you do now. And you will be even more easily aroused."

"And will I be able to make love to you with more vigor?"

She pretended to frown. "I am not certain I can stand any more vigor from you."

He turned her chin up. "But will I?"

"Yes."

"I think I will like this." She could feel him rising against her thigh. It had been too long since she had made love to Jergan. "You told me once that sometimes you took blood from your partner as you made love, that it was a most sensual experience."

She nodded, examining his expression. All she could read was softness there. No horror. No revulsion.

"Take my blood as you make love to me, Livia, and mingle my blood with your own." He kissed her, tenderly this time.

She would make it tender, too. She let him lead her to the bed. She unwound her *stola* as she went. He pulled her tunic over her head this time. She pressed her breasts to his naked chest and belly. The hair on his chest prickled against her sensitive nipples. She'd have to be careful of the healing wounds in his side and his shoulder. He lay down and pulled her down beside him. His erection strained against his belly. She lay down in his arms, and ran her hands up around the nape of his neck, under his thick black hair. His green eyes glowed. He cupped her head and kissed her, gently, yet she could feel his need, barely restrained. He was a strong man, a man worthy of centuries. Together perhaps they could do what she could not alone. Or perhaps not. Perhaps history would do what history would do. Whatever they did, they would do it together.

"You make me whole," he whispered.

That whole was about to get much bigger. He was courageous enough not to be frightened of what would happen to him. He would encompass it and use it to do good things in the world.

"Make me whole," she whispered in return, and he rolled on top of her, holding himself above her, his rod lying between her thighs. She spread them. She was wet and ready and she wanted him inside her *now*. He felt her to see that she was ready for him. She was so ready. He entered slowly, easing himself into her until she was filled. "Yesssss," she hissed as he began to slide in and out, slowly, almost tenderly, in spite of the passion she could feel in him.

He kissed her shoulder. Then he threw back his head, baring his neck to her. She wouldn't take much blood. The last thing she wanted to do was weaken him for the ordeal ahead. But she would show him that this most intimate exchange of fluids could mirror and augment the other exchange they were performing. She placed her hands on his buttocks, feeling them clench as he pushed in and out of her. She breathed faster as she pushed in counterpoint.

Companion.

Power rushed up her veins and the world turned red. She felt her canines run out. She had done this thousands of times, yet it felt as though this time were her first. The pain would be minor for him. Like being pricked by thorns, no more. He quickened his pace. Her own sensation ramped up. She must wait for exactly the right moment. She kissed his strong, muscular neck right over the artery under his jaw. Her Companion thrilled in anticipation. Jergan thrust inside her. She wrapped her thighs around him and held his head, her fingers burying themselves in his thick hair. His breath hissed in and out. The time was near.

Blood throbbed in his artery beneath her lips. Carefully, she placed her canines. She must be gentle with him. As she punctured the skin, he tensed for a moment, then relaxed. Blood welled, thick with life. She sucked at his neck and he thrust into her. She could feel his climax rising along with her own. She pulled away and bit her own lip, then sucked again at his throat, feeling their blood mingle. He groaned as he spurted inside her, and the sensation of him coming and his blood welling in her mouth as he gave her everything, his life, his future, the essence of his being, sent her over the edge. She contracted, not only with her body, but also with her soul, and then exploded outward, transformed.

They collapsed onto the linens.

"Gods, Livia," he muttered. "Why did I not ask you to take my blood before?" He raised himself up on one elbow and felt the two small wounds at his throat. "Is it done?"

Her self-inflicted bite was already healed. "Yes, my love. You can't go back."

A sigh of satisfaction from somewhere inside surprised her. *Remember to tell Leonardo what you are, and that he builds a time machine to send you back. Tell him time is a vortex. . . .*

"Donnatella?" she whispered. But there was no answer. She was fairly certain there would never be an answer again.

"Is she gone?" Jergan asked.

Livia nodded. "She got what she wanted." Things were changed forever. Livia must hope it turned out for the best.

"I don't feel different."

She smiled. "You won't. Not until after the fever passes. Then you'll feel incredibly alive. Or so I'm told. I've never known anything different. 'The blood is the life,' we say." Doubt assailed her. "You're not sorry, are you?"

He turned her chin up and he kissed her. "No regrets."

There was but one thing more. "By the way, I am with child. You will have a son."

He sucked in a breath. His gaze roved over her face, incredulous and almost tentative—afraid to believe. "Truly?"

She nodded. She must break the news to him. "He will be as I am."

Jergan took her in his arms, tenderly. His chest swelled against hers. His voice was reverent. "As we are."

EPILOGUE

Florence, 1821

DONNATELLA STOOD AT the balcony overlooking the
Piazza del Signoria as the soft summer twilight of Florence
deepened into night. She sighed. It had been a difficult day.
Her husband came up and put his arm around her shoulders.

"Brid and Belatucadros, but that Forelli is a megaloma-
niac," Giovanni rumbled into her ear. "You were right. He
cannot lead the Carbonari. Perhaps I'll have to take a hand
myself."

Donnatella turned and smiled up into his face. His dark
hair was shorter, as was the fashion these days. It curled
around the nape of his neck. The light green eyes he shared
with her son glowed in the night. No wonder Buonarroti had
thought Gian so handsome that he'd carved his statue of
David in her son's image. Gian had his looks from his father, and she had never seen a more handsome man than her
husband. In the tightly cut coats of today (his was black
across his broad shoulders) and the tight breeches that
clearly revealed his muscular thighs, his riding boots and
snowy cravat, this man always sent a thrill to the most womanly part of her, whether she called him Giovanni or Jergan
or any of the other names they had taken in their many life-
times together. "You would be a brilliant leader. But that can
wait. The time is not yet right for their rise. I can feel it."

"Then why so sad?"

"There's just a little feeling of *tristesse* hanging in the room."

Giovanni gave her a knowing look. They both thought that these feelings that occasionally wafted over her might be the original world of Donnatella still lingering somewhere near. She turned into their study and he followed. Her eyes fell on the matching paintings centered on the wall above the twin desks. The one on the left was Giovanni as Neptune rising from the waves. He had modeled for Botticelli only when she had agreed to reciprocate for the artist's rendering of Venus. All she had insisted was that the master change the color of her hair and eyes to conceal her identity. The paintings were hung as they were meant to be, so that the subjects gazed upon each other. The images spoke of a lifetime of love. How could one be sad?

"I still think I could lead them. . . ."

"Yes, you could, and no doubt you will be so stubborn about it that you will do what you want in spite of all I can say against it. . . ."

Giovanni laughed and shook his head. "Stubborn? Well, I'll give you that. It's my only defense."

He pulled her past the study they shared and toward the bedroom in the ancient Palazzo Vecchio. She nuzzled at his neck.

They were interrupted by a commotion in the square below. Someone banged on the main doors. The servants made startled inquiry. Boots took the broad stairs up from the audience room three at a time. Giovanni strode to the door and opened it.

Donnatella slid up beside him.

"What is it?" Giovanni barked as the young man tried to catch his breath.

"A ghost . . . Conte . . . risen from the crypt . . . under the Baptistery of . . . the Duomo."

"Nonsense," Donnatella said calmly. "Now tell us what happened."

"The priests heard screaming . . . from down below . . . a crypt that only a few knew existed. . . . They hauled away the stone . . . and there was a man dressed in a winding sheet, speaking only Latin. At least I think it was Latin. He didn't speak it very well. . . ."

"A winding sheet. . . ." Giovanni glanced to Donnatella. "You wouldn't mean a toga, would you?"

They had been waiting for this moment, not sure just when it would be, or if it ever would. Donnatella had lost all memory of exactly when she had decided to use Leonardo's machine to change her destiny with Jergan. She did not remember where the time machine was hidden. She no longer knew what had happened in the long life of that other Donnatella, except for wisps of feeling or occasional strange attractions or aversions. But she and Giovanni had dutifully told Leonardo what she was, and that time was a vortex, and . . . waited.

And now the time had come. The time machine was hidden in the crypts below the Baptistery, and it had disgorged its traveler into 1821.

"I . . . I don't know about any toga . . ." the young man was saying. "The priests have called for you, Conte, as the magistrate."

Giovanni took Donnatella's hand and pushed past the messenger. They hurried down the stairs. "Call out the city guard," Giovanni ordered the young man. "No time to wait for the carriage," Giovanni apologized as he strode toward the doors that opened onto a carriageway like a courtyard off the piazza. Donnatella hurried behind him.

"I'm perfectly capable of walking," she said. Servants opened the door.

"I was thinking more of running." He looked at the

dainty slippers that peeped from under her red silks. He raised his brows.

She stopped. "Oh, very well." She removed the offending slippers and tossed them at one of the footmen, who caught them deftly without even a raised eyebrow. He was used to his mistress's eccentricities. "Now I'll ruin the hem of my dress."

"I'll order you a dozen like it."

They ran through the narrow streets off the piazza, east toward the Duomo. Pedestrians and horsemen alike parted in front of them, surprised that the Conte and Contessa di Poliziano should be hurrying through the streets of Florence without even a retinue. Into the Duomo by a side door held open by a priest, they ran through the cavernous nave and down to the Baptistery, glowing with candles hastily set upon prayer tables.

Caligula was sitting in the carved seat of the priest who presided over the baptismal font. It looked like a throne. He still seemed a petulant child. Just now he was waving a scepter altarpiece at the ornate carvings and the gold everywhere.

"A perfect palace for a Caesar," he was telling an audience of priests. "Richly endowed." He was fortunate that they were perhaps the only listeners with a chance of understanding Latin as it was spoken in ancient Rome, though they would think it strange indeed.

"This is the house of our Lord," one protested.

"Whoever your lord is, he shall cede it to the emperor of Rome."

An old, decrepit priest drew himself up. "We serve Jesus Christ."

"The Christ cult has such palaces?" Caligula asked, astounded. He frowned. Once, that frown had set everyone around him to quaking. "Peasants—mere rabble. Ahhh, but the witch said they would. My first act as emperor in this time shall be to confiscate this palace and all the gold in it for the Imperial Treasury."

The priests exchanged looks as though to say, "What can one do with a madman?"

"What year is it?" the young emperor asked eagerly.

"Eighteen twenty-one, good sir," a young man in the plain cassock of a novitiate said.

"Eighteen hundred and twenty-one years of the rule of Rome?" The eyes of the man who was once Caesar went round. "That is more than a thousand years since I last ruled Rome."

"No. Since the death of Christ on a Roman cross." The old priest leaned on his stick.

"You mark all time since an impoverished carpenter was put to death in a minor province in my empire?" His brow darkened. Then he appeared to think better of his fury. He giggled and rubbed his hands. "Oh, this will be a very easy time to rule."

The old priest seemed to hear Giovanni and Donnatella for the first time as they hurried up the aisle. He turned. Relief shot through his eyes. "Conte, you are most welcome, as are you, Contessa." He made his painful way toward them. "This creature thinks he is an emperor," he whispered. "I'm not sure which one. Mad as a hatter."

Behind him, Caligula stood, blinking at them. "The witch and her slave. What are you doing here?" His eyes narrowed and he turned on the gaggle of priests. "Have you lied to me about how much time has passed since your carpenter was executed?"

"The year is as we told you, good sir, 1821, the Year of Our Lord, Jesus Christ," another priest said, carefully, as one speaks to madmen or children.

"Then how are these two here when they were in

Rome nearly . . . nearly eighteen hundred years ago?" Caligula's voice was rising. "Unless . . ." He glanced toward the stairs behind the baptismal font leading downward. "But you could not have used the bronze waterwheel. I only just left it."

"We live here," Giovanni said. "This is Florence, not Rome."

"It matters not," Caligula said. "All is part of my empire."

"You have no empire here, Gaius," Donnatella said.

Caligula looked smug. "For those born to rule, an empire is inevitable."

"Not this time," Giovanni growled. "Because this time you have no army. The Praetorians are long extinct."

"Do you know this man?" the old priest asked Donnatella and Giovanni.

Donnatella leaned in and whispered into his ear, "Isn't it obvious? He thinks he's Caligula. He even looks a bit like the busts I've seen."

Giovanni strode up to Caligula and jerked him to his feet by one arm.

"Unhand me," Caligula shrieked. "I'll have you torn apart by wild beasts in the arena."

"We're no longer so barbaric as to stage deaths in an arena." Giovanni dragged Caligula across the mosaic floor of the Baptistery. A clatter was heard in the passage from the Duomo. A troop of about a dozen city guards, some still buttoning on their blue and gold uniform jackets, appeared in the entryway. The one in the lead recognized Giovanni and bowed as crisply as he could. The others settled into some semblance of order behind him.

"Take this man." Giovanni shoved Caligula toward the troop. Two guards stepped up and took his arms.

"I'll have you all killed, and your families and your

friends." Caligula started to sob in real fear as his situation dawned on him.

Giovanni turned back to Donnatella. She could feel his inquiry. Caligula ought to be executed for all the pain he had caused. But he had committed no crime in this time, and one couldn't just execute a man for seeming mad.

Or for being mad. He *was* insane. Perhaps he had been mad all along.

She turned to the priest. "The Jesuits have an asylum in the mountains above Lake Como, do they not?"

"Why, yes." The old man nodded. Understanding drifted into his rheumy eyes.

"We will make a fat donation to provide for his care," Donnatella promised.

"It is an austere place," the old priest warned.

"He deserves worse." Giovanni glowered. He was still a warrior at heart.

Donnatella lifted her brows. "Under what Florentine law?"

Giovanni sighed and shook his head, resigned. "I let a woman plead mercy even for a snake. What am I coming to?" He motioned the guard out. "You did the same for his sisters."

"You'll be punished horribly for this," Caligula called back. His voice receded as the guards marched him from the cathedral.

"A few years of prayer may bring back his sanity," the old priest muttered, and turned to his quarters. Then he stopped. "I wonder how he got down there." He glanced to the opening of the stairway. "Brother Antonio . . . go down and see what you can make of it."

"Don't bother yourselves," Donnatella interrupted. "We shall send someone to seal up the crypt until a full investigation can be made. You belong in your beds, not down in dusty crypts at night with the rats and the spiders." She saw one priest visibly shudder.

"You are generous, Contessa, as always." The old priest nodded and limped away.

Giovanni took her arm and steered her out into the passage to the Duomo. They said nothing until they were out into the street.

"We should destroy the machine," Giovanni said.

"I know, but I can hardly bear to do it." She sighed. "Still, men weren't meant to travel in time. Or women."

"I'm glad you did."

"What if something bad happens because I challenged time? What if it has already happened?" She grasped his biceps with both hands and leaned against him.

"We've been over this before. We cannot know." He cupped her chin with his other hand and turned her toward him. They stood in the shadows of a building across the street from the cathedral. "Maybe the wrong path was the one where you did not make me vampire."

"Or maybe there is no true path, only possible paths." She sighed.

"Perhaps all versions of time exist together. Caligula was meant to be removed from power, whether by death or by Leonardo's machine. Just as you are both Donnatella and Livia, and I am Giovanni and Jergan. Regardless of our names, we are who we are, and that is right and true." He bent and kissed her, softly, not caring what revelers still on the streets saw the Conte and the Contessa di Poliziano kissing.

"I asked a moment ago what I was coming to," he said. His eyes were soft now with an expression she had learned to treasure over the centuries. "I am coming home to the Palazzo Vecchio tonight with my soul mate and we are going to eat together, and drink wine from the grapes I grew in Montalcino. And then I will take you to bed, my love, and make you scream my name as you find your release."

They turned toward the Piazza del Signoria. "I do get confused sometimes about what I should call you." Donnatella leaned against his arm. "Last night I screamed out, 'Jergan,' I am fairly sure."

"You did. I drove you to distraction." His voice was smug. He was so delightfully male.

"And am I the only one driven to distraction?" she asked in mock outrage.

"You have been driving me to distraction for near eighteen hundred years, my love," he whispered into her hair. "And I hope to be distracted for eighteen hundred more."